Down in the Flood

The second novel in the Most Secret series

by Jon Wakeham

*To Brian
Best wishes
Jon Wakeham*

CHELONIST

First Published in Great Britain in 2013 by Chelonist

Chelonist Publications
www.chelonist.com

Copyright © 2013 by Mark Errington

The moral right of Mark Errington writing as Jon Wakeham
to be identified as the author of this work has been
asserted in accordance with the Copyright,
Designs and Patents Act, 1988.

All rights reserved. No part of this publication
may be reproduced or transmitted in any form
or by any means, electronic or mechanical,
including photocopy, recording, or any
information storage and retrieval system,
without permission in writing from the publisher.

A CIP catalogue record for this book is available
from the British Library.

978-0-9573921-2-0

This book is a work of fiction. Names, characters,
businesses, organisations, places and events are
either the product of the author's imagination or are
used fictitiously. Any resemblance to
actual persons, living or dead, events or locales
is purely coincidental.

Typeset by Chelonist.com
Printed by Lightning Source
Cover design by Alex Terry

Chelonist Ltd
Knapp View
Westhope
Hereford
HR4 8BL
United Kingdom
Email: mark@chelonist.com

After he (Lenin) and Nadya arrived in Switzerland he sent a book of views of Geneva, dedicated 'to the good kind lady, Mrs Emma Yeo'. She treasured it, remembering Mr Richter as a lodger who had been 'far better to deal with than many an Englishman'.

(Lenin and his wife, Nadya lived in London in 1902 -1903 under the names of Dr and Mrs Richter. Mrs Yeo was their landlady)

Helen Rappaport - Conspirator, Lenin in Exile, Windmill Books 2010, p75

This book is dedicated to James, Veronique and, (especially), Milan Curtis Errington. When he is old enough I will give him a copy of this book.

Down in the Flood

Lord Walter Mansell-Lacey is sent on his first assignment and experiences the great flood of Paris, January 1910.

CHELONIST LTD

Tuesday 3rd January 1910

Rain squalls were blowing around the Hampshire heath-land making the soldiers shiver. They were dressed only in their PE kit of singlets, shorts and pumps. Walter had been singled out for special treatment by the drill Sergeant and was feeling picked on, but not as much as the Private who had been selected to act as his target.

'Not right, your bloody lordship. Bite the bastard; gouge his eyes, kick him in the testicles. He's no gentleman, so don't treat him like he is one. Just stop him. Put him out of action,' Sergeant Farmer barked into Walter's face, spraying him with spittle. Walter was breathing heavily from the exertions of his recent action. The soldier who had been volunteered as the target was wearing a heavily padded jacket and lay groaning on his side, having been hit several times, very hard, by some of Walter's best body punches.

'I put him down, didn't I?' Walter pointed out.

'I put him down, didn't I, Sergeant,' the Sergeant screamed back at him, thin streams of spittle flying from his lips.

'Well I did…… Sergeant,' Walter corrected himself. He wasn't much enjoying this part of his training.

''You too bleedin' posh to talk like a soldier, you great gangly bastard?' the Sergeant continued.

'Look, I really don't think I need to be here,' Walter tried to explain.

'Oh, too high and mighty, are we, too good for the likes of us,' Sergeant Farmer said very loudly, a few inches from Walter's face.

'Well, I don't want to put too much emphasis on this, but this is about fitness and self-defence. I'm already fitter and better at self-defence than anyone here, including you, Sergeant,' Walter drawled. The Sergeant's face turned purple and he seemed to burst even more blood-vessels in his cheeks.

'You really think you are better than me, do you?' Farmer screamed, 'we'll bloody well see about that. You'd better get ready to have your pretty face all bruised you posh bastard!'

'You are welcome to try, Sergeant, but I'd better warn you that I'm a pretty useful boxer. I think I just proved that with what you made me do to young Evans, there,' Walter said in an even tone with the ghost of a smile on his lips.

'What if he had a knife, eh? You wouldn't want to try to punch him then, would you?' the Sergeant barked out again. 'Wikins! Get over 'ere with that bleedin' knife.'

A tall, gangling Private with ginger hair jogged over with a large knife in his hand and presented himself.

'Right, Mr clever dick Lord fucking almighty, watch this and learn. Wilkins, attack me with that knife!'

Wilkins, the ginger-haired Private, winced visibly about being called out, but he raised the knife overhand and lunged clumsily at the Sergeant, a grimace of real intent on his face. At the last moment the Sergeant stepped sideways and elbowed the hapless and clumsy Wilkins on the chin. The Private dropped the knife, then rolled on the ground, kicking his legs and gurgling, blood coming out of his mouth from where he had bitten his tongue.

'Did you see what I did there? Think you could do that?' the Sergeant shouted.

'Yes, Sergeant. To both of your questions,' Walter answered.

'Well, see what you can do about this, then,' the Sergeant said through gritted teeth. He picked up the knife and advanced slowly towards Walter, knife held underhand, swinging the blade in a figure of eight. Walter retreated in good order until he realised that he was being forced back against a fence. He feinted to move to his left then instantly moved forward, stepping inside the swing of the knife, and then hitting the Sergeant's upper right arm with the edge of his hand. This stopped Farmer's advance and caused him to wobble slightly before he dropped the knife from nerveless fingers. Walter leaned backwards and knocked the Sergeant's legs from beneath him with a scything kick. The Sergeant went down on his back, his head bouncing on the ground. As he lay winded and stunned Walter scrambled to his feet, then he knelt down hard on the Sergeant's groin. The Sergeant let out a wheezing groan, and the recruits around all let out a loud cheer, breaking ranks to get a better look at their tormentor's discomfort.

'And that's a couple of acres for you, Sergeant Farmer,' Walter said, getting to his feet. He patted his damp hair down and brushed the worst of the grass and mud from his drill shorts with the flat of his hand.

There was the noise of a galloping horse, with the sound of hooves on wet turf getting louder as it approached. A junior Lieutenant in olive drab, apart from gleaming brown riding boots, rode up to the struggle of men gathered around the prostrate Sergeant.

'Is Lord Walter Mansell-Lacey here?' he asked of no-one in particular.

'That's me,' Walter replied, stepping towards him.

'There's a major wants to see you back at HQ straight away,' the rider said.

'Right-ho, I'll hop along as soon as I can. Got any transport？ Walter said, looking round for a vehicle.

''Fraid not,' said the Lieutenant.

'Lend me the nag then, will you. Damn sight quicker than walking all the way back,' Walter said, motioning towards the horse.

'Not sure I can do that, my lord. That wasn't what I was asked to do. I was just delivering the message,' said the Lieutenant, looking a little anxious.

'You did say it was urgent, didn't you. So use your initiative. Isn't that what you're supposed to do as an officer?'

'Oh, alright then,' the Lieutenant reluctantly agreed.

Walter held the bridle for the Lieutenant while he dismounted, then lifted himself easily into the saddle.

'Do send my apologies to the Sergeant, will you. Explain to him that I was called away,' Walter said with a smile. He turned the horse, a tall black gelding with a white star on its forehead, and rode in the direction of the sprawling mock gothic house which was the unit HQ.

Walter dismounted outside the stables, leaving instructions that the horse should be returned to the young Lieutenant as soon as possible. He found a coat with the badges of rank of a Captain on a rack. It was two sizes too small for him and far too narrow in the shoulders. He made his way into the house. His shorts and legs were liberally splashed with grey-brown mud.

Walter had to navigate through the corridors of dark oak panelling and up a wide, sweeping staircase to a first-floor room where he had been told the Major was waiting. He rapped loudly on the door.

'Come in,' a voice called out loudly.

Walter pushed the door open and strode into the room. He approached the desk and made a sloppy attempt at a salute, which the Major ignored.

'Forget the salute, but please slouch to attention,' the Major suggested. He continued to write, his head bowed towards the table. His light brown hair was thinning and the scalp was sunburnt in places, indicating that he had returned only a few weeks ago from a warmer climate.

'You've got a job for me, then,' Walter said, with a slight hint of excitement in his voice. The Major studied Walter's face as if trying to read his thoughts. He was a fleshy man of about fifty years with a moustache like a yard broom

Down in the Flood

'Colonel Cumming has asked you to do a little job. You've been asked to get ready to travel for a few weeks. You're to go up to London first, as he needs to brief you about the job.'

'Does this job mean working abroad?' Walter asked.

'I believe so,' the Major answered, in a slow and meticulous fashion, 'But, as I said, you need to ask Colonel Cumming about the details.'

'I'd better be on my way, then,' Walter said.

'He's expecting you in two hours. I'll get a driver to take you to the station,' the Major said, 'In the meantime I suggest you put some proper clothing on and return that poor Captain's jacket to where you found it, and let us hope that you haven't stretched it beyond use.'

'Yes, Sir,' Walter agreed.

'You should just make it if you take the next train. I'll get my driver to take you to the station now,' the Major said. He pressed a button on his desk. An orderly came smartly in and gave a sharp salute.

'Get my driver to take this gentleman to the station immediately,' the Major ordered.

'What about my things?' Walter asked.

'They're in the car, waiting for you,' the Major said.

'Right; thank you, I suppose,' Walter murmured.

'And surpass expectations,' the Major shouted as Walter left.

◊

The offices of newly formed Special Intelligence Services were in a prepossessing building at 64 Victoria Street, which had many turrets and towers in its construction and used more red terracotta brick than good taste allowed for. The office of the joint Directors was on the third of seven floors and was cramped and not well designed. To make it even more inconvenient, Colonel Mansfield Smith-Cumming shared his office with Vernon Kell, the head of home security. Cumming's desk had neat piles of papers arranged around a blotter which was edged with green tooled leather. Standing behind Cumming was a small, balding, square-faced man in a dull grey suit and round celluloid collar who studied Walter as he came into the room.

'Ah, Walter, good of you to come so quickly. Not to beat about the bush, I think we might have a little job for you. How's your French?' Cumming said.

'Erm, not bad, I suppose. Not exactly perfect, though,' Walter answered, a little confused.

'That's alright, it will probably be enough. I don't suppose you have any Russian?'

'No, none at all,' Walter admitted, wondering what the job might be.

'That's a pity, but I'm sure you'll muddle through. We want you to do a little job for us in Paris. There are some political exiles out there, revolutionary types, and we need to find out what they are up to. This is partly because we think they are organising trouble over here and partly because we need to keep the Russians sweet, as they are on our side, and these revolutionaries certainly want to get rid of the Czar. Think you can manage that?' Cumming asked. The little man winced slightly at this exposition.

'Sorry, but I'm not exactly sure what you want me to do,' Walter said, genuinely puzzled by Cumming's elliptical explanation.

'I want you to seduce the chief revolutionary's mistress and then get her to spill his secrets,' Cummins said with greater precision.

'Well, I'll give it a go. I'll need some more information, before I leave,' Walter said carefully.

'That's where Mr, errr.... Detective Fitch comes in. He's from Special Branch and can give you all the information you need.'

'Don't I need to receive a bit more training on codes and things?' Walter asked

'Oh, don't you worry about that. It all takes too long. But what I'm more concerned about is making sure that you're willing to do the dirty on this woman. I want you persuade her to tell us what's going on. You've got to be willing to use her in any way that will work, and have no conscience about it. Think you can manage that?' Cumming said, almost without drawing breath.

'If you ask any of my former lady friends they will tell you that is exactly what I am like,' Walter admitted with a slightly twisted smile.

'Splendid, that's exactly what I wanted to hear. Think you can be ready to leave by tonight?' Cumming asked.

'Yes, I suppose so. Like I said, I was expecting a bit more training first,' Walter answered.

'How is your training going, by the way?' Cumming asked.

'Well, to be perfectly frank, it's no bloody use to me. It isn't exactly what I was expecting, doing PT with a bunch of army recruits, instructed by an idiot of a Drill Sergeant. I thought it would be about learning secret stuff, like codes and things,' Walter complained.

'Damned if I know why they put you in the charge of a Drill Sergeant. From all the reports I have received from your instructors you are judged to be lazy, insubordinate and thoroughly arrogant. They seem to think your attitude is that there's nothing they can teach you there that you don't already know. We'll be setting up some proper training place next year, so when you come back, we should have something that'll prove more useful to you. You'll just have to pick it up as you go along in the meantime,' Cumming said, nodding to the other man.

'I'll pack my bags and be on my way, then,' Walter said, turning to leave.

'Take this gentleman with you. I'm sure he has a great deal to tell you. Best of luck in Paris,' Cumming called out.

'Right-ho,' said Walter. Detective Fitch followed Walter out of the office, staying just behind his shoulder. Walter turned his head to speak.

'What should I call you? I mean, I have to call you something, don't I?'

'You can call me Fitch',' said the man in a slightly squeaky voice, after a few seconds consideration.

'I suppose you are looking for a more discrete place to talk,' Walter commented. Fitch coughed slightly but otherwise didn't reply. He overtook Walter and led him along.

They walked down the corridor, then up a flight of stairs to a cramped room which was half filled with papers. Sitting behind a small desk was Godiva Williams, Walter's friend and sometime flatmate. The top of the desk was mostly covered by a new Imperial typewriter, He blinked in surprise at seeing her there, and she smiled back at him in a professional way. Fitch carefully shut the door after checking for anyone who might be listening in the corridor.

Godiva was comparing two type-written reports. She was dressed like a respectable typist in an insurance office.

'Oh, hello, Walter. You did well getting here so quickly. As soon as Cumming gave me a time for your arrival I checked it with the trains. I really don't know how he manages to organise his department,' she said, smiling up at him.

'Well, I suppose it's a bit different for him. He doesn't need to keep tabs on all those refugees and immigrants like your lot do,' Walter answered. 'Mind you, there are times when we need a bit of organising, which is why they sent me to see you, I suppose.'

'It's very good to see you Walter. I hope the training isn't too painful,' she said with an awkward giggle.

'Not painful for me,' Walter replied with a slightly twisted smile, 'Now, what is it that you wanted to tell me?'

'Oh, do sit down, you're making the place look untidy,' Godiva said.

'Well, I would if there was a chair,' Walter answered.

'Oh, fetch one from out there,' Godiva said, waving a hand in the direction of the door. Walter fetched a small bent wood chair from the outer office and placed himself in an elegant pose in front of the desk, his gloves in his hat on his lap and his feet crossed at the ankles.

'Bloody awful room, isn't it?' said Walter, looking around.

'Better than the accommodation your fellow recruits have,' Fitch said in his reedy voice. He was standing next to Godiva.

'Yes, I suppose so. Now, will you please give me some indication of what I'm supposed to be doing in Paris?' Walter enquired, looking towards Godiva. It was Fitch who spoke first.

'Like the Colonel said, it's about some political exiles living there. Normally we would just keep an eye on them, and let them quietly rot. However, this lot are a bit different. They have quite a lot of money, which is unusual, and they are a pretty tight group, and we haven't found a way into the group yet. It seems that someone is advising them on how to organise themselves and is also providing them with money. The group that is causing us concern consists of Latvian, but they are co-operating with one Russian group in particular. They call themselves Bolsheviks. Now, Russia's in a bit of a mess at the moment, but we need to keep them on our side. The Czar's a fool, and he's ruled by his wife. She, in her turn, takes far too much advice from some rather dubious friends. The whole country could quite easily descend into anarchy. The Czar's an absolutist, and there are lots of aristocrats who are very unhappy. The middle class have been anxious about the way things are going for years. You don't have revolutions unless you really annoy the middle classes. If the money is coming to the Bolsheviks from

Russia it would be difficult, but if it is coming from somewhere else, like Germany or Austria, it would be a good deal more serious'.

Godiva spoke next.

'The leader of the Bolsheviks is Vladimir Ulyanov, but he has many other aliases. He's a polemicist and passes for an intellectual. When he writes he usually goes by the name of Lenin. He's thirty something years old, and he's Russian, of course. His family are quite middle class, and his father got some kind of gong from their civil service. Mind you, his brother was hung for trying to blow up the Czar, and the whole family is quite radical. He was in internal exile in Siberia, but had to leave Russia after sailing a bit too near the wind. He's been moving around lots of European cities, including London. He writes and edits his own radical newspaper and also produces rabble-rousing pamphlets which advocate the violent overthrow of the government in Russia. Many people think that he is the most influential of the exiled revolutionaries. The thing you need to bear in mind is that the Bolsheviks, unlike the other groups, never want to negotiate or organise a peaceful transfer of power.'

'I thought that you of all people would have a certain amount of sympathy for his aims,' Walter commented, knowing Godiva's socialist sympathies.

'For his aims perhaps, but not for his means. The way he wants to go about bringing reform will leave a lot of innocent people dead. From my moral standpoint, getting people killed is almost universally a bad thing to do,' Godiva answered with a slight grimace. 'As it happens, I have a lot of sympathy for reform in Russia. Did you know that there are almost two thousand topics of conversation that can't legally be mentioned? We had a lot of Russians at our house. My father is very keen on constitutional reform, and he says that in violent revolutions the very worst sort of people rise to power, and I tend to agree with him. This man,

Ulyanov, has been in London, and I've got all the details of his time here. A lot of the information comes from Detective Fitch. Ulyanov's dedication to his cause and sheer hard work are really admirable, but he's a miserable man, with no sense of humour or proportion. His stated aim is to increase the happiness of the people of Russia. Trust me when I tell you that if he ever gets any power he will make most of them very miserable.'

Fitch took over the explanation, 'We need this information quite urgently. The Home Office and the Foreign Office are both quite keen to know what's going on so they can work out new policies. Normally SIS wouldn't involve anyone like you, but the Colonel has convinced me that we need someone with your talents. There's a woman who works for the leader of the group. We are just about certain that she is, or was, his mistress. Lately they seem to have disagreed about something and she's none too happy about it. We thought we could use you as bait.'

'So what's the name of this woman?' Walter asked.

'The woman's called Armand, Inessa Armand, sometimes she calls herself Stephane. She's half French and half English and she was married to a Russian and grew up in Russia. She's thirty four now, but still a bit of a looker. Be careful, mind, she's still a dedicated revolutionary,' Fitch said.

'How do you propose that I introduce myself to her?' Walter asked.

'The idea we are working on is for a couple of toughs to threaten her. You come to her rescue and get to know her as her knight in shining armour. It is essential that you make the rescue look convincing though, as we don't want her to suspect anything. I understand that you will be posing as some kind of artist. That gives you a reason to be in Paris and makes you sound suitably bohemian. If you insist on buying her a coffee or a brandy, just to make sure she's alright, it ought to give you enough time to get to know her.

Perhaps you could tell some story about being involved with the Suffragettes,' Fitch continued.

'Strangely enough, one of my best friends is involved with the women's suffrage movement,' Walter said, half smiling at Godiva, 'I'm not sure about the plan, though. It sounds a bit thin to me.'

'I'm sure we can refine it once you are in Paris. Anyway, I've got all your documents. Can you be ready to leave in a couple of hours?' Godiva said.

'That sounds fine to be. I'd quite like to get back to Paris. There are some old friends I'd like to look up,' Walter said.

'Absolutely not!' Fitch insisted, 'You will be staying there under an assumed name. We can't have you being recognised while you are in Paris. You will have to keep well away from anyone who is acquainted with you, and any places where you might be known. This isn't a holiday, you know, it's a serious job.'

'Then I take it that I'm not staying in a good hotel,' Walter said with a sigh.

'We have a house near to Ulyanov's apartment on Rue Marie Rose. Somehow I doubt that anyone will recognise you in that district. The good nightclubs and theatres are definitely out of bounds as well,' Fitch said.

'That all sounds rather depressing,' Walter commented.

'The Colonel's going out on a limb for you here. You're not properly trained as yet, so he really shouldn't be sending you. I really hope that we can trust you,' Fitch said in a worried voice, 'Now, do you have any questions?'

'Well, quite a lot, actually. I'm going to need a good deal more background information, and what about telling the French security people what I'm doing?' Walter continued.

'I've arranged for you to liaise with the French security agency. Call themselves the Tigers or some such nonsense. One of their people will get in touch once you are in Paris. As for the background,

I'll leave that to Miss Williams. She's been working on Ulyanov's case for a little while now. In fact it was her who flagged up the connection between him and the Latvians. Clever girl, Miss Williams,' Fitch said, ending with a short, sharp laugh. Godiva blushed slightly.

'So, in what way does this man pose a threat to us?' Walter asked.

'He is the spider at the centre of a web of intrigue. There are many groups who rely on him for their planning, and for the money to support their causes. You must remember the Tottenham Outrage about a year ago. A Policeman and a ten-year old boy were shot. Two Latvians tried to rob the wages from a factory. There was a chase, during which the Latvians were shooting all the time. They were eventually cornered and killed. The thing is, they were members of an anarchist group who want independence for Latvia. They attempted the robbery because they needed the money for the group, to build bombs and buy more guns. However, they are far from being the only revolutionary group hiding in England. Mostly these groups are grateful for the shelter we offer. We try to keep tabs on them, or Captain Kell does. Recently, another Latvian group set up, and these ones are closely linked to Mr Ulyanov, the puppet master in Paris. This group is much better organised and funded than the Tottenham people. They pose a threat to our security, and we're sure they are planning more robberies and possibly bomb attacks,' Fitch said.

'So, tell me a bit more about this spy-master in Paris' Walter asked Godiva, half closing his eyes in order to listen better.

'I've been looking at his notes for two weeks now. I started out thinking he had a righteous cause, but a couple of days in, I realized that he had systematically removed any potential rival from his organisation. He is totally obsessed with security, and won't let anyone near him. He lives his life through codes and ciphers. And he's the sort of person who would lay down the life of his friends to save his own reputation. His greatest scorn is reserved for anyone who might wish to negotiate or compromise. Having looked at his books and newspapers I can tell you that his writing is just awful, full of cliché and cant. This man is capable of anything.'

'So I was right. You really don't like him,' Walter said with a smile and a nod.

'What I think about him is not important. The fact is, he supports armed struggle and doesn't care who gets hurt. He encourages all sorts of groups and teaches them how to act as revolutionaries. Some of these groups are active here in England, especially in London, and we expect them to try to raise money by armed robbery,' Godiva continued.

'I thought this Ulyanov man was supplying these groups with money?' Walter questioned.

'Not directly with money, much more with support and training. He's taught a lot of people how to avoid detection and disappear into the background. There is some evidence that he gets them instructed in bomb making and such. There's one man in particular we want to find out about. This one's a Latvian anarchist we know as Peter the Painter. Of course, they all have loads of names. The point is, this Peter the Painter character is very active and is based in London. He used to be a part of Ulyanov's group, but he split away. That's something Ulyanov is not at all keen on, but he might forgive him because he's not a Russian. The thing is, Ulyanov appears quite polite, almost respectable. He even wrote a thank you letter to his landlady when he stayed over here. Also, the policy of the Home Office is to let most of these groups alone, while keeping a watchful eye on them. The policy we have been pursuing is to allow these groups to let off a bit of steam rather than let the pressure build up. If we tried to keep a lid on all their activities things would just build up to an explosion, just like what is happening in Russia.

Down in the Flood

Ulyanov even had a couple of meetings in London for Russian exiles, and we had to use the police to guard them from attack by people stirred up by the reporting in the Daily Mirror. Ulyanov know which side his bread is buttered and wouldn't want any attacks to happen here. This Peter the Painter is very different in that he doesn't mind biting the hand that feeds him. He's a very dangerous man, and we know he's already killed several people in his community. If he knew how to build bombs I am certain he wouldn't have any problem setting them off here,' Godiva explained.

'So is Ulyanov sponsoring this Peter man?' Walter asked, struggling to take in the flood of information.

'The service Ulyanov really supplies is expertise. That and the attitude that everything you do is alright, provided it's in the name of the revolution. He tells them how to organise the cells so it is difficult for us to put agents in, and he has other people who can teach them how to build bombs and where to get guns. I told you about the newspaper, but he also produces pamphlets that get delivered to the groups, which tell lurid stories of atrocities. I mean, Russia is in a pretty awful state, but I can't believe some of this stuff,' Godiva continued in an animated way. 'Oh, and that reminds me, be careful, be very careful of the Russian secret service, the Okhrana. If you come across any of them, run a mile. They are particularly vicious.'

'But we should be working on the same side,' Walter protested.

'If they even suspect that you are not sharing with them they won't hesitate to force the information out of you,' Godiva said.

'Well, if I spot any of these Okhrana I'll certainly let you know. Now, tell me, who's doing the translation of all these documents for you?' Walter asked.

'Detective Fitch speaks Russian very well,' Godiva said, nodding towards her colleague, 'and there's a little man we use, but recently I've started learning some Russian myself. I can't speak a word, of course, but I can read it quite well. Anyway, I need to tell you about how Ulyanov's household is set up. He shares a pretty decent apartment with his wife and mother in law. Look, this is stuff you'll need to know by the time you get to Paris. I've got some photos here, and a précis of the notes from the time he was in London.' She pushed a thick sheaf of notes across the desk towards him.

'Ah, a little light reading!' Walter said with a crooked smile.

'Don't worry, you'll have time to read it during your journey,' with a slight smile.

'And when am I supposed to leave?' Walter asked.

'As I said before, in about two hours,' Godiva replied as she consulted her fob watch.

'Oh, dear. I was hoping to spend an evening in town,' Walter said, sounding a little disappointed, 'Try to catch up with a few friends, perhaps.'

'You'll just have to make new lady friends on the boat train,' Godiva said knowingly. 'I've got your tickets here. And I've a request from 'K' that you go easy on the expenses. We've put some money in an account, but it is a modest amount. There should be enough Francs to be getting along with for a few days and the tickets are there. The details of the account are clear and you can access the money from any Thomas Cook office. Please provide receipts for all of your expenditure, unless you want it taken out of your wages, and remember that the person you are supposed to be hasn't much money. We've booked you into a room not far from Ulyanov's house. The address is in with the other stuff. You'll need to take some of your painting gear with you, enough to travel with.'

'So who am I supposed to be?' Walter asked, 'And since when did Kell become 'K'?'

'We've got you down as a struggling artist. It's easiest if you keep the name Walter, but from now until you return, your surname is Davies. You are the son of the Headmaster of a small Private school in Sussex. You've quarrelled with your father who refuses to support you while you try to realise your artistic ambitions. It seems quite natural that you would go to Paris, don't you think?' Godiva explained.

'Righty-ho,' said Walter, 'But what about some background on Ulyanov's mistress?'

'Well the details are in the folder, along with some photographs. She's not unattractive, so it shouldn't be too difficult for you to act the part of seducer. Sometimes Ulyanov sends her on missions when he can't turn up, and he has to brief her. So she can provide a good deal of useful information as to who he's been writing to, and what is going on,' Godiva explained in a slightly testy voice.

'What about the wife?' Walter continued.

'She's a few years older than Ulyanov, and a dedicated revolutionary herself. If she's ever shown any sign of human feelings we have yet to find any evidence. Intellectually she is not in the same league as her husband, but I'm sure she does vital work for him. We think she's a dead loss as a target. She's prepared to live off a little black bread and some water, look after her mother and any whim of Ulyanov and has no fun at all,' Godiva said.

'Is there any more background you need to tell me about?' Walter asked.

'Just a little, I suppose. This is about the Bolsheviks. The word means something like 'the majority of men'. Their main opponents are known as the Mensheviks, or 'the minority of men'. It all came about after a conference not long ago here in London. The biggest group got fed up with Ulyanov's endless hectoring speeches and left at the end of the evening. Ulyanov then took a vote with mostly his supporters there, and, surprise, surprise, he won it. It was totally unconstitutional of course, but it is typical of the man that he immediately went about shouting about how the vote showed who was the real leader of the revolutionaries. You'll probably come across some of the Mensheviks along with disillusioned Bolsheviks in Paris. There are a lot more of them than of Ulyanov's people, and they can be found in the cafés and bars, discussing things quite openly. We don't think they're a real problem. Mostly, they are quite reasonable men, and, as I said, Russia really does need a lot of reform. They are the sort of people we can work with, when Russia gets into an even worse state, which it will do. Of course, we can't be seen to be plotting against the Czar, as the Russians are our allies, but just a little reform would go a long way to calming things down there, but their rulers don't want to consider any change,' Godiva said, reeling off the facts like an encyclopaedia.

'I hope this is all in the folder, because I'm sure I haven't taken most of it in,' Walter said, feeling a little overwhelmed.

'Yes, of course. You'll find all that, and plenty more besides in the folder. Please don't flash it about in public. We don't want the French intelligence people, the 2ieme Bureau, to know exactly what we know, and they won't tell us everything they know. That's the thing about diplomacy; you need to keep a careful eye on your friends, as well as your enemies. The Bureau are not in favour with the president, and he has given many of their responsibilities to a new agency, called The Tigers. You'll be met by a Tigers agent when you get to Paris. Our relationship with the French agencies is none too warm, so don't be too open with the French. Now, I've divided the folder into two sections. At the front are things you can tell this French agent. At the back are the more sensitive papers. That's a much smaller folder. So, for once in your life, Walter, please try to be discrete,' Godiva urged.

'I thought you said I would be dealing with this Tigers mob, now you tell me the proper French intelligence agency is the 2ieme Bureau,' Walter commented.

'Ah, yes,' Godiva started, 'You see the 2ieme Bureau is the established agency and they are largely responsible for external intelligence gathering. They don't really have anything to do with counter intelligence. The Brigades du Tigre were set up through Clemenceau by the head of Police, Hennion, to combat the criminal gangs, but the Prime Minister has broadened their remit, so they are looking into the activities of foreign political groups and refugees. The other thing is that the 2ieme Bureau doesn't trust us British, we are the old enemy. We can only hope that the Tigers are more likely to co-operate.'

'I'd better get myself ready, then,' Walter said, his head spinning from an excess of information, 'I haven't got much time to get my stuff together before I go to the station. Nice to meet up again, Godiva. Perhaps we can have dinner sometime, after I get back.'

'That would be very nice,' Godiva said, 'but I'm not sure when you'll get back.'

'I'll send you a note when I return,' Walter said. He had realised that his relationship with Godiva was now very different to how it had been. He hoped that outside of work they could get back to being friends. He left after giving Godiva a brotherly kiss on the cheek, shook Fitch by the hand, then hurried outside to get a taxi to his studio in Pimlico, from where he could pick up a set of painting gear suitable for travel. From there he travelled to Victoria Station, to the platform where the train for Dover Marine station would leave.

The ticket he had been given was third class, which was just right for the character he was supposed to be creating, but he had some cash in his pocket and upgraded the ticket to first class for the journey to Dover.

◊

A vicious easterly wind was whipping sea-spray around the platforms of Dover Marine station. It stung the eyes of the people descending from the train at the end of the line. As it dried it would leave white flecks of salt on the dark overcoats of the travellers.

When Walter reached the ticket barrier and the path to the ferry, he found the route blocked and a notice informing passengers that the crossing was suspended due to storms. Accommodation was to be provided at a hotel on the harbour front. A charabanc was laid on to transport the passengers the one mile to the hotel. The driver was wrapped in several coats, with a hat, scarf and gloves, but all this did not stop him shivering. As they approached they could see him slapping his arms against his sides to encourage some blood flow.

There were fourteen of them who needed to get into the charabanc, assisted by the railway porters. With their luggage they filled the vehicle. When they were settled in their seats, huddled against the wind and the showers of sleet, the bus was encouraged into spluttering life and they were jerked into motion. The street lights were reflected in the glassy surface of the wet road. This surface was tar macadam bonded with granite chips. The quartzite in the stone reflected the light back like cut diamonds. After a very few minutes they arrived at the front of the hotel. This was a white stuccoed structure three stories high which formed part of a crescent that ran along the sea front. Fancy iron work fronted the balconies facing the harbour. Streaks of rust discoloured the stucco where the iron was embedded into the walls. Their luggage was carried inside by two grumbling porters and dumped in the entrance.

The travellers queued to get their keys at the reception desk. When it came to his turn, Walter decided to pay extra for a room with its own bathroom. He was still feeling the effects of his exertions at the training camp and had mud to wash off. The bath would have to wait for some time, as the dinner gong rang to tell guests to go to the restaurant. Walter only had time to send his luggage to his room and change for dinner before dining.

The meal was not good. It looked appetising enough, but lacked flavour, and was unevenly hot. The wine was cheap, thin and unpleasant, and Walter regretted choosing it. A pint of Bass would have been a much better selection. Across the room he noticed a table at which two women were eating. They were both quite thin, but the younger one had a good bone structure and a certain physical presence. The older woman was severe and mousy, which was an unattractive combination. The younger woman, a girl in reality, gave Walter a small smile, and, when she noticed, the older woman scowled at both the girl and Walter.

◊

Walter was taking a leisurely bath in an oversized tub before sleeping. He had just washed his hair and rinsed off the suds by lying down and dipping his head under the water. As he raised his head he heard the outer door of his room being softly opened. In an instant he switched from being relaxed and sleepy to full attention. In sitting up suddenly he slopped some water from the broad rim of the bath onto the floor. After blinking the water from his eyes he fixed his gaze onto the door of the bathroom, which was partly ajar. He placed his hands on the side of the bath and prepared to spring from the tub. Part of a face appeared in the crack of the door, and some minimal pressure caused the door to open inwards. The girl who had been at dinner was looking at him with the same interest and curiosity that he was feeling himself. She was dressed in a respectable dressing gown and ankle slippers. Neither gown or slippers were particularly suited to her slim frame.

'Oh, you're in the bath,' she said, stating the obvious.

'Yes, I'm in the bath,' Walter agreed, wondering where this conversation was leading.

'This is a much nicer room than ours. We have to share a bathroom. It's not very nice having to share with other people, especially if you don't know them,' she continued.

'Is there some reason why you have come into my room; other than to admire it, that is?' Walter asked, feeling more perplexed than anxious.

The girl shuffled into the room and stared down at him as he sat in the bath. Then she giggled. 'Gosh, I've never seen a man with no clothes on before. Well, not a young man, anyway. I think you're very handsome. I hope you don't mind me looking at you like this, only I saw you in the restaurant, and I couldn't help noticing how good looking you were,' she said in staccato phrases.

'Well, thank you for those words of admiration. Look, I'm a little disconcerted by this. I'm sure young ladies aren't supposed to come into the bathrooms of gentlemen, especially if they've not been introduced,' Walter said softly.

'How was I supposed to get introduced to you? I couldn't march up to you in the restaurant, could I? Especially with old Cauldicott guarding me the way she does', the young woman continued, now looking down the length of Walter's torso to his groin.

'So, Miss Cauldicott is your companion. But I still don't know who you are, nor what you're doing in my bathroom,' Walter said, with a small note of impatience in his voice.

'Cauldicott is the dragon of a companion my parents have sent to guard me on the journey. Before we went to bed I put an extra sleeping draft into her warm milk. She won't wake until the morning, so we won't be disturbed.'

'If you won't make the introductions, I'd better help you,' Walter said patiently, 'My name is Walter Davies. I'm an artist.'

'I'm Annabella Aphrodite Saville, and I'm going back to my finishing school after the Christmas break,' said the girl.

'I heard your companion call you Bella in the restaurant,' Walter admitted.

'I hate that name, it's so unromantic,' she said, peevishly, 'That's why I always try to use my full name.'

Down in the Flood

'And now that I know your name, Miss Annabella Aphrodite Saville, could you please tell me why you came to my room?' Walter asked, now thoroughly amused by the situation.

'Well, I was wondering if you'd like to have sex with me. We talk a lot about sex in the school, and some of the girls boast that they have already lost their virginity, but the men these girls chose were usually unsuitable, you know, quite common types. When I saw you, and noticed that you didn't have anyone with you, I thought you looked just the right sort of man to do the deed. It would mean so much to me if I could arrive back at school with some really juicy event to talk about. My life's mostly pretty boring,' she said, the words spilling out,' You don't look much like an artist. You're too clean and not sort of bohemian enough,' she added.

'I am an artist, though. My money mostly comes from my father, and he knows some rich people who buy my paintings. It's easier to sell them if I don't look too scruffy,' Walter explained. 'And how did you know which was my room?'

'I was listening when you were talking to the man at the desk,' she answered.

'I didn't notice you at the time,' Walter admitted, 'Very remiss of me. How old are you, Annabella Aphrodite?'

'I'll be eighteen next month,' said the girl.

'So, you're only seventeen. You really are a very bold girl,' Walter said.

'Shall I go away, or do you want to have sex with me?' the girl asked directly.

'I'll tell you what; you take that dressing gown off and get into the bed and I'll get myself dried off and join you in a minute,' Walter said.

'Do you want me to take my nightdress off as well?' the girl asked.

'That would save a bit of bother later,' Walter agreed.

'Righty-ho,' the girl said. She handed the towel to him, kissing him chastely on the cheek as she leaned forward, and then turned to leave the bathroom. Walter towelled himself dry, dropped the towel onto the damp floor and put on his nightshirt. With a slight smile he reflected that he could hardly be accused of seduction in this case. It should be an amusing way to spend the night. He put on his nightshirt and walked out of the bathroom to join the girl who was waiting for him in the bed, between the cool starched linen sheets.

Wednesday 4th January 1910

Walter awoke to find himself alone in his bed. He yawned, coughed, scratched and stretched, then rose, found his slippers and walked to the window to look at the day. It was a little before eight o'clock, and the sun was just rising above the newly completed Eastern arm of the huge Admiralty Harbour. The storm of the previous night had blown itself out, and pink-tinged broken clouds were scudding across the sky from the South West. In the Harbour the water was relatively calm, but beyond the great breakwater the waves were marching in battalions across the channel. Walter dressed and went down to breakfast. This was a much more satisfying meal than he had consumed the previous evening. Annabella Aphrodite Saville was sitting with her companion at a table some way from Walter, and didn't seem to notice him. Walter was relieved to be able to finish his meal in peace. The next meal he would have would be in France, and would probably be very good.

A clerk was passing around the room informing the delayed travellers that the ferry would be departing in an hour from the Western Arm, and the charabanc would be ready to take them there in twenty minutes. As no-one had properly unpacked there was no great rush to get ready to depart. There was a small queue at the reception desk, and they did not make it to the charabanc until five minutes after the supposed departure time.

The party from the charabanc were quickly ushered through immigration control and onto the ferry, which was under steam and scattering smuts of soot onto the crew and passengers on deck. Walter could feel the slow vibration of the engine through the planking of the deck and then through the soles of his boots. It was not an unpleasant sensation, and it felt good to be travelling at last. Within a few minutes of their boarding the ferry was untied from the dock and, with much churning of the water behind, it started to accelerate towards the gap between the Western Arm of the harbour and the breakwater. Imbedded into the western end of the breakwater was the barracks for the men who were to man the naval guns which faced out into the channel. All the concrete surfaces of the wall were already stained with the droppings of the seagulls which roosted there. As the ferry moved past the breakwater the gulls took off in a screaming swarm, their cries like sarcastic laughter. Then they were through the gap and out onto the choppy water of the English Channel.

Looking behind and to his left, Walter could see the outline of Dover castle. He reflected that while some castles, like his father's in Herefordshire, were comfortable homes, this one was meant to deter any attempt at attack, and to make obvious just how counter-productive any such attack would be. The entire structure seemed to scream obdurate defiance and swift and merciless revenge at any potential enemy, especially the old one across the channel.

As the size of the waves increased, so did the number of passengers being sea-sick. Walter was not a particularly good sailor, but his stomach and constitution were strong. He was used to rowing on rivers and lakes, but the water in those places did not move in this way. He half regretted the large breakfast he had consumed, but managed to hold onto it well enough. Standing at the rail of the ferry was exhilarating, and the cold wind was bracing, provided you were well enough wrapped. The crossing to Calais took a little over two hours, and the waves subsided well before the harbour grew large in the vision of the passengers on deck.

The Calais Maritime railway station was close to the Avant-Port on a loop of track around the citadel which was the only architectural interest in the entire town. Porters grabbed passenger's luggage and hauled it to the station on trolleys, demanding a tip, or pourbois, holding out grubby hands until sufficient coins had been given.

Experienced travellers too mean to pay knew they had to keep tight hold of their bags and refuse help with loud cries of 'Non!' There was a great deal of pride in the painting and decoration of the station, but it was as sooty as any such place always was. Walter had time to pour a brandy down his throat in the station buffet to settle his stomach before he boarded the Paris bound train. From this point he knew he had to act the part of a genteel but impoverished artist, and he found himself trapped in a compartment with a couple and their five noisy and argumentative children. With the number of bodies inside the air became hot and moist. Vapour accumulated on the inside of the windows until it trickled down in rivulets. This effectively screened the landscape from the sight of the travellers, but, Walter reflected, the Pais de Calais is not the most scenically interesting part of France, and so this was not a great disadvantage. The train was swift, which was just as well, as the seats were decidedly uncomfortable.

By the time they pulled in to Gare du Nord Walter could hardly wait to get off and stretch his legs. He was wondering if he would be met at the station, and, if not, how he would manage to navigate around the Metro to the suburb where he was to be based. He was still lost in thought when he was approached by a swarthy man in an elegant but well worn coat. The man touched the brim of his grey hat momentarily, in a minimal gesture of salute.

'Mister Davies?' he enquired in a deep, slow voice in accented but accurate English.

'That's right,' Walter answered, slightly guardedly. Looking at the man's face he could see a slightly hooked nose and deep-set dark brown eyes.

'I am Officer Gaston LaDavide, and I've come to guide you to your lodgings,' he said.

'Do you have any identification?' Walter asked.

'Do you, Mister Davies?' LaDavide said, with a grin.

'Fair enough,' Walter agreed, 'do we take a cab?'

'You are not nearly rich enough for that,' LaDavide said, 'we shall take the Metro.'

'Lead on, then,' Walter said and picked up his bags. LaDavide made no attempt to help him.

It was not far to the Metro station, but long enough for Walter's arm to ache with the effort of carrying his heavy bag of artist's materials. They had to descend a long flight of concrete stairs edged with grooved iron strips which were shiny with wear. In the ticket hall there were queues to purchase passes. Even at lunchtime the station was bustling. It was several minutes before LaDavide could get to the front of the queue and purchase the tickets. After returning to the place where he had left Walter he helped to carry one of the bags, if only to speed their progress.

The Metro platform was windswept and damp and smelled of domestic tobacco, sweat and cheap red wine. In a very few minutes a train rattled to a halt. There was a general scrimmage to board which was less polite than at any London station, but the carriage was more spacious and better appointed than the few underground trains which Walter had travelled on before. Walter had expected to be taken across the city to the south western suburbs where he knew he was to lodge, but LaDavide nudged him in the ribs with an elbow as they approached the fifth station.

'My office is just around the corner. We shall go there first and we will talk. Besides, it is time for some food, and I need to instruct you on how to choose a cheap restaurant in Paris, and what you should eat if you have little money. We will go to the house later,' LaDavide said as the train jerked to a halt.

The office was on the second floor of a nondescript building that had somehow managed to escape any trace of the elegance of the bulk of the city's architecture. Walter left his belongings by a cabinet in a cramped and untidy room. He then followed LaDavide out of the office, around the corner and into a shabby restaurant. The soaking rain continued to fall in a steady manner, and there were deep puddles in the gutters. Inside the restaurant the atmosphere was thick with tobacco smoke and steam. A small waiter in a half apron guided them to a table near to the back of the room, close to the kitchen and took the food order from LaDavide before leaving them.

Walter took out his cigarette case and offered one to LaDavide.

'Ah, English cigarettes. May I see the case?' the Frenchman asked.

Walter handed the case over and his host closed it and slipped it into an inside pocket.

'Excuse me,' said Walter, 'You have my cigarette case.'

'Yes, and I shall keep it until you leave Paris. You must stop being the English Milord and become a poor artist. If you do not act in the right way, dress in the correct clothes and learn to speak as a poor artist would, no-one will believe you are who you say you are. You will smoke French cigarettes and eat French peasant food. Start with the cigarette,' LaDavide said. He reached into an outside pocket of his jacket and withdrew a crumpled pack of a common brand of cigarettes, handing one to Walter.

Walter tapped the end of the cigarette and some dry strands fell out. The paper was yellow and quite thick. On sucking in a lungful he almost gasped at the roughness of the smoke. After exhaling he coughed slightly.

'What do you think?' LaDavide asked, with a crooked smile

'They're a little rough, but I suppose I'll get used to them in time. Will you supply a receipt for the cigarette case?' Walter answered.

'Of course, later,' LaDavide said with a dismissive wave of his hand.

The waiter brought two steaming bowls of some garlicky stew and placed them onto the table with an unnecessary flourish. Walter put out his cigarette and picked up a fork. He stirred the surface of the food and sniffed. There was a strong smell of aromatic herbs and some unidentifiable lumps of meat and vegetable within. He ventured to try some and found it to be excellent.

'This is very good,' Walter said, 'What is it?'

'It is a ragôut from Provence, made with lapin, err, rabbit. I'm glad you like it. You will find that most of the food is very good. Even the food from Alsace is good, if you like sausages, beer, potato and cabbage. This food is from the south of France and this restaurant is quite typical. Look for a restaurant where the workers eat, because the food will be good and it will be cheap. If the restaurant is empty at lunchtime the food will be no good.'

Walter finished his food and laid down his fork. The waiter brought a bottle of vin rouge ordinaire and two glasses, banging the items roughly on the table. Walter poured out decent measure into each glass and pushed one across the table to LaDavide.

'Merci,' said LaDavide, taking a swig of the wine before slamming the glass back down onto the table. He smiled up at Walter.

'Santé,' said Walter in salutation. The wine was almost as rough as the tobacco, but both were full of flavour. Perhaps he could get used to this. 'Now tell me who you are, and why you have been assigned to me.'

'You know my name,' LaDavide said, with a shrug, 'I work for a government agency which deals with security. We are separate from the Police. Our two countries sometimes work together. When they let us know that you were to come over, my boss told me that I was to look after you. I do not suppose that I know your real name, but that is not important. I know that you come from a rich family. This I can tell from your clothes, and from your boots and from your cigarette case. Your manners are those of any Englishman who is not a working man. That is why I am showing you how to fit in. You may be able to get away with the clothes and shoes. Most

Frenchmen, and most Russians could not tell the difference. You could explain it by saying that your father has stopped giving you money, but you still have good clothes.'

'I've already used that excuse. It's not quite a lie, anyway. My father never approved of me trying to be an artist. Now, I don't mean to be too inquisitive, but do you have some Arab blood in you?' Walter asked.

'Yes I do,' laughed LaDavide, 'My mother is Algerian. My father was a civil servant who was sent to work over there. If you wished to insult me you could call me a pied noir.'

'Black feet?' Walter questioned.

'Insults are difficult to translate. I suppose that mulatto is quite close in English usage,' LaDavide said.

'That's alright, I share an apartment with a man from India. He's a Muslim,' Walter said.

'Please do not tell me anymore. It would be too easy to identify you, and that is not good. You must learn to be discrete,' LaDavide observed.

A man in his thirties with pouchy cheeks, like a bloodhound puppy, hurried over to their table through the fog of the room. He whispered something loudly into LaDavide's ear.

'This is my friend Pascale, Walter. I will introduce you properly later. We've got to go,' LaDavide said, 'I'll leave you back in the office. Some work has come up. I'll take you to your room a little later.'

They hurried out of the restaurant, leaving the money on the table. Back at the office they found the other officers were frantically dashing around, seeking instructions and gathering guns and boxes of ammunition.

'La Villette!' someone screamed at LaDavide as they entered. He hurried into his office and returned with a revolver and was busy stuffing a handful of bullets into his pocket.

'Wait here, we will be back quite soon,' he shouted to Walter above the din.

'What is it?' Walter asked.

'We are making a raid on a group of Apaches gangsters in the La Villette district. There must be a meeting going on, and the intelligence has been sent to us. This could be quite dangerous,' LaDavide explained.

'It sounds exciting. Can I come along?' Walter pleaded.

'If there is room in the car,' LaDavide replied, 'But only if you come now.'

They ran down the steps to a waiting big Peugeot and ended up standing on the running board, clutching the doors or anything else which projected from the bodywork. The car drove faster than was safe over the cobbled streets and swung alarmingly around the right angle junctions of the city grid. All the time the rain continued to fall, and only his overcoat provided any protection for Walter as it flapped around his legs. By the time they arrived at their destination Walter's hands and face were stinging from the lashing of the cold rain. His hat had disappeared almost as soon as they had started and his blond hair was plastered darkly to his scalp. Overall the journey had taken about fifteen minutes.

The driver applied the brakes hard and the car skidded slightly on the slick cobbles, coming to rest at a slight angle to the curb. Walter leapt onto the pavement and allowed the officers inside the car to pile out. They pushed past a concierge and into the dark interior of a large apartment block. Walter decided to stay on the pavement and to guard the entrance. It would have been more exciting to join in the raid, but the numbers were such that he would have only got in the way in such a confined space.

From above came the noises of a door being battered open, with a great deal of shouting and a single loud report from a pistol. Walter judged that the noises were coming from the floor above street level.

Things seemed to be quietening down, when there suddenly came the sound of breaking glass and a small man in dark clothes dropped from the window, landing lightly a dozen feet from where Walter stood.

He was dressed in a black beret, a shirt with horizontal stripes and a spotted neckerchief, corduroy trousers and black shoes almost like dancing pumps. He had a short canvas jacket and a bright red cloth wound around his waist, with a tassel down his left hip in the Spanish fashion. For a second the two men stood looking at each other, both trying to make out what the other might be.

'Arrete! Voleur!' screamed a voice from the window above.

This interruption made both men's minds up. Walter decided he would stop the man, and the man decided he would get away. Seeing flight as an easier option than fight he turned and sprinted down the street. Walter was a little hampered by the weight of his near sodden coat and the smaller man's acceleration took him into an early lead, but within a few yards Walter was making up the distance between them. As they skidded round the corner Walter managed to get a grip on the collar of the man's jacket. The wrench of the grip caused both men to slip and fall on the wet paving stones. They went down, spinning apart. Walter's momentum took him feet first into a post box with a loud clattering noise. The smaller man rose more quickly from his fall, and he reached onto his waistband to retrieve a curious weapon. This appeared to be a snub-barrelled revolver with knuckledusters for a handgrip. A knife blade was mounted directly under the squat barrel of the revolver. Walter was just about on his feet when he saw the gun. As the man raised his arm to fire, Walter flung himself behind the post box. There was a dull crack from the weapon and the cast iron casing broke with a noise like cracking ice. Staying low, Walter launched himself at the man, performing a very effective rugby tackle around the man's knees. The Apache fell backwards under the weight of the tackle but still managed to swing the blade at Walter. It caught in the stout tweed cloth of the overcoat and remained there. Walter pushed hard with his arm and the brass knuckle-dusters of the weapon rang as they hit the granite curb of the pavement. The little man was surprisingly strong and almost wriggled his right arm free of Walter's grasp. His forearm was now overhanging the curb, halfway up to his elbow. Walter slammed the flat of his hand onto the man's wrist, and it broke with a sharp crack as it made contact with the stone, the weapon drooping uselessly into the stream of water that ran down the gutter. The small man screamed.

When Walter looked up he saw LaDavide grinning down at him.

'Pas mal! The officer said, in genuine admiration. He helped Walter up. The little man was now whimpering with pain as he was dragged upright by another officer, who then found that he could not effectively handcuff the man. Instead he grasped him by his injured arm, causing him to scream once again. The Apache pistol dropped with a clang on the pavement.

'I think your coat is a little torn,' LaDavide said, 'Now you will look right for the part you are to play.' He picked up the weapon from the pavement, thumb and forefinger between the smallest hole of the knuckle duster. He would need to take this to the fingerprint expert.

◊

The apartment was in a block near a junction to the Rue du Loing. A grim Parisienne concierge guarded the doorway from behind a window which opened into her room. She said nothing, but as Walter and LaDavide passed she glared at them, lips compressed and arms folded. After walking up three long flights of stairs, passing the smells and noise of the other occupants, they came to the corridor leading to the room. LaDavide handed the key over to Walter who had some difficulty in unlocking the door. The mechanism was stiff in movement but loose in fit. Having mastered the lock Walter opened the door and between them they put Walter's belongings inside. Looking around the room Walter noted with a certain sinking feeling that the furnishings were poorly made and considerably worn. The wallpaper was a ghastly print of bouquets of delphiniums in faded and stained yet unnatural colours. What was worse was the lack of heating. Their breath could be seen in the air between them when they spoke. Walter went to the window and observed the scene over the rooftops, northwards across the Seine and into the heart of the city. The rain had mostly cleared and he could make out the phallic iron thrust of the distant Eiffel Tower.

'The concierge says she has to notify the gas company before she can turn on the gas. It may take a day before you have any heating,' LaDavide said, with a shrug.

'Then I'll go to a café and get myself dry before I come back here,' said Walter.

It was getting dark outside and Walter had to light a candle, as the gas lamp, like the heater, was not working.

'I'll find you tomorrow morning,' LaDavide said, moving towards the door.

There was a soft knock at the unfastened door. When it opened a young but tousled head appeared in the gap.

'I thought I heard English being spoken,' the mouth of the head announced.

'Good evening,' LaDavide said to the stranger as he passed him in the doorway.

'Mind if I come in?' the stranger enquired, coming in anyway.

'Make yourself at home, by all means,' Walter said guardedly.

'I'm Franklin Skinner,' the man started, 'As you can probably tell by my accent, I'm an American. I'm a sort of artist, or at least, I'm trying to make a go of being an artist. And I do a bit of writing as well.' He was edging nearer to Walter, grinning nervously.

'And I'm Walter Davies, and you can tell by my accent that I'm English,' Walter answered. The American was strongly built, of middle height, and looked like he had been sleeping in his clothes. His eyes scanned the room, looking for something more interesting than anything Walter could see.

'It's good to hear a voice speaking English. I've been here for a couple of months now, and I've hardly heard any spoken. Trouble is, my French ain't quite so good.'

'Is there anything I can do for you?' Walter asked.

'Oh, thank you. I was really just trying to say "hello". Look you haven't seen a bald man, have you? He seems to be hanging around these apartments. He's quite a young man, but he's bald. I know who he is. He's a Mexican,' Skinner said.

'No, I can safely say that I haven't seen anyone like that round here. Are you worried about this hairless Mexican?' Walter asked, more amused than concerned.

'It's just that when he appears, I seem to have bad luck. I was just about to sell a painting and then he appeared. The woman I was selling it to caught sight of him and changed her mind. Then I had to move out of my previous apartment, after I saw him again,' Skinner blurted out.

'Tell you what, I'll let you know if I see anyone like him. I suppose your room is opposite, or you wouldn't have been able to hear me,' Walter commented.

'Sure, that would be good of you. You know, it really is cold in here,' Skinner said, frowning.

'The gas isn't switched on yet,' Walter explained.

'It took them a week to turn on the gas when I came,' Skinner said, unhelpfully.

'And there's a bad draft when the door is left open,' Walter continued.

'Oh, sorry,' said Skinner. He closed the door and then sat down, uninvited on a hard wooden chair which creaked slightly under his weight.

'Are there any decent cafés round here?' Walter asked, 'Only I was going to find a place to get warm and dry.'

'Sure, there's plenty of places. You get yourself all sorted out and I'll call round again and take you to one that I know. It doesn't look like you've got that much with you, so we'll say ten minutes,' said Skinner, and he left.

'Now that you've made a friend, I think I can safely leave you. I'll call again in the morning,' LaDavide said.

'Thank you for what you've done, I'll see you tomorrow,' Walter said.

◊

It wasn't exactly a café, although it sold food of a sort. This consisted of some charcuterie and bread, and saussison, chou-croute and potato for the hungrier. There was a small stage, with some crude lime-lights and a four-piece band. A swaggering, loudly dressed man was acting as master of ceremonies and tried to whip up enthusiasm among the audience. Below the stage most people were drinking, flirting, conversing and laughing, and paying little attention to the entertainment which was offered. There was little chance for Walter to hear what Skinner was saying above the din. This was not a situation which Walter objected to. Instead, he ate his sausages and drank a large glass of Alsace beer in relative peace. His overcoat was placed on the back of his chair, and was steaming lightly in the heat of the room.

The MC introduced another act and a drum roll immediately followed. The audience went quiet, except for Skinner whose voice was suddenly very loud. He reduced the volume after realising he was shouting.

'This is the thing we have come for. Take a look at this. There's nothing to be seen like this in Columbus, Ohio, I can tell you.'

A young woman came onto the stage in an outlandish costume with a feathered head-dress which made fanciful reference to the Far East, and heavy smudges of khol around her eyes. To the sawing of a violin and the warbling of a clarinet she started to dance, or rather to take up various positions and to sway and gyrate between poses. After a minute or so she made a swift movement and removed the heavy skirt with vertical pleats covering her legs. Beneath this she was wearing diaphanous trousers of peacock blue. The drummer joined in at this point and the tempo of the dance became faster. To this heavier beat she began to twist and jump. At the end of this period of the dance she removed the cerise silk bodice she had been wearing. Beneath this she wore only a contraption of narrow straps supporting bejewelled saucers which covered her slim breasts. The music slowed, and the drummer ceased, to be replaced by the pianist who repeated a modal phrase to a strange time signature. The dancer squatted, legs apart and swayed side to side. She stood, reached behind and deftly removed the trousers. She was now naked from the waist down, or appeared so. She resumed her squat and now swayed forward and back. The drum joined in once more and at the climax of the dance she removed the saucers, walking around the stage naked but for the headdress for a minute before grabbing a silk robe and leaving the stage to great roars of applause.

'Who was that?' Walter asked Skinner after the hubbub had died down.

'That was Rosa Languedoc,' Skinner answered with a toothy grin which was minus one upper tooth, 'She's just one of the exotic dancers in Paris. I suppose they've all kind of imitated Marta Hari, who was the first to do that kind of thing, according to the true aficionados. But I've seen her act, and I can tell you, young Rosa is the coming thing. Not so much as good as the original as better. If you want to, I can get you in to meet her. It won't be cheap, mind, if you want to enjoy her favours.'

'Well, I wouldn't mind doing a picture of her, but I suppose she's got lots of us artists bobbing around in her wake,' Walter said.

'You bet she has. And I'll bet you haven't got anything like that in London!' Skinner said, with a sharp laugh.

'Not in the sort of places I have been to. Not taking all their clothes off, like that,' Walter admitted.

'Yeah, I thought so. Mind you, I wish I was a bit better at portraits, so I could ask if I could paint her. She's quite a gal,' Skinner said, with a slight sigh.

'Do you paint landscapes, then?' Walter asked, being polite.

'Yeah, that's right. Landscapes and still life and such stuff is what I do. Not very exciting, I'm afraid,' Skinner admitted.

'Why did you come to Paris then?' Walter asked, and he lit a cigarette.

'Just to get among other artists, I suppose. Where I come from there aren't many people who like drawing and painting and stuff. I thought that if I came here, my art would improve, just being around other artists,' Skinner mused.

'And has it?' Walter asked, breathing out a wreath of blue smoke.

'Yeah, I reckon so. Of course, I still rely on my mother sending a few bucks every now again, but I have sold a few paintings. I'm trying to keep up with the modern stuff. You know, Picasso and Braque. How about you?'

'Well, I mostly do portraits in oils,' Walter said, 'and I've been following a couple of Welsh artists, Augustus John and James Dickson Innes. They do a lot of landscapes. You'll have to show me some of your work, but I haven't brought any of mine with me. The idea of this trip was to do some new work. Just like you, my father still gives me an allowance.'

'I think I've met that John feller's sister, name of Gwen. Not sure about the work of the other man. Don't suppose it's as radical as Picasso's though,' Skinner said, putting his hands on the table and leaning forwards.

'The thing about Picasso is that every time I think I'm getting to understand what his work is about, he changes his style to something completely different. It may be a bit old-fashioned, but I do like really good draftsmanship,' Walter explained.

'Why come to Paris, if you're doing the same stuff that you used to do in England?' Skinner asked.

'Because Paris is the capital city of the art world. You have to be here in order to be noticed by the people who matter. I'm just drinking in the atmosphere, same as you,' Walter explained, 'Besides, maybe I can get some new ideas.'

'Talking of drinking, how about an absinthe?' Skinner asked, his face lighting up with a wicked grin.

'Not for me, thanks. One of the few flavours I do not like is aniseed. I'll just have a brandy, if you don't mind,' Walter replied.

'But it's not just the alcohol but the wormwood in it that helps to free the mind for artistic endeavour,' Skinner said with some passion in his voice.

'I still don't like the taste,' Walter started, 'Not that I'm against some artistic stimulation. I've found that cocaine helps me, provided I don't use it too often, and I've smoked some wog hemp that a friend had, and that was quite good.'

Skinner called the waiter over and gave his order. A few minutes later the waiter returned with a very large and rather rough brandy for Walter and all the paraphernalia required for the preparation of the absinthe. There was a special drinking vessel, like a large tulip glass that bulged at the base and had a line etched into it. A full dose of absinthe filled the glass to this level. One dose would be about three or four spirit measures in England, Walter observed. Onto this glass the waiter placed a slotted silver spoon, in the centre of the bowl of which he carefully placed a sugar cube. An absinthe fountain was positioned next to the glass. This was a brass and glass container raised above the table by a column like a candle stick. The container was filled with ice and water. A small tap was fitted to the base of the bowl. Iced water dripped slowly from the tap onto the sugar cube and thence into the dose of absinthe. The steady drip of sweetened ice water caused the absinthe to turn from pale green to cloudy. When the drink was diluted about four parts water to one of absinth the tap was turned off.

By the time the drink was ready, Walter had finished his brandy. He called for another and for another dose for Skinner, who was drinking down the green fairy in mouthfuls. The waiter started the process off again and left the tap slowly dripping onto the new dose.

It was difficult to tell if it was the wormwood or the alcohol that affected Skinner's behaviour. Walter assumed that it was the alcohol which had the greater effect, for he had to help Skinner back to his room and place him on the bed, dressed but minus his boots. Perhaps he would have interesting dreams which he could afterwards use to inspire his paintings. He would certainly have a hell of a hangover.

Walter went back to his cold room and undressed for bed. His coat was now dry, and he placed it over the scratchy, thin blankets to help him to stay warm. A gusty wind made the window frames rattle, but the brandy he had drunk helped him to get to sleep very quickly.

Thursday 5th January 1910

Walter was awoken by an urgent knocking on his door. Although the sun had already risen the day was dull and grey. He walked to the door in his nightshirt and opened it to find LaDavide looking at him. The officer appeared much as he had the previous day. Walter invited him in while he dressed, then they went to a café for coffee and croissants. It was not quite nine o'clock.

'Are you awake now?' LaDavide asked as they sat smoking their first cigarettes of the day.

'Yes, thank you. And I'm beginning to warm up now. That room is really cold. Anyway, what are we doing today?' Walter asked in return.

'I hope it will be a little less noisy than yesterday,' LaDavide laughed, 'I'll show you Ulyanov's apartment in a little while and introduce you to the men who have been watching him. And there is someone else I would like you to meet, just as a courtesy; a man who works at the Russian Embassy.'

'Ah, Okhrana I suppose,' Walter mused.

'Not directly. He is mostly a diplomat. You will understand when you meet him. He is not a thug,' LaDavide explained.

'He may not be a thug himself, but he might give other people orders,' Walter said, thinking out loud.

'All I can say is that you must see for yourself,' LaDavide continued, 'We will go to his house, as we don't want to be seen going into the Embassy. He is expecting us sometime after noon. If you have finished we will look in on Ulyanov.'

Walter stubbed out his cigarette, which was rasping his throat, put his overcoat and hat on and followed LaDavide out of the café. He had paid the bill without question and was wondering how long his cash would last.

Down in the Flood

They made their way on foot a few blocks south east to the Avenue d'Orleans. Rue Marie Rose was a side-street to the right, about a hundred metres down this road, close to the Parc Montsouris. Ulyanov's apartment was on the first floor in a large modern block, not big, but much more luxurious than Walter's room. It seemed strangely grand for a Marxist revolutionary. As they approached a small man, well wrapped in overcoat and muffler came up to greet them. LaDavide introduced him as Fournier, a police Detective. He spoke rapidly in a thick Parisian accent which Walter found difficult to follow, only understanding one word in three.

'He says that we will shortly see Monsieur Ulyanov. Everyday at the same time he rides his bicycle to the Biblioteque Nationale. Tell me what you think of our revolutionary,' LaDavide said, partly translating.

A short stocky man with a clipped ginger beard came out of the entrance to the block pushing a cheap black bicycle with pneumatic tyres. Having positioned the machine to his liking at the curb he made an old-fashioned sideways mount and rode off down the road, wobbling slightly until he built up some speed.

'So that's Ulyanov,' Walter observed, 'He's not very impressive, is he?'

'Do not underestimate him, he is a very determined man,' LaDavide said, turning to accept a cigarette from the other officer.

'What about the women in the apartment?' Walter asked. LaDavide translated this question for the benefit of the other man, who replied in another rapid outpouring of harsh syllables.

'He says that they are not nearly so regular in their habits. There are two women there almost all of the time, the wife, who looks like a pig, and her mother. Sometimes a secretary comes to help Ulyanov. Then there is another woman who visits quite often, a tall, good looking woman of about thirty. I think she is the one you are looking for. The wife does the shopping, or sometimes her mother does. The secretary just comes and goes like a ghost,' LaDavide translated.

'How am I going to meet this woman visitor, then?' Walter asked.

'That I can tell you, as it is already arranged. This man here, Fournier, will telephone from that café over there to a local police station where two of our men will be waiting. He will do this when your visitor is about to leave. She is quite regular in her habits. After ringing the police station, Fournier, or one of his men, will come to fetch you. We have a motorcycle or car waiting. The two police officers will pretend to try to rob her. You will come to the rescue and after saving her you will get to know her. It does mean that we need to know where you are during the day. I suggest that you paint in your room for most of the day, using the daylight. Please be careful with our men, I've seen the way you fight and I do not want them to get hurt, and,' LaDavide said, as though explaining a difficult problem to a surly child.

'Do you have any idea when we can expect this woman to arrive?' Walter asked.

'She usually comes on a Friday, so we expect to see her tomorrow, but she may have other business. As for today, I think it would be good for you to get an idea of the arrangement of the streets around here, so that you will know where you are when you meet this woman. It would be better if you looked like you were on your own, I think,' LaDavide replied.

'Right, then. I'll have a look around and get to know the territory. I'll see you here in about half an hour,' Walter said. He pushed down the collar of his coat, and taking the time from his pocket watch he made a mental note of when to be back.

'You will find me in the café when you come back. I will have a coffee and a cognac ready for you,' LaDavide said.

Walter quartered the ground for several blocks around, stopping frequently to memorise the relationship between the intersection of streets and the local landmarks. It was somewhat over an hour before he returned to Rue Marie Rose. LaDavide was sitting by the window in the shabby café, and motioned him in. Just as he had been promised, Walter found a cup of coffee and a cognac to warm him.

'Perhaps it is time for you to start work on a painting,' LaDavide suggested.

'When is it that we are supposed to meet this Russian diplomat you were talking about?' Walter enquired.

'About half past twelve would be a good time. I will call for you at midday. Please do not look too smart. This may be a visit to a diplomat, but it is not a diplomatic visit. You must convince this man that you are what you are pretending to be. The clothes you are currently wearing will do very well, but I advise you to shave first. Two days' growth of beard would seem to be a little disrespectful,' LaDavide said, sipping his own cognac.

'Then I hope that there is some hot water to be had,' Walter said, with a touch of bitterness.

'Is your gas supply still not connected?' LaDavide asked, without any interest.

'I'll ask the concierge when I go back,' Walter answered, 'And I think I should go back now, while I still have time to shave and set out an easel.'

'You could always go to a barber for a shave,' LaDavide suggested.

'That sounds like a good idea. I'll see you about noon,' Walter said, getting up.

'A bientôt,' LaDavide said as he walked out the door.

Walter found a barber's shop which was not crowded on the way back to his room, and received an adequate but expensive shave. He longed for the attentions he received from his manservant, Dorkins when he was in London. It was nearly eleven thirty before he returned to his room. As he set up his easel he could hear the noises from Skinner's room. The American had woken up with a stinking hangover and started groaning. On a small canvas Walter tried to sketch the face of Ulyanov, as he could recall it from the brief look he had managed, using a soft pencil. The face which appeared on the canvas was just about recognisable by the time LaDavide returned to fetch him.

'So, you really are an artist,' LaDavide said, a considering sort of expression on his mouth and giving a slight shrug.

'It's quite difficult to capture an image of him. The eyes are quite interesting. They're a bit Asiatic, I think,' Walter said, thoughtfully.

'It does look like him. Anyway, you should fit in well enough among these artists,' LaDavide observed, 'Time to go now.'

◊

'I should warn you that the man you are about to meet is a Russian prince,' LaDavide stated as they approached the house, which was three storeys tall and had an entrance that led through ornate wrought iron gates with gold leaf picking out the details on the finials.

'That's not a problem. I've met a few European princes. They seem to be ten a penny. For the Habsburgs the title is three or four rungs down from the Emperor. I suppose it is about the equivalent of being a lord in England,' Walter replied.

'Of course, we had a revolution here and chopped off the head of the King a hundred years ago,' LaDavide said with a laugh.

'We did that two hundred and fifty years ago,' Walter replied, 'only we were stupid enough to let his son back in.'

They walked through the unfastened gates and to the front door. It was opened for them before they had a chance to knock. The man who opened the door was a monstrous creature, even taller than Walter, with a head devoid of hair except some coarse black stubble poking out from his collar without any intervening neck. He had massive shoulders and a hugely distended belly which hung in folds over the belt of his footman's uniform. Without uttering a sound he ushered them into a small sitting room to the left of the central tiled hallway. After tapping lightly on the ornately panelled door the footman received a sharp acknowledgement from within. Opening the door quietly, he allowed LaDavide and Walter into the sanctum, then closed it noiselessly.

The Prince was a small spry man of about fifty. He stood to the left of the fireplace with his left foot raised on the fender, a cigar between the index and middle fingers of his gloved hands. He had curling grey moustaches which were elegantly shaped, but was otherwise clean shaven. The lounge suit he wore had a narrow jacket, and there was a fancy braid on the seams of his trousers. His mouth smiled, but the eyes failed to join in. He gave a small bow in the direction of his visitors.

'Prince Pechorin, I have the pleasure in introducing Mr Davies from England,' LaDavide said in French, returning the bow, but only from the neck. The Prince looked Walter up and down, pursed his lips and frowned.

'What do you think, my dear?' he asked of someone else in the room. With a rustle of taffeta a tall slim woman appeared from the shadows near the curtains. She was dressed in peacock blue silk dress. This looked far too dressy for this time of day. Her cheeks were set high and her eyes were truly blue, matching her dress, which also set off her hair, which was nearer to white than to blond. She looked Walter up and down with a cool, appraising air before replying.

'Yes, I think he will do very well. To an unsophisticated woman he has just the right look of a romantic hero.

Walter was on his guard, but tried to look relaxed, even a little bored, even despite having a strong desire to seduce this desirable woman, at least twenty years younger than her preening husband. Remembering the words of warning about the Okhrana he had received from Godiva he waited to see what would happen next. He realised that they were completely familiar with the ploy that British Intelligence had devised, and he was unsure who had told them, though he strongly suspected that it was LaDavide's superior. He would have to report this meeting back to London as soon as he could manage. Such a breach of security should not go unreported.

'Pardon, Monsieur Davies,' the Prince said, pronouncing the name as "day-vees", 'je vouz presentez ma femme, la Princess Eugenie Pechorinova.'

'Enchanté, Madame la Princess,' Walter said with the faintest of bows. She came forward and presented her hand to be kissed.

'No, this won't do at all!' the Prince insisted in French, 'His manners are far too aristocratic.'

'Monsieur le Prince, I can act the gentleman or the man of the people, depending on who I am talking to,' Walter said in slow but good French. He turned around to look at LaDavide, who shrugged disinterestedly.

'I am sure he will do very well,' the Princess said, in perfect English.

'Then I must rely on your judgement, and defer to you, as always,' the Prince said, 'And now, gentlemen, let us have something to eat and discuss how this matter is to proceed.'

A table was spread with a variety of cold meats, bowls of caviar, some pickled vegetables, black bread and tiny yeasted pancakes. For drink there were magnums of champagne and bottles of vodka in ice buckets, with glasses for each.

The Princess glided over to Walter, frowning slightly in the way that Walter recognised as a sign of long-sightedness. Close to, there were subtle signs of age on her face and neck, but she was still very attractive, and would make an excellent subject for a portrait.

'Mr Davies, I understand what your job is in this matter,' she said in good but accented English, 'I am a little curious as to what your talents are. Tell me, how would you go about seducing me?'

Walter thought for a few seconds before replying. 'I would find it a little difficult to start while your husband is listening to every word I say,'

'My husband doesn't speak a word of English, and I assure you, I will not show any reaction should you make an improper suggestion. I should not want to arouse his suspicions,' the Princess said, with her face relaxed but her eyes taking in all the details.

'In which case I would first attempt to play on your vanity and suggest that you sit for me. Then, when I had you in my studio I would suggest that you change into a suitably revealing costume, help to pose you in a sensual position and continue the flattery while making you laugh,' Walter said slowly.

'And has that worked in the past?' the Princess asked, this time adding a slight smile.

'Oh, I assure you that it has,' Walter replied.

'Are you a good painter of portraits?' she continued.

'He has already made a very good likeness of our suspect, after seeing him from a distance for a few seconds only,' LaDavide interrupted. He was carrying a glass of champagne and a small plate with delicacies piled on it.

'That was just a sketch, a sort of test for my memory,' Walter explained, 'With a proper sitting I can get a much better impression of a person.'

'Very well, then. You must paint my portrait,' the Princess said in a very decided fashion.

'What is this? What are you plotting?' the Prince asked in French. He looked a little upset at not understanding the conversation between Walter and the Princess and downed a shot glass of iced vodka in a single swallow before throwing the glass at the fire. The few drops of vodka clinging to the fragments of the glass flared for a second with a blue flame.

'I was just asking Mr Davies to paint my portrait,' the Princess replied in the same language, 'It seems he is a very good painter of portraits.'

'That is one way of keeping an eye on our young friend,' said the Prince, 'Just make sure you don't fall for his obvious charms.'

'When have you ever known me be carried away by any emotion?' the Princess asked with acid sweetness.

'Never, my dear. You know that I trust you entirely,' the Prince returned with a hesitant smile. He took out a gold and white Faberge cigarette case with diamonds studded into the clasp, extracted a black cigarette with a gold band, lit it and began smoking. The smell of the tobacco was quite exotic.

'I cannot call you Mr Davies always. Do you have a Christian name?' she asked, turning round to Walter.

'My name is Walter,' he replied.

'Then that is what I shall call you, Walter.' She walked to the table and poured champagne into two glasses, bringing one back for Walter. 'Now we must arrange a date and time for you to start on my portrait.'

'I'm afraid that I am probably otherwise engaged tomorrow,' said Walter, 'would Saturday be a good day for you? Preferably sometime in daylight.'

'Can you spare me at some time on Saturday, Cherie?' she asked of her husband.

'I have business at the Embassy for most of the day,' he replied.

'In that case, we need to arrange a suitable venue. I think I should like to be painted in the Chinese room. Would you like to see it beforehand?' she asked Walter.

'No, I'm sure that it would be very suitable. I shall come when the light is good. Would half past ten be a good time?' Walter said.

'That would be perfect. Now, please have something to eat,' she answered, and with an elegant sweeping gesture with her hand indicated the food and drink.

Walter picked at a few small pancakes with caviar and drank his champagne, both of which were very good.

◊

When they arrived back at the apartment block Walter stopped at the concierge's room and asked for the gas to be turned on. The concierge shrugged and made a 'Poff' sound, reminding Walter that no-one can match the Parisians for rudeness. He then smiled sweetly and asked if a deposit for the gas he was likely to use would help, and how large that deposit might need to be. The concierge then insisted that it was the gas company he should be talking to. LaDavide butted in at this point and counter-claimed that the gas supply was to the block, and that it was the responsibility of the owners of the apartments and rooms to turn the gas on and collect the money for gas from the tenants. This last statement was followed by a lot of shouting until LaDavide produced his warrant card to show his official status. The concierge, with the kind of expression that can curdle milk at thirty paces, glumly accepted an over-large deposit, for which a receipt was given and agreed that the handyman would come round later in the day and turn the gas on.

When they reached Walter's room LaDavide fumbled in a pocket and found a small open ended hexagonal spanner. With this, he managed to turn on the tap which controlled the gas supply to the room.

'Why didn't you let me wait for the handyman to turn it on?' Walter asked.

'Because the concierge will take the money and never get around to calling the handyman. If you wanted him to come you would have to pay him separately. Now we have the receipt she cannot deny that you paid her. She will have to pay for the gas you use. As she charged you twice as much as it costs it means she has made a good profit, and she will not mind,' LaDavide said with the smile of someone who knows the way things work. He used a match to light the gas fire, which burned fitfully in the draught from the window.

'Well, thank you for that,' Walter said, 'Now tell me about the Prince and Princess. How did they get to know what we were intending to do?'

When he replied, LaDavide spoke softly and in French. 'Most of the men who work on the Russian section were born in Russia. Some of them have divided loyalties, and one of them must also be working for the Okhrana. I imagine that if we were to look we would find another who is working with the revolutionaries. I need to encourage you to be careful in dealings with the Prince, and even more careful when you are in the company of the Princess Eugenie. She is a Princess by marriage and not by birth, and she is a very ambitious woman. All Russian aristocrats want to come to Paris and to speak French. All Russian revolutionaries want to go back to Russia and speak Russian. The Princess is not a real aristocrat and is happy to live in any country where she can speak the language. She also knows German and Italian, and probably others. She is a very subtle woman, and much more able than her husband. Be very careful with her.'

'What about that servant of the Prince's?' Walter asked.

'I've never known him to say a word, but I do not think he is stupid. He is the Prince's bondsman, and completely loyal. If he comes after you, at least you will see him first,' LaDavide answered.

'I have to send a telegram now, and let them know how I am getting on,' Walter said.

'Of course,' LaDavide drawled, 'I shall see you tomorrow morning. In the meantime, I must get back to my work.' He left in a slouch and at a slow pace, indicating that the prospect of work was none too appealing.

Not long after LaDavide left the door opened and Skinner's face appeared in the gap. Walter was looking through his instructions on sending coded telegrams at the time, trying to work out how to tell Cumming that the Russians knew of the plans that had been made. Unhurriedly putting the papers back in their folder Walter looked at to see what Skinner wanted.

'Who's that French fellow that was just here?' Skinner asked.

'He's my father's agent in Paris and he's been told to keep an eye on me,' Walter lied.

'He looks a bit like a policeman to me,' Skinner said, narrowing his eyes.

'No, he isn't a policeman, I can assure you of that, on my honour' Walter said, 'But why should be worried even if he is?'

'I just don't like the police being around me. I don't trust them,' Skinner said, 'And what were you talking about in French?'

'You shouldn't have been listening,' Walter said, suddenly angry, 'Anyway, I need to practice my French if I'm going to be here for a while.'

'Sorry for that, I didn't mean to offend you,' Skinner apologised.

'Look, if you don't mind, I need to do a bit of urgent work now. I've got to report back to my father and let him know about some business,' Walter said, directing Skinner out of the room and closing the door.

Walter saw how inadequate the lock on the door was and spent some time looking for a place he could conceal his paperwork. There was an obvious loose floorboard, and he put the least important papers in the gap beneath. After replacing the floorboard he placed a scrap of paper in the gap to indicate if anyone had looked there. The few sensitive papers he placed between the back of the cloudy mirror above the wash stand and the wall, after first roughly encoding the message he needed to send. He left the mirror at a slightly askew angle, so he would know if anyone tried to straighten it. At the end of the message he asked for some indication of the relationship between the Russians and the French authorities.

The nearest Thomas Cook office was the agreed communication point. It was a moderate walk away, and there were queues at the desks, into which some people would push rather than join at the back. This behaviour annoyed Walter, but he kept patient and eventually made it to the front of the queue. By the time he had sent the message it was nearly time for the office to close. It would not be worth waiting for a reply. He would have to come back the next morning to find the response to his query.

◊

When Walter returned to his room he checked the hiding places he had used. The mirror and the sliver of paper were positioned as they should be. The room was just beginning to warm up, and the damp and clammy coldness was being dispersed. Despite it now being nearly dark, he opened his paint box and started to colour his sketch of Ulyanov in rough blocks of near primary colours. It was not a great painting, but it was good to get back to something he knew he could do well, and at a steady and satisfying pace. With the room warming he no longer felt restless and hungry, so it was with some surprise at the amount of time which had passed when Skinner knocked at his door at eight o'clock.

They returned to the Blue Barge club where they sat at the same table, watched the same acts and drank the same drinks, though Skinner was more moderate in his consumption of absinthe. He did not have to be helped back to bed, and they called their 'Good night's' to each other. When Walter examined his hiding places he found that the scrap of paper was missing from the gap in the floorboard. He wished the visitors luck with the papers, with their low security level he had placed there and got himself ready for bed.

Friday 6th January 1910

The Thomas Cook office was much less crowded when it opened than it had been the afternoon before. The reply to his telegram was waiting for him behind the counter, and he retrieved it after a short argument with the clerk about who he was and who the telegram was for. On opening the cheap, stiff envelope Walter read the short reply.

COUSIN FRANK ENGAGED TO MISS EAGLES

He did not need to return to his room to translate the message, or the warning it contained. It was hardly a code at all. 'Cousin Frank' was clearly a reference to the French, and the Imperial Russian symbol was the eagle. The French were now more closely in league with the Russians. He needed to be careful in his dealings with the French authorities and their agents. The trouble was that he was completely dependent on the Tigers organising the attack on Lenin's mistress. He was also fairly certain that it was French agents who had searched his room.

Just how this suspicion would affect his plans for later in the day was unclear, but for the present he would let things take their course and see what turned up. As he did not know what time to expect a message from LaDavide's people he returned to his room and continued to work on the background of his painting of Ulyanov. The work was both engaging and satisfying, and he was very pleased with the results. It was one of the best works he had ever created.

Shortly after eleven o'clock there was a sharp knock at his door and Fournier stood outside, looking much as he had done the previous day. Walter understood that he must go immediately. Only stopping to put on his overcoat, he followed the Detective rapidly down the steps and towards Ulyanov's apartment. When they came to a group of mean little shops near to the café where LaDavide had treated Walter to a coffee and brandy, Fournier pointed to a plain woman in a headscarf carrying a heavy bag of groceries. This woman resembled neither the mistress nor the secretary of Ulyanov, but his wife. He recognised Madame Oulianoff from the photographs in his folder. It seemed that the plans had become mangled in translation.

'C'est la femme?' Walter whispered urgently to Fournier.

'Oui, la femme,' Fournier agreed, unhelpfully.

The woman had crossed the road and was being approached by two toughs in Apache clothing. It appeared that this part of the plan was still in operation. Walter sighed and decided to go to the woman's rescue. He ran across the road, avoiding a horse-drawn bus and placed himself between the woman and the policemen disguised as thugs.

One of the men was as tall as Walter, but slightly gangling and awkward, the other was of middle height, with a barrel chest and huge hands. A bicycle chain was wrapped around the knuckles of his right hand, and he unwound this expertly before swinging it around in a whipping motion. Close up, the taller man had a pock marked face and a long scar down his cheek. He had reached inside his coat and pulled out a butcher's cleaver of dull grey steel. They certainly looked the part of thugs. In fact, they were rather too convincing, and their target appeared to be Walter rather than the woman.

The shorter man advanced towards Walter, a strangely detached expression on his face. He swung the chain in a figure of eight pattern, closer and closer to Walter's face. A glancing blow caught Walter on the cheek and drew a spot of blood. Walter sought shelter behind a convenient lamp-post, the chain flicking chips of paint from the surface of the metal, which the wind blew into the man's face. One piece landed in the man's eye, and he tried to blink it out. Taking advantage of this momentary distraction Walter leapt from behind the lamp-post and planted a solid straight left jab onto the man's nose with a splintering noise which was followed by a rush of blood distracting the man even more. Walter followed up with a right uppercut to the chin that lifted the man off his feet, and dumped him unconscious onto his back on the pavement.

The taller man now advanced at Walter, the meat cleaver held vertically. His steps were almost like a dance, indicating that he knew about balance and timing. Walter had been backed onto the frontage of an ironmonger's shop. He slipped slightly as he tried to avoid the first swing of the cleaver, and half fell onto a stack of galvanised steel buckets. Reaching around he grasped the handle of the bucket at the top of the pile. He swung the bucket upwards and managed to deflect the cleaver as it was slashed at him for the second time, at some cost to the shape of the bucket. Scrambling to his feet, Walter started swinging the bucket in short arcs. The reach of the bucket was greater than that of the cleaver, and the attacker now began to retreat. He turned and sprinted off, leaving Walter triumphant on the field of battle.

The shopkeeper came out of his store, complaining bitterly about the damage to his stock and demanding payment for the bucket. Walter was reaching for some coins with his right hand to pay for the damage, his left hand still grasping the bucket, when a cord was looped around his head. There had been no warning of this attack, and Walter was left almost helpless and gasping for breath as the cord was tightened. Another attacker appeared in front of Walter, armed with an apache pistol; gun knife and knuckle duster combined. Walter was being pulled back and was off balance and incapable of adequately resisting the assault. He fully expected to die, when the cord around his neck suddenly slackened and there was a clattering noise like tin cans falling onto paving stones. Walter swung his head backwards and head-butted the man who had used the cord. This was probably unnecessary, as the man had already been struck on the head with a shopping bag half full of tins, but it hastened his journey to the pavement. In an attempt to free himself from the cord Walter twisted ninety degrees to his left. The attacker in front had committed to a stab with the blade of his weapon and he lunged forward, striking Walter in the arm, through the thick tweed sleeve of the overcoat. The knife blade slipped easily through the faux silk lining and the sleeve of his shirt, into the triceps and past the fibula. In a sudden rush of pain and anger Walter turned back and swung the bucket onto the side of the attacker's head, just below the temple. The man slumped to the ground with a soft groan. The weapon was still stuck in Walter's arm, and its weight as well as the position of the blade caused him exquisite pain and a slight loss of balance. Gradually becoming aware of his surroundings Walter noticed that he was still by the Ironmonger's shop, that the shopkeeper was still complaining to him and that Ulyanov's wife was looking at him with concern and thanks.

'Monsieur, comment allez-vouz?' she asked with a thick Russian accent.

'Je ne sais pas,' Walter answered through teeth gritted with pain.

'Est-que vous habite?' she continued.

'Pas la!' Walter said, indicating the direction of his room with his left hand.

She reached down and picked up her shopping bag. At the same time Walter carefully withdrew the blade from his arm and dropped it into the damaged bucket. The blood was now flowing freely from the wound and Walter put his left hand over the area. Madame Oulianoff guided Walter down the street to a Pharmacie where she bought some bandages and a bottle of iodine, then, following his directions they came to the Block where Walter lived. She helped him to his room, then out of his coat, the arm of which was now soaked in blood. She delicately bathed his wound with warm soapy water and then dabbed it with iodine, placing a piece of lint over the wound and winding the whole area in clean bandage.

Turning around after completing her nursing duties she noticed the nearly complete canvas on the easel.

'C'est mon mari!' she said in huge surprise.

'Votre mari?' Walter said in a good simulation of amazement, 'Vraiment?'

The woman said something in Russian, then complained that her French was inadequate to express her meaning. Walter asked if she spoke any German, and between them they found a language they both understood tolerably well.

Walter explained that he had seen the man riding the bicycle and was so taken by the image that he had come back to his studio and painted the picture from memory. The woman clucked around the painting and back to Walter.

'My husband is a very important man. He is a leader of the Russians in exile. You must have seen the greatness in him and understood exactly what he was. Only a true artist could see this quickly. If you knew him as well as I do you would truly know what a great man he is. But we have many enemies, not only in Russia, but also among some groups in exile. We have to be very careful. We must look out for these enemies at all times,' she said.

'How do you know that I am not an enemy?' Walter asked.

'Because of the way you acted to save me today. You are a brave man to fight so many criminals. All the traitors are cowards,' she answered.

'And I want to thank you for saving me when I was being garrotted, and also for helping me back here and for bandaging my wounds,' Walter said.

'You really need a doctor to dress the wounds. You will need some stitches. I will send a doctor round to see you. We know which doctors can be trusted. Now I must get back to my husband. I would very much like you to meet my husband and to show him your painting. He would like to thank you as well,' she said.

'I would be very pleased to come,' said Walter, 'You must let me know when it is convenient for you to see me.'

'I will send you a note. Of course, it would help if I knew your name,' she said.

'My name is Walter Davies,' he explained.

'That is an English name. I thought you were German,' she said, slightly puzzled.

'It's a Welsh name. It's a small distinction, but we are a proud people,' Walter said.

'I'm sorry if I insulted you in any way,' she said, sounding slightly embarrassed.

'There is no need to apologise at all. We are a very small country, and are quite used to this. But I do not know your name, Madame,' Walter said.

'I am Nadya Oulianova', she said, 'But you must understand, that is not my real name. We all live under assumed names here.'

'Of course I understand. You probably still have family back in Russia,' Walter said.

◊

Walter went out to find a bottle of aspirin to dull the pain in his arm. He was sitting in the only chair in the room facing the gas fire and feeling rather sorry for himself when LaDavide came in without knocking.

'You really must stop attacking our criminals. Soon there will be nothing left for us to do,' he said, looking at Walter with his head cocked slightly to the side.

'Just tell me what went wrong,' Walter said, barely looking up at the Frenchman.

'Well, it seems that our colleagues in the Gendarmerie have someone working for them who is also working for the Apaches. You see, the boy whose arm you broke was the son of a local gang boss. He set out to get you and used the Police to find out who you

Down in the Flood

were and what you were doing. As you may have guessed, the men who turned up to meet you this morning were not policemen. They were sent by this crime boss. I find this a little embarrassing, as you are a guest in our country, but you can now understand why we do not entirely trust the Police, and why they are not very good at dealing with the Apaches. Did you know that you put two men in the hospital? One has a broken nose and jaw, the other has a fractured skull. There was quite a scene next to that shop, and you know how to attract a crowd. Have you ever thought of going on the stage? Fournier was very annoyed that he had to deal with it all. It will mean a lot of paperwork for him,' LaDavide said.

'Well, you'd better get someone to teach him to read and write, then,' Walter said bitterly.

'I understand you had some help from a passer-by,' LaDavide said.

'Yes, I did, but none from Fournier. This woman hit a man over the head with her shopping bag. She must have had tins in it, as she knocked him out. He was trying to garrotte me at the time, by the way,' Walter said, determined not to admit who the woman was.

'That's quite a common way for the Apache to attack people. Normally they only rob them, but I guess this one intended to kill you,' LaDavide said in a nonchalant tone.

'What's to stop this boss from sending some more of his thugs to attack me,' Walter asked.

'As for that, well, I went to have a quiet word with him. I explained that we would concentrate almost exclusively on his operation for the next three months if he didn't leave you alone. He is a business man, and will listen to what I say,' LaDavide said with a shrug.

'Do you think I should change rooms? Just in case he changes his mind,' Walter mused.

'That will not be necessary. You will be safe now. By the way, do you know who the helpful woman was?' LaDavide asked, carelessly.

'I'd rather not tell you, in case the information is somehow discovered by the Apaches,' Walter said, 'She was just a middle aged French woman who came to the aid of a stranger.'

'Did you see Ulyanov's girl friend?' LaDavide continued.

'She wasn't there. I never saw her,' Walter said, flatly.

'So who was it who was getting attacked by the Apaches?' LaDavide asked.

'Whoever she was she didn't stay after the fighting started. I've seen photographs, and it wasn't Ulyanov's mistress,' Walter said, adding to the confusion.

'I'm sorry to be questioning you in this way, but we need to understand what went on today,' LaDavide explained.

'Who do you mean by "we"? Do you mean the Tigers or the Okhrana?' Walter asked pertinently.

'We are not working with the Russians quite that closely,' LaDavide said, 'But I cannot help it if my boss is playing politics. This is quite a dirty business.'

'But I can decide whether or not to play,' Walter said, 'And that whole affair this morning was a complete disaster. That man, Ulyanov, and the people around him, would never believe such a stupid attempt. It would never have worked.'

'Then you had better practice your charm on the Princess tomorrow,' LaDavide said with a smirk, 'Look, I would like to say sorry to you for what has happened. Would like to come out with me tonight?'

'Where were you thinking of taking me?' Walter asked.

'It is just a little place I know. You should find it amusing. I promise that it will be clean and safe. It is approved by the Government,' LaDavide answered with a self-satisfied smirk.

Down in the Flood

'It would be better than staying here all evening or going out to a club with the American in the next room,' Walter said in resignation.

There was a knock at the door and a cadaverous looking man carrying a medical bag looked into the room.

'Looks like your doctor is here. I'll see you later,' LaDavide said, leaving.

'Monsieur Davies?' the Doctor asked, removing his hat.

'Oiu, sais mois, monsieur le Medicine,' Walter admitted, gesturing the doctor to come in.

The doctor unwound the bandage gently from Walter's arm and tut-tutted over the wound. He gave a small injection of morphine before cleaning and stitching it. He then applied a clean dressing and bandage. By the time he had finished the opiate was giving Walter a sense of wellbeing like dull euphoria. Not long after the Doctor left he was curled up on his bed, sleeping soundly.

◊

LaDavide was smartly dressed and ready for a night on the town when he turned up some hours later. Walter had to search through his clothes to find a clean shirt and decent jacket. His overcoat was badly ripped, covered in blood and would have to be replaced the next day. Outside it was raining heavily and he was likely to get wet. Walter stayed by the concierge's door while LaDavide found a motor taxi for them. He splashed through puddles as he ran to the taxi. The driver's cab was open and he looked thoroughly wet and miserable, but the inside the car was dry enough, even if it was drab, dirty and dusty. Walter had very little idea where they were going through the dark wet streets until he recognised the Louvre. They had hardly gone past when the cab stopped outside an elegant six storey building. LaDavide and Walter dashed together for the entrance to the block.

The entrance hall was stone lined and meant to resemble a cave. This was in stark contrast to the exotic rooms inside. A pair of deliciously discrete doormen approached them and LaDavide produced a letter on headed notepaper which seemed to act like a cry of "Open Sesame", for the doors to the inner sanctum were immediately opened. They were escorted by an attractive, flashily dressed middle aged woman into a lobby, blazing with electric lights. These reflected off many mirrors and shiny polychromatic tiles. A curved sweeping staircase led to the promise of the upper floors. It looked like a fantasy palace from a pantomime.

'What is this place?' Walter asked, hardly able to believe the opulence of the interior.

'This is a maison close, or rather, it is THE maison close,' LaDavide explained.

'This is La Chabanais?' Walter asked in great surprise.

'Ah, so you have heard of this place,' LaDavide said with satisfaction.

'What English gentleman hasn't heard of this establishment. This is where the King used to come,' Walter said in awe.

'It is the greatest palace of pleasure in Paris, probably the greatest in the world. My boss managed to get an official visiting pass for you, in the hope that you might forgive us for the incident which took place today. You have a choice of any of the lesser rooms, with any girls you choose for as much of the evening as you require,' LaDavide said.

'I had heard that you use this place for entertaining visiting dignitaries. I suppose that the first class rooms are for royalty and presidents,' Walter said with a slight smile.

'Yes, that is right. But even the second class of room is better than the best anywhere else. Did you know that there is a room above that was especially built for your King when he was the Prince of Wales. It has his coat of arms above the bed and a big copper bath that he had filled with champagne and bathed in with the ladies. Then there is the chair that was made for him, to allow access of a certain kind. I do not want to go into more detail. This is a great honour. This place has been here for many years, but this is my first visit,' LaDavide said, looking just as impressed as Walter.

'Then you must come with me and enjoy the facilities,' Walter said.

'No, no, I am only supposed to bring you here,' LaDavide protested.

'Well, I'm not going to tell anyone, and I don't suppose the girls will say anything. Besides, I'm still worried about my personal security, aren't I?' Walter hinted.

'You are too kind,' said LaDavide.

'It's not costing me anything, and anyway, you should keep your thanks for the girls,' Walter suggested.

The flashy woman returned and guided them to the lift. On the way they passed a series of tableaux which Walter recognised as the work of Toulouse-Lautrec. The lift carried them to the fourth floor and a room decorated like a Turkish Sultan's harem by someone with a large budget and a lurid imagination. The woman then presented them with a menu containing photos of girls and a list of the services they would provide. Small sliding flaps indicated those girls who were absent or otherwise engaged. As with all expensive menus the price was not displayed.

'Is all this paid for?' Walter asked.

'In principal, yes. But the girl will expect un petit cadeaux if she has performed to your satisfaction,' LaDavide explained.

They looked down the lists and made their selections, consulting each other to ensure that the girls they chose were attractive to the other. Walter chose a slim mulatto girl with full lips and skin that shone like bronze, while LaDavide selected a Dutch girl with silver-blond hair and a Junoesque figure. There would be a good contrast in their choices. The Madame gushed with praise for their selections and went to fetch the girls that they had chosen, and to order some good champagne and oysters.

'I have a pamphlet from a few years ago that advertises this place. It shows the main rooms and has several good pictures of what they are like. There is one which is designed to look like Louis fifteenth's bedroom in Versailles. When I was younger I dreamed of saving up enough money for one evening there. I am s good republican, but it would be such an experience to live like a king for a night,' LaDavide said dreamily as they waited for the girls to arrive.

'Didn't one of the rooms win a prize at an exhibition?' Walter asked.

'Bien sur! That was the Salon Japonais. It won a prize at the World Fair, nearly ten years ago. Of course, the decoration was at the exhibition at the time,' LaDavide answered.

'I'm glad you explained. I was just imagining the judges being shown round a brothel,' Walter said.

'But this is not a common brothel, this is a maison de luxe, this is where you can live out your fantasies. There is nothing to match it anywhere in the world,' LaDavide said, bursting with pride, 'Here are all kinds of fantasies, rooms which suggest places where sex is completely natural.'

The girls arrived at the same time as the oysters and champagne and the group settled on the couch to have a drink and to introduce themselves. LaDavide's girl had put on a little weight since the photograph had been taken but she bounced with life force and good nature. The other girl was surprisingly tall, and much more reserved, though she had a smouldering presence that hinted she could erupt at any moment. Both girls soon disrobed to the laciest and briefest of garments. There was a gramophone in the room and the Dutch girl wound the handle and put on a disc of a ragtime band. Both girls jigged about to the music, enthusiastically enough, though neither should have attempted to become a dancer.

After more champagne and some oysters they transacted their business to the entire satisfaction of both men, swapping partners half way through. Walter had some sharp pain in his arm when he changed position and put weight on the injured limb, but overall he came through the experience with almost unalloyed pleasure and no pangs of conscience.

Saturday 7th January 1910

Walter awoke late and hurried over to turn on the gas fire before attempting to wash and dress. He would need to buy a new coat and hat before he could go to visit the Princess, so he examined his dwindling pile of coins and decided that he must change one of his banknotes. Even a cheap but decent coat would be more than the few francs he had left. He had only been in Paris a few days and yet he had spent almost half the money he had been allocated.

There was a shop selling men's clothing just down the road from the apartment block. Walter went in, uncomfortable that he was not in the fashionable tailor's in Burlington Arcade that he habitually used. He was pleasantly surprised to find that the ready-made coats available fitted him well enough, though the cut and the quality of the cloth were not to the standard he was used to. It was excusable in that it would help with his disguise for the few weeks he would be in Paris. He also selected a narrow brimmed hat that was reasonably weatherproof and would not blow off in the wind.

He returned to his room, wearing his purchases, and fetched his painting kit, placing markers in both the places where he had secreted papers before he left. He took the tram down to the Prince's house. In full daylight he was more aware of the proximity of the house to the River Seine. The banks of the river were filled with a rushing mass of turbulent brown water. If much more rain was to fall on the headwaters the river would flood. Walter had seen small streams turned to raging torrents after heavy rains, and remembered a time when an ornamental bridge and a tall aspen had been washed away by a usually tiny stream known as the Paradise Brook, which ran at the bottom of the hill on which his father's house stood.

Unseen in the swirling brown river flowing through the arches of the Pont de Sully was the corpse of a small balding man swathed in an overcoat the same colour as the rushing water. The mortal remains might have passed thousands of people without notice. It was not until the coat snagged in the branches of a toppled tree that the corpse came to the attention of a man who hired out rowing boats in the summer. Having spent an exhausting morning trying to drag the boats to higher ground, he was just completing his task when he saw the man's hair trailing in the flow like water weed. Using a boat hook he managed to drag the corpse to the bank and haul it ashore before calling the Police.

After entering through the gates and knocking at the door, Walter was allowed into the house by the same monstrous servant who had greeted him two days before. Having taken his coat and hat the servant guided Walter to Princess Eugenie Pechorinova, who was waiting for him in a small but elegant sitting room well warmed by a roaring fire. The walls were covered in opulent dark red fabric with an embossed pattern that included the Imperial eagle of the Romanov dynasty. Having wisely chosen not to wear this shade, the Princess was instead dressed in ivory silk with ribbons of the same peacock blue shade she had previously worn. She was well aware which colours suited her pale complexion. She held out her hand to Walter to be kissed and invited him to sit on the heavily upholstered sofa which squatted on the window side of the room. She sat herself in an armchair which was upholstered with fabric that matched the walls. The arms of the chair were decorated with gilded scrolls. Walter mused that such furniture could well have been one of the minor rooms at Le Chabonais.

'Thank you for being so prompt, Mr Davies. I have an appointment with my dressmaker early this afternoon. Now please have a cup of coffee and decide how you would like me to appear in my portrait,' she said in her excellent English before pouring him a coffee in a delicate porcelain cup decorated with the Prince's coat of arms. Walter took his coffee without cream or sugar and sipped it whilst studying the Princess's face and figure and her icy demeanour.

'Would you like to be painted in informal wear or dressed as for an occasion?' Walter asked.

'What would you advise?' she asked in return.

'That rather depends on whether the portrait is meant for your husband or for your own pleasure,' Walter answered.

'In that case, you had better paint two pictures for me, one of each kind. I presume the preliminary sketches will not require me to change today. I trust that you will find that acceptable,' the princess said with a slight smile.

'Then we must arrange another sitting in a few days time,' Walter said, finishing his coffee and placing the cup and saucer on a small round occasional table covered in chased silver with a slight lip around the edge. He took out a sketch pad and pencil, looking around the room for the best place in which to light the princess's face in three-quarters view. 'Perhaps you would like to stand over by the window, facing that lacquer cabinet, or, rather half way between the cabinet and the window.'

The Princess glided across the room and Walter instructed her in the exact position and pose that he required. It took three attempts and nearly an hour to get the sketch to his satisfaction, before he felt it suitable to show the Princess. When she came over to look at it she sighed slightly.

'Is that how you see me?' she asked with a note of disappointment in her voice.

'My preference is a less formal pose, and for a quicker process of catching your likeness. This sketch is for the formal portrait only,' Walter said, sounding a little defensive.

'That is better. This style is far too stiff for my taste. The other painting should be much more of a boudoir piece. I fancy being shown in a reclining position, possibly reading a book,' she said.

'And how would you like to be dressed for that?' Walter asked.

'I would like to be naked, so that when I get to be an old woman I can look at my painting and remember what an attractive figure I once had. Are you willing to paint me in that way?' she said softly.

'Of course,' said Walter, 'I'll do it in any pose you ask for. But I wouldn't want to do sketches for that. I'd much rather paint directly and give my immediate impressions.'

'In which case we must find somewhere where I can get some privacy. My husband's servant is very diligent in performing his duties,' she mused.

'I'll try to find a suitable location,' Walter said.

'When are you available to do the next sitting?' she asked.

'It will take me about two days to get the canvas prepared with your outline and face blocked out. Is that suitable for you?'

'That would be Tuesday, I think. Yes, that would be a good day. Shall we say the same time as today?' She suggested.

'Then I will come on Tuesday,' Walter agreed. When he got to the door Walter heard the creaking of the floorboards outside, as though a quiet but heavy person had just moved out of the way.

◊

When Walter returned to his room he found two notes waiting for him. The first was from Madam Oulianova, inviting him to bring the painting to her apartment at 3 pm following day. The second was from a secretary at the British Embassy asking him to visit an address in the 6eme arrondisement at 2 PM the same day.

If he were to keep both appointments he would find it difficult to spend much time at the first appointment or to get between them. Distance was not a great problem, as the 6eme arrondisement lay just to the north and west of his room. He knew the area because it contained the École des Beaux-Arts de Paris where he had spent five weeks learning some classical techniques a few years ago.

Walter studied the papers he had been given about Ulyanov, now calling himself Oulianoff, and tried to prepare for the visit the next day. As for the visit to the diplomatic house, this would probably prove to be a meeting to update him on some new information. He carefully replaced the papers behind the mirror before going out for a late lunch.

During the afternoon he sketched out the formal portrait of the Princess and blocked out the main colours, except for her clothes. For the other painting he recalled the chamber at la Chabanais he had shared with LaDavide and the two ladies of the night, using it as a suitably exotic and erotic background for the figure. Walter had some idea of how the Princess would look without her clothes, but would need to arrange the pose to best show those features of her body she was most comfortable displaying.

Having worked until the light faded, sometime after 4 o'clock, Walter decided to call on Skinner and find out how he did. Skinner was lying fully dressed on his bed reading a dime cowboy novel. There was no evidence of artistic work anywhere in the room except for a few dusty sketch pads. A two-thirds empty bottle of cheap brandy and a glass beaker were on the stand by the bed along with an ashtray showing the butts of several of the small strong cheroots he habitually smoked. The entire room looked as though he had never unpacked. He could have disappeared and not have left any sign that he had in any way affected this environment.

'Sorry to disturb you,' Walter said, I was wondering if you wanted to go out to the "Blue Barge" again tonight.'

'Sure,' Skinner agreed, 'How about eight o'clock?'

'Right, I'll see you then,' Walter said.

With three hours to fill, and no chance of working he decided to go for a walk. The rain had mostly stopped and it was quite mild. There would be enough light from the streetlamps to guide his way. Putting on his new overcoat and hat he strolled down the staircase and out into the street. It was not long before he realised that he was being followed. Walter had stalked deer and had to put himself of the mind of the stag when he did so. Overall he took the view that the discrete follower was working for LaDavide's people, making sure that he was safe. He hoped that it wasn't the Apaches the Police or the Okhrana.

He wandered down a slight slope, towards the river. The banks were totally full of sluggish brown water and there was insufficient clearance at the bridges to allow even small steamers to navigate through the reaches of the city. Small whirlpools appeared where the water was forced between the arches. The water was lapping at the top of the wall which ran around the Île Saint-Louis, but there were better flood defences around the Île de la Cité and the buttressed walls of the Cathedral of Notre Dame. And still it carried on raining.

◊

Walter had eaten before going to the Blue Barge and had taken a sketch pad with him to capture details of some of the performers on stage, the customers and the whores. He selected a few faces and swiftly drew his impressions of those interesting people who spent so much time at the club. With a few deft pencil strokes he could capture the expressions of desperate enjoyment, greed and arousal. He had never been so productive in his life. Soon he would need to purchase more materials.

The portrait he made of Rosa Languedoc as she swayed at the end of her act was satisfyingly good and unpretentious. The dancer, having noticed that she was being sketched, joined Walter and Skinner at the table and insisted on being shown her picture. She still wore the clownish stage makeup, and close up her complexion was far from perfect. Her dressing gown slipped slightly as she leaned forward to view all the sketches, lingering on her own and returning to it. She drew the outline with her finger a little above the pencil lines, her lips pursed in concentration and a slightly puzzled look on her face. Skinner alternately stared at her and away from her. He hardly managed to stammer more than a few words and that in the most execrable French.

'Is this how I look?' she asked Walter.

'That is how I saw you when you were dancing,' Walter answered.

'You've made my breasts look small,' she complained.

'Dancers don't often have large breasts. Besides, you could hardly dance like you do if your breasts swung around too much. I think they are the perfect size for your dancing,' Walter said. Rosa smiled, showing a small gap between her top front teeth.

'This picture is very good. I like it very much. Could you do one for me in colour? I would like to use this on my posters. But I cannot pay you very much,'

'I'd be very happy to do that without payment,' Walter said with a gracious smile, 'But it might be better if I did a few more studies of you.'

'Then you had better come to one of the rehearsals,' she said sweetly, 'We are doing a new part of the act next week. Come along on the afternoon of Tuesday or Wednesday.'

'I've already got an appointment for Tuesday. We'd better make it Wednesday,' Walter said.

'Can I come along as well?' Skinner asked, 'I'm an artist too.'

'No, I don't like to be stared at while I'm practicing. It will just be your friend. He knows how to behave,' she replied with a toss of her head before standing up and leaving. She had not asked his name or given a time in the afternoon.

'Well, of all the luck. How come you get to be with her? Hell, I would give a lot of money to be there,' Skinner protested to Walter.

'Well, why don't you do a drawing of her and see if she likes it,' Walter suggested.

'That's exactly what I'm going to do. I'm not so bad an artist,' Skinner said, puffing himself up a little.

'I haven't seen any of your work yet,' Walter observed.

'That's because I haven't been doing much of late. You know what I do? I draw the covers for those dime cowboy novels. I came to Paris to do some proper work, yet I've hardly done any. Now my money's run out and I'll have to ask my mother for another loan to keep me going. I'll need to show her that I've been working. I was wondering if I could show her some of your sketches. She's down in Nice at the moment, but she'll be in Paris in a few days,' Skinner said slyly.

'I'll have to think about that,' Walter said, unsure how to react.

'What's to think about? It's not as though they're earning you any money. If you do get some offers, I'll give them back to you right away.'

'It just doesn't seem right. It's not that I think it might be criminal, but that is my work and I'm quite protective of it. How about if I let you copy it?' Walter said, measuring his words.

'OK, that would be great. Just drop some off tomorrow morning and I'll let you have them later,' Skinner agreed.

Sunday 8th January 1910

Besides lending some drawings to be copied, Walter also had to give Skinner a good deal of instruction as to the method of execution. Although Skinner had canvasses and paints Walter had to lend him two good pencils and some sheets from his sketch book. The American had a good grasp of drafting, but held the pencil far too rigidly to achieve flowing lines. It took a good hour and a half before Walter felt he could leave Skinner to his task. By that time it was nearly late enough to set out for the meeting with the diplomat.

Walter collected the portrait of Ulyanov before leaving, knowing that he would not have time to come back to the room between the meetings. For once the rain was holding off and he enjoyed the brisk walk to the house where the first meeting was to take place. The houses in this district were solid and respectable, older than the blocks further out in the suburbs. The front door was decorated with chipped and faded red paint. Walter knock knocked on the door and had to wait a minute before someone came to let him in.

The door was opened by a fat young man with a smooth round hairless face set off by round eye-glasses. He motioned Walter towards a side room at the back of the house, glancing over his shoulder for signs of anyone following his visitor.

It came as a surprise to Walter that the room was already occupied by his friend, Godiva Williams. She was sitting at a large writing desk with piles of documents and photographs in front of her. Looking up at him she smiled and motioned Walter to sit on a chair next to her.

'Hello, Walter. I'll bet you didn't expect to see me here. Still, it's nice to be out of the office. I say, what have you got there?' she waved a hand in the direction of the painting Walter was carrying.

'It's a painting I did. After I leave here I am going by invitation to visit the subject of this portrait. See if you recognise him,' Walter said, smugly, unwrapping the picture and handing it over to Godiva.

'Oh, my word! This is really rather good. It is Ulyanov, isn't it? You must have managed to get in to see him. That is using your initiative,' Godiva said in an admiring tone.

'I've become acquainted with Madame Ulyanova. She helped my back to my room after that unfortunate incident,' Walter said.

'What unfortunate incident was that?' Godiva asked, looking a bit puzzled.

'You know I was supposed to fight off a couple of pretend thugs and save Ulyanov's mistress, well, it was Ulyanov's wife and four real thugs who were after me, not her, so it all went rather wrong. Anyway, I managed to deal with three of them, but one had a cord round my throat, and she bashed him on the noggin with her shopping bag. I'd got a bit of a scratch from a knife, and she helped me back to my room, where she saw the sketch I'd done of her husband. And yesterday, when I got back to my room I got your note and another from Madam Ulyanova asking me to go round today, in an hour's time. Oh, and she organised for a doctor to stitch up my wound. I thought the Tigers would have told you about it,' Walter explained.

'They didn't say a thing to us. I suppose it was a bit of an embarrassment for them. Anyway, you look none the worse. I see you've changed your coat and hat. That's very suitable,' Godiva said.

'It was a necessity. The old one was rather covered in blood. I've had to spend a lot of my money on replacing them. So I was rather hoping that you could stump up the cost before I go broke,' Walter continued.

'Well, possibly. Just leave it with me and I'll see what I can do,' Godiva prevaricated.

'I'd rather have it today, please. There have been other expenses which I couldn't avoid,' Walter said firmly.

'I hope you have receipts for everything,' Godiva said. Walter handed over the receipt for the coat and hat. Godiva sighed and reached inside her bag, producing five one hundred franc notes. 'Try to make this money last, please. This is already proving to be a rather costly operation.'

'Now, what was it you wanted to see me about?' Walter asked.

'There have been a few developments you need to know about. The main thing is that Peter the Painter has moved on to pastures new. We last heard of him in Copenhagen. He's certainly not in Paris. So don't bother to find out about him. Concentrate on what you can find out about Ulyanov's plans. It looks like you're making good progress on that front, anyway. With a bit of luck we can have you out of here in a few days,' Godiva said, not even consulting her notes.

'What was that about the French becoming friendly with the Russians that someone sent me in that telegram?' Walter asked.

'It's just the way things go. At the moment the French are rather more anxious than usual to butter up the Russians. In a month or two it will have come back to how it was before. In the meantime, we have to be a bit careful about not upsetting the Russians any more than usual. So make sure you are on your best behaviour,' Godiva said, sounding like a games mistress.

'LaDavide, the agent from the Tigers I am talking to, took me to see some Russian diplomat, one Prince Pechorin to be precise,' Walter said.

'He's the security representative at the Embassy, so he's the local representative for the Okhrana. I hope you were properly discrete with him,' Godiva said, sounding a little worried.

'I'm painting a formal portrait of his wife in a couple of days,' Walter said with a slight smirk.

'Look, Walter, on no account have an affair with his wife. Can you imagine the trouble it would cause if there were to be any kind of incident? For once in your life, control your baser instincts,' Godiva pleaded.

'I have no intention of doing anything in that line. Her husband's got some kind of dancing bear as a servant who watches everything she does. I dare not touch her, if only for my own safety,' Walter said, smiling.

'I should hope not. There's a couple of things that might be useful to us if you are seeing Ulyanov. It would be really good if you could get some kind of introduction to his people in London. Well, it's a lot more useful than finding out who his people in Paris are,' Godiva said.

'And a lot cheaper, I should imagine,' Walter said with a small sigh, 'I'll spout the sort of stuff Beatrice and Sidney Webb come up with, that usually goes down well.'

'It's probably not radical enough for our Mr Ulyanov,' Godiva observed, 'But I'm sure you can act a bit less moderately than usual. Just don't push it, and agree with all he has to say. The one thing he can't stand is people arguing with him. He has to win every argument. The man's a positive monomaniac. He lives, breathes, eats and sleeps revolution. I suppose we must rely on your famous charm in the mean time,' Godiva said, 'And, for heaven's sake don't let him know that you've been to see Prince Pechorin.'

'How will we keep in touch from now on?' Walter asked.

'Just leave a note with Mr Campbell at this address. Drop it through the door. If we have any message for you he'll drop it off at your room,' Godiva said. She stood up and smoothed her dress down. Walter stood and was just about to say his goodbyes when she raised a hand to his face and kissed him full on the lips. This took him so much by surprise that he failed to respond in the usual way.

'Thank you, I suppose,' Walter stuttered.

'See you back in London, Walter,' Godiva said, shooing him out of the room, 'Make sure you're not late for your appointment with Mr Ulyanov.'

◊

Madam Oulianova greeted Walter like an old friend, hugging him in a maternal embrace and kissing him on both cheeks. She then took the painting from him and hurried him through to the kitchen. A small stocky, balding man with a neatly trimmed ginger beard was working on the kitchen table, over which a black oilskin had been spread. Various books and papers were in front of him, in meticulously neat piles, along with a stack of writing paper, pens and ink. He looked up at his visitor, smiled and then stood and shook Walter firmly and formally by the hand, adding a little twisted bow.

Walter decided to speak in German, as he knew that he would be understood in that language.

'Gutten tag, mein herr, ich bin Walter Davies,' he said.

'Yes, yes,' Ulyanov said, 'Now where is this painting you have done of me that my wife talks about?'

The painting was unwrapped with some ceremony and handed over by the wife. Ulyanov studied it from close to, at arm's length and from every angle before pronouncing his opinion.

'This is very good. I am not sure it gives the right picture of me, though. I look more like a bank clerk than a worker,' he said.

'Bank clerks work too,' Walter said, 'And they are not well paid.'

'The thing is, they are not very revolutionary. We want factory workers to man the barricades. It is hard to imagine a bank clerk manning a barricade,' Ulyanov corrected.

'Of course, you are completely right,' Walter agreed, remembering the role he was supposed to be playing.'

'I think it makes you look like a man of the people and a great thinker, Volodya,' Madame Ulyanova said.

'When I saw you in the street I instantly recognised that here was a great man,' Walter added sycophantically, 'So I fixed the image in my mind and painted it as soon as I got back to my room.'

'I think the bicycle looks too new, Nadya' Ulyanov continued, 'Of course, my last bicycle was wrecked by a French Marquis in his car, Mr Davies. I am pursuing him in courts at the moment. I had thought the French had chopped the heads off all their aristocrats. Still, we have some way to go in Russia in that way.'

'The bicycle looks very good. You know how well you look after it, Volodya. You are always cleaning it and greasing it,' Nadya said.

'Well, you know what I say, you look after your bicycle, and your bicycle will look after you,' Ulyanov said, and he beamed, 'Your painting is very good. I think my dear wife has taken to it very much.'

'Then your wife must have it. I would like very much for you to have it, Madam, for the kindness you showed me after that attack. It was very kind of you to show me home and arrange for that doctor to visit. I am very grateful to you,' Walter said, smiling at Nadya.

'Please tell me what happened that day,' Ulyanov instructed.

'I don't think it was much to do with your wife, sir. It was just after I arrived in Paris. This man tried to rob me. He had a knife. We fought him and I broke his arm. It seems he is the son of a local criminal boss. He knew I would come to the aid of a woman, so he arranged to have some thugs to pretend to attack your wife. In the end, she came to my aid, and hit one of the thugs over head. It probably saved my life,' Walter said, quite slowly.

'And how did you know about the thoughts of this criminal boss?' Ulyanov enquired.

'There is a man who has a room in the same block as me. I think he has some criminal connections. He told me after the attack,' Walter answered.

'And are you not afraid of another attack?' Ulyanov asked.

'I wrote a letter of apology to this criminal boss. The man in the rooms told me what to say and who to send it to. It is a matter of honour, apparently, and I have to show him the necessary respect,' Walter invented.

'I will never understand the French,' Ulyanov muttered.

'So, how is your painting going?' Nadya asked Walter.

'Very well, thank you. I don't think I've ever done so much in such a short space of time. Currently I am doing a portrait and a picture of a music hall artiste,' Walter answered. Ulyanov stood up at this point and motioned Walter to sit on the hard dining chair he had been using. He then proceeded to put his face close to Walter's and to glare into his eyes without blinking. He needed Walter to be sitting before he could do this, such was the disparity of their heights.

'Have you been to the Gaité theatre, Mr Davies?' Ulyanov asked, 'Most people call it the Bobino. That is real entertainment for the workers. It is not far away, and they very often have good singers. Have you heard of Gaston Montehus? He is a singer I have a great admiration for. Such passion, and what a fine revolutionary message. He is a real man of the people. You must go and see him while you are in Paris and paint his picture,' Ulyanov said firmly.

'I'll make sure I go to the Bobino and I hope I will see Monsieur Montehus there. When I am in London I like to see the Music Hall, but I do not know of any singer there as you have described. We are very bourgeois in our tastes,' Walter said.

'But you have political freedom in England. We have much better causes for revolution in Russia. There are some good thinkers in England. Do you know of Beatrice and Sidney Webb?' Ulyanov continued.

'I have seen Sidney Webb speak, and of course I have read their books. I especially admire their work, 'The Theory and Practice of Trade Unionism',' Walter prompted.

'Ah, that is very good. It was I who translated that book into Russian. Of course, my English was not too good, so I mostly worked from a German translation. I do not care for German philosophers, especially Kant, but it is a language you can be precise in. You, Mr Davies, speak excellent German. How is that?'

'My mother was German, so I spoke both German and English from an early age,' Walter said, deciding to keep his lies as close to the truth as he could.

There was a coded knock at the door and Nadya went to answer it.

'What are your views on social justice, Mr Davies?' Ulyanov asked, again glaring at Walter.

'I would have to say that I share the belief in the historical inevitability of the rise of the working classes as Marx defined in Das Kapital,' Walter answered. He had never actually read Das Kapital, except for a resumé provided as a revision aid. It seemed to sound right, however.

'Good, very good. I hope you do not stray from the orthodox views on most matters,' Ulyanov continued.

'It seems to me that Marx and Engels envisaged the revolution taking place in an advanced industrial economy, but Russia is still mostly an agrarian economy. I was wondering how far the views of Marx need to be adjusted to fit with the situation in Russia,' Walter commented. He was not to get an answer because a woman entered the kitchen with Nadya at that time, and her arrival seemed to knock Lenin slightly off his line of argument. He stood up straight and smiled at the visitor.

'Inessa, you are very welcome. I would like to introduce you to our English friend, Mr Walter Davies. He has painted a very fine picture of me,' Ulyanov gushed.

'I am very pleased to meet you, Mr Davies,' the woman said in perfect English. She was in her thirties, but what is referred to in some parts of society as well preserved. She had wavy chestnut hair, large green eyes, a perfect bone structure and a fine figure complemented by a fetching blue dress. Compared to the squat figure of Nadya with her dull black skirt, unkempt hair and slightly popping eyes she appeared very beautiful indeed. She held out her hand for Walter to kiss. 'I must see this fine picture you have painted of my friend,' she said in the carefully modulated tones of an actress or singer.

Walter nodded to Nadya and suggested in German that she show the painting to Inessa. Her glance at the painting was not that of an artist or a critic but one of a lovesick girl looking at the portrait of her lover. Ulyanov looked on at Inessa, drinking in her rapt expression. If they were not actually lovers, then they were very near to the act. Their mutual attraction was completely obvious to all in the room.

'Oh, this is a fine painting. It makes you look so serious and handsome,' Inessa said. Ulyanov barked out a laugh. 'How did you come to paint this?' she asked Walter.

'I just saw this gentleman in the street, and there was something about him that made me want to paint his picture. I suppose I must have been struck by his intellect and personality,' Walter answered, not telling the whole truth.

'I love this painting. Please will you leave it here, so that I can see it when I visit my friends?' she pleaded.

'I've already said that I would. And I was wondering, do you think that I might paint your portrait?' Walter asked.

'No, no, no; I really don't think so. I am not important like my friend here,' she protested.

'But you must, my dear,' said Ulyanov, 'This young man is an excellent painter and he holds very sound opinions. I am sure that we would both like a nice picture of you.'

'I'm still not sure,' she said in German, 'but if you really want it, I shall try to arrange a sitting with Herr Davies.'

'Madame knows where I am staying,' Walter said with a smile, 'so maybe we can arrange a sitting sometime next week, perhaps Thursday, if that is agreeable to you. You think about how you want to be painted and I will come to you at a time that suits you,' Walter said.

◊

Walter spent the evening in a café close to his room and used a small part of the money he had taken from Godiva by buying better brandy than a struggling artist ought to drink. He flirted with a couple of girls who were touring the bars, but felt insufficient desire to follow up on the acquaintance. When he considered the course of the afternoon he could hardly believe the success of his endeavours. He felt some small moral qualms about betraying the Ulyanovs. He liked and felt grateful to Nadya, and her husband may have been slightly ridiculous but there was no doubting his zeal and force of character.

Monday 9th January 1910

Walter started work immediately after breakfast, getting ready for the portraits he was to do that week. He blocked out the surround for the nude portrait using his memories of the room in La Chabanais he had shared with LaDavide. The centre of the picture was reserved for the reclining nude figure he was to draw. Having produced something he liked he decided to base the picture of Rosa Languedoc on his sketch, which Skinner had borrowed. On trying to rouse Skinner from his room he received no answer. Whether he was asleep or his mother had arrived in Paris was unclear, but he didn't respond. The pose would be difficult to recreate without seeing the dancer rehearse, but that shouldn't prove be too difficult.

Back in his room Walter drew a basic outline of Inessa Armand's face, remembering for the first time that the corners of her mouth drooped slightly. It would need a piece of judicious work to make sure she did not look permanently disappointed.

He was just completing this task when there was a knock at the door and LaDavide entered without invitation. The agent looked at this picture without any apparent recognition. The reclining nude was covered.

'Is that another of your conquests?' he asked.

'Not yet, but I live in hope,' Walter replied.

'She's a very good looking woman,' LaDavide said.

'She is, but I've improved her looks a little. Let us hope that she appreciates it and rewards me properly,' Walter said with a sly smile.

'Do you have some time to spare today?' LaDavide asked, changing the direction of the conversation.

'Might it be another trip to La Chabanais?' Walter joked.

'I don't think the department's budget will run to that. No what I would like to do is to take you to a café where they know all about your Russian. They used to be his friends, but he has a rare talent for losing friends. You will be able to find out more about him there. It might be best if you didn't use the name I know you by, so try to think up another one,' LaDavide explained, walking up and down the room as he did so.

'Would that be this evening, then?' Walter asked.

'This afternoon would be better. Most of the Russians don't have enough to do, so they hang around the cheap cafés and talk about politics and mother Russia,' LaDavide answered.

'It's lunchtime now. We might as well go and get some food, and you can tell me more about this,' Walter said, sounding interested.

◊

The café had seen better days, but was still bright, warm and cheerful. Walter was introduced to the group as a young German socialist called Karl, from Cologne, who was visiting Paris for the first time. LaDavide looked the part he professed, that of a trade union activist who had lost his job for being too militant.

The Russians fell into one of two states. Some were jolly and outgoing while others looked gloomy and haunted by some great sorrow. During the course of the meeting the moods switched between the majority of them, and the jolly became morose while the introspective became outgoing. None of them seemed to be able to maintain an emotional equilibrium.

Some were drinking a foul form of tea from a samovar while other preferred the Alsace beer. Black bread and sliced dry sausage with pickled vegetables were on the table and the group would come over when they were hungry and browse. Everyone seemed to be smoking heavily, and a thick acrid cloud hung around the ceiling.

'Who do you think I should listen to while I am here?' Walter asked the group.

'There are plenty of good speakers, but they tend to be able performers rather than deep thinkers,' a big man called Igor said. His spade-like beard brushed the table.

'The thing is, we sit around the table and argue. That's the method we use to come to a conclusion. One man will propose something and we all discuss it. Sometimes there are heated arguments, even fights, on occasions. The process is one of thesis and antithesis,' an emaciated man with a prison cough answered.

'Are there many exiles in Paris?' Walter asked in an innocent tone.

'Many of us come here for a time. We are gypsies. We travel to any city where there are other Russians who have fled exile or escaped from prison. Myself, well, I've been to Geneva, Munich and London before I came here,' said a bald man who needed a good wash.

'Sorry for being curious, but how do you live?' Walter asked, genuinely interested in the reply.

'Those of us with jobs spread the money round. Some people have money from home, others beg or steal. The Georgians and the ones in the party often rely on exes,' the emaciated man said.

'What does that mean?' Walter asked.

'Expropriations is what it is short for. That means bank robberies, extortion, blackmail, even a bit of kidnapping,' the bearded man said with a fruity chuckle.

'Do they do that in Paris?' Walter asked.

'No, all that sort of stuff is done by the Apaches. We don't want to take their living away,' the smelly man added.

'I hope you only expropriate from the rich.' Walter said.

'Either the rich or the bourgeoisie,' Igor said with a hollow laugh.

'So do you rob in Germany or England?' Walter asked.

'Well, we don't but the desperados might. Our opinion is that it is wrong to be a criminal in a country which offers you some protection,' the emaciated man said. Walter nodded.

'I was reading an article by a man called Lenin,' Walter said 'Someone told me he is in Paris.'

'Oh, he's in Paris, alright. We see him here sometimes, but he doesn't come here very often. He makes big speeches that go on for hours and he gets speckles of spit on his chin. You don't want to talk to him, he'll bore the shit out of you,' Igor said with a dismissive grunt.

'The article was a bit wordy, maybe boring, but it seemed really sincere,' Walter said.

'Yeah, he writes all the time for underground newspapers. I suppose he works hard, but he's not as clever as he thinks he is, otherwise he'd learn something from all that study. If he reads something he agrees with he pretends it's his idea. If he reads anything which contradicts his ideas, he ignores it or publishes articles about how wicked it is,' the smelly man said, and he thumped his fist onto the table.

'Then I had better look for some better person,' Walter said.

'Just stay around here, then. We are all better men than he is,' the bearded man said with a guffaw.

'Does anyone go to the Bobino music hall?' Walter asked, innocently, 'I heard that it is a proper worker's place.'

'Yes, it's a very good place. Mind you, the girls are not very clean,' the emaciated man said.

'Then I'll go there tonight,' Walter said.

'Monday nights aren't the best. You'd be better off going on a Friday or Saturday,' said the smelly man.

'I suppose that I'll just have to take my chance, then. I don't know how much longer I can stay in Paris,' Walter said.

'I will do my best to come with you tonight,' LaDavide said, 'I've got some other business to deal with, but I should be able to put it off. In fact, I really ought to go now. He stood up and Walter followed him out of the bar after saying a few hurried goodbyes and receiving a bear hug from the smelly man.

'What's happened?' Walter asked as they were back on the street.

'A body has been found a little downstream from here. We think it is a Russian called Lermontov. He has something of a Police record and he was working for the Apaches in a small way, so it came to our notice.' LaDavide said with a shrug, is if the matter were of little importance.

'What did this Lermontov do?' Walter asked.

'He was a forger. An art forger,' LaDavide replied.

◊

Walter decided that his success at Ulyanov's apartment the previous day warranted a note to be dropped off at the house and sent on to Godiva. Having written the note he decided on a strategy for delivering it safely. As it was not a good idea to walk to the house with someone following him, he went to the local Metro station at Port Royale, purchased a ticket and went on two stops southwards towards the University. He then crossed over the bridge between platforms and headed back north, getting off at Luxembourg station. This was within easy walking distance of the safe house. As he approached the house he pulled his hat down over his eyes and adopted a shuffling, stooped gait.

There was no-one at the house, so he dropped the note through the letter box, first checking as best he could that he was not being watched or followed. He walked smartly away from the house and climbed aboard a moving trolley bus to avoid anyone following him on foot.

◊

Skinner was still not at home when Walter returned. It had seemed like a good scheme to invite Skinner out to the Bobino, and Walter did not want to go on his own. His problem was solved when LaDavide turned up later in the afternoon, as Walter was completing his preparations for the next few days of painting.

'I am a little worried about you,' LaDavide mused, 'You may become a full-time artist if you go on like this. That would not serve our purpose at all.'

'Very droll,' Walter said with a small smile of pleasure, 'Now Monsieur Oulianoff has recommended a theatre and a singer to me. How would you like to come to the Bobino tonight?'

'Well, it's a little worthy for my taste, but it is certainly the place to meet the internationalists,' LaDavide said with a Gallic shrug.

'I need to get some idea of their tastes in order to get to know them better. If I can find out what they really like I can spark some interest and enthusiasm. They might think me a good painter, but that won't help me to win their confidence,' Walter explained.

'Is this how you go about seducing your women?' LaDavide asked.

'It's just one of the techniques,' Walter answered.

'As for me, I usually try to make them laugh,' LaDavide said

'That can work just as well,' laughed Walter.

'So I will see you a little before ten,' said LaDavide, 'The theatre is only a short distance away.'

'That's rather late,' Walter observed.

'It may be a worker's theatre, but not many of the audience have to get up early for work,' LaDavide explained. He left to go back to work, not noticing the man following him across the streets of the 14eme arrondissement and back to the headquarters of the Tigers.

◊

An enthusiastic and noisy crowd smelling of tobacco, wine and garlic pushed Walter and LaDavide through the door of the Gaieté Workers Theatre, universally known as the Bobino. The entrance was far more cavern-like than the hallowed portals of La Chabanais, where a fortune had been spent trying to achieve just this effect. The interior of the theatre was ill-lit, smoky and noisy. Friends greeted each other with bear-hugs and laughter. Bottles of cheap red wine were plonked onto plain deal tables with tumblers. The ashtrays had been emptied but not washed. With the noise of chairs scraping across floors, the customers settled down to watch the start of the performance.

A squat man dressed in a canvas jacket jumped onto the stage and shouted out the order of the evening's entertainment in a voice like a trumpet. When Montéhus' name was mentioned at the end of the list a great cheer arose from all the tables.

The Master of Ceremonies told a few jokes about people Walter had never heard of. LaDavide chortled and cheered, slapping the table with his hand and slopping wine from the well filled tumblers. They were seated with a middle-aged couple. The man was small and thin with an extravagant moustache, the woman was tall and fat with a much smaller moustache and both of them were rolling drunk.

Next on the bill was a juggler who used unusual and delicate objects rather than balls or clubs. He was skilful without being wildly entertaining. He was followed by a woman just beyond the first flush of youth who belted out some sentimental songs, her barely covered breasts rising in a hypnotic rhythm of increased breathing rate as she sang the high notes at the climax. This was a good populist performance and was better received. The third act was a trio of tiny Chinese acrobats who gave a supremely gymnastic performance despite the constrictions of their slightly wrinkled leotards. Their performance was good, but they should have sacked their agent for booking them into this venue.

The table were onto their third bottle of wine by now, and LaDavide was going slightly red in the face. It was nearly midnight, and things had hardly started. An ill-matched couple performed a dance that seemed to be about a street girl getting the better of a rich old man, which Walter did not quite understand, but which was clapped enthusiastically. A comedian came on and clowned around, pulling faces and doing pratfalls. The audience laughed, and it seemed well suited to their inebriated state. Then the MC came on again and introduced the final act, Montéhus.

The singer was a wiry man of about forty with greying and receding hair, deep set eyes and a hooked nose. He was dressed in a canvas jacket and muffler, baggy trousers and scuffed workman's boots. After the initial cheering his appearance had prompted, the audience fell into a reverential silence. The man had a genuine stage presence. Even when doing nothing all eyes were drawn to him. When he started singing his voice proved to be rough and deep, but rhythmical, with a thick Parisian accent. He emphasised the message of the lyrics with clenched fists and sweeping arm movements. As the volume increased at the end of the song Walter was able to observe a vein throbbing in his neck. As for the meaning, it appeared to be a paean of praise to the workers of the Paris Commune. At the end almost all the audience stood up, whistled, cheered and clapped.

Montéhus quietened the audience with a gesture and launched into his next song. This one was about a regiment who had refused to fire on some striking workers. The title was 'Gloire au 17ème', and it was a popular song with the audience who joined in the chorus with gusto. The atmosphere was like that of the crowded terraces of a football match. The cheering at the end of this song was even more enthusiastic. To an outsider it might have seemed that such a song might inspire a revolution, but Walter was wise enough to know that the effect it had was to relieve rather than intensify the passions of the audience. It provided a feeling of unity and purpose, but that would fade in the cold of the early morning journey home.

As they left the theatre LaDavide turned to Walter and asked. 'Was that at all useful to you?'

'Yes it was. It gave me a very good idea about the man I am dealing with,' Walter answered, thoughtfully.

Tuesday 10th January 1910

Walter was going down for petit dejeuner at his usual local café when he noticed that Skinner's door was ajar. The sudden absence of his neighbour and the need to use the sketches that had been loaned combined to make Walter justified in knocking briskly on the door. He was surprised to find Skinner not only fully awake but also smartly dressed.

'Oh, good, I really wanted to see you,' Skinner said, brightly

'And I wanted a word with you too. Where are those sketches of mine? I need one of them immediately. I'm painting a picture from it tomorrow,' Walter said, with a trace of annoyance in his voice. Skinner twisted his fingers and his mouth seemed to be trying to form a suitable expression.

'Look, now, I've done something a bit bad, but it has turned out wonderfully for you, so please forgive me. My mother came up from Nice, as I said she would. I showed her your drawings, and I didn't say they were mine or anything. Not to put too fine a point on it, she immediately knew they weren't mine. I never did get to have the right technique with a pencil. Now, I thought she would be really angry with me, but she wasn't. She liked the pictures so much she took them round to a friend of hers who runs a gallery, and he really admired them too. So I acted as though I'd been the one who discovered you and I seem to be acting as your agent. Anyway, he's still got the sketches, and he really, really wants to see you,' Skinner said in staccato bursts.

Walter stood slightly open mouthed, unsure of how to take this news. If he rejected the offer his cover as a struggling artist would be blown, but he had very little extra time to spare over the next few days. Of immediate importance was recovering the sketch of Rosa Languedoc. He had attempted to recreate the position several times, but it always defeated him. There was a curve as she stood one leg which went from the raised foot through leg, hip, spine and shoulders to the wrist like a recurve bow used by the Chinese. It was an elegant and striking pose, which was also dependent on the position of the artist, the perspective, the lighting and a slight foreshortening of the foreground. He must reclaim the sketch before imposing Rosa's figure on the background he had created.

'Are you going to this gallery now?' Walter asked with a frown of concentration.

'Sure I am. You want to come along?' Skinner returned.

'Alright, but only as I really need that sketch of Rosa Languedoc,' Walter agreed, 'Just let me get my other jacket and I'll be right with you. Not that I can stay long, I've got another appointment later this morning to do a portrait'

It was Skinner's turn to feel somewhat confused. Surely any artist would want his work for sale at inflated prices in this gallery? Still, Walter was coming along. While Walter changed his jacket Skinner reflected that if he couldn't make it as an artist he might still make a living as an agent or at a gallery. After all, you didn't need to be Anna Pavlova to know if someone was a good dancer.

Walter returned after a minute and they made their way to the Gallery together, using the Metro to go to the Bastille station, from where it was a short walk to the gallery on Rue Jacques Coeur. The Gallery Etienne was one of those expensive establishments where the clientele do not window shop. If you wanted to see anything you had to go inside, where the salesmen were both discrete and insistent, and none of the items displayed a price. If you had to ask the price you couldn't afford it.

Skinner took a deep breath and patted down his damp, spiky hair before entering the shop. Walter followed looking entirely less overawed. The art on display was mostly Russian Avant Garde, with several canvases by a woman called Natalia Goncharova who painted a little in the style of Paul Gaugin.

The owner of the shop was a man of about forty, running slightly to fat, who was wearing a beautifully cut dark blue suit with a scarlet cravat. He had a trimmed and waxed moustache and lifted a monocle to his eye as Skinner and Walter approached him.

'Ah, Monsieur Skeener,' he said, smoothly, 'And would you like to introduce your friend?'

'This is Mr Walter Davies. He is the artist who did those sketches you liked so much,' Skinner said, 'Walter, this is Monsieur Etienne, the proprietor of this here gallery,'

Etienne held out a hand, more in the position to be kissed than shaken. Walter grasped the hand firmly. It was like handling a wet fish. Close up the man had a strong smell of cologne.

'Enchanté!' Etienne murmured, a smile playing briefly across his lips.

'A votre service, Monsieur Etienne,' Walter said without smiling.

'Vairy good,' said Etienne in English, 'When The Countess Podolski came to see me yesterday she brought along some of your sketches. They are really very good. These I could easily sell for a good price. If you have some paintings for me to see which are as good, they will fetch a much better price.'

'I have not been in Paris for long, but I'm very busy painting now. In fact I have a portrait to do today, and another study tomorrow. The thing is, I need the sketch of the dancer to work from before tomorrow. So if you could let me have it I would be most grateful. I promise to let you have first refusal on the painting of the dancer once it is complete,' Walter explained.

Etienne blew out a little breath and shrugged slightly, 'Unfortunately, someone has already purchased this sketch from me,' he said.

'Do you still have it? I mean, it must be here or at the framers,' Walter said, a note of quiet desperation in his voice.

'No, Monsieur. This client bought the sketch for cash and said that he would get it framed for himself,' Etienne said sadly.

'Do you have an address for this client?' Walter asked.

'As I said, this was a cash sale, which is most unusual. The lady refused to give an address,' Etienne replied. Walter swore under his breath.

'Mr Skinner had no right to allow you to have these sketches without my permission,' Walter protested.

'But Mr Skinner represented himself to me as your agent,' Etienne said with a sad smile.

'Then I shall have a word with Mr Skinner in a short while,' Walter said through gritted teeth. At this very moment he felt like hitting someone.

'Of course, I can give you the money you have earned from the sale,' Etienne said in a soothing way.

'Then you had better give it to my agent,' Walter growled.

'And when you have completed the painting I would be very interested in selling it,' Etienne continued. He was somewhat surprised to find an artist so disappointed by a sale of his work.

'Of course,' said Walter, 'Now I must be going, as I have an appointment to do a portrait.' He stormed out of the gallery without talking to Skinner.

'These artists, they can be so unpredictable,' Skinner said to Etienne, 'Now you mentioned the money from the sale. I would be very happy to pass it on to Mr Davies. I'm sure he will be very grateful to receive it. It would make him much more likely to want to do business with you again.'

Etienne sighed and went into a back room for a minute and returned with a plain white envelope and a receipt pad. The amount of money was good for a sketch, but Etienne never mentioned his percentage of the sale.

◊

The Princess Eugenie Pechorinova was waiting for Walter in her study, dressed in a high necked, long sleeved blood-red silk gown. Walter had brought the two paintings, his paints, brushes and an easel. The monstrous servant had escorted Walter to the room in silence, but had managed a throaty grunt when Walter had thanked him after he had opened the door. The princess dismissed her maid, a woman of indeterminate age, with thin lips and hooded eyes beneath a single eyebrow, who scowled as she left the room.

'Do come in, Mr Davies,' the Princess insisted. She motioned him in and then locked the door, leaving the key in the lock.

'Thank you, Princess,' Walter said as he tried to place his equipment in suitable places, 'Perhaps you would like to pose as you did at our last meeting.'

'You will have to remind me. I think I have entirely forgotten how it was. You had better show me what you have done so far, if that is allowed,' she said softly, turning her head to one side and smiling.

'I have no objection to that at all,' Walter said as he set up the easel and fixed the unfinished portrait to it. Turning the painting towards the Princess, he instructed her on how to return to the position she had previously taken up. This took a few minutes to get exactly right. Walter prepared his paints and brushes and then turned the painting around to face him.

'I do believe that the face in the painting is almost finished,' the Princess said with a sleek smile.

'The mouth and the eyes are not ready, and your neck is not quite right. That will need a bit of work today,' Walter said, 'And then there is your new gown, as well. That will take me some time, but I can finish that back in the studio.'

'Am I still standing correctly?' she asked after a few seconds. Walter had been busy squeezing paints onto his palette. He had to look up to answer the question.

'Could you turn your head a little away from the window, please; and back a little. Right, that is perfect', Walter said.

'Help yourself to some wine,' the princess offered as Walter began to paint dots of light and rays of colour in her eyes.

'Perhaps, in a little while. Just for the moment I'll carry on while it is going well,' Walter answered. He filled in a few fine hairs at the back of her neck. Then he worked on the mouth. Seeing where his intent gaze was directed, the Princess licked her lips with a pale pink tongue.

Walter mixed the colour for the base of the lips and drew this in with a few swift strokes. The fine work of vertical lines and the shadows had to be filled in on the top of this layer. The finishing touches for the face could be done later. The figure was drawn onto the background in light lines of white and a sample dab of paint mixed to judge the background colour of the dress. The shadows and highlights would be added later. Now was the time for a glass of wine.

'I have finished as much of the portrait as I need to do here,' Walter said, 'Would you like to see your likeness?' the Princess nodded.

'So I can stop posing, now, can I?' she said.

'Of course you can,' Walter said, turning the easel towards her.

'That is very good. My husband will be very pleased with it, I'm sure,' the Princess murmured, 'And now, when do you want to start on the other painting?'

'I have roughed out a background, not one that is in this house, but I haven't drawn in the figure yet. I'm not sure that I know quite how you would like to appear,' Walter said thoughtfully.

'Let me see the background and I will decide,' the Princess said. Walter dutifully unwrapped the second canvas and showed it to her. She studied it for a few seconds and then looked around the room.

'I think that chair would do very well,' she said, indicating a plush high-backed armchair.

'It would have to be moved nearer to the window, and it rather depends how you drape yourself over it,' Walter said.

'You move the chair while I get undressed, said the Princess, 'And keep your back turned until I tell you to look.'

'Of course I shall,' Walter agreed. It took him a few minutes to position the chair. In a mirror on the wall he could see a reflection of the Princess disrobing completely. Her figure was long and lithe. She had light brown pubic hair and pinkish nipples. There were several blemishes on her white skin including a large mole under her right breast, and the blue veins showed where the skin was thinnest. On closer examination there was a long scar under her left shoulder blade and some bruises on each arm where strong hands had held her. The bruises were partly covered by makeup, but the purple colours were showing through.

'You may look now,' the Princess commanded. Walter looked around, smiling to himself, having already seen all there was to see. She positioned herself on the chair, raising her right knee almost to her chin with her head bent forward and her hands wrapped around the raised shin. The pose was three quarters towards Walter and was more Rodin than Monet. 'Will this do?' she asked in an innocent voice.

Walter moved to her chair and arranged the position of the furniture so that it made best use of the optimum light from the window. This involved him in a series of moves forward and back to check how the scene looked. As he was standing close to the Princess she unwrapped her hands, took hold of Walter's right hand and guided it, palm downwards to the parted lips of her vulva, urging his fingertips to caress her clitoris. Walter looked in her eyes and saw that she was urging herself on to this action and that there was a measure of fear and disgust in her eyes. He gently pulled his hand away and gave her a sad smile before moving back to his easel. The bruises showed that she was maltreated by her husband and Walter suspected the Prince of encouraging his wife to do this. Whatever the combination of causes, the effect was not in the least erotic. The Princess grasped her shin again with a sigh. Walter half closed his eyes and placed his finger tips together. He decided to pretend that nothing had happened.

'Yes, that will do very well,' he said slowly, 'I'll do some sketches now and base the figure in the painting on those.'

'Well, do hurry up, it could be warmer than it is in here,' she said. Walter thought, but did not say out loud, that the cold was keeping her nipples erect.

In a series of lightening sketches he captured the pose from various angles and was well pleased with the result. There was a noise of heavy footsteps outside the door.

'Don't worry, it is only my husband's man, and he cannot look in,' the Princess said, 'But it is time that I was dressing again. Perhaps you can complete the paintings and show them to me in a few days.'

'Of course I shall,' said Walter, 'And I will be discrete with the second canvas, if you are worried about your husband seeing it.'

Despite her undress there had been no hint of sexual impropriety nor anything more than artistic interest from Walter. He was unsure whether this unusual lack of interest in a woman was from him or her. He decided that the crude signal of interest from her had been prompted by instructions from the Prince and not by any desire she might have felt at the time.

The Princess dressed quite rapidly, with only a little help from Walter, and within a few minutes he was outside again, dodging a brief squall of rain. The level of water in the river had fallen just a little, but it would not take much more rain on the sodden ground of the tributaries to make it flood.

◊

There was a note from Godiva waiting for Walter when he arrived back at his room. It asked him to go to the diplomatic house and collect something from Campbell. Walter sighed at the interruption to his artistic endeavours, and cleaned his brushes and the palette thoroughly before going out to collect his instructions.

Campbell acknowledged him with no particular warmth and offered neither food nor drink. Walter was not even invited to sit, but he did so anyway. Campbell produced a note and Walter decided to read it through before leaving in case he had any questions. He didn't as the questions were all answered by the note. In typical fashion Godiva had set everything out very clearly. This included notes concerning his mission and a series of questions for Walter to ask Inessa Armand. It added a useful additional note that Armand was trusted sufficiently by Ulyanov to undertake what amounted to diplomatic missions. After taking skeletal notes into a pocket book Walter burnt the original note before leaving the house.

Skinner was waiting for him back at the room and insisted on handing over exactly half of what Etienne had passed on from the sale of the sketch, despite Walter's insistence that all he wanted was the sketch back.

Wednesday 11th January 1910

Walter was taking his breakfast when LaDavide sat down next to him. He sat there in polite silence until Walter had finished his coffee and croissants, blowing cigarette smoke across the food. The only greeting Walter offered was a brief lift of his head.

'Right, we need your help,' LaDavide said.

'Then how can I help you?' Walter asked, resignedly.

'We have arrested the men we think attacked you. We would like you to identify them, if you can,' LaDavide explained. Walter sighed, placed some coins on the table for payment and stood up.

'Are we going to your office, then?' Walter asked.

'No, we do not take such men to our offices. They are at Montparnasse Police station. It is only a short distance away,' LaDavide said. He stubbed out his cigarette and stood up.

'Is this likely to lead to another attack on me?' Walter enquired with a raised eyebrow.

'Not at all. That matter is entirely settled now. This is so we can get these men back to their master. They have to be bailed, but before that can happen they need to be identified and properly charged,' said LaDavide, 'The law must be seen to be done.'

'Well, you'd better take me there now. I've got some appointments to keep later today,' Walter said. He followed LaDavide down the street.

They walked into the police station, LaDavide slouching ahead of Walter and calling to some of the smartly dressed officers. The room where the prisoners were housed was at the back of the station, facing onto a grim, high-walled compound. The windows were barred and a heavy door with a heavier lock blocked the exit. The men inside were sitting on benches and they quite closely matched Walter's memory of those events. One of the men had a bandage across his nose and large purple bruises showing under his eyes.

Another had his jaw fixed shut and a bandage like a sling from the top of his head to under his chin. A third had a bruised and cut cheek.

'Are these the men?' LaDavide asked Walter.

'Yes, I do believe they are. It is a little difficult to be exact, because of the bandages and bruises, but it seems to be them,' Walter replied.

'They wouldn't have those bandages and bruises if it wasn't for you,' LaDavide laughed.

The tallest of the prisoners looked up at Walter with an expression of stoical resignation and nodded with a hint of respect, as of one taught a valuable lesson.

'Is that all?' Walter asked.

'Of course it is. In most circumstances we would need you to fill in some paper work, but it will not be necessary in this case. We have made you an honorary Tiger to allow this. I hope you don't mind joining us, if only for a short time,' LaDavide said.

'I think I would be honoured,' Walter said, deciding to go with the flow and he nodded his acceptance.

◊

It was about half past three in the afternoon when Walter went to the Blue Barge. It took some time for him to persuade the doorman that he had been invited to come by Rosa Languedoc. Inside there were the noises of the band practicing their parts and the musical director shouting instructions at the musicians. Rosa was sitting at a table wrapped in her dressing gown, with a glass of clear liquid in front of her. With her was a moustachioed man of about forty who was cradling a large cup of café au lait in his hands. Walter walked up and greeted her.

'Bonjour, Walter, do you know Monsieur Joseph Pujol?' she asked in French, 'He is a very distinguished performer.

Walter racked his brain but could not recall who this man might be.

'Pardon me,' he said, 'I am just an ignorant Englishman. Your name is familiar, but I cannot quite place you.' The man laughed a deep, fruity laugh.

'I am better known by my stage name. I am Le Pétomane. Perhaps that helps you. I have performed in front of your King, when he was Prince of Wales.'

'Of course, you are indeed very famous and I do apologise,' Walter said.

'Well, I do not perform so very often now, so you are unlikely to catch a show in Paris any time soon. I just came here today to see my friend, Rosa,' Pujol said. There was something about the way he said it that suggested that he and Rosa had been lovers.

'Walter has come to paint my picture,' Rosa explained.

'Unfortunately I must be going now. I have to discuss a tour with my agent,' said Pujol. He placed his cup down on the table, shook Walter firmly by the hand, kissed Rosa on both cheeks and walked over to the coat-rack to collect his hat and coat.

'Has Monsieur Pujol performed at the Blue Barge?' Walter asked. Rosa emitted a sarcastic laugh in answer to this question.

'The Moulin Rouge cannot afford Le Pétomane. How could the Blue Barge pay his fee?' she laughed. Walter shrugged.

'I haven't been in Paris long,' he explained, 'Now, have you been rehearsing yet?'

'Not yet, I have been waiting for the band to get their parts ready. It will be any time now. I see you have brought your sketchbook with you. Be sure to make me look good!' she giggled.

The musical director coughed loudly and when Rosa looked up he motioned her over. Walter set himself down in the chair where he had been seated when he drew her before and set out his pencils in readiness. When he looked up Rosa was standing on the stage, in full costume but without her dressing gown. She was looking rather nervous and was twisting a strand of hair between her fingers.

With a tap of his baton the director started the band up. Rosa took a breath and composed her features before gathering herself into the starting position for the dance. The band hit an arpeggio and Rosa began to sway. Walter began to draw rapidly, waiting for certain poses and flexing to add new lines. After about a minute either the music or Rosa went wrong. They stopped and began again from the beginning. The new section of the dance consisted of dramatic sweeps of hands with the head thrown back in a simulation of ecstasy. After one more attempt the rehearsal was deemed to have been successful. By the end of the dance Rosa was naked and Walter had made five sketches.

Rosa put on her dressing gown and gathered up her clothes from the stage. She looked over at Walter and beckoned him to come to her.

'Let us go to my dressing room. You can show me what you have done when we are there. I must put on some clothes and turn from being a goddess to a normal young woman,' she said when he was close enough to hear over the noises from the band as they rehearsed another turn.

The dressing room was large enough for a rack for clothes a hard chair and a small table loaded with makeup, over which was a mirror. Rosa went over to the table and took off her stage makeup using a piece of muslin and some cold cream. When she had finished she turned back to Walter, her skin a little blotchy after the scrubbing.

'Show me your drawings,' she commanded.

'Of course,' said Walter. He produced the sketchbook and handed it to Rosa. She studied all of the drawings carefully, then pointed to the fourth of them, which closely resembled the drawing Walter had made on his previous visit.

'I like this one best. Could you make a painting of it for me?' She smiled, leant forward and stroked Walter's cheek.

'I can let you have it next week,' Walter replied. Taking the sketchbook from her, he placed it on the chair before turning back to her. He undid the loosely fastened belt and opened up her dressing gown to show her naked. She in turn lifted his waistcoat a little and undid his fly buttons.

It took a little while to find a position where she could place her feet on the edge of the table. She had her legs already wrapped around his waist and her arms looped round his neck. His hands supported her little weight under her buttocks. The bottles on the table were soon rattling to the urgent and increasing rhythm of their mutual thrusts. When she came she was uttering hoarse guttural noises. Walter allowed himself to come shortly after. All in all it was the best exercise he had managed for the last few days.

◊

Back in his room there was yet another note. This one gave details of how to get to Inessa Armand's apartment. He was due to meet her there at eleven o'clock the following day. Walter checked the papers in their hiding places and found that the floorboard had been moved slightly, but the mirror still seemed to be exactly in its proper place. Skinner came round a little later and proposed that they go and spend some of the money they had earned from the sale of the sketch on a few absinthes, and then go on to the Blue Barge and see Rosa's new act. Having nothing better to do, Walter agreed.

Thursday 12th January 1910

When Walter awoke the next morning the wound on his arm was itching and a little hot to the touch. If it did not improve he would have to see the doctor again. He swung the arm in an arc, attempting to ease the stiffness, without avail. Outside of his normal routine of exercise Walter was beginning to feel a little sedentary and in danger of getting plump. To overcome this he performed a set of exercises which allowed for a decent workout even in a small room. After completing these he was in need of a good wash. He fetched water in the jug and proceeded to sluice himself down thoroughly from head to toe.

Staring at his reflection in the mirror he decided that he could do with a good shave and haircut, but only the shave was really necessary. Fingering his upper lip he tried to decide whether or not a moustache would suit him. With his blond hair it would take a good deal of effort to grow one that would not look scruffy for more than a month, so he decided against it. He decided to dress, get some breakfast and then search out a barber before he went to Inessa Armand's apartment.

◊

The interior of the apartment had a bohemian yet comfortable family atmosphere. Inessa overflowed with life and seemed to have enough to spare to enthuse those around her. She was the mother of four children, a revolutionary and the mistress of a revolutionary leader. The apartment was alive with bright colours, the laughter of children and the smells of good food and coffee. The kitchen was its centre and was the beating heart of the place.

She sat Walter down in a kitchen chair and gave him a cup of coffee topped up with some brandy. Meanwhile she bustled around and made arrangements that would keep the children away from her for enough time to allow the sketches for the portrait to be made.

Taking him into the living room, she cleared one corner of toys and children's books and sat down in a chair, looking out of the window.

Walter sat in a position where he could draw her from the three-quarters view he always preferred for portraits. As he sketched Inessa could not sit still. Her body was wracked with a steady tubercular cough.

'Sorry, I must get a drink,' she apologised. She returned in a few minutes with a glass of water. There were a few beads of sweat on her forehead.

'That is a very nasty cough,' Walter said.

'It is a souvenir of a prison in St Petersburg. Last time I was in Russia I was locked up. It is all part of the game. They know I want revolution, but my husband's family has money and influence. The police lock me up and my husband's family get me released after a month or two. There is no brutality towards me, but the conditions in the prisons are not so good. It is not easy for me to go back to Russia these days as the Okhrana agents all know me,' Inessa explained.

'When do you think things will change in Russia?' Walter asked, trying to lead up to his other questions. Inessa shrugged.

'When it comes it will have to come from inside Russia. We can talk and plot and argue with each other, but the people who could make a difference in Russia are all tired of our little games. You will find Bolsheviks all over Paris, and the only thing they have in common is that they disagree with each other. We need to show a lot of discipline if we are to make any difference. Only Volodya keeps the faith. He is the only one who is consistent and will not compromise for a comfortable life.'

'He's your lover, isn't he?' Walter asked.

'Yes, we are lovers. How could you tell?' Inessa asked, surprised.

'It was the way you looked at him, and the way that he looked back at you,' Walter answered.

'Is it that obvious?' Inessa mused.

'Well I think it is, but other people might not notice. What does Nadya think about it?'

'We haven't discussed it, but I think she understands. What matters is the revolution. If Volodya is to work he must be in good health, in body and mind. If he has needs they must be met. We have to subsume our needs if we are to work for the revolution,' Inessa explained with conviction.

'But you like him as well, don't you?' Walter asked.

'I'm sure we like each other very well. He is very fond of me, but the revolution is more important. And I admire him so very much. I am honoured to be in his company,' Inessa said with a wistful smile.

'Are you going to be in Paris for long?' Walter asked.

'I'll be here for as long as I am needed. We are planning a school for some Russian workers. We can educate them in how to operate within Russia. I think Volodya wants the school to be somewhere in France, probably quite near Paris, in some quiet place. I'm not much of a teacher, but I'll do what I can. I'm better at organising and at keeping everyone happy. Volodya will decide what I should do,' she answered in a resigned tone.

'There must be Russian exiles all over Europe,' Walter said, 'I've met a few in London.'

'Yes, there are. It is difficult to go anywhere without meeting some. They are in Munich and Zurich, London and Copenhagen. There are even some at Gorki's house on Capri. Volodya has been everywhere. He likes to stay where there are good libraries so he can do his work. He only has a modest allowance and Paris is so very expensive. I think we must find another place in a while, perhaps nearer to Russia,' Inessa said, thoughtfully.

'What is the situation in the countries around Russia, like Poland or the Baltic states?' Walter asked.

'I don't know much about that, but no small country likes being next to Russia. We are not good neighbours,' Inessa said with a shrug, 'Was there any reason why you were asking?'

'Well, not really, it's just that we've had a Latvian group in London causing trouble recently. In most cases the police just leave these groups alone, and the members of the groups are grateful for some freedom and safety. These Latvians have been committing robberies and even killed a few people, and it's given all the exiles a bad name. The newspapers ask for action to be against them. There was a robbery in London a little while ago and a policeman got killed. Now anyone who comes to London talking in a Russian accent is under suspicion,' Walter explained.

'There are always casualties in a revolution,' Inessa said mechanically.

'But this isn't our fight. It's difficult to explain to an English working man why his neighbour has been killed for something that is happening over a thousand miles away. Those of us who want social change in Russia find that our cause is hurt when someone acts like a bandit and claims it is done in the name of revolution', Walter insisted. He was beginning to gesticulate with his pencil.

'I don't know anything about any Latvians, and neither does Volodya!' Inessa said with emphasis.

'I'm sorry,' Walter apologised, 'And I agree about the necessity of revolution in Russia. I'm just trying to help.' Inessa seemed a little mollified but neither spoke for a few minutes. Walter resumed his drawing.

'I'm sorry if I got angry,' Inessa apologised in turn, 'It's just that we know there are agents sent to spy on us. You can have no idea how careful we have to be. Even here in Paris there are agents of the Okhrana who want to see us expelled or even killed. The French allow them to operate without hindrance. I'm sure that could not happen in England.'

'I'm sure you are right, and I understand that you need to be very careful about what you say and who you say it to,' Walter said smoothly.

'I wish I could make the exiles see how lucky they are to be safe. They already know how bad things are in Russia, but they will not come together to make things better. They just argue pointlessly with each other. But I suppose that is what happens to exiles,' Inessa said, her voice trailing off to near silence.

Walter could sense that she would not supply any more information to him on this visit. He would have to store up some of the questions, especially those about finance, until the next visit. He was not hopeful that Inessa knew any of the answers anyway. If he was able to seduce her he might be able to glean some extra details, but she was so well drilled in secrecy and so obsessed with Ulyanov that even then she was unlikely to provide much that was of use. He finished the sketch he was working on, looked up and smiled at her.

'I'm just about finished for today. Do you want to see what I have done?' he asked.

'Thank you, I would,' Inessa answered. She glanced at the sketches with interest but with none of the vanity that Rosa had shown on the previous day. 'You've made me look much prettier and a little younger than I am.'

'I'm not sure that they even do you full justice,' Walter said. He started to pack up his pencils and prepared to leave. Inessa followed him to the door of the apartment.

'Let me know when the painting is finished,' she said.

'I might need to add a few touches; I usually do,' Walter explained, 'Could I come back sometime next week?'

'Of course. You would be most welcome. Just leave a note with Nadya,' Inessa said as she ushered him through the door.

As Walter walked back down the street he realised that he had overplayed his hand and that some trust would need to be built up before Inessa could be regarded as a useful source of information. Perhaps he considered this too deeply, because he never noticed the discrete little man who was following a few yards behind him.

◊

Rather than return to his room Walter decided to report directly to Campbell about the results of his meeting with Inessa. Following his previous plan he doubled back on himself using the Metro and tram system. By the time he had arrived at the house he had certainly lost his shadow. Campbell was no more pleased to see him than before, but permitted him a table, chair and writing materials to record in detail the information he had been able to gather that morning. Leaving Campbell to encode the contents of this paper Walter left to get a shave and some lunch.

It was a little after two o'clock when Walter returned to his room. He decided to spend the few remaining hours of the day finishing the pictures of the Princess and of Rosa, and starting the picture of Inessa. Looking around the room he realised that he did not have any spare canvasses and that his paint was in short supply. He would have to buy some more paint and two canvasses before working the next day. In the meantime he had sufficient to complete the pictures of the Princess.

He had hardly started his work when there was a knock on his door and Skinner invited himself in.

'Hello, there,' Skinner started, 'How are the paintings going?'

'I'll let you be the judge of that,' Walter said, continuing to work on the canvas of Rosa.

'It looks pretty good to me, and I think I'm a pretty fair judge. You've really caught the way that she looks when she does that part of the dance. But you're also working on a couple of portraits, I can see. Mind if I look at them?' Skinner asked.

'Be my guest,' Walter muttered as he tried to add reflections to the costume gems which glittered on Rosa's breast covers. Skinner looked at the other two paintings and considered their content.

'These are fine looking women. You must let me know where you met them,' Skinner said admiringly.

'Just my indisputable charm,' Walter said.

'So, who are they?' Skinner asked.

'One is a Russian aristocrat, the other is of French, English and Russian ancestry and is a revolutionary. I'll leave it to you to work out which one is which,' Walter replied.

'Well, this one looks like an aristocrat, or at least she does to my American eyes,' Skinner said, pointing to the portrait of the Princess.

'Uh-huh!' Walter agreed.

'So what's with all these Russians?' Skinner asked.

'Somehow I seem to have been thrown in with them,' Walter said, still trying to finish the picture of Rosa.

'My mother does a lot of business with the Russians,' Skinner said dreamily.

'How's that?' Walter asked, suddenly taking note.

'She imports Russian art. Her new husband is Polish, but he's into some kind of deal with some people in Russia and brings out paintings and things. My mother takes them back home and sells them to museums. Of course, that's only the old stuff. All the modern stuff gets sold in Etienne's gallery,' Skinner explained.

'What kind of old stuff does your step father bring in?' Walter asked, with some genuine interest.

'Those religious paintings, mostly. Really old ones from churches and monasteries,' Skinner said as he looked through Walter's sketchbook, whistling when he saw the nudes of the Princess.

'Do you mean icons?' Walter asked.

'Yeah, those are the ones. Funny looking things, kind of flat and stylised. I don't really like them myself but the museums back home go for them in a really big way. They pay good money for them,' Skinner replied.

'Can you get me a cigarette? There's a packet in my coat,' Walter asked, 'I don't mean to ask, but I've got paint on my hands.'

'Sure, not a problem,' Skinner said. He retrieved a cigarette, put it between Walter's lips and struck a match to light it. 'I don't know how you can smoke these things. I think they're disgusting.'

'Someone took my English cigarettes from me when I came into this country. These are pretty rough but you can get used to them,' Walter explained.

'If you want to sell these pictures I'm sure Etienne would get you a good deal,' Skinner said, the light of an agent's fee glinting in his eye.

'Alright, I'll do a copy of the nude, in a slightly different pose, and with Rosa's face,' Walter agreed, 'I'm sure Rosa won't mind.'

'Say, could you get me a date with Rosa?' Skinner asked.

'Sorry, my friend, I don't think I can. She just doesn't seem to be interested in you, and I'd never encourage a woman to go against her instincts,' Walter drawled.

'I really want to have that woman. Do you think she would be interested if I had the right sort of money?'

'You'd have to ask her that for yourself. From what I've seen she would rather sleep with a man who is a celebrity rather than a rich man, or just because she desired him,' Walter said.

'Have you had her?' Skinner asked, angrily.

'If I did enjoy her favours I wouldn't tell you,' Walter replied softly.

'You have, haven't you?' Skinner demanded. Walter did not reply. A minute of silence followed while Walter continued to paint.

'So, tell me, who are the Russian artists that Etienne is showing?' Walter asked.

'I've never heard of most of them. There's a woman called Natalia Goncharova, who paints a bit like a Russian Gaugin, only not so good. Her paintings seem to sell well,' Skinner said, a note of resentment continuing in his voice.

'I'll have to take a look at those paintings,' Walter mused.

'Sure. You can have a look at them when we take that painting of yours over to the gallery,' Skinner suggested.

'I'll have the picture finished in a couple of days,' Walter said.

Friday 13th January

Walter had been to an artist's supplies shop and had returned with three new canvases, several tubes of paint, two new brushes and some turpentine. This cost him a large part of his remaining cash, but could be regarded as an investment if he sold the nude to Etienne for a good fee. As he was about to enter his building he was joined by LaDavide, who came into step with him.

'How are you Walter?' he asked politely.

'Very good,' Walter admitted, 'My career as a painter is coming on very well. And how are you my friend? I presume you have some reason for calling on me.'

'Yes, I do,' LaDavide said as they walked past the concierge's booth, 'I'll tell you when we get to your room.'

They walked down the corridor without talking; though their walk was scarcely silent, their boots echoing on the floorboards of the upper floor. LaDavide closed the door behind them once they entered Walter's room and waited for him to put the parcel down before talking.

'Do you mind if I talk in French?' LaDavide asked, 'Just to make sure we are not overheard by your neighbour.'

'Mais oui,' Walter agreed, 'But I may have to ask a few questions if I don't understand.' He sat down on the bed and invited LaDavide to take the chair.

'That is no problem,' LaDavide said, sitting down and switching to French, 'This is about the discovery of a body in the river. The body was fished out two days ago, but it took some time to identify who the man was. It turns out that the man was doing something which is a little associated with what you are doing. His name was Lermontov, and he was a Russian émigré with links to the Bolsheviks. Now the story gets a little more complicated. You see, Lermontov was an artist and a forger. He started out as a restorer of old paintings, but he then began making his own quite convincing copies. They were good enough to fool the experts for a time. Because he was committing criminal acts he came to the attention of the Apache, especially as he was making good money. They offered him protection, in exchange for a large part of that money.

Lermontov was used for some scheme we don't really know much about, but it was to do with forgery and seems to have involved an art dealer who was himself working for someone important. We suspect that he was doing some business with Prince Pechorin, which is where the Russian link comes in again. Only Prince Pechorin is not associated with the Bolsheviks. On the contrary, he operates the Okhrana agents in Paris, who are working against the Bolsheviks. You can see how this complicates everything you are involved with. You now know both the most determined of the Bolshevik leaders and the counter intelligence officer for the Imperial Russian government. What I am trying to tell you is that you may well be in danger from one side or from both. If Lermontov knew something which got him killed, then you too may be in danger.

There is another coincidence in this matter which I do not like. The Apache boss who was running Lermontov is known as le Baron. It is his son whose arm you broke, and his men you put in hospital.'

'Do you think that Pechorin has been involved in something criminal?' Walter asked after a few seconds of thought.

'Who can tell? It may be that he needed money for some reason. All these Russian aristocrats pretend that they have got money, but many of them are quite poor. It must be expensive to keep up the pretence. Perhaps Pechorin borrowed some money from le Baron,' LaDavide said.

'And what is the link between Lermontov and the Bolsheviks?' Walter enquired.

'He ran errands for them. They paid him to deliver the plates for a printing press which published their propaganda. He wasn't a political exile, so he wasn't suspected of involvement by the Okhrana. As he was working as an art restorer he was able to travel freely to and from Russia carrying artist's materials,' LaDavide explained.

'So, Lermontov might have been killed by the Bolsheviks or by the Okhrana or by the Apache,' Walter mused, 'Now tell me, who is this art dealer you were talking about?'

'His name is Etienne. He has a gallery near the Louvre,' LaDavide said with a rueful smile.

'I've met him,' Walter admitted, 'We were introduced by my friend, Skinner.'

'Which is precisely why I wanted to hold this conversation in French,' LaDavide said. He took a cigarette out of Walter's confiscated cigarette case and started smoking.

Walter rose from the bed and walked around the room, smoothing his hair down in a thoughtful way.

'I can see that this complicates things a little. I must be very careful about what I say, and to whom,' he said as though thinking out loud.

'Yes, that is right. But there is more. It would be very useful to us if you could find out who might have had good cause to have Lermontov killed. We cannot expect you to put your mission or your life in danger, but if you do happen to hear anything, please tell us, as it might help in our investigations,' LaDavide said.

'Alright,' Walter agreed, 'If I do hear anything I will let you know.'

'Excellent,' said LaDavide, 'I'll call round for you on Monday, if not before and find out how you are doing.'

'In the meantime, I have some paintings to finish, including one for Etienne. I'll certainly tell you how that meeting goes,' Walter said.

◊

After a brief lunch Walter returned to his room where he found Inessa Armand waiting for him. She was looking through his canvasses with the air of a kindly-disposed art critic and smiled up at him as he entered.

'I'm sorry for coming unannounced. I got your address from Nadya,' she said, smiling.

'That's alright, I wanted to see you anyway. I need to finish the picture,' Walter said, smiling back, 'What do you think of it?'

'It's very flattering. I'm sure I'm not really that pretty. You've made me too young and slim. I have four children, you know,' Inessa said modestly.

'I didn't know you had four. I'm sorry if you find the picture a little too flattering. I'll add a few laughter lines to your face if you like. But you must know how attractive you are. Do you want me to finish the picture now?' Walter asked.

'That picture, the nude, it's very intimate,' Inessa commented.

'That's the way she asked to pose. I can honestly say I didn't encourage her to sit like that,' Walter said in explanation.

'And that dancer is wearing very little in the other painting,' Inessa continued.

'It's her act, and she wanted me to do that as a poster for her,' Walter said.

'Do you have many lady friends?' Inessa asked with a slight trace of coquetry in her voice.

'Well, probably I have more friends who are women than men,' Walter answered, 'Now, can you tell me what they call that garment the dancer is wearing over her breasts?'

'I do believe that it is called a soutien gorge in France. That is the cloth version. This one with stage jewels may have some other name,' Inessa replied.

'So, do you want me to finish the picture now?' Walter asked again.

'Yes, why not. Where would you like me to sit?' Inessa replied.

'I'll just move the chair by the window,' Walter said, moving the furniture at the same time. Inessa sat on the chair and Walter set the canvas of Inessa on the easel and fetched paints, brushes and a palette.

'Are you looking at me the same way you look at that other woman, the nude one?' She asked.

'If you are asking if I find you attractive, the answer is a definite 'yes',' but I wouldn't ask to paint you in a state of undress unless I believed you wanted me to,' Walter replied as he prepared the paints on the palette, 'So, do you want me to?'

'I don't think so, but you can make love to me if you want to,' Inessa said casually.

'Thank you for the offer. Yes, I would like to do that, but I'll do a bit more on the painting first, if you don't mind. Work before pleasure, you know. Anyway, I thought you were in a relationship with Monsieur Oulianoff,' Walter returned.

'Yes, I am, but you must understand that we have to take our pleasures where we can, it is a part of the freedom of the revolution. You can make love to me, but please don't ask any questions about my relationship with him, as I won't answer,' Inessa said.

'I promise I won't ask a single question,' Walter agreed. He started to make a few changes to the canvass, giving the face a few more years and a good deal more character. Inessa sat very calmly, watching his face as he worked. It took about half an hour to make the alterations, after which Walter showed the results to an appreciative Inessa.

They made love on the thin mattress of the narrow bed, only partly covered by the blankets and warmed more by their own exertions than by the efforts of the gas fire on the other side of the room. Inessa was able to join in the rhythm with little effort, like an experienced dance partner joining in with a waltz, and her embrace was warm and welcoming. This wasn't ecstatic, but it was very satisfying. She moaned softly and let out a gasp as she came.

Her body showed the signs that age was creeping up and the results of four births, but it was a body she was comfortable inhabiting and she showed neither shame nor embarrassment in appearing naked, without any sign of exhibitionism. She hadn't long left before Skinner made an appearance at the door.

'How the hell do you manage it?' he asked.

'I suppose I just have the knack,' Walter answered.

'Perhaps you can teach me,' Skinner said wistfully.

'It's something you'll just have to learn for yourself. I'll give you a tip if you like. What you have to do is to listen to women and treat them as people. If you can make them laugh with you rather than at you it usually helps,' Walter explained patiently.

'That's easy enough for you to say, but I don't happen to be, what are you, six feet three or four? And I don't have blond hair and brown eyes. I can see why a girl would go for you. Look at me, I'm five feet seven with mousy, thinning hair and grey eyes. What chance do I have?' Skinner complained.

'Just follow the first rule and have some confidence in yourself. It's not what you are but how you can project who you'd like to be that really counts,' Walter said.

'Yeah, I'll try that,' Skinner said with a sigh, 'Do you want to help me practice sometime? I thought we might go out to the Blue Barge.'

'That's not a good place to meet women. Tell you what, I'll take you to another place. Just pretend to be a man of the people and I think you should have some success. They won't be flashy women, but they will be friendly,' Walter said thoughtfully.

'Right, that sounds good,' Skinner said, 'Unfortunately I can't make it tonight, I'm having dinner with my mother.'

'Well, how about tomorrow night instead, then?' Walter suggested.

'That would be great. What sort of time should we go?' Skinner asked.

'They don't start to late, maybe half past ten, and I don't think they do absinthe there. The wine's quite good, though', Walter said.

'Then I think I'll go to a bar for a couple of drinks first,' Skinner said.

'How are the drawings going?' Walter enquired.

'Oh, not bad, quite good, really,' Skinner lied.

'You'll have to let me look at them sometime,' Walter said.

'Sure, I'll get a few of them ready for you, when you come round tomorrow' Skinner said without conviction.

Saturday 14th January

Having fulfilled another part of his brief by starting an affair with Inessa Walter wondered whether it was worth trying to contact Campbell to inform the office about the events of the previous day. But it was Saturday and the fat young man was unlikely to be present. He would drop a note in on Monday.

Walter looked at himself in the age-spotted mirror and decided he needed some fresh air and exercise. He was looking pale and felt a little bloated. The enforced lack of exercise was having an effect on his health and well-being. He could not hire a horse or go to a gymnasium, take boxing lessons or swim. What was left to him was a spot of sculling on the river. The weather was grey and overcast but there was no worse rain than a fine drizzle. But would some hardy souls be out on the water or were all the rowing clubs closed for the winter? In order to find the answers he would have to go to the Post Office and look for the telephone numbers of the club secretaries and make a few calls. He felt that he would not be able to paint another stroke until he had flexed some muscles and breathed in some moving air.

Before going to the Post Office, he decided to have some breakfast at his usual café and kept to his routine by ordering coffee, croissant and jam. Skinner had shown his ignorance of custom by asking for a 'café noir' at their previous visit. If you wanted milk you asked for it. If you merely asked for a coffee it came black. Any visitor to Paris should know this.

There were long queues at the Post Office, and the telephone directories were not available for public use or abuse. Walter sighed and decided to walk down the river in the hope of being able to hire a skiff. After a short walk he came to the river and looked at the turbulent brown water which rolled in oily swirls. If anything the level had gone down some. This was the South Bank, and when he looked to this right he was looking east. There was nothing other than factories and houses in that direction. The curve of the river to the west prevented him seeing what lay in that direction, but it looked more promising than the other way. He turned and walked for some distance along the bank.

He was just coming to the line where city met suburbs when he noticed a partly flooded playing field onto which some skiffs had been dragged. A large man with a shambling gait was putting worn and damaged tarpaulins over some of the boats. He was wearing a caped Mackintosh and had a drooping, sad moustache which hung like a ragged curtain over his lips.

Walter walked over and tried to engage the man in conversation. All he received in reply to his efforts were a few non-committal grunts. The man then went to haul another boat a little way up the slope of the field. His grip on the wet turf was very limited and the boat refused to move. Walter walked over and helped the man. The boat was broad-beamed and could carry six people. It took their combined efforts to shift it to slightly higher ground. The man now became friendly and talkative. His accent was more Normand than Parisian and Walter had a little difficulty in understanding him.

'Thanks, I couldn't have managed that without you,' the man said smiling broadly and showing where several teeth had once been resident.

'The river's very high, isn't it?' Walter said as an opening remark.

'I've been here for fifteen years and I've never seen anything like it. I tell you, if we get any more rain we'll all be flooded out,' the man replied with some animation.

'I don't suppose that you've got much trade at the moment,' Walter continued.

'No-one's going to want to go on the river with the water as it is. They all want to row when it's a nice sunny day and the river looks placid, so there's not much happening at this time of year,' the man said sadly.

'Oh, by the way, my name's Walter Davies. I've done quite a bit of rowing, at all times of year. I'd really like to get out on the river if I could,' Walter said.

'Oh, you're English, are you? Well the English are all mad. I suppose you've tried the rowing clubs, but they won't set out on water like that. No-one should if they don't know what they are doing. It's easy enough to drown in these conditions. I found a body, myself a few days ago. Don't know if the man fell off a bridge or was thrown in, but he ended up wedged under a fallen tree. It was a devil of a job getting him out from there,' the man said with a shake of his head, 'My name is Guillaume Maupassant, but everyone calls me Willy.'

'What did the Police say about the body you found, then, Willy?' Walter asked.

'What do the Police ever tell you? They just took my statement and took the body,' Willy said with a shrug.

'Yes, I suppose so. They never tell you anything, do they?' Walter agreed, 'Now I was wondering if I could hire a small boat for an hour. I really am a very good sculler, and I'm used to cold and rough conditions.'

'I really don't think I should let you. You don't know the river and you don't know the conditions. Besides, the landing stage is under water. What are you doing in Paris at this time of year anyway?' Willy said.

'My uncle has some business in Paris and asked me to come along. I can speak a bit of the lingo, so I can help him out a bit. The thing is, I'm supposed to be trying out for a really good eight in a few weeks time, and I really could do with the practice. All I do in Paris is go out to clubs and eat too much. My uncle's gone off to a spa for a couple of days to work off the food, and I thought it would be more fun if I could get in a bit of rowing. I'm willing to pay you well,' Walter said in a tone that was somewhere between jollity and pleading.

'Well, if you are sure that you can manage it I won't stand in your way. And because you helped me earlier, I'll only charge you the usual amount for a hire. Look out for the river, mind. It really is not so good at the moment. You can choose one of those skiffs up there,' Willy said, gesticulating towards a group of five small slim boats.

Walter paid five francs in advance and Willy helped him to drag the skiff to the edge of the water. The oars had to be fetched from a wooden shack which needed a good coat of creosote. There was a good deal of water in the bottom of the boat and Walter had to turn it over before he could get in. As Willy had said, the landing stage was a few inches beneath the water. This came up to the lace holes of Walter's boots as he clambered in and set the oars in the rowlocks.

With three good pulls Walter was able to get into the centre of the stream, where the current was at its most swift. It was a considerable effort to row against this current, but it would be better to get the effort done with at the start, so he headed east along the river for nearly half an hour, during which time he had managed to make less than half the distance he had walked along the bank in just ten minutes. After a break of a few weeks the rowing was proving to be more tiring than usual, but Walter exalted at the effort and the sweat required to make even this little progress. His muscles ached and his lungs burned but he was happy to be away from the noise and bustle of the streets. He rowed on for another ten minutes before turning in the quieter water close to the south bank. The journey back took much less time, with a few gentle strokes taking him much faster than a walking pace, and he was back at the partly flooded landing stage with some minutes of his hour to spare. Willy helped him to haul the skiff back onto the dry ground. Together they put a tarpaulin over the boat and then Willy returned the oars to the shed.

'I am most impressed with your rowing. Most men would have just have gone with the current. I think you will have no trouble in getting into your rowing eight. I think you would even be good in the single sculls,' Willy said admiringly.

'Thank you, although I don't think so. I don't have the speed for that. But I do have some endurance, I think. Thanks for letting me take the boat out. I really do appreciate it,' Walter said, tired but satisfied.

'Come back anytime. Now I know you can row like that I will not be at all concerned for your safety,' Willy said.

Behind the boatshed a small man was taking note of everything that had happened.

◊

Campbell was loitering by the door to the apartment block when Walter returned, looking obviously British and very awkward. A steady drizzle was soaking everything, including Campbell's coat and hat, and he looked very unhappy with the world.

'I've been looking for you. Where have you been?' he said peevishly.

'I've been for a row on the river,' Walter answered casually.

'In this weather? Are you completely mad?' Campbell asked.

'Quite possibly,' Walter said, deciding to answer the impolite question, 'You'd better come up to the room and dry out.'

They trudged up the stairs to Walter's room. Campbell was puffing with the effort by the time they got to the top of the house.

'So, this is what is meant by an artist's garret,' Campbell observed.

'Hmmm, yes, I suppose so. Well, welcome to my humble abode. You can see that a very vast sum has been invested in my accommodation,' Walter said sarcastically, 'Anyway, what was it that you wanted to see me about?'

'I don't know how you've managed it, but you've well and truly poked a stick into the hornet's nest,' Campbell said as he looked around the room with obvious distaste.

'Why don't you sit down on the only chair and tell me all about it?' Walter said. Campbell unfolded a handkerchief and placed it on the seat of the chair before sitting down.

'The Russians have got into a funk about you. They say you are getting too close to Ulyanov and his faction, and that your behaviour with the Princess Pechorin is decidedly inappropriate. Moreover they complain that you are not only keeping information from them but actively spying on them,' Campbell said in a flat tone.

'It's actually the Princess Pechorinova. That's how the Russian names work for a woman,' Walter corrected him, 'And my behaviour towards the Princess has been nothing but gentlemanly. In fact, I have had to reject her advances, which were, I strongly suspect, prompted by her husband. As for getting close to Ulyanov. Well, yes, I have been successful, because that was what I was supposed to do. It isn't the Russians who are giving me orders. And I don't see how it could be my fault if I succeed. Are the Foreign office getting windy about the Russians?'

'Not to put too fine a point on it, the Russians have been getting into bed with the French, and we need to make sure we don't offend either of the parties involved,' Campbell declared.

'So, tell me, which hat are you wearing at the moment? Is it Foreign Office or SIS?' Walter asked with a certain amount of acid in his voice.

'I'm the former. I don't pretend to know much about your outfit. And I'd rather you didn't mention the names here. Just in case someone is listening,' Campbell said, sotto voce.

'Well, I don't take my instructions from you. I think you had better approach my seniors,' Walter said smoothly.

'Don't worry, we will do that,' Campbell said, his face flushing with anger.

'In the meantime I will continue doing what I was sent here to do,' Walter said, 'Was there anything else?'

'There's the small matter of the Tigers and their investigations. You've caused no end of trouble and expense because of your actions. Their patience is coming to an end, and you can't rely on their co-operation or protection from now on,' Campbell said.

'That's a pity, I quite like my contact. He's a thorough rogue, but a reasonably honest man. But don't worry, if I contact him it will be outside of his working hours. I wouldn't want to make myself unwelcome,' Walter drawled.

'My advice to you is to go home right now and stop upsetting people,' Campbell said haughtily.

'Then I thank you for that advice, and will ignore it completely. My job is not finished yet. In fact I am making real progress at the moment. And besides, I have a few commissions for paintings to complete,' Walter said with a smile of satisfaction. Campbell snorted in derision.

'Well then, complete your daubs and leave. And try not to make too many waves in the meantime,' he said dismissively.

'Those daubs look likely to earn me a good living,' Walter said with undisguised pride.

'Good God, you mean that you're actually selling them?' Campbell said in amazement.

'Quite by accident, I assure you. And it has led me to an entirely new line of enquiry,' Walter replied.

'Well, I've said what I came here to say. If you have anything else you wish to pass on to me I think you'd better do it now,' Campbell said.

'The trouble is, I don't seem to be able to trust you anymore,' Walter said, 'I'll have to establish a new line of communication.'

'Then I wish you luck in that. Just don't come to me expecting any kind of help in the future,' Campbell said peevishly.

'Perish the very thought,' Walter said carelessly, disguising the concern he was feeling about becoming isolated. He would need to encode and send another telegram to Godiva before the end of the day.

◊

Walter arrived with Skinner at the Gaieté Workers Theatre before the crowds had begun to assemble. As this was Saturday night there was likely to be a big crowd. They easily found an available table neither too far nor too near the stage and a mildly inebriated Skinner went to fetch wine. Montehus was not performing that night, having a more lucrative engagement elsewhere. His place at the top of the bill was taken by a woman Walter had never heard of but who was enthusiastically recommended by the man who sold the tickets.

The show proceeded much as it had done on Walter's previous visit, but before the end of the first turn they had been joined at their table by two young women who boldly sat down beside them. One was barely five feet tall, but prettily buxom with a gap-toothed smile and a mass of fair curls, the other was tall and willowy with dark auburn hair and the sort of face which can be either beautiful or ugly depending on the lighting and the expression it wore. The smaller woman was showing a good deal of décolletage to augment her obvious charms. She smiled and simpered at Skinner, who tried stammering a few opening phrases in his broken French. The taller woman looked appraisingly and directly at Walter with an intelligent but tolerant expression. She seemed to approve of what she saw, but did not attempt to speak before a break between acts.

'I am Sylvie and my friend is Brigitte. I have not seen you here before. Are you American, like your friend?' she asked in good English overlaid with a strong Parisian accent.

'My friend, Mr Franklin Skinner is American. I am English, and my name is Walter Davies. We are both artists who have come to Paris to work. I have been here once before, but it is Mr Skinner's first visit,' Walter replied in good French. Sylvie gave him a slightly pitying look as though she had met struggling artists before and knew the stories they told.

'So, you are an artist, Mr Skinner,' she said across the table.

'Well, it's Mr Davies here who really makes a living from his art. I just hang around most of the time trying to make and sell my paintings. Walter is a real artist and has people queuing up to buy his stuff. He is working all the time, apart from when I drag him out in the evenings,' Skinner said with a sheepish grin.

'But it is Mr Davies who has been here before, not you,' Sylvie corrected him.

'Sure, but I took him out when he first came to Paris. He's just returning the favour,' Franklin said.

'And how did you get to know about this club, Mr Davies?' Sylvie asked.

'A Russian gentleman told me about it, a Mr Oulianoff. He is a great admirer of Montéhus and thought I would like to see the man perform,' Walter answered in English, for Skinner's benefit, 'And call me Walter, please.'

'Yes, Montéhus is a great man of the people. You must be very good if you are earning a living as an artist. But tell me, how do you make a living, Mr Skinner?' Sylvie asked.

'Well, I must admit that I get most of my money from my mother, but I am starting to get some money as an agent as well as selling my own paintings. I reckon I'll be earning a living soon. And tell me please, what is it that you do for a living?' Skinner replied.

'We work in a factory. What we do is very tedious and repetitive and what we make is not glamorous or exciting. It pays us a meagre living, but men doing the same work are paid more. We look forward to the time when the workers control the means of production,' Sylvie said with a tone somewhere between anger and sadness.

'Yeah, well don't hold your breath, from my little experience, that could be some time in coming,' Skinner said with a chuckle.

'You should talk to one of my friends back in London. You would have a great deal in common with her. Her father is a well-known socialist but wants the women to sacrifice their claims for equality until after the revolution. It has caused a lot of bad feeling between them,' Walter said in French. Sylvie looked at him with cool approval.

'But what is your friend's name?' Brigitte asked in her Parisian accent.

'She is asking what your name is,' Walter explained to Skinner.

'Franklin,' Skinner said, pointing a finger to his chest, 'Et votre nom?'

'Brigitte,' the fair woman said with a lecherous smile, 'Veux tois avec mois a couché cette nuis, Franklin?'

'What did she just say?' Skinner asked of Walter.

'She just asked if you wanted to share her bed tonight,' Walter translated with a smile.

'Really? That's terrific,' Skinner said, almost bouncing in his seat with enthusiasm and impatience, 'Vouz ettez tres gentil, Brigitte,' he stumbled through.

'I think you can address her as 'tu' from now on,' Walter said, 'you're not talking to your bank manager.'

'So, you are a socialist, Walter?' Sylvie said.

'Yes I am. Does it make a difference?' Walter replied.

'Of course it does. I won't sleep with any capitalists,' she returned.

'Is that an invitation?' Walter asked.

'The problem is, I cannot invite you back to my room, as I share it with Brigitte, and there is only one bed. Do you live nearby?'

'About two hundred metres away, but I only have a very narrow bed,' Walter explained.

'That is alright, I do not have to be in work tomorrow. I can sleep during the day, and I'm sure we can get a little sleep, even in a narrow bed,' Sylvie said to their mutual satisfaction.

Brigitte left with Skinner before the end of the show but Walter stayed on with Sylvie to see the main act, the woman singer Laila Boucheron. The songs were delivered in a husky and impassioned tone with many dramatic gestures. It all felt a little too contrived to Walter, as though she were trying just a little too hard to achieve the effect.

Sylvie turned out to be a willing and skilled partner in the act of lovemaking and neither managed much sleep during the night. Walter dropped off into a deep sleep shortly before dawn and did not awake until the late morning, by which time Sylvie had gone, leaving a socialist pamphlet on his chair as a memento of the night of politics and passion.

Sunday 15th January

Walter decided to find a bath-house and get properly clean. The washing facilities in the room were very limited and there were only so many places a wash cloth could reach. He knew there must be one locally, though he did not know if it was open on a Sunday. He was also hungry and needed some breakfast. He was just about to go out when Skinner came into the room looking very pleased with himself. He walked around making almost random remarks and grinning at odd moments with a faraway look in his eyes. There was no doubt about it, Skinner was in lust with Brigitte.

Walter invited Skinner down to the café and ordered enough for two, even though Skinner insisted that he was not hungry.

'Anyway, Brigitte has invited us both to eat over at their place tonight, so I was wondering if you'd come along,' Skinner said.

'Will Sylvie be there?' Walter asked, just to check.

'Sure, it will be the four of us, together. You know, this is something really new for me,' Skinner said, absently eating a croissant.

'You mean it was your first time?' Walter said sympathetically.

'Well the first time I didn't pay for it,' Skinner said, spraying flaky brown crumbs on the table, coughing and drinking some of Walter's coffee.

'My experience is that you always pay for it, one way or another,' Walter mused.

'What was that?' Skinner said with no signs of having heard.

'Oh, it doesn't matter,' Walter said.

'Say, what was your first time like for you?' Skinner asked.

'It was good. The girl taught me quite a lot,' Walter answered.

'How old were you at the time it happened?' Skinner continued.

'It was a long time ago,' Walter mused, 'I think I was nearly fourteen.'

'You were only thirteen?' Skinner said, incredulously.

'I suppose so. It was the daughter of a family friend, a few years older than me, and she decided to show me the ways of love,' Walter said with a thin smile.

'And how many women have you known? You know, I mean in the biblical sense?' Skinner asked.

'I really can't tell you. After I got into double figures it seemed a little impolite to keep count,' Walter answered modestly.

'What would that be? Twenty,? Thirty,? Fifty?' Skinner said, leaning over the table and taking another croissant.

'As I said, I really don't know. I used to keep a diary, and I could probably work it out for those years, but since then there have been quite a few women passing through my life, and I've never set out to keep count,' Walter said, determined not to give out any further information.

'Well, how many have you had since you came to Paris?' Skinner persisted.

'It doesn't matter, really it doesn't,' Walter said, firmly.

'It kind of matters to me,' Skinner said, taking another swig of coffee, 'Please tell me.'

'Oh, alright, it's three. And there was another on the journey over,' Walter said with a note of impatience, 'And I refused another offer.'

'My God! You really are amazing!' Skinner said with grin and a cackle of ribald laughter.

'I really don't like to talk about it too much. It sounds a lot like boasting. Can we choose another topic of conversation, please?' Walter said

'Yeah, sure, whatever you like. Say, what do you know about Socialism? You see, Brigitte seems awfully keen on it, and I want to have something to talk to her about,' Skinner said after a few seconds of thought.

'I think we'd better get you a book on the subject. It had better be in English. Let's go to a bookshop in town,' Walter said, pushing the plate away and motioning a waiter over, with a sign indicating he wanted the bill, 'And we'll get some decent wine for the dinner tonight.'

'Have you got that painting ready for Etienne yet?' Skinner asked.

'Yes, I have, but the paint needs to dry and it's Sunday, so the gallery won't be open,' Walter said.

'We could always take it to his house. I know where he lives. He's a friend of my mother, you know,' Skinner said.

'Yes, you told me. But, as I said, the paint is still too wet to wrap it up,' Walter said as he stood up. The waiter appeared with a slip of paper, like magic as Walter was threatening to leave. Walter dropped some coins onto the plate to the value indicated and added a small tip.

◊

There was a socialist book shop near to the Bobino theatre and Walter took Skinner somewhat reluctantly inside. There were sections for books in various languages. In the English section Walter was able to find cheap editions of 'Das Kapital' and 'The Communist Manifesto'. Skinner looked at these as though they were artefacts of some ancient and rather unpleasant civilization which specialised in ritual cannibalism.

'There you are,' Walter said with a slight smirk, 'If you read those you will be the first American to do so since they were written. It's probably all there, but let's look for something a bit more digestible.'

They looked around for a little longer and Walter found a book by Sidney and Beatrice Webb, 'The History of Trade Unionism'.

'Do I really have to read this stuff? It looks like a load of bunk to me, and I was warned about reading things like this,' Skinner stuttered.

'Ah, but who told you that, and what were their reasons for saying it?' Walter said, lightly.

'Yeah, maybe you're right. But it looks awfully heavy to me,' Skinner complained.

'I'll give you a hint,' Walter said with a smile, 'Read the introduction and the notes and just glance through the rest. That will tell you what you need to know.'

As they passed the Russian section they came across two of Walter's old friends, Igor and the bearded man, who were leafing glumly through some well-worn tomes with Cyrillic writing on the spines. The bearded man greeted Walter like an old friend, and Igor insisted on being introduced to Skinner before admiring his purchases.

'Those are very good books. Make sure you read them carefully. Karl Marx was a genius of the highest order,' he said in good French. Walter had to translate for Skinner's benefit.

'Well, thanks for the kind words, I guess I have a lot of catching up to do. Say, are you fellows Russians?' Skinner blurted out. Walter now had to translate as best he could for Igor's benefit.

'Is your friend an American?' Igor asked in mild amazement, 'I didn't think they read such books.'

'Only when they are in Paris, and only if they have a friend like me,' Walter explained with a chuckle.

'Anyway, I'm glad to see you here, Walter. That man who brought you to the bar where we met. There is some talk that he may be a police informant,' Igor said, giving Walter a piercing look.

'Thank you for that warning. I'll bear in mind that I have to be careful when I see him,' Walter said seriously, 'And I'm really glad I found you here. There is a Russian man who was recommended to me to do some work on an old painting I've got. His name's Lermontov, and he claims to be a Bolshevik. I was just wondering if you had ever heard of him.'

'I don't think I know the man. I'll ask Sergei here. Perhaps he knows about man,' Igor said, and he asked something of the bearded man in rapid Russian. The only word Walter recognised was 'Lermontov'.

Sergei screwed up his face in an effort to prompt his memory before giving a long answer. Igor nodded several times during this stream of words and then turned to Walter to translate.

'Sergei says that he knew a man of that name, but this person is little more than a common criminal. He hasn't been seen for some time. He was involved in some 'exes' a while ago, before he came to Paris. He was closely involved with some Georgians, and they are scarcely better than bandits. Sergei thinks he took up with some criminals when he got here. Whether he was ever involved in the movement, we do not know. It may be that he is part of Oulianoff's end of the movement. That could explain why we know little of him.'

'Well, I'm glad I didn't employ him. Do you happen to know what kind of crime he was involved with?' Walter asked, trying to sound like he was just making conversation.

'Something to do with forgery, Sergei says,' Igor said with a knowing smile.

'That's someone else I need to be careful with, then,' Walter said thoughtfully.

'Why don't you come to the bar a little later, and bring your friend with you,' Igor offered.

'We've got a dinner date with a couple of ladies, but we may have time to call in on the way,' Walter said.

'If you can't make it, don't worry. We're there most evenings,' Igor said, pumping Walter's hand.

'By all means,' Walter said, managing to extract his hand. Sergei gave a curt nod to both Walter and Skinner as they left the bookshop.

'What was all that about?' Skinner asked as he paid for the books he had taken.

'It's a couple of Russians I came across a few days ago,' Walter explained.

'They're not dangerous revolutionaries, are they?' Skinner asked.

'Well, revolutionaries, possibly, but dangerous, erm.., I don't think so,' Walter said with a slight smile.

'You were talking about someone called Lermontov, I worked that one out,' Skinner said.

'I was asking them about a Russian who is involved in the art world, but they didn't know much about him. He was supposed to be doing some framing for me, but it appears he's a forger, so I won't be using him,' Walter explained.

'As far as I'm concerned, the biggest criminals are the ones running the galleries,' Skinner complained.

'Now it's you who is sounding like a dangerous revolutionary,' Walter laughed.

'Well, don't tell my mother, will you, or she'll cut me off without a penny,' Skinner said with a grim smile.

'You must introduce me to your mother sometime,' Walter said.

'I'm not sure that's a very good idea. Not a man with your reputation,' Skinner said with a hollow laugh.

'I knew I shouldn't have confided in you,' Walter complained.

'Now let's look for some wine to take with us tonight,' Skinner said.

◊

The dinner was a reasonably civilised affair, with the added comic touch of watching Skinner trying to communicate with Brigitte. If Skinner was expecting another sexual encounter he was to be disappointed. The women were anxious to get to bed at a reasonable time, as work would start again tomorrow. And so both men walked back through the rain to their own rooms. Walter was glad of the opportunity for a good night's sleep. He would have to find out what had happened to Lermontov if he were to identify where funds for Ulyanov were coming from, and he had three main suspects, the Bolsheviks, the Apaches and Etienne.

Monday 16th January

Leaving it until a decent time when Etienne was likely to be working at the gallery, Walter called for Skinner, got him breakfasted and organised him into going to the studio. With the new canvas safely wrapped with brown paper and string the two young men set out on their journey via the Metro. It was late morning, approaching lunchtime when they arrived at the gallery near the Louvre.

They entered by the front door but were immediately ushered to a back room by an assistant. Etienne, as elegant as ever joined them, a small hot-house orchid on the lapel of his elegant grey suit.

'Ah, Monsieur Skinner, it is good to see you again. I trust that your mother is well,' he started, 'and I see that you have brought your friend, Mr Davies. I do hope that you are carrying a painting for me to sell.'

'I am, and I trust you like it,' said Walter, unwrapping the package. Etienne lifted the painting and held it at arm's length, then he placed it on a bentwood chair and viewed it thoroughly from a distance, the knuckle of his left forefinger on the cleft in his chin.

'Yes, that will do very well. It is difficult to know how to price a painting by an unknown artist, but I think I can get you a decent sale price on my recommendation. Do you wish me to negotiate with Mr Skinner, or shall we continue talking together?' Etienne said as he stood in his completive stance.

'I'm perfectly happy for Mr Skinner to act on my behalf in this matter,' Walter said, and he went out to look at the art in the main part of the gallery. He had not come to Paris to make a living as a painter, so he could be relaxed at the progress of the negotiations. It still gave him a thrill that someone was willing to pay handsomely for something he had created.

Down in the Flood

The pictures and small sculptures on display were all artfully and tastefully lit and arranged to show them off to best advantage. Walter was looking at a series of pastoral scenes he did not quite recognise, but the slight resemblance to Gaugin made him think about Skinner's comment about a Russian woman artist. These were quite good, with subjects which were vaguely familiar whilst being at the same time foreign and exotic.

A small stout man in a black coat and old fashioned top hat came into the gallery accompanied by a tall gaunt woman with a horse face. They studied the art on show and studiously ignored Walter in his working clothes. The few words they spoke were in a rustic form of German which Walter recognised as coming from Vienna. In order not to embarrass these customers, Walter moved silently back to the room behind them, where Skinner was concluding the deal with Etienne with a handshake. Walter did not enquire about the price which the other two had agreed until after they left the gallery.

'So how much am I getting?' Walter asked as they walked in the direction of the Louvre Rivoli Metro Station, close to the Pont Neuf.

'You are getting eight hundred francs, my friend. Now what do you think about that?' Skinner said with a grin. Walter thought that the painting would be sold for nearer to four thousand francs, and it was time he got a new agent, but he didn't say so.

'So where is my eight hundred francs?' Walter asked, already knowing the answer.

'Of course Etienne has to sell the painting first. You can't expect him to pay up front. If it's anything like the sketch you shouldn't have long to wait, though,' Skinner said, still smiling, 'And he says he's more than willing to take on some more work from you, as soon as you can come up with it.'

'I'll have to think about that. If the paintings are selling that well I ought to get a bit more money from painting them,' Walter said, with a mock note of bitterness in his voice.

'Now, don't get greedy. You ought to realise how lucky you are. There are so very few artists who make much money from the sales of their early work. Just do a few more and build a reputation and we'll see how it goes, right?' Skinner suggested, putting his hands in his pockets. The day was colder and brighter than any the previous week.

'Well, I've got an exhibition of my work in London later in the year. I need to keep a few canvasses back for that,' Walter said.

'But that's London, we're talking about Paris. If you can make your reputation here, then you're made for life. You can name your own price,' Skinner said, encouragingly.

'I need to finish these few paintings first and take them to the sitters. I'll think about it in a few days, and see if that painting has sold,' Walter said, putting his own hands in his pockets.

'You know, I think this is a real opportunity for you. You really ought to take it,' Skinner urged, pulling a hand out of a pocket to lift up his collar.

'Maybe you're right. I'll give it some thought,' Walter said, 'It's just that I don't like Etienne. I don't trust him at all.'

'Right now, he's your best option. The thing is, you need to get a reputation before you switch dealers. Once your work is selling, we'll have a bit of a Dutch auction and get really good prices,' Skinner said with some definition.

'Remind me how it is that you came to know Etienne anyway,' Walter inquired.

'He's a friend of my mother, didn't I tell you? She buys and sells a lot of art, not so much as a business, but as a collector, and he's one of her contacts in Paris. I guess they just became friends over the years,' Skinner said less animatedly.

'What about your step-father? You've never said much about him,' Walter probed.

'What's to say? He's a Polish aristocrat, with lovely manners, expensive habits and no money. My mother grew up poor. She got her money from my father, and he made his in mining. When he died he left it all to her, with barely a penny for me. She decided to come to Paris and Monte Carlo and spend some of the money collecting art and other forms of gambling. She collected my step-father as well. The thing is, she's got a real head for business. If anything, I think she's got more money now than when my father died. Not that she spends any of it on me, at least not more than she thinks I can live on. She thinks I should make my own way in the world. That's the phrase she uses. She has this idea that you don't value money unless you have to live without it. She may have a point, but I sure could use a few more francs right now. That room is really getting me down. Say, how about you and I getting an apartment? We could have our own rooms and invite the girls to stay anytime.' Skinner said, changing subjects without prior warning.

'I think we need to make a bit more money first,' Walter said, bringing the conversation down to earth, 'Besides, I've got to go back to England in a few weeks.'

Skinner stopped dead, raising an arm and pointing into the distance at a small group of men near the Metro station. 'It's the Mexican, the bald Mexican. He's still following me. Oh God! That's bad. Every time I get myself going he interferes. I hope he's not seen us in Etienne's place,' He said, finishing slack jawed and shocked.

'Are you sure it's him?' Walter asked, aware that this might well be an irrational fear on Skinner's part.

'Of course I'm sure. I'd recognise him anywhere. He follows me around, bringing bad luck with him, or worse,' Skinner said, looking close to tears.

'Now look. Since I've been around your luck has turned, right? You've sold a few things for me and got the commission and you've improved your drawing a lot. And you've got yourself a girl. Maybe your luck has changed now,' Walter said soothingly. Skinner drew in a deep breath and held it for a few seconds before replying.

'Yeah, you're right. I really don't need to worry about him anymore. I've just got to get on with my life.'

'Is your mother still in Paris?' Walter asked.

'I suppose so. Why do you ask?' Skinner said.

'It's just that I think you should tell her about selling that painting for me and the commission you're getting. That will show her that you are trying to make a living. It might make her a bit more generous,' Walter reasoned.

'You're right. I'll go and see her and tell her all about it. I might even tell her that I've got myself a girl,' Skinner said, suddenly smiling at the memory of his night in the arms of Brigitte.

◊

It took Walter over an hour to code his message for Godiva. He then had to queue at the Telegraph office for a further half hour. He was informing her of his suspicions that the Bolsheviks were smuggling art treasures out of Russia in order to fund the revolution. The telegram was more expensive than he had hoped, despite his cutting down the words to a minimum. It would take several hours for a reply to come, so it was not worth waiting around until the office closed. He decided to pay a visit to LaDavide and ask about the connection between Lermontov and the Apaches. It took half an hour and two changes on the Metro to get near to the Tiger's offices, and even then it was a decent walk. At least the fine weather was persisting and most of the puddles were drying. He never noticed the discrete man following him.

LaDavide was taking an early lunch break and was seated with a colleague in the café where he had taken Walter at the beginning of his visit. Both men were hunched over their coffees, smoking cigarettes. Walter nodded to LaDavide and sat down opposite him. The follower came in, ordered a coffee and sat not far from them.

'Pascale,' LaDavide said, waving a hand in the direction of his colleague, a barrel-chested balding man with a big nose. Walter did not know if this was the man's forename or surname.

'Have you found out anything about the death of this Lermontov man?' Walter asked without preamble.

'Someone knocked him on the head and threw his body in the river,' LaDavide said with a shrug, 'Why do you want to know?'

'Because some of the Bolsheviks knew Lermontov. I think he was doing a job for them,' Walter answered in French.

'And what kind of job would that be?' Pascale asked.

'Well, this is just supposition, but I've got some clues. I think the Bolsheviks have been smuggling art works out of Russia. But I haven't heard about any thefts. Lermontov was a forger. He could copy these art works and get them replaced as if they were the originals. If you had someone who was working as an art restorer the paintings could be taken away and the copies substituted without anything being discovered for years. There have been many works of art appearing in America in recent years and selling for enormous sums. You would need the help of someone who is a respected figure in the art world to verify the authenticity of the paintings and give them something called provenance. I think I know who that man is. Now Lermontov was working on behalf of the Apaches for a while, and you don't stop working for them. If I have got it right, I can explain how it is that the Bolsheviks have so much money, and give a plausible reason why Lermontov was killed,' Walter explained.

The other two thought for a while. Pascale took a large swig of coffee and LaDavide Sucked on his cigarette.

'So who do you think killed Lermontov?' LaDavide asked.

'It could have been just about anyone in the chain. If Lermontov got greedy or developed a conscience then almost all of them had a motive to kill him,' Walter answered. There was another gap in the conversation while the implications were taken in.

'So, are these paintings worth much?' Pascale asked at last.

'Millions of dollars. Some of them are almost priceless,' Walter stated, baldly. Pascale opened his eyes in surprise.

'I think that is much too big for the Bolsheviks,' LaDavide said in a whisper.

'But think of it, the smugglers get their share, the art dealer has his part of the profit, as does the auctioneer and the forger. Everyone gets a cut of the deal. It doesn't mean that the Bolsheviks get more than a small part of the money, but it would still be a lot of money by their standards,' Walter continues, patiently.

'So, who is this art dealer?' Pascale asked.

'I've got a suspicion about one man, but I'll need to do some more asking around. I'll get back to you on that. What I need from you is some idea who was the Apache group that Lermontov would have been working for,' Walter said. Pascale grunted.

'It would have to be le Baron,' LaDavide said slowly, 'He's the only one with pretentions to be a gentleman and links to the art world.'

'In that case I had better steer clear of him, given our history. Perhaps you could find out a bit about that,' Walter suggested.

'That could be a little difficult,' Pascale said thoughtfully, 'But I don't see why we shouldn't ask a few questions.'

'Come back and see me in two days time. You can tell us what you have found out and we might be able to tell you a little more,' LaDavide offered.

'Right, then. I'll call back in a couple of days,' Walter agreed.

◊

Walter was applying some finishing touches to his nude painting of the Princess as the light in the room faded, when Skinner came in.

'Just thought I'd let you know that you have got an invitation to dinner,' Skinner said.

'Is that at Brigitte and Sylvie's place?' Walter said.

'No it isn't. It's at my mother's place. Are you free tomorrow night?' Skinner asked with a wry smile.

'I should think so. Do I need to make a formal reply?' Walter returned.

'No, that's alright. I said I'd bring you along. My mother wants to meet you,' Skinner said with a sigh, 'And my step-father will be there as well, and his sister.'

'I'm not sure I have any suitable clothes,' Walter protested.

'You'll do just fine. It will look just right if you go as a struggling artist. Just clean yourself up a bit,' Skinner suggested.

'What sort of time would this be?' Walter asked.

'We'll get there for eight. I'll show you where the house is,' Skinner confirmed.

'And are you taking Brigitte?' Walter asked mischievously.

'Somehow I don't think that would be a very good idea. Maybe they'll meet a little later. Frankly, I don't think either could handle the other at the moment,' Skinner answered.

Tuesday 17th January

Walter was outside the door of the Telegraph office when it opened in the morning. There was a brief message waiting for him from Godiva. He spent much less time decoding this than he had spent encoding his last missive. It stated quite blandly that he should pursue this line of enquiry a little further, but ought to concentrate on the main task of identifying links between the Bolsheviks and the Latvians. There was a final note which said, Peter is back in Paris. Walter decided he needed to see Inessa Armand again. First, he would have to deliver the painting to the Princess. There was time before he did this for some breakfast and reflection. He folded the note and positioned it carefully behind the mirror, placing a hair on the frame which would fall if the mirror was moved. Then he wrapped the painting of the Princess in re-used brown paper and string before going down for his usual meal at the usual café.

◊

When he got to the Prince's house he found that the Princess was out or unavailable. The massive servant was either unable or unwilling to specify what the cause of her absence was. All Walter got out of him was a single low grunt. Not wanting to leave the painting behind in case the Prince were to view it first, Walter left a message that he would return again at the same time on the next day. With a shake of his head he left to return to his room. Before he got inside he found his way partially blocked by LaDavide's colleague, Pascale, who evidently wanted a word with him.

'I've found out a little about your art swindle,' he said, motioning Walter towards the entrance of the flats and the concierge's kiosk, 'It's not who you thought it was.'

'Alright, but it would be easier if we went into the café over there. We won't be overheard,' Walter said.

Down in the Flood

They walked over to the café, Pascale turning round frequently to study the faces on the street. In the cafe they found a table away from all listening ears, but quite close to a window. Walter ordered some coffee and two cognacs. He could see that Pascale was in a state of nervousness, and the agent kept looking out of the window in a wary way. Walter was sitting with his back almost parallel with the window, on the opposite side of the table from Pascale. He placed his hat on the table and propped the wrapped painting against the wall.

'I went to the Russian embassy to have a word with our contact there and asked if there had been any art thefts in Russia in the last few years. The clerk went away for a while and came back to tell me that he had looked up the figures and there was no significant increase in the theft of art, as far as he could tell,' Pascale said in a low voice. The waiter came over with the drinks and there was a silence which lasted until the waiter had returned to his station.

'But you didn't let it rest there, did you,' Walter guessed, 'And besides, if the paintings were replaced by good copies no-one would have known about the thefts.'

'That's right, I didn't stop there. I went to see an informer I use in le Baron's gang. He's not always reliable, but I can usually read him well enough. When I mentioned the art business he said he knew nothing. Then I mentioned Lermontov's name and he couldn't get away quickly enough. I've never seen him frightened like that. I don't think he was any more frightened of le Baron than he usually was. This was something different. If Lermontov was mixed up in the politics of the Russian exiles, he probably had links to some real desperadoes. Most of the émigrés talk politics but not many of them are real maniacs. Mind you, a small number of them are. They will do anything, kill anyone and they don't care if they get killed in the process,' Pascale said. He gulped down his brandy in one.

'Do you know who these desperadoes are?' Walter asked.

'They've got many names and they move about a lot. There's one I know about. This one works with the Russians, but he's not a Russian. I don't know what he is, but I do know what he looks like. We had him in for questioning once, but we had to let him go. Anyway, after I left the meeting with my informant I thought I'd come and see you, in case you knew something more. I noticed I was being followed, and I'm sure it was that man. I won't lie to you, I'm frightened. If he is following me, then he probably means to kill me. That's what he does. Mind if I have your cognac?'

Pascale reached across the table and took the glass before Walter could say anything. As he lifted his glass to his lips there was a loud bang and a simultaneous shattering of glass. A large calibre bullet had broken not only the window but the brandy glass on its path from outside the cafe window to the wall behind where Walter and Pascale were sitting. The other damage caused by the passage of the bullet was to Pascale's throat and spinal cord. His head was almost severed from his neck and after a short but almost interminable moment, it lolled back at an obscene angle. The dead man still held the remnants of the shattered brandy glass. There was a lot of blood from the severed arteries and some of it gushed onto Walter. A woman screamed and the waiter fainted. Walter noticed that several shards of glass had hit him and that he was bleeding from a small scalp wound. He removed a splinter of glass from his hand.

Walter tried to get past Pascale's corpse and at the gunman but was hampered by the table he was behind. Pascale's body was blocking his way out. It was too impolite to push the corpse out of his way, and so he had to clamber around and over the furniture. By the time he got to the door there was a crowd looking in at the broken window, some open mouthed with shock but more enjoying the spectacle and the entertainment. Walter screamed, asking if anyone had been seen running away, but no-one answered him. Someone grabbed at his shoulders, as though he were the assassin, then other joined in the effort to restrain him and Walter was protesting his innocence when the gendarmerie arrived and started their own round of shouting and pushing.

Walter was hauled off to the local Police station where he was questioned by a detective who evidently did not believe his story. It was only after three uncomfortable hours being shuffled between cells and interview rooms and repeating his story several times that LaDavide arrived and was able to confirm Walter's identity to the satisfaction of the detective. Still splattered with Pascale's blood and also with some from the scalp wound he looked a sorry sight. He was tired, hungry, shocked and thirsting for revenge against Pascale's killer. LaDavide was tight-lipped and looked both sad and angry, almost frog-marching Walter out of the Police station to a waiting Peugeot.

They drove along like the first car in a funeral cortege. Neither spoke or even looked at each other. It began to rain again. Walter realised that he had left his hat on the table at the cafe. The painting had been propped against the wall near where they had been sitting. They drove on to the Tiger's offices and processed solemnly in. Walter was sat in a hard upright chair in the office of LaDavide's superior. The senior officer was a prissy looking little man who wore pince-nez and had neatly cut greying hair with rather too much pomade scented with rose. He wore a neat old-fashioned suit and looked like the manager of a branch of a provincial bank.

'Tell us what happened and what Pascale said to you,' the boss said.

Walter explained all that had happened and all that Pascale had said up to the time of the shooting. Having told the story three times before at the Police station he was now getting to the point of retelling when the additions the mind makes start to outweigh the actual events, but Walter was sufficiently aware of this trap to keep the descriptions to a minimum. The boss sat in silence, his finger tips touching and his face expressionless.

'Did he mention who this desperado was?' the boss asked at last.

'He just said that this man used many names. He did say that you had interviewed him here and released him without charge. The other thing he said was that man was not a Russian, but sometimes worked with them,' Walter replied. The boss nodded and whispered some instructions to LaDavide, who nodded and left the room to return in a few minutes with a pile of folders which he placed carefully on the desk in front of the boss.

'There are a few men who might meet the description you gave. We will look through these files and get back to you. There is only one more small question I have to ask you. Do you have any knowledge of any non-Russian criminals who might have dealings with the Bolsheviks?'

'The only one I know of is supposed to be based in London, but he travels around. He is known to our Special Branch as "Peter the Painter". I was supposed to look out for him, just in case he was in Paris,' Walter answered, aware that he was telling more than he should but thinking it better to co-operate than obfuscate after the killing of Pascale.

'What do you know of this man?' the boss continued, leaning forward slightly.

'All I know is the name he uses, that he is a Latvian and that he is involved in criminal acts, mostly robberies. He is also suspected of several killings within his own community,' Walter answered slowly, 'And that is absolutely all I was told of him. I don't think it can have been him in Paris. He's supposed to have gone to Denmark.' The boss nodded slowly.

'Thank you for answering that question so honestly. We will look in our records and see if there are any matches to this Peter man. Because you answered so completely I will share any information we have on him. Our files are quite extensive. The search will take some time,' the boss said, 'And now, LaDavide, you had better take our friend here back to where he is staying. Goodbye, Mr Davies.'

The traffic was bad that early evening and the journey took much longer than it would have if they had left an hour earlier. LaDavide mumbled something about coming to see Walter on the following day, and Walter nodded in response to this offer. Even talking seemed to take more effort than he could manage.

When he got to his room Walter found his hat and the painting had been returned by some unknown person. The brown wrapping paper and string were still splashed with blood. In almost all other circumstances he would have mused on how those objects had got there. Just at the moment it didn't seem important. After a very few minutes he was joined by Skinner who, for once, knocked before entering. Walter raised just enough enthusiasm to invite the American in.

'Say, how are you feeling, Walter?'

'Oh, alright, I suppose,' Walter sighed.

'I was passing by the cafe when the owner called me in and told me to bring back your hat and the painting. I hope you don't mind me bringing them into the room. The door wasn't locked'.

'I'm sure I locked it before I went out,' Walter said, seeming slightly more lively in his delivery.

'Anyway, I thought I'd better bring them back. The owner told me what happened, and that you were right there when that man was shot. Must have been a really bad thing to have seen; to be sitting next to that man when he got killed.'

'I've had better days,' Walter observed.

'Now it's probably not the right time to say this, but I thought I'd remind you. I don't suppose you remember that we were supposed to be having dinner with my mother this evening,' Skinner said.

'In truth, it had slipped my mind, but, why not? It's bound to be better to go out to dinner than to stay here all evening,' Walter decided.

'Right, then, we'll need to be ready to leave in an hour. I think you'd better get yourself cleaned up before we go out,' Skinner advised.

'Don't worry, I intend to have a really good wash and put on some clean clothes,' Walter said with a half smile. He needed to have some goal to get himself through these hours.

◊

Skinner's mother, the Countess Podolski, was at home in a large rented apartment just off le Place de la Concorde. A liveried lackey took Walter's damp hat and coat with some distaste as he entered through the front door, giving a look of distaste at the poor quality of the cloth. Skinner was greeted with a little more enthusiasm by the domestics, as he was the son of the Countess, known to them and rather better dressed than Walter. Both men were ushered into a reception room where the other guests were waiting with their drinks. The Countess left the small, civilised throng and came to see them.

'Franklin, you did manage to persuade your friend to come. How very delightful. You must introduce me,' she trilled.

'Sure, mother, may I present Mr Walter Davies, and Walter, may I present my mother, the Countess Podolski,' Skinner said. The Countess raised her hand for Walter to kiss, giggling in a slightly girlish way, showing large teeth. She was above average height with a heavily corsetted waist, and very defined hips and bust. She motioned over a small, slim immaculately dressed man with black dyed hair and a carelessly artful curl on his forehead.

'Mr Davies, may I present my husband, the Count Podolski, and this, dear, is Mr Walter Davies, that young artist whose work I like so much,' Her voice was quite deep, and showed signs that it had been coached to lose some of the previous mid-west accent. The Count bowed stiffly, but the curl did not move, being glued to his forehead. Walter and Skinner were then guided around the room by the Countess and introduced to the various well dressed people who were making polite conversation in a mixture of English and French. Walter was more comfortable in this situation than Skinner, who seemed to withdraw into himself. The procession took them both round the room until a point near to their entry, when Skinner suddenly stopped dead in his tracks.

'Mr Davies, may I present Mr Hugo Ramirez,' the Countess intoned. Walter shook the outstretched hand of a man of less than forty years, of medium height and dark complexion. What little hair he possessed had been shaved to the skull.

'It's him!' Skinner hissed into Walter's ear, 'The bald Mexican!' It was as audible as a stage whisper, and Ramirez laughed delightedly.

'And you must be Mr Skinner. We meet face to face at last,' Ramirez said.

'I hope you don't mind, Franklin, but I've had Mr Ramirez keep an eye on you over the last few months, just to make sure you don't get into trouble,' the Countess said.

'But I haven't needed to look in on you since Mr Davies came to stay at your house,' Ramirez said to a scowling Skinner.

'Mother, You should have told me. I thought I was going mad. Everywhere I went I could see Mr Ramirez out of the corner of my eye. It really upset me.' Skinner stammered.

'But I told him to keep a discrete eye on you, just to make sure that you weren't getting into trouble. It was the first time you had to live on your own, and just wanted to make sure you were doing alright. I hope you don't mind,' the Countess said with a winning smile. Skinner continued to scowl.

'I was really getting anxious,' Skinner protested.

'Now, don't make a fuss, we are trying to have a pleasant dinner. Do make up with Mr Ramirez,' the mother said to her son before walking away to talk to the other guests..

'Pleased to meet you, Mr Ramirez,' Skinner mumbled.

'And I to meet you,' Ramirez said with an elegant bow, 'And to meet you too, Mr Davies.'

'Charmed,' said Walter, 'But I must admit I never noticed you around the apartments.'

'Oh, I can be very discrete when I need to be,' Ramirez said in his smooth voice with its transatlantic tone.

'And what is it that you do for a living?' Walter asked.

'Well, I have some little money of my own that I supplement by performing services for people and by trading in some luxury items,' Ramirez said blandly.

'I'm not sure that I quite understand,' Walter said, 'but I'm sure you make a good living. May I ask if you were around the apartments today?'

'As I said, I have not needed to come to the apartments since you arrived. You have been taking good care of Mr Skinner, and I have told the Countess about that. Is there a particular reason for you asking that question?' Ramirez asked. He took a sip from a crystal glass of champagne he was holding. A waiter came up and offered glasses to both of them, which they gratefully accepted.

'It's just that there was a murder committed very nearby, and the police are looking for witnesses,' Walter said sweetly.

'How very dreadful, but I suppose that such things happen. I'm afraid that I was elsewhere today, so I am unable to help,' Ramirez said with a note of regret in his voice. Walter gave a brief nod which both men took to be an indication that this topic of conversation was over. He turned away.

With a slight shock of recognition, Walter saw that one of the guests was an acquaintance of his from London, a mostly useless gadfly called Algernon Twisden. He was the sort of well-connected man who pops up at parties but had no known interests or means of support. He waved a glass at Walter and grinned inanely before coming over.

'Walter, what are you doing here?' he asked in a loud, braying voice.

'Look, Algernon, I'm in a bit of a fix here,' Walter said in an urgent whisper, 'I'm trying to make a go of being an artist, so I'm known here as Walter Davies. If my father found out what I was doing he would stop me, and it's all going very well. So please don't shout out my real name, just in case my father gets to know and drags me away. Promise me that you won't tell who I really am. Just say I'm someone you met in London, please.'

'Of course, old boy. I wouldn't dream of saying anything. Your secret is safe as safe can be. Now, don't you worry about it. We'll have a little talk later. Must dash now,' Twisden said before turning to find someone else to talk to.

Walter was concerned that Twisden could not resist telling his story. He was just the kind of person who could not bear to be discrete if the opportunity to gossip presented itself.

It was time for the start of the meal and the guests all filed in to find their carefully marked places. Walter found himself wedged between a stout Italian matron and a small bird-like French woman of indeterminate age. When Walter looked up he saw his sketch of Rosa Languedoc framed and hanging from the wall opposite. He now knew who had bought the sketch from Etienne. He was marginally surprised that the gallery owner was not present at this dinner. He had half expected him to be there.

The food arrived in numerous small courses, all with the appropriate wine, and the entire meal dragged on for hours. The food was much like the French haute cuisine which could be found in London since Escoffier had worked there. It was very good but rather too formal for Walter's taste, and his neighbours provided him with little amusement. It was nearly midnight before they finished at the table.

The gentlemen went into the library for brandy and cigars while the women went into a sitting room for coffee and gossip. Walter took a very large measure of brandy, but selected a Turkish cigarette in preference to a cigar. He noticed that Ramirez had been very abstemious with the alcohol and didn't smoke. The Count bore down on Walter like an admiral's launch, decorative and impressive, but with little practical function in serious situations.

'My wife seems to like your work very much,' he said to Walter in heavily accented English with an American twang.

'I saw my drawing on the wall. It is very good to be appreciated,' Walter said politely.

'I'm sure she would like to buy some more of your drawings or paintings,' the Count continued.

'I've just put a painting of mine in Monsieur Etienne's gallery,' Walter said. At the mention of the name of Etienne the Count bristled slightly. He changed the subject abruptly.

'Have you been to the South of France, Mr Davies?'

'Not yet, but I'm sure I shall in time. I was thinking of going to Provence later this year. Everyone says how good the light is there,' Walter replied.

'We have just returned from Monte Carlo. It is not quite France, but it might as well be. The food, the entertainment and the company are good. If it was not for my wife wishing to return to Paris to see that her son was well, and for some other business, I would have preferred to stay there all of the winter,' the Count said.

'But what about the casinos? Isn't it expensive there?' Walter asked.

'My wife has plenty of money, and she doesn't lose it on the gaming tables,' the Count said with a short guffaw.

'You must meet all sorts of people of quality in Monte Carlo,' Walter said without much interest.

'Oh yes, we know many people from the ruling houses of Europe and beyond. We number among our friends a Russian Prince and his wife, a Maharajah, and several English lords,' the Count said with a note of pride. Walter was going to ask if the Count knew the Duke of Radnor, but refrained from blurting out that his father was well known in Monte.

'What was the name of this Russian Prince. Perhaps I have heard of him,' Walter said.

'I should not think so. He is a very distinguished diplomat,' the Count said dismissively.

'Probably not then,' Walter said, thinking that maybe he did.

'Do you spend much time in the United States?' Walter asked.

'We have travelled over several times, but my wife prefers to be in Europe. She finds the atmosphere more suited to her nature, I think,' the Count said, 'If you will excuse me I think I have someone else to talk to,' responding to a gesture from a man across the room.

Skinner appeared at Walter's elbow. 'I think we ought to make our excuses and leave soon,' he said.

'Righty-ho,' said Walter, 'Just give me a minute to make my apologies and good-byes.'

'I hope you haven't been too bored by all this,' Skinner apologised.

'Not at all, it's been very instructive,' Walter said.

'Well, you took to it like you were born to it,' Skinner remarked.

'In fact, I was brought up to it, though the dinners were a lot less fancy than this,' Walter said, meaning the food but implying that he meant the company.

'Whatever it was, you looked at home here. I'm sure we can get you to paint some society women. That sort of work pays really well,' Skinner suggested.

'Well, possibly. I'll give it some thought,' Walter said, without much enthusiasm.

Wednesday 18th January

After a sleepless night Walter woke up late to find his sheets in a twisted mess. It had taken a long time to get to sleep and now he awoke to a cold room with the memories of the previous day still vividly coloured in his memory. His mouth tasted bad, and the fractured sleep caused him to feel woolly-minded and slow. He wandered over to the mirror and found that the hair he had placed there the previous evening was still in place. There was a knock at the door and LaDavide entered, looking just a little less grim than he had on the previous day.

'Could you give me just a minute to get dressed?' Walter asked.

'I'll see you downstairs in a few minutes,' LaDavide answered.

Walter performed a hasty toilette, and didn't bother to shave. After dressing quickly he made his way downstairs, past the concierge's booth and out into the street where LaDavide was waiting for him, smoking a cigarette. He had his collar turned up, his broad-brimmed hat pulled down and his left hand thrust deep into the slit pocket of his overcoat.

'Where do you want to go?' Walter asked.

'Just around the streets, I think. I don't want to go to that café at the moment,' LaDavide said in a flat tone.

'Alright, I can understand that,' Walter agreed, 'For some reason I don't feel inclined to go there either.' They wandered off in the general direction of Ulyanov's apartment.

'I just wanted to ask you a bit more about what might have got Pascale killed,' LaDavide said in a measured way. Walter nodded.

'If we can work out who might have had a reason to kill Pascale, we might be able to find out who ordered the killing,' Walter mused.

'What I really want to know is why they didn't kill you,' LaDavide said.

'You said that you spoke to le Baron, he agreed to leave me alone. Might that have anything to do with it?' Walter asked.

'It might well have been the reason, and the Apache leaders have been known to order executions. But I'm certain the killer was not an Apache. I've asked around and no-one thinks it was. Maybe they changed the way they do business, but, overall, I think someone else ordered it,' LaDavide answered.

'How about the Bolsheviks? If they were involved in smuggling art they might want to keep things in the dark,' Walter suggested.

'As for those exiles, mostly they don't want to antagonise the local police, but you mentioned a man called Peter the Painter. There are always a few desperadoes among the community. It could have been one of them,' LaDavide responded.

'I have a theory that an art dealer in Paris might be involved. He would have to have criminal connections, but if he was doing something illegal, he might know such people,' Walter said, as though thinking aloud.

'There is another possibility you haven't mentioned. It may be that another Russian is organising the transport of paintings out of Russia and the copying of the originals. This would be a man with connections in the highest circles. It could explain why both Lermontov and Pascale were killed; Lermontov because he knew too much and Pascale because of something he had learned,' LaDavide stated in a measured voice.

'I agree that the deaths are linked. I'll see what I can find out about Lermontov. One thing I ought to tell you is that I saw a couple of our Bolshevik friends at the nightclub a couple of days ago and they know you are a policeman. So it would be better if I asked them about Lermontov. They are not sure exactly what I am, so it might come better from me,' Walter said, looking at LaDavide with a serious expression. LaDavide gave a shrug.

'It was bound to happen sometime. I'm sure they can spot an Okhrana agent at fifty paces, and a policeman at twenty. I need to be sure that you tell me what you find out as soon as possible. It doesn't look good when one of us is killed. We need to clear it up as soon as possible,' he said. They stopped while LaDavide lit two cigarettes and handed one to Walter.

'What time do those Russians go to their café?' Walter asked, blowing out smoke at the same time.

'Two or three o'clock. They are there almost every day,' LaDavide replied.

'Is there anything you would like to know, if they are willing to answer my questions, that is?' Walter said.

'Just find out all you can about the links between the Bolsheviks and Lermontov. Look, I'll pass on anything I find out. It might be that something I learn links to something you discover or already know. The important thing is to make the connections. I'll come to see you this evening,' LaDavide said before inhaling a deep lungful of smoke and gently easing it out.

'I think I'll find a different café for my breakfast,' Walter said, changing the conversation.

'Do you mind if I join you, I am rather hungry, but the knowledge of what happened in the usual café would make the food indigestible,' LaDavide said, with a sad, slight smile.

◊

Later, when Walter entered the Bolshevik café he was greeted warmly by the smelly man, who had, thankfully, washed in the interim and was only moderately offensive to the nose. Walter ordered some brandies and sat down with the motley crew of expatriate Russians. There was little space for the drinks next to the chessboard which took up most of the table. Walter knew he had no innate talent at the game, and had been too lazy to learn to play even moderately well, but he observed how the game was progressing with a little interest. It seemed better to develop some friendly relations with the Bolsheviks before starting to question them, so he held his tongue, smiled and tutted as the game progressed. He could think of more exciting ways of spending an afternoon, most of which involved young women and privacy.

More brandies were produced, and tea from a samovar. The chess game dragged on almost interminably, with long gap between moves. The emaciated man eventually knocked over his king in surrender and a burst of applause and some back-slapping greeted the victor, a small jolly looking man with round eye-glasses.

'It's Karl, isn't it?' the man called Igor asked Walter.

'That's right, and your name is Igor, Walter said back to the man with the black spade-like beard.

'Ha, so you remember me, then,' Igor chortled.

'I'm still looking for one of your number, a man called Lermontov, I think I mentioned him last time we met,' Walter said.

'Of course I do. I'm afraid that we have bad news for you. His body was found in the river. He won't be able to do that job for you now,' Igor said. Walter acted slightly shocked.

'How did that happen?' he asked.

'Who can say? He was a man with many criminal connections. Maybe he fell in by accident or he ended it all. Many of us are very homesick and some become depressed and kill themselves. We are a very emotional people, you know,' Igor explained.

'Do you know where he lived, or who he was working for? It seems bad to speak this way of the dead, but he promised to do a job for a friend of mine, and I promised to find out what happened to the painting,' Walter said in a solemn voice.

'I shall ask everyone. There are a lot of people here. Maybe one of them can answer your question,' Igor said, immediately turning to address some of the other exiles in Russian. There was a good deal of talking and some animated disagreements.

'Apparently he used to live in La Villette,' Igor said, 'But no one seems to know exactly which street his house was on. He was doing some work for a local gangster, something to do with art forgery.'

'Was he doing any work for one of the Russian groups?' Walter asked.

'If he was, then he was taking his life in his hands. These gangsters don't take kindly to their people working outside the gang. They are a little like our revolutionaries. It is to stop the group being infiltrated. There are people from various groups here, but none of them admits knowing anything much about Lermontov and his business. I don't think they are lying. It is possible they are not telling the whole truth, but I didn't notice any guilty silences,' Igor replied.

'In that case it must have been someone else outside who was employing him. I wonder who it could have been?' Walter mused. Igor shrugged.

'Who can say? Not us, that is for sure,' Igor said, 'Now, do you want some tea?'

'I'd rather have another brandy,' Walter said, 'Don't worry, I'll pay for it.'

They were sitting down with their drinks when Walter introduced another subject of conversation.

'Do you have any contact with any of the Latvian people?'

'I don't know any Latvians in Paris. There may be some, but not Bolsheviks. I think they must all be anarchists. These are very bad people. Why do you ask?' Igor replied.

'One of them's a painter. I was wondering if he was in Paris. We have some business, you know, money. He ran away from London and is supposed to be here. Sometimes he calls himself Peter.'

'Like I said, I don't know of any Latvians here.

◊

As Walter was returning to his room the concierge stopped him as he passed the kiosk and handed him a note. It was from the Princess and said that the note had been delivered by her maid. Walter was not to come to the house or to try to deliver the painting again until it was safe to do so, several days at least. She would send the maid again with a further note when the coast was clear. If he wished to reply to the note he should send it via a dressmaker's that the Princess used and who she could rely on be discrete. The dressmaker's address was included. Walter folded the note and put it in an inside pocket.

Skinner heard Walter unlocking his door and came over to talk.

'I got a message from Etienne. He's managed to sell that painting of yours, so we are to collect the money from him. The trouble is, he's going to pay us by cheque, so I'll have to open an account at a local bank, and that could take a couple of days,' he said, between excitement and concern.

'That's alright, I'm not desperate for cash at the moment. I can wait a couple of days,' Walter said with a slight smile at Skinner's worries.

'And my mother wants to see you. I think she wants you to do her portrait,' Skinner continued.

'In that case, I'd better see her,' said Walter.

'Anytime within the next twenty four hours, knowing my mother,' Skinner remarked, pointedly.

'So when am I supposed to talk to her, then?' Walter asked.

'She asked if you could go to the house tomorrow afternoon, about three o'clock,' Skinner said.

'I suppose so,' Walter said, 'I haven't got any appointments then. You'd better tell her I'll be coming.'

'Oh, I won't need to do that. She has commanded and you will obey. That's the way she does it,' Skinner said with a grim smile.

'Do you want to go out tonight?' Walter asked.

'How about the Blue Barge?' Skinner suggested.

'I take it that you are not seeing Brigitte tonight,' Walter commented.

'She said that she will see me on Saturday. She's got to get up for work every morning, so I guess she's too tired to go out during the week,' Skinner said.

'The Blue Barge sounds good to me,' Walter said, thinking he could make use of the break from reality, 'I've got to send a couple of messages first'.

Skinner returned to his room and Walter entered his own. He would need to contact Godiva to update her on what was happening and acknowledge the note from the Princess. The second note was easy enough, but he would need to spend some time encoding the former. The note would need to be short but precise, and that required some thought.

◊

The Blue Barge was much as usual, except that Rosa Languedoc was working elsewhere and had been replaced with a woman who did a dance with swirling skirts and fabric that blossomed around in a cloud of printed silk. Skinner became very inebriated on absinthe again. This was beginning to become a habit, and Walter had to help him home as before.

Thursday 19th January

Walter rose late and decided to see if a message had come from London before eating. There was a short reply waiting for him at the telegraph office. The clerk was getting used to Walter and smiled at him before handing the note over. It had lain in a pigeonhole overnight and even before he opened it Walter felt that he should have dealt with it earlier. The reply simply said that he should expect the arrival of a friend tomorrow, which meant later that same day. He was to go to the Gare du Nord to meet the train.

Walter cursed softly under his breath and checked his watch. He still had two hours to get to the station, and there would be time for a coffee and croissant when he got there. He made his way to the nearest Metro station and proceeded to try and navigate its labyrinthine passages and nodes where the lines intersected. There was a delay just south of the Montparnasse station and Walter arrived at the Gare du Nord a few minutes late to meet the train, and had no time for any breakfast. As he got to the platform where LaDavide had met him just two weeks ago, he saw his friend Godiva Williams. She had already arrived and was standing with her luggage by the exit from the platform.

Godiva was ordering a porter about in commanding schoolgirl French. The porter merely shrugged and held out the palm of a hand to receive payment. The luggage consisted of two capacious leather bags, one somewhat bigger than the other. It amused Walter to see the attitudes of an Englishwoman abroad and her interactions with the locals. Suppressing a smile, he hurried over to offer her assistance. As he approached Godiva scowled suspiciously, then broke out into a relieved smile. Walter handed a few sous to the porter and grabbed the bags before the man could query the fee.

'Ah, Walter, glad to see you. I had horrible visions that you might have missed my message,' Godiva said, relieved.

'I was a bit late picking it up, then there was a delay on the Metro. Sorry not to have been here when you arrived. I thought I'd have time for a coffee before meeting you. Would you like one now?' Walter said in a rush.

'I'd rather have a cup of tea,' Godiva replied.

'Believe me, the tea here is disgusting. If you don't like coffee I can recommend the chocolate,' Walter continued, 'There's a café in the station or several in the streets around.'

'If we are going to talk, I think a café outside the station would be best. Not the nearest,' Godiva decided.

'Follow me, then,' Walter said. He picked up the luggage and led Godiva through the Station concourse and onto the Rue de Maubeuge. There were several cafés on the side streets and Godiva chose one some two hundred yards distant from the station. They sat as far as possible from any inquiring ears and talked in low voices, which carry much less well than whispers. Walter had croissants with some butter and apricot conserve while Godiva had a slice of cold tarte tartin with her cup of chocolate. There were periods of silence while they ingested and appreciated the food and drink, and they did not discuss business until after they had finished.

'This has all become a bit of a mess, hasn't it, Walter,' Godiva said.

'I suppose it has,' Walter sighed.

'In fact, I'm not sure that it wouldn't be wiser to send you straight back home,' she continued, 'Only the Tigers have asked for you to stay on for a few days.'

'Did you hear about that business with Pascale?' Walter asked.

'Of course we did. We heard about it in great detail; gory detail, in fact. It must have been horrid for you,' Godiva answered.

'I suppose the Tigers want to help me find out who it was who killed Pascale,' Walter mused.

'Have you thought that the shot which killed Pascale might have been meant for you?' Godiva enquired.

'If it was, then the man who fired must have been a terrible shot,' Walter replied, 'He can't have been very far away.'

'But consider the refraction through the glass of the window. If the man with the gun fired at an angle to the window he could well have judged it wrongly,' Godiva said, wiping her lips with a serviette to remove any crumbs.

'I'd never considered that. It could be true. I'd always thought that Pascale was the victim of an expert assassin, but it could just have easily have been an incompetent one,' Walter mused.

'So, the question is, who would want to kill you?' Godiva asked.

'Where do I begin with that? How many cuckolded husbands would you like me to name? To be a bit more serious, I don't think there are that many husbands in Paris who are after me. I have done some physical damage to a few men since arriving, and they are gangsters,' Walter answered.

'How did you injure them?' Godiva asked.

'Well I broke the arm of the son of a local gangster chief, then I put two more of his men in hospital, one with a broken jaw and nose and another with concussion and things. But this boss, le Baron, well he's supposed to have promised to leave me alone,' Walter said.

'Why on earth did you do that to these men?' Godiva asked with a good deal of surprise in her hushed voice.

'I suppose it happened because they were trying to kill me at the time. Besides, I had a bit of help from Ulyanov's wife. She hit one of them over the head with a bag of shopping. There were some tins of Alaskan salmon in the bag. That's how the gangster got concussion. She came to my rescue, and I'm grateful to her for that,' Walter replied, thinking that it sounded like something which happened to somebody else.

'Does anyone else want to kill you?' Godiva queried, the pitch of her voice getting higher.

'There's some kind of criminal conspiracy going on about smuggled Russian art and forgery, but I'm not sure who's involved in that,' Walter admitted.

'No offence intended, Walter, but you are supposed to be doing the work for us, not the Paris police,' Godiva commented, a note of exasperation in her voice.

'The forger was a Russian who had links to the Bolsheviks,' Walter said.

'Why do you say "was"?' Godiva asked, 'Has he left the group or something?'

'You could say that. He's dead. His body was found in the river a week ago. One of the theories I have is that he was copying pictures which were smuggled out of Russia and substituting his copies for the originals. It may be that this is one way that the Bolsheviks were funding their activities,' Walter continued.

'I'm glad to hear that there is a link. But how did you come to learn of all this?' Godiva asked a little more calmly.

'Believe it or not, I'm beginning to sell some of my paintings. I'm quite in demand. It all came through my contacts in the art world,' Walter said, smugly, 'In fact, I've got an appointment with someone this afternoon. This woman buys and sells art, and she's an American, and that's where the originals are ending up, so she might well have something to do with all this.'

'So what are you going to see her about, and what time is your appointment?' Godiva enquired.

'As to the first question, I think she wants me to paint her portrait, and the answer to the second question is three o'clock. Now tell me something, what time did you set out?' Walter said.

'Oh, I took the sleeper late last night and got into Calais quite early. I managed to do another little job there before coming on to Paris,' Godiva said.

'It must be inconvenient for you to have to come out at such short notice,' Walter said sympathetically.

'It would have been more convenient if you had not quarrelled with our Mr Campbell,' Godiva commented with a slight touch of acid in her voice.

'The man is an idiot,' Walter said with some anger.

'The man is a diplomat, a straight diplomat, and he doesn't like what we are doing very much. It upsets his idea of propriety,' Godiva came back.

'He's still an idiot,' Walter said with a smile.

'You'd better go off for your appointment. We need to arrange a time and place for us to meet up later,' Godiva said bossily.

'Where are you staying?' Walter asked.

'At the Hotel Ariadne,' Godiva replied.

'I believe that is in the general direction I need to go. I might as well help you with your bags,' Walter offered, 'Then I'll know which room you are in.'

'That would be very much appreciated,' Godiva said.

Walter paid for their refreshments and picked up Godiva's luggage.

'How long are you staying for?' he asked, feeling the weight of the bags.

'Sorry, but I don't like to travel unprepared,' Godiva replied.

◊

Having left one strong and opinionated woman, Walter now found himself travelling to the house of another. Everything was new and gleaming and screamed of a high-cost rental. The servant who answered the door was in a brand new uniform with gleaming brass buttons. By his expression he was not a native Parisian, as he looked grave and respectful.

The Countess was sitting in a high armchair in a bright new sitting room taking whatever the French habit was for high tea. Tiny cakes were symmetrically arranged on delicate porcelain plates alongside small cups of china tea. She motioned Walter to sit opposite her before placing her plate down and dabbing her mouth with a lace serviette.

'Thank you for coming to see me, Mr Davies. It was good of you to come at such short notice,' she said with quiet precision.

'Not at all. Franklin tells me that you might have some kind of commission for me,' Walter said with extreme politeness.

'That's right. I had planned to commission a portrait of my husband and myself, and I seem to have taken a liking to your work, at least the work that I have seen. So I thought I would ask if you were interested in us sitting for you,' the Countess said, smiling with mouth but not eyes.

'I will certainly be very pleased to take your commission. Would sometime next week suit you?' Walter said.

'I'm sure that would be very suitable. I shall pass a message onto you via Franklin. It will probably be earlier in the week, before we go back to Monte Carlo at the end of week,' the Countess said, 'But please tell me if you have been misleading me. You were introduced to me was Walter Davies, but a little bird tells me that you are really called Lord Walter Mansell-Lacey.'

'I make a point of never using my title. I find it gets in the way when I am trying to do something serious. The reason I came to Paris was to get away from the social circles I was in and to find some real artists. I presume it was Mr Twisden who felt he had to tell you, despite, or probably because of me asking him not to. I really had no intention of deceiving you, it is just that I wish to be taken seriously,' Walter said by way of explanation.

'I believe your father is a Duke. The Duke of Radnor, in fact. Is that correct?' the Countess asked.

'You are completely correct, but I am just a younger son with little money and no likelihood of inheriting the title. The only reason for my having a title is that, if you are a Duke, then all your sons will bear the title of 'Lord' without ever having to have done anything to deserve it,' Walter continued.'

'That sounds very much like socialism to me. Surely you should be one of the greatest supporters of the aristocracy, given your background,' the Countess protested. Walter had to take a deep breath to stop himself replying in immoderate tones.

'Do you still wish me to go ahead with commission?' he asked.

'I wish it even more than before. Just to think, we will get our portrait painted by a real English Lord!'

'Please do not spread my story around. You see, I need to prove to my father that I can make my living as an artist in my own right, without relying on the family name,' Walter pleaded politely.

'I think that is very silly of you. You really ought to make best use of all the advantages you have. Poor Franklin thinks much the same as you, but he keeps coming back and asking for extensions to his allowance. The terms of his father's will are very specific; the money will not come to him unless he takes up the business and does a proper job of it. This painting idea of his is very silly. He really has no talent for it. If you could, I would like you to encourage him to give up on his plans and come back into the family fold,' the Countess said, smiling genuinely at Walter this time.

'I'll certainly have a word with him this evening,' Walter confirmed.

'Thank you so much for that. I am so very much looking forward to going back to Monte. The climate is so much better there,' the Countess said, changing the subject.

'It is possible that you will run into my father there,' Walter said.

'It may well be possible. We were in the company of a Russian Prince and Princess last time we were there. Such a charming man and his wife is quite lovely. They have a place in Paris too,' the Countess said with pride.

'Would that be Prince Pechorin?' Walter asked, making mental links as he said this.

'That's right. Do you know him?' the Countess returned, surprized.

'Not at all. It was just that someone mentioned his name to me once,' Walter lied.

That is a pity. He is, as I said, a very charming man. You should make his acquaintance,' the Countess suggested.

'Not in my present situation, I think,' said Walter, 'But I will make sure that I do your portrait before you leave.'

'Then thank you, Mr Davies, or should I say Lord Walter? I look forward to seeing you next week. And don't forget what I said about Franklin,' she said by way of dismissal.

On the way back to Godiva's hotel Walter dropped a short note to the Princess in at the dressmakers her note had specified.

◊

Godiva was waiting for Walter at the hotel in a sitting room decorated in the Art Nouveau style that had gone out of fashion at least five years before. She was making notes in a black memorandum book and was wearing her gold-rimmed spectacles. No-one else was in the room. She looked up and beckoned Walter to sit next to her on an over-stuffed sofa. He sat down and smoothed his trousers, then crossed his ankles. Godiva closed the memorandum book and turned to face him.

'How was your meeting?' Godiva asked him.

'Oh, quite interesting. I've been asked to paint a portrait of a Polish Count and his American wife. She's a dreadful old snob, and she's managed to find out who I really am,' Walter admitted.

'Tell me, how did that happen?' Godiva asked, in a controlled voice, with tight lips.

'I had to attend a dinner at her place and an acquaintance from home happened to be there. I asked him to be discrete, but he went and told his hostess who I was. When I see him again, I will return the compliment. I've sworn her to secrecy though, and I don't think she's in any way connected to the situation. She's the mother of the American who has the room next to mine,' Walter said.

'Is there any way that she could be connected?' Godiva asked.

'Well, the only way I can think she might be is through a mutual acquaintance, a Russian Prince based here in Paris. He's a diplomat of some sort and LaDavide, my contact at the Tigers, introduced me,' Walter answered.

'What is the name of the Countess you saw? And please tell me the name of the Prince,' Godiva said, opening her memorandum book again and taking out a pencil which she raised and held poised above the page.

'The Prince is called Pechorin and the Countess is called Podolski,' Walter answered.

'How is the Prince's name spelt?' Godiva said, taking notes. Walter spelt it out.

'Let's hope that there is no connection between them. Did you know that Pechorin is in charge of the Okhrana in Paris?' she continued.

'I'm not in the least surprised by that. There is definitely something a bit sinister about him. His manservant is a real monster,' Walter said, 'And I'm sure he is beating his wife.'

'It sounds like you know the Princess quite well,' Godiva commented.

'I painted a portrait of her, and another picture, a nude which I haven't delivered yet. The nude was her idea, and she tried and failed to seduce me. It wasn't just your warnings, but the sight of the bruises which put me off. It made me feel all brotherly, which is quite a strange sensation for me. She had tried to cover the bruises with makeup, but they were easy enough to see if you were looking closely,' Walter said. Godiva had been tapping the point of her pencil on the page of the book while he said this.

'Oh, Walter, I don't know whether to congratulate you or tear you off a strip. All I can say is that I'm glad you were honest with me. It sounds like she was trying to entrap you in some way. The bruises were probably a result of her husband's attempt at persuading her to do that. I do hope that he forgives her for failing,' Godiva said, closing her memorandum book.

'You know I wouldn't fail to boast about my sexual conquests to you. If what you said is true, then I feel rather guilty about putting the Princess in danger,' Walter mused.

'Right now I am going to make some enquiries about your Countess Podolski. Perhaps you can take me out later to some place where we might run into your Bolshevik contacts,' Godiva said.

'How about a sort of socialist nightclub? It's called the Bobino, and we are bound to see some people I know there. I might even introduce you to my American friend, and hope that he doesn't fall in love with you. He has a very romantic disposition,' Walter said with a slight laugh.

'Then why don't you collect me later?' Godiva suggested.

'I'll see you about seven o'clock and we can find somewhere to eat before going on to the club,' Walter said, decisively.

'I'll see you here later, then,' Godiva said, standing up and walking to the door. Walter followed her out.

◊

The Bobino was crowded for a Thursday night, probably because Montéhus was performing. Walter and Godiva had to squeeze into the back, and there were no unoccupied seats or tables. The meal had been very good but it had taken longer than anticipated, being one of those Normand affairs that drag on for hours. Godiva had not talked business at all during the meal and Walter had not prompted her. Instead they discussed mutual acquaintances and recent events in England. In the club there was no chance of being overheard, though the noise was such that Godiva had to talk directly into Walter's ear, in a way which looked more intimate that it was.

'Your Prince is a bit of a gambler,' Godiva said, 'He lost a good deal on the roulette tables in Monte Carlo last year. I asked some questions about him and about the Countess. Now the interesting thing is that it seems that your friend the Countess has bailed him out. She's a very serious business woman, so she had to have some reason for loaning the Prince that money. She helped out her husband even before he became ill. His finances were not exactly transparent, and there was something a bit funny going on, as far as we can tell. His declared income was negligible but he lived like a king. If nothing else, he was cheating on his taxes. So, maybe, she's continuing the family trade. The word from the Americans is that his business was not entirely legal. The trouble is, we don't know what that business might be at the moment.'

'I can hazard a guess about that. Now bear with me while I explain. Firstly, there was a Russian I was interested in, a forger called Lermontov. He was found dead in the river a week ago, probably murdered. He was supposed to be working for a local gangster boss, but seems to have taken on other work. I thought he was working for the Bolsheviks, but I don't think they have the resources to have employed him. Secondly, there is a gallery owner called Etienne who is involved in dealing in Russian art. He is also well known to the Countess. Thirdly, the Countess seems to be connected with a scheme to acquire art for the American galleries, whether legally bought or not. What I think happened was that the forger, Lermontov, was creating good copies of paintings kept in noble Russian houses. The Prince was able to get access to these houses and swap the pictures for Lermontov's forgeries. Etienne helps to get the genuine paintings out of Russia and the Countess gets them to America. That way, the Prince pays off his debt and the Countess and Etienne get their share of the profits,' Walter said into Godiva's ear. She looked serious and nodded.

'But why was the forger murdered?' she asked.

'I can't be exactly sure, but I think it was probably the gangster boss, because Lermontov should have been working for him. But it could have been the Prince, if Lermontov had tried to blackmail him. Take your pick, really,' Walter answered.

It was at this point that Montéhus came out onto the stage. He had such presence that Godiva immediately paid attention to the radical singer until he had finished his first song. Walter had been looking round the room and had spotted someone he knew, sitting at a table quite near to the stage.

'He's very good, isn't he?' Godiva observed, 'I didn't understand all of the song completely, but I understand what it is about.'

'Stand on tip-toe and look at that man with the short beard sitting at the table to the left of the stage,' Walter instructed her. She had to crane her neck to see what Walter could make out due to his great height.

'Is that Ulyanov?' Godiva asked in some surprise.

'Indeed it is. If I get a chance I shall introduce you to him,' Walter promised. Montéhus started his second song at this point and the room went quiet. Walter started to edge forward, Godiva following in his wake. There were some muffled protests from those who had come to see the singer and found their view interrupted. It took two more songs for Walter to get to the front, by which time Montéhus had come to the last song in his first set. When he had finished, and the thunderous applause had died down Walter was able to edge over to the table where Ulyanov was sitting with Inessa Armand and a solidly built dark man with deep-set eyes. Inessa spotted

Walter first and motioned him over. Walter brought a somewhat shy looking Godiva with him.

'Hello, Walter, how are you, and who is your friend?' Inessa said in good English.

'Hello, Inessa, this is my friend, Godiva Williams. Godiva, may I present Inessa Armand, Monsieur Oulianoff and I gentleman I haven't been introduced to,' Walter said in French.

'I am very pleased to make your acquaintance,' Oulianoff said, confusingly for Godiva in German. He held out a hand to be shaken in British fashion, 'This is a colleague of ours in the party who is visiting.'

Godiva gave a half smile at the unnamed stranger and shook Ulyanov's hand.

'Godiva is the daughter of the socialist writer, Offa Williams, and she has collaborated in the writing of his later work,' Walter said, 'perhaps you have heard of Offa Williams.'

'Indeed I have,' Ulyanov said, 'I came across his work when I was in London. He is one of your more enlightened thinkers. Now, tell me, Miss Williams, what do you think of our friend, Montéhus?'

Godiva struggled to find the proper words of praise in French. Her knowledge of the language was too formal to fully form the everyday expressions used in Paris. With help from Walter and Inessa she made her meaning flatteringly clear.

Ulyanov nodded and smiled at Godiva. 'It may be that Monsieur Montéhus will join us later,' he said, and banged the flat of his hand on the table, rattling the glasses.

Walter managed to waylay a passing waiter and order drinks for the table, but only the cheap red wine he had tasted before. Five tumblers and two opened bottles arrived and Walter paid the waiter the cost and added a small tip. He tipped out the wine into the tumblers and handed them around the table. Everyone except Godiva drank deeply. She sipped her wine more delicately.

'I have read some of your articles, Monsieur Oulianoff,' Godiva said in moderately good French.

'I had no idea they had been translated into English,' Ulyanov said in bad French.

'I learned to read a little Russian, but I can't speak a word, I'm afraid,' Godiva excused herself. Ulyanov gave a short chuckle.

'That is quite remarkable. I'd like to see this,' So saying he produced a pamphlet in Russian from his pocket. Godiva, tired though she was made a brave stab at translating the words into English, with Inessa translating them back into Russian. When she had finished, Ulyanov clapped and smiled. 'That is truly remarkable. I have never known anyone be able to do that before. How did you learn the language?'

'From a Russian / English dictionary. That was all I had,' Godiva answered.

'Now you must learn to speak the language. Russian is a very beautiful language for poetry and song,' Ulyanov continued.

'I shall try to find some Russians living in London who will be able to teach me,' Godiva said, 'That is, when I get back to London.'

'Will you be in Paris long?' Inessa asked in English.

'Only for a few days. I came over to see how Walter was getting along,' Godiva answered, glad to be able to use English again. The two women smiled at each other. In other circumstances they might have become close friends.

'Walter is doing very well. He is busy with commissions for paintings. He has made portraits of Monsieur Oulianoff and myself, and they are very good,' Inessa said.

'I'm pleased to hear that he is doing so well,' Godiva said with a slightly twisted smile, 'Perhaps we can meet again while I am here. I would like to talk further with you, about the party and what I could do.'

'I'll tell you what, I'll get a message to Walter to pass on when I know what I am doing. We could do with more help in London,' Inessa said, translating rapidly into Russian for Ulyanov's approval. He nodded and smiled.

Montéhus came from backstage to sit with Ulyanov. There was insufficient room at the table for them all and Walter and Godiva bid the others a good-night. It was a long walk back to Godiva's hotel and there were no cabs or buses to be had. The rain had started to fall again. It was the steady sort of soaking rain which permeates any number of layers of clothing. Godiva made good use of her trusty umbrella, but Walter became soaked.

'You know, if this is a criminal conspiracy, then we ought to pass it onto the police,' Godiva observed.

'I'm not sure we can trust the Gendarmerie,' Walter said, 'But it might be safe to tell my contact in the Tigers, LaDavide. He's working on the Lermontov case and on Pascale's murder.'

'Didn't he introduce you to the Prince?' Godiva asked.

'I'm still not sure about the motives for that, but I think he has to tread a fine line sometimes. I've met his boss and he's too much of a politician to make a good policeman. I'm certain LaDavide knows that the Prince is the local head of the Okhrana, but he must have thought that we were basically working for the same side,' Walter replied.

'Then you'd better introduce me to him tomorrow,' Godiva conceded.

'I'll bring him round to the hotel tomorrow morning,' Walter said, delivering Godiva to the door of the hotel at almost exactly the same time.

'Good night, Walter,' Godiva said, kissing Walter on the cheek before hurrying through the door. It was well past midnight.

Friday 20th January

LaDavide knocked at Walter's door at nine o'clock the next morning. He found Walter already dressed and wanting breakfast. They went together to the further cafe and sat at a table at the back, well away from the window. They both ordered coffee and croissants.

'Would you mind meeting a colleague of mine?' Walter asked. LaDavide shrugged.

'If you think it would be useful,' he replied, 'Who is this man, anyway?'

'I'll introduce you when we get to the hotel,' Walter said with a slight smile, 'Now, has there been any progress in your investigations?'

'It is a little odd, but we have heard almost nothing. All our usual sources are completely silent. No-one can imagine why anyone would wish to kill poor Pascale,' LaDavide said with a sad shake of his head.

'My colleague has a theory you might want to hear,' Walter said, taking a bite out of a croissant liberally spread with apricot conserve.

◊

Godiva was waiting for them in the same sitting room where she had met Walter on the previous day. This time there were other guests using the room and they had to find a quiet corner. LaDavide had shaken hands with Godiva at the time of the introduction, but had not changed expression much to register even moderate surprise that Walter's colleague was a young woman, and an attractive one at that. Godiva signalled to a lurking waiter that some coffee would be required, something she must have arranged earlier.

'Godiva, may I present Monsieur Gaston LaDavide; LaDavide, this is Godiva Williams,' Walter said, making the introductions as quickly as he could.

'Hello,' Godiva said, holding out a hand. LaDavide shook it briefly and nodded but did not smile or speak. The waiter arrived with the coffee and proceeded to pour out the steaming liquid into delicate porcelain cups. With a jug of cream and a bowl of sugar lumps in front of them the three participants performed an impromptu ballet of passing receptacles and spoons and making the coffee as they wished it. Godiva started the conversation.

'What we really need to do is to define the limits of what each side is entitled to do. If it is solely to do with a criminal act committed in France, then, obviously, it is a matter for the French authorities. If there is anything linked to what Walter has been doing, then I hope he will be allowed to continue,' she said to LaDavide.

'I understand what you are saying,' LaDavide said with a nod, 'And there has been some pressure from within my own department to exclude Walter from our operations.'

'Do you mind if I put in a word here, as you both seem to be talking about me,' Walter said, a little peevishly, 'It seems to me that it is almost impossible to separate out what has happened into neatly divided responsibilities. Now, please, Godiva, just tell your idea of what might have happened at the shooting.' There was a slight but significant delay before Godiva spoke.

'I only suggested that Walter might have been the target at the shooting, and not your colleague, Monsieur. It seems to me that the shot was most likely fired through glass that had been viewed at an angle. There would have been a certain degree of refraction. Also, the shooting may have been done by someone who was not an expert shot,' she explained.

'We did briefly consider that, but the shot seemed to be very expert,' LaDavide commented.

'Well, I am by no means an expert, but I believe that an assassin would have aimed for the torso or the head. The neck is too small a target to aim for with a relatively inaccurate pistol,' Godiva continued.

'There is something in what you say,' LaDavide agreed after a little thought, 'Although I think our assassins might have different methods than those in England. It would certainly be worthwhile considering your opinion and asking if Walter might have been the target. Unlike my unlucky colleague, Pascale, Walter seems to make enemies very easily, so there will be no shortage of suspects. I will tell my boss what you said and we will see what happens. If it gives us some more information it will be useful. Sometimes when you ask the wrong question you get the most interesting answers.'

'Well, in that case, it looks like I am still involved in the investigation,' Walter said to both of them.

'Yes, I suppose it does,' Godiva conceded. LaDavide just nodded and fumbled in his pockets for a cigarette. He offered one to Godiva, who politely declined before giving one to Walter.

'I've come up with a theory about the other crime as well,' Walter said.

'What other crime is that?' LaDavide asked., lighting his cigarette.

'The death of the art forger, Lermontov,' Walter answered.

'Oh, that. Well, you had better tell me, as you have started,' LaDavide said warily.

'I believe Lermontov was being paid to copy paintings which were being smuggled out of Russia. There is a man who imports Russian art. His name is Etienne, and he runs a gallery near to the Louvre. The real paintings were replaced with the copies made by Lermontov and the genuine ones smuggled out to the United States,' Walter said.

'Then I think I should ask Prince Pechorin about this. He has a large private collection and will know if there is any criminal activity with paintings going on in Russia,' LaDavide said.

'I don't think that would be a very good idea,' Godiva interrupted, 'The prince could well be involved in this because he needed to pay off his gambling debts.'

'Do you have any proof of that?' LaDavide asked.

'What I have is a suspicion, but I know he is friendly with a woman who imports art into the United States. In fact, the Prince owes the money to her, so it all fits together rather neatly,' Godiva said with a slight smile. LaDavide gave a low whistle.

'You will understand that this matter must be approached with the greatest amount of discretion. It is not easy to accuse a diplomat of any crime. He could just claim diplomatic immunity,' he said.

'Well, I'm sure you would be much more diplomatic about it than Walter,' Godiva commented.

'Thank you for that vote of confidence,' Walter said. LaDavide shrugged and stood up.

'And thank you, Miss Williams, for the coffee and for your thoughts. I will take them back to the office now and talk to my boss. I will see you tomorrow, Walter, and let you know what has happened,' LaDavide said. Godiva stood to bid him farewell and he kissed her on both cheeks before pressing a business card into her palm. He clapped Walter on the back before leaving.

'I somehow think he'll try to take credit for coming up with those ideas,' Walter said after LaDavide had left.

'Does it really matter, if we get the results?' Godiva said.

'But they were your ideas. I think you ought to get some of the credit,' Walter replied.

'Oh, Walter, you really have no idea what it is like being a woman,' Godiva said with a little laugh, 'But, you know, I think we can trust him, so I don't mind telling him what we know.'

'There was one thing I didn't tell him,' Walter admitted.

'What would that be?' Godiva asked with a touch of weariness in her voice, knowing that she was about to be told this secret anyway.

'I'm still in touch with the Princess Pechorinova. She is using a dressmaker's as a means of getting notes to and from me. I'm going to go there and see if there is anything waiting for me. I'll probably try again tomorrow, if there is nothing there,' Walter said.

'Do you mind if I come along?' Godiva asked.

'Not at all. I'm sure it is easier for a man to go into a dressmaker's if he is accompanying a woman than if he is alone. It is almost entirely a female preserve.'

They left the hotel together, with Godiva using her trusty umbrella to keep out the persistent drizzle. The establishment was just a few streets away from the hotel, sandwiched between a milliners and a photographic studio. They entered together. Though his message had been taken, there was no note waiting for Walter. He decided that he should come back every day, just to check that the Princess was still well.

'So, where are you taking me tonight?' Godiva asked as they left the shop.

'I really hadn't made any plans,' Walter admitted, 'I suppose we could always go to the cinema.'

'I'm not sure I like the idea of that. The few film shows I have been to in London were held in rather dirty little halls,' she said.

'They take cinema rather more seriously here in Paris. There are especially built halls, and it is quite respectable,' Walter said.

'Alright, then, I'll give it a go. I shall expect you at about half past seven this evening. In the meantime I must go and ask a few questions which the London office can answer. I shall see you this evening,' Godiva said. With that she turned on her heel and left. Walter wondered what he was to do during the intervening period. He decided to work on some of his paintings and see if Skinner had received the cheque from Etienne.

◊

Skinner was in his room trying to do an illustration for the cover of a dime novel. The scene he was attempting to show included the hero, white hat removed, confronting a villain, black hat on, at a poker table. Both men had six-shooters in their hands and angry expressions on their faces. In the background was a stage with a dancing girl who looked a lot like Rosa Languedoc about half way into her dance, but with western dress. Of its type, it was very adequate. Walter praised it as best he could and Skinner seemed pleased.

'Are we seeing Brigitte and Sylvie tonight?' Walter asked.

'No, I'm afraid not. They are working tomorrow. We'll see them tomorrow night, if that's OK with you,' Skinner answered.

'I'm not sure, I've got a friend who has come over from England, and I'm having to do some entertaining. In fact, I'm going to a cinema show tonight,' Walter said.

'Oh, I was going to ask if you wanted to go to the Blue Barge,' Skinner said.

'Sorry, not tonight. Maybe you can meet my friend tomorrow,' Walter said, 'Now I really must get on with some of my own work. I'll see you a bit later.'

'Alright, and I've got to finish this thing. I need to send it off tonight,' Skinner said.

'Any news of the money from Etienne?' Walter asked.

'I'm putting it through one of my mother's accounts. I should be able to draw on it tomorrow,' Skinner said.

'I'm getting a bit short of money, sorry to push you,' Walter said in a serious tone.

'Don't worry, you'll get your money tomorrow,' Skinner replied.

'Thanks, ' Walter said and he turned and went to his own room.

Painting for two uninterrupted hours proved to be a useful period for meditation. Walter tried to make sense of the paths he had taken which had led to his current position. The connexions between the various threads of the case proved not so much elusive as transitory. He tried to make the links every way he could imagine, and, if he didn't come to any definite conclusion, he felt he had still managed to free his mind of some preconceptions that had hampered his progress.

When he had finished doing the drawing and blocking he looked in detail at his work. It was a picture of Godiva talking to LaDavide, based on the scene in the room at the hotel earlier that day. He had replaced the dour furnishings in the room at the hotel with a remembered picture of the sofas in the reception area at Le Chabanais. The heavy, vividly coloured silks with the embroidered pictures of exotic birds transformed the picture, drawing the viewer into the work. Godiva was talking, with her chin lifted in that typical way of her, and LaDavide's expression seemed to indicate that he was trying hard not to look interested.

◊

The cinema was nearly full for every short performance, and though the entrance price was cheap, the throughput of paying customers was enough to turn a good profit for the owners. Walter found it hard to recall the film afterwards, though he remembered the time that the film broke and had to be repaired and when the reel stuck. The frame showing to the audience blistered and twisted in the gate. Godiva was left unimpressed by the dumb-show acting and the limited ambitions of the script.

'Perhaps we should have gone to a proper show,' Walter confided.

'Oh, not at all. It's been an experience,' Godiva assured him, 'But not one I intend to repeat in a hurry.'

'I'll come to see you tomorrow morning, at your hotel,' Walter said.

'Could you make it at half past ten? I've some work I need to complete first. And try to be punctual, just for once,' Godiva said.

Saturday 21st January

Walter decided to visit the dressmakers again as soon as he had finished his morning coffee, though this time without Godiva. At least the manager there knew who he was now. There was a note waiting for him there. It read,

Come to the house as soon as you can and rescue me. Marie will let you in at the back door. Please hurry!

There was an indecipherable squiggle at the base of the note, but the message seemed clear. He set out for the Prince's house at a trot, splashing through the puddles on the pavement. It was raining steadily and the number of puddles was growing. Most people seemed to be avoiding the rain, but there were some hardy types who were walking around with umbrellas. He had to dodge their spokes which were at his eye-height.

As he crossed the Pont du Neuf Walter noted that the level of the water in the river was once again rising and would soon fill the banks. The pedestrians crossing the bridge partially blocked his route and he had to dodge around them and into the road, where he had to avoid. While on the road he had to avoid busses, cabs, carts and the occasional motor car.

Although he was soaked by the time he got to the Prince's house the effort of the run made him warm. Having only entered the house through the front door previously, Walter had no idea how to approach the back of the house. There was no entrance through the front around the side of the house, but, logically, there had to be another way in via an alleyway at the rear of the houses. It took Walter some time to find the narrow passage leading to the alleyway, which was partially blocked with a pile of building rubble. The alleyway was little more than a muddy paved track with grass growing through in places. He had to count back to find the correct house. The rear of these houses was much less grand than the front, and had no distinguishing architectural features. After all, it was only servants who would see the house from this side.

Having found the correct house, Walter climbed gingerly over a slippery locked gate whose rotting wood threatened to collapse under his weight. The path beyond was green and slick with moss. Dodging behind the shrubs in the garden, and trying to hide behind the evergreen bushes of holly and ornamental spruce, he wove up the length of the garden to the rear door. It was set off centre to the right of what must have been the kitchen. It had once been painted blue but the paint had peeled and faded and was streaked with rust from the iron of the door furniture. Walter stood to the side of the door and knocked softly. A shuffling noise of feet on wooden floors was followed by the door opening slightly. The ugly face of the maid, hair tied tightly back and mostly hidden behind a mob cap, appeared, acknowledged Walter's presence, and motioned him in with a swift toss of the head. Walter followed cautiously, opening the door no more than was necessary to squeeze in. He shut it softly behind him. There was no-one else to be seen, other than the maid at the end of a short corridor. She waved him along, scuttling in front.

As Walter passed an open door to what may once have been a lamp-room he looked up to see the maid motioning him forward. He took a short stride and was then grasped with huge strength by a pair of enormous arms. A pad soaked in chloroform was clamped over his mouth. He kicked out behind, raking heels down his assailant's shins and twisted with all his strength, all the time trying not to breathe in the chloroform fumes. His eyes were watering but he could see the maid laughing at him. He was in danger of passing out from lack of oxygen when his body made the decision for him and he gasped air in through both nose and mouth. The air was mixed with chloroform fumes. Within a few seconds he was deeply unconscious and hanging limp in the encircling arms of the giant servant.

As he gradually came around from the chloroform Walter began to take note of his surroundings. He was in a damp and musty wine cellar, securely manacled to a wall. He had been stripped to his shirt and was very cold. There was no blanket or any other form of cover and warmth. How long he had been there he had no idea. His watch was in his jacket pocket, and the jacket was nowhere to be seen. Damp leaked out of the bricks and there was a coating of white mould on the outer walls. He would have cried out, but there was a gag tied across his mouth. He tested the shackles by pulling on the chains as hard as he was able, but they were securely fastened to the wall. The metal was hardly spotted with rust yet, so must have been newly installed, probably with him specifically in mind. Walter looked around the little room as much as he was able to. Above was a rough ceiling below the ground floor of the house. Walter made a rough estimate that this cellar must be below the current level of the water in the river.

Whatever the purpose of his imprisonment, his captor seemed in no great hurry to question him. For a full half hour he tried to move, both to avoid cramps and to keep warm, but his movement was very limited. He could scarcely move his arms more than six inches, and his feet less than that. Then he heard the noise of the rusty bolt being drawn and the dry hinges of a door being opened. This was followed by the sound of footsteps gradually increasing in volume as they approached. Marie the maid appeared in front of him and spat copiously over the top of his face. With his hands fastened the way they were Walter was unable to wipe the spittle away, and it dripped down his brows. Without saying anything to him she went to fetch his captor. Soon he would find out why he had been so ungraciously treated.

Down in the Flood

A few minutes later the Prince appeared. The monstrous servant was with him, stooping under the low roof of the cellar and carrying a lit oil lamp which cast strange wavering shadows on the walls. With the return of consciousness he began to feel the after-effects of the chloroform. Walter had a sick headache and a burning sensation around his mouth and nose where the pad had been clamped. His eyes were streaming and felt sore and bloodshot. Through his bleary eyes Walter could make out the rictus smile on the face of the Prince, or it might have been a sneer. One thing Walter knew for certain was that he was about to be questioned and not within the rules of any government or police force. The monstrous servant pulled the gag from Walter's mouth. Then the Prince started to talk in bad, slow French.

'You have fucked my wife,' the Prince said.

'Have I?' Walter returned after a short pause.

'Have you?' the Prince continued.

'No,' Walter replied. The Prince said something in Russian to the servant. The huge man handed the lamp to the Prince, loped across the cellar and struck Walter in the solar plexus with a massive fist. The pain was excruciating and it felt like he had no more air left in his lungs.

'Did you fuck my wife?' the Prince asked, seeming to recall the correct words.

'No, I only painted those pictures of her,' Walter replied, struggling to get the words out. The Prince nodded to the servant and another blow was delivered, this time just below the ribs on Walter's left side.

'Say that you fucked my wife!' the Prince shouted.

'Why? Are you going to hit her again?' Walter asked, 'I've seen the bruises.'

The Prince looked confused. His French vocabulary was insufficient to understand what had been said to him. He scowled, said something to the servant and left the cellar. In a few minutes he returned again. This time he was accompanied by a slight man dressed discretely in grey who had no memorable features and whose image seemed to melt into the bricks of the cellar wall. The Prince said something to the grey man, and it was the latter who now spoke.

'You have insulted the honour of the Princess,' he said in immaculate French, 'You painted a picture of her which is completely obscene. You took advantage of her and forced yourself on her. You will admit this now. If you do not, then the Prince's manservant will continue to hit you until you do.'

'I just told the Prince that I never fucked his wife. She tried to seduce me, probably on his instructions, and she failed. I saw the marks of the bruises he gave her, and I'm sorry if this earns her another beating,' Walter said.

The grey man translated for the benefit of the Prince, who grew very angry. He shouted something to the servant who pulled Walter forward until his arms were forced behind him and nearly wrenched from their sockets. Then he forced Walter's head down on his chest. Finally he gave Walter a punch in the kidneys before releasing him.

'What you told the Prince is not what he wanted to hear. I think you should agree with him unless you want more of a beating,' the grey man said in a bored voice.

'I'm only telling him the truth. Why should I lie?' Walter said once he could talk without groans of pain interspersing the words.

'You don't have to lie, you only have to sign a paper. Then he will let you go,' the grey man explained.

'What will he do with the paper I sign?' Walter asked.

'He will use it to divorce his wife,' the grey man said.

'I'll need to read it first,' Walter said, playing for time.

'It is in Russian. I will read it to you. You don't speak Russian do you?' the grey man said.

'Niet!' Walter said in a soft voice.

The grey man removed a paper from an inside pocket, unfolded it and started to read, but stopped after a few words. 'This is all the usual legal stuff. I will just translate the relevant section for you. 'I Walter Davies admit to having sexual relations with the Princess Pechorinova on Tuesday 17th January 1910 during the afternoon when I was supposed to be painting her picture,' he said in a flat tone.

'If I signed that I would be telling a lie,' Walter persisted.

'If you do not sign it would mean more of a beating for you,' the grey man said.

'Oh, alright,' Walter agreed. After all, he had every right to claim the confession was obtained under duress. Also, he knew no Russian and Walter Davies was an assumed name. Such a document would never be admissible evidence in court. The greater worry was that this document could be used to discredit him in other ways.

Walter was allowed to move himself painfully back against the wall and to free up his right hand sufficiently to hold a pen and move it across a small part of a page. The grey man produced a fountain pen, unscrewed the cap and handed it to Walter. He then held out the paper to be signed.

'Where do I sign it?' Walter asked.

'Here,' said the grey man, leaning forward and pointing at the bottom of the page.

Walter took his brief opportunity of extracting some revenge to head-butt the grey man as hard as he could, with his restricted movement. His forehead made good contact with the bridge of the man's nose, splintering the bone and causing a great gush of blood. He reeled away, clutching his nose in his hands and splattering blood all over the paper that was to be signed. The monstrous servant then landed several blows on Walter's head and body, temporarily rendering him unconscious. When he came round the grey man was standing over him, clutching a handkerchief to his face. As Walter's eyes fluttered open he received a kick to his ribs, at least one of which seemed to be broken already. He winced with pain.

'You could have been released, you know,' the grey man said, his voice muffled by the blood and the handkerchief, 'Now you will be asked more questions while another copy of the document is typed.'

'Lay on, McDuff,' Walter said.

'What was that? Oh, it doesn't matter. Now, tell me, what is your real name?' the grey man asked.

'Only if you tell me who you work for,' Walter said. He received another kick in the ribs.

'I asked you what your name was,' the questioner continued.

'My guess is that you work for the Okhrana,' Walter said between short breaths,

'What is your name?'

'My name is Walter,' Walter replied.

'What is your surname?'

'What is yours?' Walter asked in return. He got another kick for his pains.

'Your name is not Davies. What is your name?'

'My name is Walter,' Walter said.

'Your name is Mansell-Lacey,'

'Why am I imprisoned here? Why have you kidnapped me?' Walter blustered. He hadn't expected them to have his real name. Where had they got it from?

'Your name is Walter Mansell-Lacey,'

'I thought you were asking me questions, not making statements,' Walter said. It suddenly occurred to him that he had been interrogated in English since coming around the last time.

Down in the Flood

'Your name is Walter Mansell-Lacey, and you work for the British intelligence agency SIS. You came here to investigate one of our dissidents, Vladymir Ulyanov.'

'If you already know so much, why are you asking me these questions?' Walter asked. He decided that his best option for keeping alive might be to add some truthful answers among the dissembling and lies.

'You need to know that you cannot lie to us. What do you know about another Russian man, Lermontov?'

'I know he was an art forger. I know he used to work for a gangster called le Baron. I know he was found dead in the Seine. That is all that I know about him,' Walter said.

'Why did you concern yourself with this man?'

'I thought he might have been working for the Bolsheviks. It turns out that he wasn't. I asked some of them and none of them really knew him,' Walter explained.

'That is not enough. Why have you spent so much time trying to find out about him? It was not what you were sent here to do.'

'I thought the Bolsheviks were raising money for their revolution by smuggling art out of Russia. I really thought there was a link between Lermontov and the Bolsheviks. I was wrong,' Walter admitted.

'What else do you know about this art smuggling?'

'I really don't know anything else. I have some suspicions, but no proof, and no hope of finding any. I'd given up on that investigation,' Walter said.

'That is not true. You talked to your friend LaDavide. He has started some investigations. Why did you do that?'

'There seemed to be a link between the death of Lermontov and the killing of LaDavide's colleague, Pascale. As I was sitting next to Pascale when he had his head blown off, I was asked to help in that investigation,' Walter said. The interrogator considered for a minute before continuing.

'You will be asked some more questions later. I will send Marie down with some food.'

'I'll look forward to that,' Walter shouted at the retreating figures of his captors. The monstrous servant returned and replaced the gag over Walter's mouth.

Walter wondered how they knew his name and the details of his mission so exactly. His name could have been passed on to the Prince by the Countess, but that supposed a degree of contact between them which he hadn't suspected. LaDavide would not have given details of his mission, he was certain of that, so that information must have come from another source.

Walter examined his body as best he could and came across several areas which were very sore. His bladder was uncomfortably full but his mouth was dry and tasted as if a small rodent had died in it several days before. There was no immediate possibility of rescue and another round of questioning could start at any time. At least they hadn't hit him in the face.

◊

Godiva had waited for Walter for nearly an hour before she decided that he wasn't coming. Although he was habitually late, he would always turn up eventually. Something must have happened to him. She decided to go to his room and see if anything could be learned of him there. With stout boots, overcoat and umbrella she set out from the hotel across Paris to a place she had not previously visited. Outside the hotel she found herself walking in the direction of the dressmakers and decided on a whim to see if he had called in there. In the dressmakers she found that neither the owner nor her assistant spoke any English, so she was forced to resort to her primitive French to describe Walter.

'Un homme avec les cheveau blonde. Il ettez prez de deux metres... oh, dammit, what was the word for height?' she stumbled through. Luckily this proved to be sufficient.

'Ah, ouis, le milord, l'artist. Il ettez ici depuis dix heure du matin,' the owner said.

Godiva managed to find out that Walter had been at the shop a little after ten in the morning and that he had taken a note which caused him to become very excited. Wasn't he a handsome young man, and wasn't the Princess lucky to find such a lover, especially because he was so keen that he had run out of the shop and seemed to be going in the direction of the Princess's house. She was such a charming woman, and so beautiful. No, she hadn't read the note, that would not have been right, and it was the Princess's maid who delivered the note, the sour-faced woman.

Godiva thanked the dressmaker and left the shop feeling like her brain had been pummelled with the insistent rush of gossip. Walter must have gone to the Prince's house and become stuck there for some reason. He would be too polite to forget their appointment, so it wasn't an urgent call to a love affair which had taken him there. The other possibility, one that seemed more likely, was that this was some kind of trap, and Walter had walked into it. She would need help to find out what had happened to him, and the only person she could turn to was LaDavide. She retrieved the business card from her handbag and tried to work out how she was to get to the offices of the Tigers he worked from. There was a telephone number on the card and she walked around until she found a telephone in a Post Office.

It took some time for Godiva to make herself understood. LaDavide was out on a case but would be back later, probably in the mid-afternoon. A note would be left for him. Where did she wish him to meet her? She decided that the hotel would be the best place.

Finding that she needed to get involved in some work to calm herself she decided to go to the embassy and find out all she could about the Prince. This man was supposed to be a friend but was acting more like an enemy, and it was important to know your enemy.

◊

LaDavide walked into the sitting room of the hotel looking rather piratical in his undercover outfit. He was dressed as an Apache. Godiva invited him to sit down and explained the situation. LaDavide sat impassively and listened without showing any great degree of interest.

'I was supposed to meet Walter at half past ten this morning, but he never came. I had someone from the Embassy check, but he was not in his room. Walter may be late, but he can be relied upon to come eventually. What I did find out is that he had received a note, supposedly from the Princess Pechorinova, Godiva said.

'Since I received your telephone call I have been checking myself. I believe that Walter has been taken by the Prince. The questions we need to ask are where he is being kept, and how do we rescue him?' LaDavide said, and he lit a cigarette without seeking permission.

'Could he still be in the Prince's House?' Godiva suggested. LaDavide shrugged.

'It is possible. The Prince is not very bright, and besides, he has diplomatic protection. It is possible that the Prince is holding him there,' LaDavide replied.

'I suppose that we first need to find out if Walter really is there,' Godiva said.

'Then I shall go to the house and try to find that out,' LaDavide offered.

'Before you go, I think we ought to tell each other what we know about the Prince. I was trying to look up some details today, ones that are held on our files,' Godiva said.

'He is a diplomat. This is mostly because of family influence, as he has no real talents, other than strutting round and losing money. He is supposed to be head of the security at the embassy, which should mean that he is in charge of the Okhrana in France. There is another man there who is supposed to be a clerk, but who is treated with some deference. We suspect that this man is the real head of their service there. It may be that this clerk is more interested in what Walter knows than the Prince is,' LaDavide said with no hint of holding back any information.

'My information is that the Prince is very well connected, and that he tries hard to look like a wealthy aristocrat. He has mortgaged his lands to pay for things to make him look rich. It seems that his wife was the mistress of Czar's cousin, but when it became inconvenient for her to remain single, with gossip in St Petersburg, she had to be married to someone from a respectable family. The Prince was convinced to marry her because he owed the Czar's cousin a favour, and because he thought she had money. But she didn't bring any money into the marriage, and her lover deserted her soon afterwards. It is not a happy marriage, and he beats her. He is very fond of gambling, and he has large debts. It seems that he is already on a warning because of his behaviour, and he would be recalled if he failed to repay the debts. It might well be the case that he was persuaded into some criminal activity to raise money to pay them off. Our information agrees with your impression. He isn't very bright,' Godiva said in return.

'One of his largest debts is to the Countess Podolski, just as you told me yesterday, and she is involved with an art dealer called Etienne who imports art from Russia. We have been looking closely at the business affairs of Monsieur Etienne, and we do not believe he can make enough money from his gallery alone to live as he does. It seems that the Prince has been identifying good works of art in private collections and offering to get these restored and cleaned through his Paris connections at a bargain price. When these works get to Paris he has them copied and sends the copies back to the owners while selling the original to the Countess Podolski. He needed someone in Paris who knew a forger, and that is where Etienne becomes involved. He knows a good forger, a Russian called Lermontov who has done some very creative restoration for him. Etienne has a way of smuggling stolen art out of Russia disguised to look like modernist works. The customs in Russia will not recognise these paintings as old masters. When he gets them in his gallery the new paint is taken off, then they are once again sold through the Countess Podolski, who knows so very many rich buyers in the United States, especially the ones who are building galleries and museums to show how very cultured and public-minded they are,' LaDavide said.

'And you know all this for certain?' Godiva asked.

'It would not be the kind of evidence which comes to court, but it is true,' LaDavide replied with a shrug, 'it was what I was doing today before I got your note. I was checking with my contacts in the criminal world. Some of them are very well informed and because neither the Prince nor Etienne are proper criminals, they are willing to talk to me about it. There is that much honour among professional thieves.'

'What can I do to help?' Godiva enquired.

After some thought LaDavide said 'You could come with me to the Prince's house. You could tell him that Walter has gone missing, and that he told you he was going to see the Princess before he left. We will see how he reacts. If Walter is in the house he will attempt to smuggle him out, and if Walter is not there he may lead us to where he has him hidden.'

'Let's go now, then,' Godiva said with some urgency.

'Before we go I need to put some men to watch the house, from both the front and the back. It will take a little time to arrange, perhaps half an hour. I must make a telephone call. He sauntered off to the reception desk at the hotel, showed his warrant card and commandeered the telephone to make his call. After getting in touch with the duty officer he briefly explained the situation, gave the address of the Prince's house and asked for four men to be assigned to this duty.

Godiva was impressed by LaDavide's organisational abilities and his general air of confidence. This was an ally she could work with.

'We have a few minutes to spare before we go to the Prince's house. If you don't mind, I will have another cigarette before we leave,' LaDavide said, sitting down again.

'Of course I don't mind,' Godiva said, smiling at him.

As LaDavide smoked his cigarette they sat together in companionable near silence. A porter hurried in with a message and Godiva found herself whisked out of the room and into the rear of a large Peugeot car which was waiting outside to take them to the Prince's house.

After receiving instruction from LaDavide the driver made reasonably sedate progress towards their destination. It was necessary that the other officers were place before they could attempt to find out where Walter was being kept. As they travelled along the tyres of the Peugeot threw sheets of water from the puddles onto passing pedestrians. The rain was still falling steadily as they reached the Prince's house. LaDavide was first out of the car and held out a hand for Godiva. She opened her umbrella and together they made their way to the gates. LaDavide pressed the bell and they heard it sound within the house. Godiva held the umbrella so that it covered both of them. After about a minute without any activity from the house, he pressed it again. The thin, foxy face of a woman appeared at a ground floor window and looked out at them before disappearing. Another minute passed before the front door opened and a maid hurried to the gate to let them in, a shawl held above her head. Her face was hidden by the shawl until she was almost upon them. When they could see her they recognised the face which had looked out of the window. The maid opened the gate and led them to the house. The door was slightly ajar and they hurried in to the dry warmth of the interior. Godiva shook out her umbrella and furled it before entering.

The Prince was waiting for them near to the staircase. He stood formally with his right hand behind his ram-rod straight back. His eyes took in Godiva without any sign of enthusiasm and he never looked directly at LaDavide.

'What can I do for you, lieutenant?' he asked.

'We are looking for the gentleman who came with me when I last visited, Mr Walter Davies. This lady who is with me is his colleague, Miss Williams. It seems that he was supposed to meet her this morning, but he never arrived,' LaDavide explained.

'Ah, yes, I remember the gentleman. But I am afraid he did not come here. He must have had something else come up which caused him to forget his appointment with the young lady,' the Prince said in a bland voice.

'It seems he received a note which asked him to come here,' LaDavide continued.

'All I can say is that I know nothing of any such note and he never came here. Are you sure you are not mistaken?' the Prince replied.

'Unfortunately for you, the dressmaker read the note,' Godiva interjected, adding with another lie, 'She told me what it said.'

The Prince's eyes blazed with sudden anger, but he controlled himself and his face adopted an expression of dislike as he turned towards Godiva.

'We have not been properly introduced and you will not address me in that manner,' he said in an aggrieved drawl.

'Would you mind if we looked around the house?' LaDavide asked.

'You have no right to do any such thing. I am a diplomat. I am protected by your law,' the Prince said angrily.

'That is only partly true, I'm afraid,' LaDavide said, 'You have diplomatic immunity, but this house is not a part of the embassy. As such, it is subject to the normal laws of France.'

'In that case you will need a piece of paper from a magistrate allowing you to perform such a search. Do you have one?' the Prince said with distain.

'The necessary paperwork is coming shortly. It would save us all a good deal of trouble if you agreed to the search now,' LaDavide suggested.

'If you attempt to search the house without observing the legal niceties it will be defended against you,' the Prince stated grimly.

LaDavide was about to speak again when there was a noise of a door being forced open on the floor above. A few seconds later a slim woman with silvery blond hair streaming around her ran down the stairs dressed in a dressing gown. She shouted out as she came down the stairs.

'He's in the cellar. They've been torturing him,' she screamed.

The Prince turned, walked up two stairs and struck her on the jaw, very hard with the back of his left hand. She stumbled and struck her head on the banister rail. LaDavide strode over and punched the Prince in the face, knocking out a tooth and causing his mouth to bleed freely. Godiva ran over and helped the Princess to her feet. There was some shouting and the noise of a pistol being fired into the air from the back of the house. LaDavide, wiping the blood from his fist, ran down the corridor to the kitchen, where the maid was barring his exit to the back yard. He pushed her aside, turned the knob and swung the door open.

Out in the yard a huge bald man was standing facing the two armed Tiger agents who had been assigned to guard the back of the house. Hanging over the huge man's shoulder was Walter's limp body. He was able to carry Walter's not inconsiderable weight seemingly without effort. His thought process may have been slow, but he had enough intelligence not to try to argue with two men who had large pistols pointed at his chest. Godiva and the Princess now appeared at LaDavide's side. The Princess shouted something to the servant in Russian. He turned and walked back to the house, dropping Walter's body quite gently just within the door.

LaDavide bent down and examined Walter, checking his pulse and opening an eyelid to look within. Then he sniffed around Walter's mouth.

'Chloroform,' he said, 'He'll be awake again in a little while. He doesn't appear to be too badly hurt. I will get a doctor to look at him, but he should be alright.'

After he stood up the Princess knelt down and kissed Walter on the cheek and smoothed his damp hair down. Godiva helped her to rise again. The maid screamed some obscenity at the Princess which meant nothing to Godiva, but the tone of voice was unmistakable.

'Shut up, you ugly pig,' LaDavide shouted back at the maid, and he strode over to her in a menacing fashion. The maid shrank back into a corner, muttering under her breath. LaDavide turned back to the others and seemed to find the need to take the lead.

'I think we should get Walter out of here. Perhaps we could carry him between us. And the Princess must come with us. It will not be safe for her here. Perhaps you can look after her, Miss Williams. Now let us see if we can get Walter to the car.'

Godiva lifted Walter's feet while LaDavide took him by the shoulders. Together they lifted him and started to make their way out of the kitchen. The weight was not so much a problem as Walter's height. His body flopped at the waist and he was in danger of having his buttocks drag across the floor. The Princess took hold of Walter's waist and together they struggled out of the house, through the gates and into the waiting Peugeot. The most difficult task was getting the unconscious body into the car, and the driver had to help in this task. With the body spread across the back seat the other three had to squeeze themselves in as best they could into the two remaining seats. Godiva and the Princess had to perch on one, and they were in danger of falling off as the car went round corners.

'Shouldn't we have searched the cellar?' Godiva asked.

'No magistrate would have agreed to a search warrant. I was bluffing the Prince. We had to get out as soon as possible. I'm sure the Prince will have been in touch with his embassy by now. They will have contacted my department. No doubt I shall be hauled up before my boss on a charge of assaulting a diplomat. I think I shall have to ask the Princess to confirm what happened today. I might be able to get away with it. What the Prince was doing was against every principal of diplomacy, and I think he'll be sent back in disgrace,' LaDavide said.

'Would you like to stay with me at my hotel for the moment?' Godiva asked the Princess.

'Thank you, that is very kind,' the Princess answered, 'but I really need to get some other clothes.'

'You can borrow some of mine for the time being. They will be a bit too big, but that is better than being too small,' Godiva said, practical as always.

'I'm sure the department can arrange for some clothes until we can get yours from the house,' LaDavide added.

'In that case, I would be very happy to accept your kind offer, Miss Williams,' the Princess said in gracious acceptance.

The car pulled up at the offices of the Tigers and four officers moved Walter's still unconscious body into a waiting room and onto a bench covered in green leather. A doctor was sent for and arrived only a few minutes later. He produced a bottle of smelling salts from his medical bag, waved it under Walter's nose and Walter coughed himself back to partial consciousness. As he began to come round he groaned and clutched his ribs.

The doctor examined Walter closely, prodding gently where he found his probing caused pain. He announced that Walter had two broken ribs and severe bruising to his torso. As Walter was in considerable pain he administered a dose of morphine. This reduced the pain but left Walter almost unable to communicate about what had happened to him in the cellar.

LaDavide arranged for Godiva and the Princess to be taken back to the hotel. A bed was found for Walter in a nearby house that was used by the Tigers when on extended duty. All the questions to be put to Walter would have to be asked on the next day.

Sunday 22nd January

When Walter woke up in the darkness of the Tiger's house he had a splitting headache and felt nauseous. He tried to get off his bed to find a bathroom and winced with pain. The effect of the painkillers he had taken the previous day had worn off and he was in considerable discomfort. His last unfogged memory was of being shackled to a wall in the cellar of the Prince's house. There was a vague sense that Godiva had been there, and some other people he knew, but the details eluded him. Quite where he was now, and how he had come to be there were mysteries to him. He called out for some assistance and was answered by a call from the other side of the room. The voice was one he recognised; it was that of LaDavide.

'How are you, my friend?' LaDavide asked in a soft voice.

'I really need to use a toilet,' Walter answered with a gasp of pain.

'I'll not be long,' LaDavide said, and he returned in a few seconds with a chamber pot.

As it was very painful for him to stand, Walter had to suffer the indignity of being assisted in emptying his bladder. The feeling of relief afterwards more than made up for this.

'Did you want something more to take the pain away?' LaDavide asked.

'Yes, I think I do, if only because I need some more sleep,' Walter answered with gritted teeth.

LaDavide prepared a syringe and injected Walter with a dose of morphine. Within a few minutes Walter was deeply asleep again.

He slept through the day, turning fitfully on his bed every few minutes. LaDavide remained the faithful nurse though most of the day, only taking breaks for meals and catching up on his paperwork as he watched his patient sleep.

◊

Godiva was woken to the sound of gentle sobbing. She had slept on the divan couch and her neck was stiff. After a somewhat restless night she had fallen deeply asleep at a time when she would normally be waking up. The Princess lay curled up in a foetal position and her body could be seen shaking a little through the covers, although the top of her head was all that could actually be seen of her. Her silvery hair was damp, either from tears or sweat. Godiva lifted the edge of the sheet and climbed into the bed beside the Princess and hugged the trembling body to her.

At first the Princess remained silent, then she started crying more and more loudly and then, coughing and spluttering. She sat up and needed to blow her nose and wipe her eyes. Having done that she looked up at Godiva with a sad smile on her face.

'Thank you. I think I shall be safe now,' she said.

Godiva extricated herself from the embrace, climbed out of bed and fetched a clean handkerchief which she handed to the Princess who tidied herself up as best she could. Godiva climbed back into the bed but remained sitting up.

'As soon as you feel better we will find you somewhere to stay. Do you have any friends in Paris who might be able to help?'

'I have friends in Paris, but they are all friends of my husband as well. I do not think that I would be safe with any of them,' the Princess answered with a sigh.

'Well, there's no need to worry about it now. I'm sure we'll find a suitable place for you,' Godiva said, stroking the Princess's damp hair.

'But what if my husband should try to take me back?' the Princess worried.

'He won't be able to get at you here,' Godiva comforted her.

'I am very frightened of his men. There is his servant Piotr, the loyal giant, and then there is a man who comes to the house. I think he is Okhrana. He is a very bad man. That one will find a way to get to me. He is a very good spy,' the Princess continued.

'Sergeant LaDavide is very good at his job. We will stop this man, I promise you,' Godiva said.

'You are a good friend of Walter?' the Princess asked.

'Yes, I am his friend. We have known each other for years, and we shared an apartment,' Godiva replied.

'And you are his lover?' the Princess asked.

'No, I've never been his lover. There have been moments when something might have happened, but they passed. We are just friends and don't want to change the nature of our friendship. We value that more than we want to enjoy each other's bodies, so we have never taken things further,' Godiva explained.

'I thought he was the kind of man who would hardly ever turn down the opportunity to make love to a woman,' the Princess said, frowning.

'He has his own standards of honour. He thought you were being threatened by your husband and were being forced to try to seduce him,' Godiva said with a slight smile.

'So that is that why he refused me. My husband was very angry. He hit me. I do not think that Walter would hit a woman?' the Princess said thoughtfully.

'He's not always that kind to women. I've known him to turn a woman out of the house who had left her husband for him. He can be quite cruel, but not violent. When he takes a woman as a lover she needs to know the limits of his affection,' Godiva explained.

'Has he never been in love?' the Princess wondered.

'There was one woman, but she was the wife of one of his childhood friends. That made it very difficult for him. But he soon got over his disappointment,' Godiva said, and she laughed gently.

'I suppose that he has known many women,' the Princess said with a slight sigh.

'Very many women,' Godiva agreed, laughing more loudly.

'Well, I shall soon get over my disappointment. I shall take a bath and then we can have some petit dejuener,' said the Princess.

'That does sound good,' Godiva agreed.

◊

The official note of complaint from the Russian Embassy and the Prince in particular had been delivered to the French Minister of Justice, Louis Barthou. It took some hours for a copy of this note to be delivered to the office of the Tigers. LaDavide's boss was summoned to make a reply, and he called in his officer to explain exactly what had happened on the previous day. Charges of assault and kidnapping were not to be taken lightly, and a diplomatic incident had already occurred. LaDavide had taken the opportunity while watching Walter to write a preliminary report concerning the events of the previous day, including as many of the gory details as possible. He also discussed the possibility of making counter charges of exactly the same nature but much better attested by the facts.

The director looked seriously at the complaint and at LaDavide's report. He shook his head sadly and laid the papers on the desk. It was Sunday and he wanted to return to his lunch and a very good bottle of Margeaux he had been looking forward to. He had no doubt that Louis Barthou would be doing exactly the same thing. There would be no-one in authority in the Ministry of Justice to communicate with until Monday. He might as well go home and forget all about this little local trouble until tomorrow.

Monday 23rd January

It was quite late on Monday morning when Walter woke up, hungry, sore and very thirsty but much better than he had seemed the previous day. He was now totally alone in the room. He struggled out of bed and shuffled out of the room dressed only in his underwear looking for a bathroom along the corridor. Eventually he came to a toilet with a washbasin.

After relieving himself he splashed his face with cold water and wet his hair down before rinsing out his mouth, which had tasted foul. The cold water made him draw in his breath, reminding him sharply of his injuries. He examined his torso with gentle fingers finding out where the worst pain was seated. Besides the broken ribs and the bruises, he seemed to have broken all the finger nails of his right hand, though he had no memory of trying to get free of the shackles that had bound him to the cellar wall. Overall there was no damage that a week's recuperation could not mostly cure.

He moved more freely back to the room and spent some time looking for his clothes, but these had been taken for cleaning. His overcoat had probably been left in the cellar and his hat was also missing. He pulled a blanket off the other bed in the room and wrapped it around himself, wondering what he should do next. There was a soft knock at the door.

'Come in,' he said, noticing how weak his voice sounded.

LaDavide entered, followed by Godiva and the Princess.

'How are you today?' LaDavide asked in a tone that hinted of a good bedside manner.

'I am very much better, thank you,' Walter answered.

'Should you be out of bed?' Godiva asked, sounding rather officious.

'Frankly, I feel rather better sitting up,' Walter assured her, 'But I really could do with something to drink, and after that, something to eat. And, if you could find some clothes for me, I would be very grateful.'

'I will see what I can do,' LaDavide said, leaving Walter in the company of the two women. The Princess looked at Walter with shy fondness.

'We have been a bit worried about you,' Godiva said softly.

'I shall be absolutely fine in a couple of days, but I am feeling a bit sore. I really must thank you both very much for what you did. I'm sure I would still be in that cellar, or dead, if you hadn't come to my rescue,' Walter declared.

'My maid, Marie told me what they were doing to you. She took great delight in telling me the details. They had locked me in my room, but I managed to break the lock when I heard the policeman talking to my husband,' the Princess said.

'If I have put you in any difficulty or danger I beg your forgiveness,' Walter said with a sad smile.

'It was not anything that you did. My husband is a silly and cruel man who only thinks of his honour and position. When I was helped out of that house I determined never to see him again, even if that means that I am completely lost to society,' the Princess said, emphatically.

'So what are you going to do?' Walter asked her.

'There will be someone who is willing to help me. It will not be easy for me to go back to Russia,' the Princess answered him.

'There are some Russians in Paris I know. I shall ask them if there is a suitable place for you. Of course, some of them are Bolsheviks but there are some decent people among the community. In fact, I have an idea which may be of use to you. I need to get in touch with someone I met a little while ago,' Walter mused.

'Who's that?' Godiva asked.

'Inessa Armand. She seems to take waifs and strays under her wing,' Walter replied.

'Who is this woman?' the Princess asked.

'She's half French and half English and was brought up in Russia. She is married to a Russian and has links to many of the exiles,' Godiva explained.

'I like her very much, and I think she can be trusted. It should put you safely out of your husband's reach,' Walter added.

'But can I trust people like that?' the Princess asked.

'A great deal more than you can trust your husband,' Walter assured her.

LaDavide returned with a jug of water and some clothes for Walter. His outer clothes were still at the laundry and these were the best that could be found in the house. The two women left the room while Walter dressed. The trousers fitted around the waist but hung half way up his calves. The jacket was long enough in the sleeves and broad in the shoulder but had belonged to a much fatter man and flapped far out from his chest. Moreover, the two garments had widely different checks in different colours. There was no mirror in the room, but Walter knew that he looked ridiculous. These rags would have to do for the time being, but he longed for his tailored suits from home more than he had at any other time during his visit to Paris. At least he still had his shoes.

Godiva and the Princess came back into the room and looked at Walter with amusement.

'Oh, Walter, you look like a circus clown!' Godiva blurted out.

'You do look a little like an Auguste clown,' the Princess agreed.

'I need to buy some more clothes. These will have to do until I can get some. My overcoat and hat were in the cellar, so I suppose I shall have to buy those as well,' Walter complained.

'There should be sufficient money to get you some more,' Godiva said, helpfully.

'I don't suppose there's any other compensation, is there?' Walter asked without much hope of a suitable reply, 'Only there was a fair bit of money in my coat pocket from the sale of a painting.'

'Somehow I don't think "K" will allow that sort of claim,' Godiva said.

'I didn't think he would,' Walter said ruefully.

'Let us get something to eat,' the Princess suggested. Walter suddenly remembered just how hungry he was, and started to salivate at the suggestion.

'There's a cafe round the corner. LaDavide knows where it is, don't you?' Walter said to the room in general.

'I'll come and get you if you are needed,' LaDavide said. He led them out of the house and pointed them in the direction of the cafe. They had to go slowly as Walter was still not able to walk without some difficulty.

They ordered coffee and a selection of breads and pastries. Walter ate slowly and steadily at first but found that he was indeed very hungry and continued until all the food was gone. He was about to order more when the Princess suggested that it might be overloading his system to eat any more, and this seemed sensible. The food and the coffee made him feel considerably better. He was still sore, but at least he wasn't hungry.

There was a man's clothes store on the opposite side of the road. To call it a gentleman's outfitters would be to suggest it had pretentions which it did not. It required a little searching for the little Jewish shopkeeper to find the right size for Walter, but he included a shirt in the price of the jacket and trousers. Walter had to be helped into the shirt by the shopkeeper. Godiva explained that the gentleman had been involved in some kind of accident and that his clothes were being cleaned. An overcoat and hat were found which, though barely serviceable, were cheap enough not to suggest wealth.

Walter dressed in his new clothes and felt that he looked much better, although he badly needed a shave.

The trio were just coming out of the shop when LaDavide approached sheepishly and asked them to go to the office where his boss, Rousseau, wanted to ask them about what had happened on the previous day. They walked together into the building and Walter handed LaDavide the old clothes, now tied in a parcel of brown paper.

Rousseau's office was on the second floor and it took Walter some time to negotiate the steps. There was no pretence to wealth or importance in the office. It was sparsely furnished and the decoration was dowdy and grubby with use and age. To Walter's surprise they were to be interviewed together. There were three seats in the office beside Rousseau's. Walter took the one to the left of the desk, the Princess sat on the middle chair, which had the least leg-room and Godiva on the one to the right.

'I would like you, each one of you, to tell me what happened yesterday. I shall ask Mr Davies to start, and he can tell me how he came to be found in the position in which he was discovered. Then I shall ask Miss, err..... Williams to continue, and then I shall ask Madame la Princess to finish,' Rousseau said. He sat back in his chair and closed his eyes while Walter spoke.

Walter explained how he had taken the note from the dressmaker's shop and had immediately gone around to the Prince's house. He described how he had been drugged and had woken up with his arms in shackles. Rousseau opened his eyes to look at the marks that the iron rings had left on Walter's wrists.

'I do not need to see the injuries which you sustained,' Rousseau said, 'The doctor has provided me with a full report.'

Walter described the beatings he had received, the questions he had been asked and who had asked them. His last memory in the cellar was of having the pad of chloroform pushed over his nose and mouth for the second time.

Godiva continued the story from her perspective from the time of her meeting with LaDavide to her visit to the dressmaker's and from there to the raid on the Prince's house, until the time that the Princess appeared on the stairs and was struck by her husband.

Then the Princess described being locked in her room and the gloating taunts of her maid, Marie, about Walter's imprisonment and torture. She went on to explain how she broke out of her room by applying a crude lever made from part of a washstand to the lock on the door on hearing LaDavide below. Then she told him how she had cried out a warning to LaDavide and had been struck on the cheek by her husband. Rousseau examined the bruise on her left cheek caused by the slap she had received.

Godiva returned to her story at this point and described how they had found the inert body of Walter being carried over the shoulder of the huge servant.

At the end of the story Rousseau smiled at them.

'Thank you for that. Your story exactly tallies with the report I have received from Sergeant LaDavide. Now I must tell you, Madame, that I have received a complaint from your husband concerning the blow he received from LaDavide. No true Frenchman could stand aside and watch a woman being struck as you were, so there is no question of further investigation of that part of the story. Unfortunately, your husband has also alleged that you were kidnapped at gunpoint. I must now ask you if you have any comment to make on that accusation, and whether you are willing to return to your husband's house,' he said.

'If it hadn't been for Sergeant LaDavide, I think my husband would have hit me more, maybe even killed me. I can assure you that I went with the Sergeant. I went very willingly. I was not kidnapped, in fact I led the way out of the house. And I will certainly never willingly return to my husband,' the Princess said with controlled fury.

'In that case, I believe that we can reply satisfactorily to the charges which your husband has made. Also, if you are willing to make a report, we can insist that his acts were criminal and against the law codes of France, which place him outside the limits of his diplomatic immunity. It may be that he has to return to Moscow in disgrace,' Rousseau continued.

'Good! I hope he is sent to Siberia,' the Princess retorted with a snort of derision.

Then, may I ask you to return this afternoon to make your official report with a notary to be present?' Rousseau asked the Princess.

'Of course, I will be most happy to do so,' the Princess said.

'If you could be back at two o'clock, then, please,' Rousseau said. He stood up and shook hands with all of them and then ushered them to the door.

'I think it will be necessary for me also to obtain another set of clothes,' the Princess said as they walked back to the entrance of the offices.

'Do you want to go back to the dressmaker's shop where we swapped notes?' Walter said with a smile.

'Somehow I do not think I am very likely to do that,' the Princess answered.

'Then I think that I had better leave you ladies to do your shopping. I need a shave and to get back to my rooms before Mr Skinner reports me missing,' Walter said, 'I don't suppose that you could lend me a little cash?'

'Just in this one circumstance,' Godiva agreed, fishing for money in her handbag.

'In that case I shall see you at your hotel this afternoon, at about tea-time. Say four o'clock,' Walter said.

'Righty-ho,' Godiva said in agreement.

◊

Because his key had been in his coat pocket Walter had to argue with his concierge about getting a pass key until his coat could be recovered. After a great deal of grumbling a key was produced from some drawer and Walter was able to go to his room. He was feeling very tired by now and lay down on his bed. Several notes had been pushed under the door during his absence and he read these in turn, even though they were out of order. One of them was from Inessa Armand, requesting to see him about a painting. Two more notes were from LaDavide and a fourth was from Skinner asking if Walter had any other paintings ready for Etienne. After reading these Walter folded them, placed them in an inside pocket, shut his eyes and was almost instantly asleep.

He was woken from his slumbers a few hours later by a knock at the door and he looked up to see Skinner standing in the doorway.

'Jeez, you look rough. Have you been out with some woman you couldn't deal with?' he asked Walter in a joking way.

'I've been a bit ill,' Walter replied, 'I got your note and I'll try to have something ready for you very shortly.'

'Sorry to hear you haven't been well. I was getting kind of worried about you. Oh, and by the way, my mother sends her regards,' Skinner said. 'You missed a great evening with Sylvie and Brigitte on Saturday.'

'Sorry to have missed that. I'm afraid that I was unavoidably detained. By the way, how is your mother?' Walter asked, more to be polite than from genuine interest.

'Oh, she's much the same as ever she was. But she's not being any more generous to me yet. You'd think she would be impressed that I'm starting out as an artist's agent, but she doesn't seem to be. I mean, it's her line of business anyway. She could really help me,' Skinner said with a slight sigh.

'I knew she helped to get art to America, but I didn't know she looked at it as a business,' Walter commented.

'Oh, sure, everything she does is business. After my father died she took over the company for a while until the stockholders kicked her out. My father was one big capitalist. He was what they call a Robber Baron, not in a really big way, like Carnegie, but big enough in his area. He could make money from just about anything and he passed almost all of that knowledge onto my mother. It seems that they didn't pass that kind of business sense down to me. Anyway, my mother got all the money and she decided she was going to change the way she did business. All these Robber Barons were trying to look like they were really good guys, wanting to start museums and art galleries and they were willing to pay big money for old European art. So my mother decided to go into the business of selling them the art. She makes a good thing of it too. The Count, well he's just there for show, and I guess the title helps her when she meets people, but she runs the show. I was hoping she might cut me in for a piece of the action, and maybe she will, if I can make a success of this,' Skinner said with a dreamy look in his eyes.

'Does she do much business with Etienne?' Walter asked pointedly.

'Well, I suppose she does. He's got contacts in Russia. There are plenty of art collections there and aristocrats who have run out of money. He gets the paintings from Russia and she gets them into the US,' Skinner answered.

'I've heard complaints that some of the art going into America hasn't exactly been obtained legally. Now, don't get me wrong, the British used to loot the world to stock their museums, but it does cause some bad feeling,' Walter suggested.

'Nah, I haven't heard anything like that, about what she does' Skinner said, and Walter was sure the American was speaking honestly.

'Look, I'm sorry to have missed the weekend. What did you get up to?' Walter asked.

'We went to the Bobino again, and got a bit drunk. Sylvie didn't have anywhere to go to so I spent the night here. But I spent most of Sunday in bed with Brigitte. She's quite a girl, that one. Sylvie was asking where you were. It might be nice if you could drop her a note and explain that you've been ill. She seemed really disappointed that you weren't around,' Skinner said, looking even more dreamy.

'What time is it now?' Walter asked. His watch had been in his jacket pocket.

'About three I guess,' Skinner answered, 'You got to be somewhere or something?'

'Yes, that's right, I've got to meet a friend shortly,' Walter replied.

'Would that be a woman friend?' Skinner said with a twisted grin.

'It is a woman, and she will have a very respectable chaperone,' Walter said patiently.

'That will be disappointing for you,' Skinner suggested.

'It's business. I'd better get myself ready,' Walter said, rising from the bed with a groan of discomfort.

'Are you sure that you are alright?' Skinner enquired with some small signs of concern.

'I'll be alright,' Walter replied.

'Oh, before I forget, I've got some money for you,' Skinner said. He reached into an inside pocket and produced a wad of ten franc notes which he handed to Walter, whe stuffed them into a pocket without bothering to count them.

'Thanks for that,' Walter said, and he smiled weakly.

The sound of footsteps came down the corridor. LaDavide looked in the room and smiled at the neighbours.

'Hello again, Mr Skinner,' LaDavide said, 'It's good to see you again. Walter, I thought you might want a lift. I understand you have a meeting quite soon. There's something I want to say to you first.'

'I'll be right with you. See you later, Skinner,' Walter said. He climbed off the bed and put on his new overcoat and hat. They left the room and Walter locked up.

There was a car waiting for them outside, one of the big Peugeots the Tigers used. They climbed in the back and the driver set off at a steady pace. As they started Walter saw a grey man watching them from the cover of a doorway. The day was so dull that there were no shadows to hide in. It was the Okhrana man Walter had head-butted in the cellar. Walter decided not to say anything about this to LaDavide. The roof of the car had been raised as it had started to rain yet again. The streets were shining a steely grey and a westerly wind blew stinging rain under the fabric of the car roof.

'Prince Pechorin has sent on your coat, jacket and hat. There was some money in the pocket of the coat, and a watch in the jacket,' LaDavide said.

'Why would he want to return those?' Walter wondered aloud.

'I suppose he didn't want to be accused of theft as well as his other crimes,' LaDavide suggested, wryly, 'He made me sign a note for them, anyway. You can come to the office and collect these things later.'

'The watch will be handy, and it was a fair amount of money. I got that from selling a painting, you know,' Walter said, a little boastfully. A few moments followed when neither man spoke.

'I've had a tip about who might have shot Pascale,' LaDavide said in a flat tone.

'Where did you get that from?' Walter asked, nearly shouting to get heard above the noise of the wind.

'It came indirectly from the boss of an Apache gang, but not le Baron,' LaDavide said into Walter's ear, 'It seems that there is going to be an attempt to shift the boundaries between the gangs soon. The tip is very interesting. It suggests that it was le Baron's son, in person, who fired the pistol. And if that is true, then Miss Williams was right to suggest that you were the person he was aiming at. It appears he thought you had shamed him when you took the gun from him and broke his arm.'

'But I don't even know his name,' Walter protested.

'It is easy to make enemies, even when you don't know their names. His name is Eric Chabal. He is what you English call a hot head,' LaDavide continued.

'So, what are you going to do about it?' Walter asked

'We will try to gather some more evidence, something we can use in court, then we will arrest him. Of course, that rather depends on what le Baron wants to do about it. If he decides that his son has broken the rules he might give him up to us. If he wants to defend his son he could make it much more difficult for us,' LaDavide replied.

'Please let me know when you are going to arrest this Chabal. I'd like to be there to see it,' Walter said.

'I'll have to ask the boss about that,' LaDavide said.

By this time they had reached the hotel. LaDavide made way to allow Walter out of the car and waved him goodbye. A clock inside the reception area showed it was nearly three thirty. For once in his life Walter would be early for an appointment. He nodded to the receptionist and made his way to the guest lounge to wait for Godiva and the Princess.

While he waited for the women to appear he read a copy of Le Monde. The story on the front page was about flooding to the east of Paris, near the border with Germany, in the headwaters of the Seine.

When Godiva entered the room she was talking to the Princess as though they were old friends. The Princess touched Godiva on the arm and laughed at some joke between them, as if she had not a single care in the world. They noticed Walter and came across the room and sat opposite him. He folded the newspaper and smiled at his companions. He generally found the company of women preferable to that of men.

'Have you had a good day?' Walter asked the question to either of them.

'Oh, yes, we have been out shopping for some clothes for me,' the Princess said enthusiastically, 'and Godiva is a much better companion than my maid.'

'Well, I wouldn't choose to be in Marie's company myself,' Walter agreed.

'My husband would always tell me which friends I was allowed and who was forbidden to me. From now on I shall be able to choose my own friends,' the Princess said.

'I've been telling Eugenie all about the women's suffrage movement,' Godiva announced proudly. Walter noted the use of the first name and what it signified.

'But the aristocracy don't get the vote anyway,' Walter said.

'My husband will divorce me. Then I won't be a princess anymore. I didn't grow up as a princess, and I will be very happy not to be one again. Of course, it may take some time for women to get the vote, but when we do I shall be the first to cast mine,' the Princess said with a jutting chin.

'Do you think you will go back to Russia?' Walter asked the Princess.

'That won't be possible for a while. I have left my husband and I will be an outcast from society. But, who knows, things may change. I'm sure that I will return sometime, but I will have to find another home for the time being,' she replied.

'I have been trying to convince Eugenie that she would be welcome in London. I'm sure that would keep you well out of reach of your husband, my dear.' Godiva interpolated.

'And I still have some acquaintances in Paris who may be happy to help me. The problem is to know which ones to trust. Almost all of them are friends of the Prince,' the Princess mused.

'We talked briefly about making contact with some Russian exiles in Paris who will not be friends of your husband,' Walter reminded her.

'Do you think they will be my kind of people?' she asked.

'As a matter of fact, I have a note from one of them on me. It was pushed under the door to my room. It's from the lady I mentioned to you, Inessa Armand. I will go and see her and see what she recommends if you want to stay in Paris,' Walter said.

'If you can assure me that she is a good woman, I will take her advice,' the Princess agreed.

'Then I will go and see her tomorrow,' Walter said, 'And now, what are your plans for this evening?'

'I've promised to take Eugenie to a meal and a show this evening,' Godiva said, 'A girls-only treat. I hope you don't feel too put out.'

'Not at all, I'm not quite up to going out yet. You go out and enjoy yourselves and you can tell me all about it tomorrow,' Walter said, without sounding at all like a martyr.

'What are you going to be doing?' Godiva asked.

'Right at this moment I think I shall be going for a light meal then retiring to my bed for a good sleep. But before that I have to collect my coat and things from LaDavide's office. It seems as though your husband has returned them to me,' Walter said.

'You just make sure that everything is cleaned before you wear it again,' the Princess suggested, 'And please call me Eugenie.'

'Don't worry. I'll take them to the cleaners first thing tomorrow morning, Eugenie,' Walter said with a smile.

◊

Back in his room after his meal, Walter was preparing for bed when there was a soft tapping at his door. He opened it to find that Sylvie was looking at him in a concerned fashion.

'Are you well?' she asked.

'I'm much better now,' Walter said, 'Please come in.' She came in, shutting the door behind her.

'I can't stay long. I have to work in the morning,' she said.

'And I am still quite sore, which means that I could not share a narrow bed with you tonight,' Walter explained.

'Franklin told me that you had been ill,' she said softly, 'I didn't come here to make love to you, only to make sure that you were well.'

'I haven't really been ill. I was beaten up quite badly, that's all,' Walter admitted.

'Show me,' Sylvie commanded. Walter took off his shirt and she looked at his chest and back. 'That is very bad bruising. What happened to you?'

'There was an important man who accused me of fucking his wife, which I hadn't. He enticed me into a trap, drugged me, tied me up and got his servant to do this to me,' Walter said, getting a little angry at the memory of his treatment.

'What are you going to do about it?' Sylvie asked.

'I'm going to give him a good beating, and his servant as well,' Walter promised. He thought that the watcher could do with a good thrashing as well.

'But not tonight. Tonight you will allow me to make love to you very gently,' Sylvie said. She unfastened and removed his trousers and then laid him down on the bed. Then she disrobed to her shift, straddled him and did as she had promised. Walter relaxed and enjoyed the treatment. Sylvie seemed to find it pleasurable as well. After she had finished she held him gently for a few minutes, dressed and left. Walter went to sleep very soon afterwards.

Tuesday 24th January

Walter was drinking his morning coffee when he remembered the notes in his jacket pocket. He had already taken his old coat and jacket into a laundry, having carefully removed the contents from the pockets first. He would collect them in two days time. The coffee tasted good and the warm croissants with apricot jam were delicious. Wiping his fingers before opening the note from Inessa he studied what it said.

Walter, could you please call round and see me sometime soon. I would like you to paint a proper portrait of our friend. I hope to see you soon,
Inessa

The note seemed both friendly and businesslike. He would get a good shave and call round that very morning. After paying for his breakfast he left the little cafe which had become his new favourite, and went to look for a barbers shop. Having once noticed the man who was following him, he found it much easier to identify him again. The difficulty was to keep him in sight whilst not letting him know that he had been spotted. He sauntered around a corner into a deserted street and, while briefly out of sight of the follower, dived down an alleyway. When the man turned the corner he looked around to see where Walter had gone. He took a few cautious steps forward, scanning all around. Suddenly he was dragged with great force into the alley, punched very hard in the abdomen and slammed against a rough brick wall. A tall, grim-looking blond man towered over him with a wolfish grin on his face.

'Hello,' said Walter with purr of satisfaction in his voice, 'How nice to meet you again so soon.' He pushed the man's head into the wall with controlled force, and then had to hold him by the lapels of his coat to stop him sliding to the ground. 'I want to ask you a couple of questions. Nod your head if you understand.'

The follower nodded dumbly and seemed to be trying to catch his breath.

'Are you Okhrana?' Walter asked.

The man did not answer, so Walter gave him a couple of hard slaps, making his head turn sharply in either direction.

'I asked you if you were Okhrana,' Walter repeated.

'Yes, I am Okhrana,' the follower wheezed.

'Who do you work for?' Walter asked, adding another slap for good measure.

'I work for Prince Pechorin,' the man said.

'Now tell me who you really work for,' Walter said, threatening a slap but not delivering.

'I work for Prince Pechorin,' the man repeated.

'The Prince is an idiot. He is far too stupid to be in charge. Who do you really work for?' Walter pulled the man's head back by his hair and flicked his larynx with a forefinger. The public school bullying he had both undergone and given in return had provided plenty of ideas for methods of torture.

'There is a sub-secretary at the embassy who handles the messages from Moscow. He tells me what to do,' the follower said, tears springing into his eyes.

'What is his name?' Walter asked more gently.

'Poliakov. His name's Poliakov,' the man said a little too easily.

Walter pretended to let the man go, then punched him again in the solar plexus. The man crumpled to the ground and vomited. After he had finished retching Walter lifted him to his feet again.

'What is his name?' Walter asked.

'I told you, his name's Poliakov. That's all I know,' the man said, looking terrified as Walter threatened to strike him again.

'Do you work for anyone else?' Walter asked.

'I don't know what you mean,' the man protested.

Walter lifted him off his feet and glared into his face.

'You people usually work for more than one master. If you ever do any jobs for anyone else you had better tell me now,' he suggested with menaces.

'There is a German man at their embassy. I sometimes carry messages for him,' the man confessed.

'And what is the name of this German?' Walter asked. The man's spirit appeared broken.

'He calls himself Tolcher, but I don't know if that is his real name. We meet in a museum sometimes. He leaves me messages there,' the man answered, limply.

'Have you told him about me?' Walter asked.

'He was the one who told me about you. He told me your real name. He said you were working for British Intelligence,' the man admitted.

'What does this Tolcher look like?' Walter demanded.

'Nothing; I don't know. He always kept his face half covered when we met,' the follower said.

'How tall is he? Is he fat or thin? What is his voice like?' Walter barked.

'He's not tall or short, he's not fat or thin. His voice is quite high and light, and I think he speaks German with an Austrian accent,' the man stumbled through these answers, obviously feeling no loyalty to his employer.

'What is your name?' Walter asked, giving the man a little shake.

'Chelakhov, Dimitri Chelakhov. That is my name,' the man said and he started to sob.

Thinking that there was little else to be learned from this shadowy little man, Walter gave him one more punch for good luck, banged his head against the wall and let him crumple to the floor. When the man had started to revive he kicked him hard in the ribs in memory of the kicks he had himself received.

'If I ever catch you following me or anyone I speak to, I will kill you. That is not a threat, it is a promise.' Walter snarled. After that simple warning he turned and left the follower curled in a foetal ball and crying pitiably. He continued on his way to the barbers, relieved that he could still deliver a punch, even if his fists were now grazed and bruised.

◊

Inessa Armand was preparing to go out when Walter arrived at her apartment, but she hadn't yet put on her coat.

'I received your note yesterday. I'm afraid I wasn't in my room for a couple of days,' Walter explained.

'Another woman, I suppose?' Inessa said with a smile.

'In a way, it was. In this case it is a young Russian woman. Her husband is an aristocrat and was beating her and locking her up in her room. I helped to rescue her, but I'm not her lover,' Walter answered.

'And just how did you come to know this woman?' Inessa asked, a little intrigued.

'Her husband asked me to paint her portrait, and I saw the bruises on her arms. She's staying with a friend of mine at the moment, a lady friend. But that friend is going back to England shortly, and the Russian lady needs somewhere to stay where she will be safe. She is still frightened of what her husband might do. I thought it would be easier if she could stay with someone in the exile community. Perhaps you could suggest someone suitable,' Walter enquired.

'If she is an aristocrat then she will not be very welcome among us,' Inessa warned him.

'She wasn't born an aristocrat, and was passed on like a trophy or a toy. Her husband is a diplomat, and I think he has something to do with the Okhrana,' Walter said, as if dropping a bombshell. A few seconds of silence followed.

'What do you know about the Okhrana?' Inessa asked guardedly.

'Only what this lady has told me, and a few things I have heard and seen,' Walter lied.

'Does her husband have agents watching us?' Inessa asked, her eyes hooded.

'She doesn't know any details, but I imagine that is very likely. I haven't questioned her closely about that,' Walter admitted.

'I will need to see Monsieur Oulyanof about this. We may be able to help your friend, and she may be able to help us,' Inessa said, 'There are Okhrana agents among our numbers. We know they are there, but we don't always know who they are.'

'I will only allow you to speak to her if you can offer her protection, and if you treat her gently. She has suffered a good deal,' Walter negotiated.

'I can promise you that this lady will be treated very well. She could be of great use to our cause, and it is yet another example of how corrupt the aristocracy are,' Inessa said.

'So would you like me to make the introductions?' Walter asked.

'That would be good. I'll drop off a note to your room to let you know a time and place for a meeting,' Inessa answered.

'Of course,' Walter agreed, 'Now your note said that you wanted me to paint another portrait.'

'Oh, yes. I had an idea about a picture to show Monsieur Oulianoff as a leader. Perhaps showing him delivering one of his speeches,' Inessa suggested.

'That's not really my style of portrait, but I may be interested,' Walter said, trying not to sound too positive.

'That can wait for the moment,' Inessa said, 'Right now I am more interested in your lady friend and what we can do for her.'

◊

'Have you been in some kind of fight again?' Godiva asked him, turning his right hand between hers.

'In a manner of speaking. I had a little encounter with the man who has been following me, the one who was in the cellar with the Prince. I had a little chat with him down an alley and managed to get some useful information from him,' Walter said.

'I really don't wish to know what you did to get that information. Just tell me what he said,' Godiva said in a cool tone.

'Firstly, the real head of the Okhrana in Paris is a man called Poliakov. He is some kind of cipher clerk at the embassy. He's the one who really knows what is going on,' Walter said. Godiva started to take notes in her little pocket book. 'Secondly, my little follower was also working for a German he knows as Tolcher, but it isn't his real name. All I really got about him is that he has a high voice and speaks in a rather rustic German accent, possibly Austrian. He may be attached to the German Embassy,' Walter said.

'That would be the first place I would ask for him,' Godiva said, taking another note and laying her pencil down, 'I'll make the necessary enquiries and get back to you this evening. But I don't suppose it is his real name.'

'There are a couple of other things that have come up,' Walter said, wondering how to give the information, 'The worrying thing is that it was Tolcher who told my little watcher who I was. That means that the Germans have been keeping tabs on me. I had thought that the Prince had found out who I was from the Countess Podolski. I know I told you about that. She got it from an absolute ass I know from London, a useless drone called Twisden. He was at the Countess' party. I swore him to secrecy, but he only regarded that as carte blanche to spread it as much as possible. I would like to have a few words with Mr Twisden.'

'I wouldn't worry about him if I were you,' Godiva advised, 'I'd be more concerned about the Countess. She's deeply involved in art smuggling and has contacts with local criminals. As for this Tolcher man, I'm sure we will be able to identify him if he is at the Embassy. If we could find a way to get at him it would be very interesting.'

'That's your problem. Just let me know what you find out,' Walter said with a snort.

'It may well become your problem once we've identified him,' Godiva commented dryly.

'One last thing; I've been to see Inessa Armand, and she may be able to help the Princess. I'm slightly worried that the Bolsheviks may try to use her, but I trust Inessa enough to think she won't allow anything too bad to happen. Where is the Princess, anyway?'

'She's gone out with LaDavide's wife to buy some clothes. I imagine that the Prince will destroy all her possessions out of pique. He seems to be that petty sort of man. Anyway, she should be back in a little while and I'll tell her about the offer from Inessa Armand. If she doesn't want to come to London she'll need some friends here,' Godiva answered.

◊

LaDavide grabbed Walter by the lapel when he came to the office and dragged him into a corner for a quiet word.

'We've got some information about your art forger, Lermontov. It seems that he was loaned out by le Baron to that gallery owner, Etienne. It was a business arrangement,' LaDavide said.

'What does that mean?' Walter asked.

'It means that le Baron had no reason to kill Lermontov. Think about it! If le Baron knew what Lermontov was doing he must have been happy with the arrangement. And if le Baron didn't have Lermontov killed it must have been someone else. Most likely it was someone in the chain that Etienne is in,' LaDavide explained.

'Let's go through the people in that chain. There's Etienne, the Countess Podolski and her husband and Prince Pechorin. Can you think of anyone else?' Walter asked, thinking out loud.

'There are certain to be other people in the chain, but they are only little criminals. Who is it who can call on someone to kill Lermontov?' LaDavide asked in return.

'The most obvious one is Prince Pechorin. He could order that servant of his to do anything. As far as I can tell, Etienne isn't the kind of man who could kill or would know people who would do that sort of thing. He'd want to stay away from that sort of work. As for the Countess, I don't think she would risk getting involved in anything like that, at least not in France,' Walter answered.

'I agree with you about Etienne, if only because he would not dare to hurt the employee of le Baron. I am not so sure about the Countess. She can be very ruthless if her business was threatened, and she probably knows many people who could be asked to kill someone who is in her way. What I would ask is why she would risk losing a great deal of money by killing Lermontov?' LaDavide said with a slight shake of the head.

'So it looks like the Prince organised the killing,' Walter stated.

'That seems most likely, but we can't be sure,' LaDavide said ruefully.

'Well, not yet anyway,' Walter agreed, 'Maybe some other information will come in.'

'Let us hope so,' LaDavide concurred, 'Now, what was it that you wanted to see me about?'

'I came across the man who was in the cellar with the Prince, questioning me. I managed to get him to answer some questions. As we are working together, I might as well tell you what he said. He told me that the man who really runs the Okhrana at the Embassy is someone called Poliakov, who is a humble cipher clerk. The other thing is that my shadow was also working for a German who calls himself Tolcher who may be at the German Embassy. He knows rather more about me than I'd like him to. It might be useful for you to know who the German spies are,' Walter said.

'I'm sure we do know him, if he is at the Embassy. Do you have a description of him?' LaDavide asked.

'Only that he has a high voice and speaks like an Austrian,' Walter admitted. LaDavide sucked on his teeth.

'That is not much to go on, but we will do our best,' he said.

'Godiva tells me that the Princess has gone out shopping with your wife. I didn't know that you were married,' Walter commented.

'You never asked me,' LaDavide replied with a sharp little laugh, 'And I never told you if I had children, either.'

'Do you have children?' Walter asked.

'Mind your own business!' LaDavide laughed.

'Is there anything else you wanted to see me about?' Walter asked

'Will you be around tomorrow?' LaDavide asked in return, this time quite seriously.

'Of course. Any particular reason you asked?' Walter returned.

'Nothing I can talk about at the moment. If this happens, it happens in the morning. Get yourself here at ten o'clock and you will not miss anything,' LaDavide said mysteriously.

'Until tomorrow morning, then,' Walter agreed.

◊

As it was a Monday, Skinner was not able to see his beloved Brigitte and was very happy to be in Walter's company. They went to the Blue Barge, which was very quiet, even for a Monday night. Rosa Languedoc was working elsewhere or else she had the night off. They drank brandy and talked of art and painters. Walter noticed the smelly Bolshevik standing at the bar with a solid man who had dark hair and eyes and a moustache like a yard broom. There was a certain Levantine air about him, and although he seemed vaguely familiar Walter could not exactly place where he had seen the man, or the man's picture before. Outside the club the rising water was lapping at the tops of the river banks and the rain continued to fall.

Wednesday 25th January

The Metro was crowded on this Wednesday morning. Some lines had been affected by the general flooding seeping into the lower levels of the city, close to the river. All trains under the Seine were stopped, as the pumps were unable to deal with the huge amounts of intruding water. Walter had to walk in the steady rain across the pont Mirabeau to the north of the river. Due to these delays it took longer than it should have to reach the office of the Tigers, and it was almost ten o'clock by the time Walter arrived there.

The office was buzzing at it had been when Walter had first been taken there. It was obvious that another raid was planned. Amid the chaos and the dashing around it was hard to find LaDavide. When Walter arrived at the office where he was generally to be found, he was somewhere else. They missed each other at a number of other points in the building and it was only when Walter stood still for a while that LaDavide could find him.

'We are going on a raid, and you are to come along,' he said.

'Happy to oblige you. I hope I don't get in the way,' Walter replied.

'Take this pistol,' LaDavide said, thrusting a large and heavy revolver at Walter. He took it, made sure the safety catch was engaged and placed it in a jacket pocket.

'I'll try not to use it, unless I really have to,' Walter said.

'I'm very glad you made it. You could be very useful to us,' LaDavide said rapidly, 'You are to come in the car with me.' He then grabbed Walter's arm and dragged him outside and into the first of the waiting black Peugeots. Other men were pouring out of the building and trying to find a place in or on one of the cars. LaDavide shouted an address to the driver, who nodded his recognition and drove off as fast as he could, to be followed by the other cars.

'Where are we going?' Walter asked above the roar of the traffic and the noise of the rain on the car.

'We are going to pay an official visit to le Baron. His son is there and I don't think we will get him without a fight,' LaDavide replied.

'That sounds good,' Walter said, 'But I don't understand why you want me to come along.'

'I really hope I won't need you. If things go to plan, you will not be needed,' LaDavide explained.

'You just keep me as the reserve. I'll be happy with that,' Walter agreed.

The car skidded round a corner, the tyres struggling to find grip on the wet cobble stones. LaDavide fell into Walter, banging him against the car door which threatened to burst open. Walter had to grab it and hold it shut. His ribs ached fearfully. The driver took the following corners more carefully and it was just a few minutes before they arrived at their destination.

The warehouse was as anonymous as any building could be. It had been selected for its total lack of features and had very nearly done a good job. If it had not been for a tip-off from a member of a rival gang, the temporary headquarters would never have been known to the Tigers. But, anonymous as it was, lookouts had been stationed on the upper floors to look down the approaches to the building. One of these lookouts raised the alarm, and by the time the Tigers had disembarked from the cars and arranged themselves for the assault, the occupants of the building were rushing into pre-arranged defensive positions. It was like a bee hive under attack from wasps.

A group of the Tigers led by a huge man in an even bigger overcoat rushed the door, which they found barred and bolted. The huge man swung a sledgehammer at the door lock, the noise booming across the street like thunderclaps. The door was resisting the attack and the blows became weaker and less frequent. Jeers came from the floors above and missiles rained down on the agents, though these were too feeble to cause any serious injury.

Giving up on the attempt to break the door down with a hammer, the Tigers changed tactics. One man shooed the others away from the door and fired five shots from a large revolver onto the area of the door lock. One bullet rebounded from the thick plate of the lock and narrowly missed the man firing the pistol. The door was damaged and the lock now useless, but the thick wooden bar behind remained undamaged, and resisted all attempts to move it. It would require a battering ram to shift. The use of a gun had also raised the stakes. Some disorganised firing came from the upper floors. One bullet struck the huge agent, but failed to pass through his coat. It had been fired from an Apache pistol at very low velocity. The Tigers were now firing at the windows behind which le Baron's men were hiding, some of them firing back. This gunfire caused the Apaches to take better guns from their arsenal. A bullet from a rifle hit one of the Tigers in the shoulder, sending him spinning to the ground in a pool of blood and bone fragments. There was no jeering now. What had started as a raid had become a siege.

Walter had not been called on to join the foot soldiers and was sheltering from the rain and the gunfire under the awning of a baker's shop. A bullet fired by one of the Tigers had injured or killed one of the men within. The cry of pain was unmistakeable. The Tigers were now finding places to fire from. Some sheltered behind the cars which were becoming increasingly bullet-ridden. If there had been a plan 'B' to the operation, Walter could not see what it was from where he was standing.

Suddenly the situation changed. A group of Tigers had managed to make their way into the building via some back entrance which was less secure. The ground floor became too difficult to defend for the handful of Apaches who had been guarding it, and they retreated up to the first floor. The wooden bar was lifted and the front door opened by the Tigers within. The main party stormed through in a matter of seconds. They had taken the lowest floor, but the way up was blocked and they would encounter deadly fire if they attempted to climb up the stairs.

A message was sent to fetch a ladder, but any attempt to climb a ladder under fire would be a forlorn hope assault with armed men in cover on the upper floors. Without any element of surprise there would be considerable bloodshed unless an alternative plan could be put in place.

'Walter!' LaDavide shouted across to him, 'I need you to help us.' Walter went to where LaDavide was standing behind one of the cars at a swift stooped shuffle that caused pain in his ribs.

'Alright, I'm here,' Walter said.

'I want you to help end this siege. If we don't do something soon there is going to be a lot of death here,' LaDavide said, his use of demotic English slipping slightly.

'What is it you want me to do?' Walter enquired, sensing that he might not like the answer.

'I want you to face le Baron's son, or to offer to do this at the very least,' LaDavide answered.

'You want me to fight a duel with le Baron's son?' Walter asked with incredulity.

'What you must understand is that these Apache like to think of themselves as men of honour. This argument is between you and the son. If you stand out in the open and challenge him to a fight he will have to consider taking the challenge. The other men will not be willing to die for him if another option is available. Of course, it will not be a fight with swords or pistols; it will be a street fight, probably with knives. Are you willing to do this?' LaDavide explained.

'You want me to stand in front of the warehouse and risk getting shot at?' Walter asked, 'I could get killed before I could help. And what good would that do anyone?'

'I'll ask for a little time of ceasefire first. You only go out front if it is agreed. Is that acceptable to you?'

'Yes, of course. But if the young man has a broken arm he might use it as an excuse for not fighting. Besides, I don't have a knife, and I don't fight that way,' Walter argued.

'Then you can offer to fight him left-handed,' LaDavide said, slightly exasperated.

'I'm not very good with my left hand,' Walter replied with a slight smile, 'but I'll give it a go.'

LaDavide found a megaphone among the equipment in the car. He held an arm up to show he wasn't carrying a gun and to ask for attention. There was a gradual decrease in sound as both sides realised some negotiation was about to take place and waited to hear what he was going to say. He raised the megaphone to his lips.

'We are trying to arrest Eric Chabal. We want to talk to him about the death of one of our officers. We know he is with you. No-one has to die. We do not think that Chabal intended to kill the officer. This was a matter of honour. Chabal's argument is with an Englishman who has done some work for us. This man has offended Chabal's honour. We understand that. He is willing to meet Chabal, here and now. We will not interfere in this combat. If he does not agree then men will die. I do not wish any of my men to die. I understand that Chabal has a broken arm. The Englishman, who is right handed has agreed to fight with his left hand. If Chabal does not agree to this he is a man without honour,' LaDavide spoke as loudly as he could through the device.

There was a good deal of movement inside the warehouse and eventually a figure appeared in a second-storey window.

'Where is this Englishman?' a ringing baritone voice asked.

LaDavide called Walter forward and presented him to the men watching from the warehouse. He then lowered the megaphone and spoke to Walter.

'That is le Baron speaking. I think you should answer him.'

'I am Walter Davies. It was me who helped to arrest your son. I was the man who broke his arm. He tried to kill me as I was sitting in a cafe by firing a pistol at me. He missed me and killed the man I was with, an officer of the Tigers called Pascale,' Walter shouted up in French, 'If he wishes to try to kill me again I will meet him down here. If he wishes to hide like a coward he can stay where he is and die with the rest of you.'

There was a distant babble of voices from above and it was more than a minute before anyone else spoke. It was le Baron who came to the window again.

'Do you promise to only fight with your left hand?' he demanded.

'I promise, on my honour,' Walter agreed.

'And do you promise that my son will not be arrested as soon as he comes down?' le Baron continued.

Walter turned around to see LaDavide nodding his agreement.

'That is agreed as well,' Walter said.

'Very well. My son will be down in a minute,' le Baron replied. He went away from the window.

'You had better have this,' LaDavide said, handing a large single-bladed knife over to Walter.

'I don't think I'll use it much. I'll probably just try to disarm him. And I didn't say that I wouldn't use my right hand to hit him,' He moved the knife around in his left hand, trying to get used to the weight and balance and the moves. It felt completely unnatural and this feeling increased his determination not to use the knife as an offensive weapon, except under dire need. He briefly handed the knife back to LaDavide as he took off his coat and jacket. He wanted to be able to move freely if he was to avoid the blade that would be used against him. The rain started to soak his shirt, but at least he could react quickly to any move.

The Tigers had pulled out of the ground floor of the warehouse and now formed a rough semi-circle around the main entrance, leaving a small arena for the contest. Walter stood in the centre of this space. Le Baron emerged from the front door, followed by a worried looking young man Walter recognised as Eric Chabal, who was also stripped to his shirt. He carried a huge hunting knife in his left hand and was trying to look careless without much success. He had to remove the waist sash as it might interfere with the movement of his left hand. His right arm was strapped into a light splint which was half supported by a loose strap hanging round his neck. Taking a deep breath he stepped out to meet Walter in combat.

Walter moved to allow Chabal into the impromptu arena and gave a curt bow of acknowledgement towards his opponent. Chabal returned the gesture, then moved into a fighting stance, legs slightly apart, knees somewhat bent, as though he were about to spring up. He moved around just beyond of Walter's long reach. Walter stayed in a more relaxed posture and stared into Chabal's eyes, trying to judge when the smaller man would attempt a knife thrust. Chabal's face was now a mask of inscrutability. He started to sway, then he shuffled across the line and back, looking for some weakness in his opponent. Walter held the knife loosely in his left hand but had his right hand almost in a fist, ready to strike.

They continued like this for almost a minute, though it seemed much longer. Then Chabal suddenly launched an attack on Walter's right side, knife aimed at his injured ribs. Walter stepped smartly back and the blade whistled past him. He then aimed a punch at Chabal, making contact with his opponent's left arm, on the biceps. It was a glancing blow, but, as this was the arm Chabal was using it had sufficient sting for the smaller man to stand back and shake out the hurt and numbness the blow had caused. Walter waited for the next attack. There was some whistling from the assembled crowd who had expected more action than this.

Chabal came in for another attack. This time he made the same feint as he had before. When Walter stood his ground this time Chabal aimed a kick at Walter's knee, connecting painfully with his shin instead. Walter swore under his breath and decided to go on the attack. He swept the knife across Chabal, not intending to hit him with the blade. Instead, he continued the turn of his body, leant forward and struck the smaller man on the chin with his shoulder, forcing him to stagger backwards. Walter then turned swiftly back and produced a very good right hook which connected with great effect on Chabal's cheek, knocking him sideways and to the ground. The elbow of the smaller man's broken right arm touched the ground first and he yelped with pain. In stretching out his left hand to break his fall he had let go of the knife, which shot across the wet cobbles with a chattering noise.

Walter stood over his opponent and waited for a sign of surrender. When none came he leaned forward to grab Chabal by the collar and lift him to his feet. If he had not leaned forward he would have been struck by the rifle bullet fired from the second floor of the warehouse. In a wild ricochet the bullet struck the mudguard of one of the cars and diverted back to explode the tyre. The man who had fired the rifle from above was hit by a bullet from the pistol of a Tiger who reacted faster than anyone else. Le Baron screamed in rage and ran inside the warehouse. Quite what he had been upset about was not immediately clear. In the makeshift arena Walter now held the unresisting body of Chabal upright. The smaller man was dragged backwards to the waiting LaDavide who promptly produced handcuffs and fastened Chabal by the left wrist to the right arm of the huge officer whose coat had been torn by the bullet earlier.

Walter handed the knife back to LaDavide and put his jacket and coat back on. Several Tigers came over and slapped him on the back. There was some shouting from behind the broken windows on the second floor. This was followed by a scream and a man's body was flung from the window, landing head down with a sickeningly dull thud on the cobbles. It was the man who had fired the rifle; he had only been winged by the pistol shot. Le Baron had found his notion of honour challenged by the action of this man who had broken the temporary truce. There was a few seconds of shocked silence before one of the Tigers ran over to make sure the man was dead.

'He should not have fired at you. He broke the rules,' le Baron shouted from the window, 'I will come and see my son in a while. He has at least acted with honour.'

'Our business is finished, for the moment at least,' LaDavide shouted, 'But if our injured man dies we will be back for you.'

'A bientôt,' le Baron shouted back.

The Tigers prepared to leave with their prize. One had covered the would-be assassin with a blanket, and an ambulance would soon be on its way. Another joked about the ambulance, calling it a meat wagon. A third was changing the wheel on the car for one with a usable tyre, assisted by a fourth, who operated the jack.

LaDavide, Walter and two other officers climbed into the back of the leading car. A bullet had pierced the door and had buried itself in the back of a seat. This had left a neat oval hole through which some of the horsehair stuffing of the seat could be seen.

◊

The receptionist at the hotel looked at Walter with a certain degree of contempt. This was not too surprising as Walter's clothes were wet and dirty and his blonde hair was plastered to his scalp in rat tails. He badly needed a shave. Godiva looked him over with same degree of acumen but more sympathy. She put down the notes she had been working on.

'You look a complete mess again, Walter. Honestly, that jacket is brand new and it looks like you've been rolling around on the ground in it,' she said with a shake of her head.

'I've just been helping the Tigers in a raid,' Walter said with a sigh, 'Mind if I get a little closer to the fire; and several cups of coffee would be good.' Godiva nodded in the direction of a waiter.

'You want coffee? Well, you are welcome to have some, but it is lunch time, you know.' Godiva said.

'I'll probably be ravenous in a while. In the meantime the coffee will be fine. Where is the Princess, by the way?'

'Oh, she's gone to meet Inessa Armand. I do hope they get on together. When you suggested it at first I thought it was a joke, but I can see that it is a really good place for her,' Godiva said, smiling up at Walter who was sitting legs apart with his trousers gently steaming by the fire.

'I'm sure they will get along just fine,' Walter said, thinking he must be picking up some expressions from Skinner.

'So, tell me. What happened this morning?' Godiva asked. A waiter came over and placed a jug of coffee, cream, sugar crystals and two cups in front of them, then left after Godiva had signed a chitty.

'There was a pitched battle between the Tigers and an Apache gang, and I fought a sort of duel with the son of the leader of the gang,' Walter answered with a sharp little laugh.

'If it was anyone other than you I wouldn't believe them. Did it all work out satisfactorily?' she continued.

'Yes, I suppose so. Only one man died; an Apache, and he was killed by his own side. There were a couple of other injuries and a damaged car. Oh, and someone shot at me but missed,' Walter answered in a slightly distant voice.

'That will do for now. You can tell me all about it later. Meanwhile, I want to get you out of Paris while you are still alive.

I see what 'C' means about you stirring things up. You really are very good at poking at wasp's nests,' Godiva commented.

'Who do you mean by 'C'?' Walter asked, puzzled.

'Oh, do work it out, Walter,' Godiva replied.

'Ah, yes, of course. When do you want me to go?' Walter asked.

'As soon as we can tie up a few loose ends,' she said, 'Probably in a couple of days.'

'So, tell me what these loose ends are,' Walter said.

'It would be good if you can get some kind of promise from Inessa to tell you if she hears anything about our friend, Peter the Painter. Then we need to negotiate with the Russians about what happened to you. They will owe us a favour if we don't pursue it through the Foreign office. If you can continue to talk to the Bolsheviks it may well prove helpful. Other than that, I think most of the issues are criminal rather than diplomatic, and I think you have done more than enough for the Tigers. You seem to get along very well with LaDavide, and that could prove to be useful later on,' Godiva listed, counting out on her fingers.

'I may have to paint another portrait of Ulyanov,' Walter mused, 'Would that be worthwhile?'

'I can't see any harm in it,' Godiva replied, 'Perhaps he will say something indiscrete for once. Not that I hold much hope of that, but it will be good to have someone who knows him, especially if he comes to London again.' Walter was finishing his second cup of coffee. His trousers were still steaming and would be horribly creased when they were dry.

'I can't tell you how good it will be to get back into some decent clothes,' he said wistfully.

'And now it is time for me to get some lunch. Did you want to come along?' Godiva asked.

'That sounds like a really good idea. I said I'd be hungry later, and I am. Where did you plan to go?' Walter said.

'It's not far from the embassy. A couple of the people from there are coming, including Campbell. I hope you don't mind.'

'I'll try not to punch the man. As it happens, I am in quite a mellow mood now, so that promise shouldn't be too hard to keep,' Walter answered her.

'Well, come on, then, or we will be late,' Godiva said, standing up and preparing to leave, 'There is a taxi waiting for us.'

◊

Walter nearly fell asleep during the lunch, his reaction to the stress of the morning. It had not been difficult to ignore the presence of Campbell, despite a few jibes about the state of his clothes. It was not the best lunch he had ever had. Neither the company nor the food was particularly good. This restaurant seemed to specialise in serving food to what it saw as the British taste. To Walter, who had become used to better fare, the one quality it lacked was flavour. He would make up for his disappointment with a good dish of ragout de lapin later.

After the coffee at the end of the meal, brandies being considered too alcoholic at this time of day, he bid his goodbyes to the company and made his way back to his room to try to finish at least one painting before he left the creative crucible of Paris. The Seine had burst its banks in several places, but the rain had, thankfully, stopped and the river did not appear to be rising any further. The Metro system across the river had ground to a halt and he had to walk back to the room. There was some deep standing water on the low points of the roads and his boots were completely soaked by the time he had walked above the low lying land close to the Seine. With some bitter satisfaction he thought that the Prince's house would surely be flooded.

As he passed the door to the Blue Barge he noted that the evening's performance had been cancelled due to the flooding. Some of the booked artistes, as well as a significant proportion of the audience would be unable to negotiate a way through the water.

◊

Skinner came into Walter's room within a minute of his return.

'Want to go to the Blue Barge tonight?' he asked as Walter was still taking off his coat.

'It's not open because of the floods. I passed by it just now and there's a notice pinned to the door,' Walter said with a wry smile.

'That's too bad, I could do with an evening out,' Skinner said with a sigh. 'Has it stopped raining, yet?'

'It's not raining at the moment,' Walter confirmed, 'In fact, I think the rain is going away for a while.'

'That's good, the floods should start to go down soon,' Skinner said.

'I don't think they will. If there is any water coming down from upstream it could get a lot worse before it gets better,' Walter warned.

'You really think so?' Skinner asked with some surprise.

'It's very likely. I've seen it happen before. Once the fields get soaked they can't take in any more water. Any rain that falls washes straight into the streams and rivers. If it happens upstream, the water takes some time to get downstream. I'm pretty certain that the flooding will be worse tomorrow,' Walter explained.

'Are we safe here?' Skinner asked, sounding worried.

'I should think so. In fact I am certain of it. We're quite high up, and the water won't come up here. Your mother should be fine too. There's a bit of a hill going up to her house. It's the houses by the river that are going to suffer,' Walter continued.

'To hell with my mother!' Skinner burst out, 'She's cut me off without a cent. The police here are looking into her business affairs and she's decided to go back to the States.'

'I'm sorry to hear that. Is the Count going with her?' Walter said sympathetically.

'Of course he is. Where else would he go?' Skinner said in a peevish tone.

'What's going to happen about you and Etienne?' Walter asked.

'Who knows!' Skinner said with a shrug, 'I should think the police are investigating him too. He's quite close to my mother, you know.'

'Yes, I thought he might be. That really is quite tough on you,' Walter said.

'Yeah, well maybe I'll have to get a job, even if it is with the family firm. I've always got that to go back to,' Skinner said, and his head slumped forward, 'That's why I wanted to go for a drink tonight.'

'I think I shall still be around tomorrow, and there are other bars to go to. I'll buy you a brandy if you like,' Walter suggested.

'That sounds good. When do you want to go out?' Skinner said with sudden enthusiasm.

'A bit later. I've got to get on with some painting first, while there's still some light,' Walter answered.

'Sure, I'll see you a bit later,' Skinner said. He put his hands into his pockets and left the room whistling tunelessly.

Thursday 26th January

It was a grey and blustery morning. The wind rattled the ill-fitting casement window in Walter's room. When he gazed out of the window he could see a great sheet of water spreading out across the old flood plain by the river. Fingers of flood-water spread up what had once been the small tributary streams that flowed into the Seine near the city. He could see groups of people trying to lay barriers across the path of the rising water, to little apparent effect. If one path was blocked the water swiftly found an alternative route. There were no busses or wagons, taxis or cars moving. The streets above the flood level were blocked with vehicles which had been moved out of harm's way.

Walter had just finished dressing when there was a knock on his door. Outside was the concierge who looked angry at having to climb the steps to the top of the building. She had a note, which she handed to Walter with no attempt at pleasantry. The note was from Inessa Armand, asking Walter to call on her at his earliest convenience. As Inessa's apartment lay on the same ridge as his room Walter felt confident that he could get there with dry feet in a very short time. Putting on his half-dried shoes and overcoat Walter pocked the note and made his way there.

Inessa was trying to organise and amuse the children who were bored and fractious at being unable to play outside. She asked Walter in and directed him to sit in the kitchen while she chivvied and mollified the children. It took some minutes for her to come back.

'Sorry to be so direct, but what is it that you wanted to see me about?' Walter asked.

'I just wanted to know if you had seen Eugenie,' Inessa said, pushing strands of hair behind her ears, 'She was supposed to be coming here yesterday evening with her luggage, but she never turned up.'

'Perhaps she was trapped by the floods. They are pretty bad, you know,' Walter suggested.

'She should have been here by six o'clock. The floods didn't really start to rise until much later. I am very worried about her. I don't think she is the kind of woman who would easily change her mind. I thought that her husband might have managed to track her down,' Inessa said, looking very worried.

'Is your apartment being watched?' Walter asked, with a sick feeling in his stomach.

'There's some police and some Okhrana sometimes, but they don't really bother me too much,' Inessa replied.

'What time did the Princess, Eugenie I mean, leave you yesterday?'

'It would have been about four o'clock. She said she didn't have too much to fetch from the hotel and it wouldn't take much time to pack. Why do you ask?' Inessa said, looking intently at Walter.

'It would have been getting dark about that time, and it was before people come home from work. The thing is, her husband is something to do with the Okhrana, and I'm concerned that she might have been snatched. I need to talk to a friend of mine. This is the one Eugenie was staying with at the hotel,' Walter said in a low, urgent tone.

'You must telephone this friend at once,' Inessa insisted.

'Where is the nearest telephone?' Walter asked, insistently.

'There is one in the bureau de tabac on the corner,' Inessa answered after a few seconds of thought.

'Then I shall call her right away,' Walter said, standing up, 'I'll be back in a few minutes.'

He ran to the tobacconists and had to argue for a minute and put some money on the counter before he was allowed to use the telephone. He then had to find the number of the hotel, get a connection through the operator and wait while the receptionist located Godiva.

'Walter, where are you?' Godiva asked without waiting to find out what Walter wanted, 'Eugenie seems to have gone missing. I haven't seen her since she left to see Inessa Armand yesterday lunchtime.'

'That's what I called you about. I've just been to see Inessa. Eugenie was supposed to be moving in with her yesterday evening, before the floods rose. But Eugenie never came back. I've a horrible feeling that she was snatched by the Okhrana from outside Inessa's apartment. The Prince could have her back again by now!' Walter almost shouted down the microphone.

'Calm down, Walter. It doesn't help anyone if you panic,' Godiva said.

'This isn't panic. The Prince is stupid. If he caught her he would lock her up in his cellar,' Walter tried to explain calmly.

'In that case we shall go and rescue her,' Godiva said, trying to calm Walter.

'Think about it! The house is down by the river. The cellar will be filling up with water. If she is locked up there she could easily drown, and I can't see the Prince letting her out. There is very little time left if we are going to save her, and there is no way through from the north side of the river. I'm just going to have to improvise something,' Walter said.

'What are you going to do, Walter?' Godiva said, sounding worried.

'I'm going to go there by boat,' Walter stated, 'See if you can get anyone else to go the Prince's house.'

'I'll do my best,' Godiva said as Walter placed the microphone back in its holder, ending the call.

Down in the Flood

He sprinted back to Inessa's apartment to tell what he had learned. The door was not properly closed and he burst in without knocking.

'I think Eugenie has been snatched by her husband. I'm going to try to get her back,' Walter said, and he touched Inessa comfortingly on the shoulder as she looked very upset.

'Please take care,' Inessa said as Walter ran out of the apartment and made quickly for the field where he knew he could find a rowing boat. There was a pain in his side from his cracked ribs, but he kept running anyway.

◊

The smaller skiffs were threatening to float away into the flood and the shed in which the oars were kept was surrounded by nearly freezing water to a depth which came to Walter's knees. Walter found a piece of scrap iron propped up against the shed and using it he easily broke the padlock away from the door. Taking the best oars which were within easy reach, he half waded, half ran, to the larger skiff he had seen on his previous visit. It lay almost at the edge of the flood and was nearly half full of water. It took all Walter's strength to turn it on edge and drain the bulk of the water out in a single motion. There was no time to bail out. After placing the oars in the boat he pushed it out into the stream and jumped in.

One effect of the flood was to reduce the current in the stream. The water was flooding inland more than it was travelling downstream. And so it took far less effort than it had previously to row upstream. With so many landmarks partially inundated it was difficult to work out exactly where he was in relation to the Prince's house. Eventually he identified the top of a small obelisk which stood about fifty metres upstream of the house.

It was quite bizarre to be rowing across the fencing which marked the edge of the promenade next to the river. The bottom of the boat scraped over the top rail. A small road led directly down to the river.

The road Walter wanted was the second turning on the right. He had to negotiate between sunken and floating hazards in the road, and because he was facing the wrong way he had passed the Prince's house before he recognised the tops of the gates. After rowing back he tied the painter of the boat to the gates, then he clambered across the side of the gate where the barrier was lowest and waded, waist deep, to the front door. The level of the water had reached the top step leading to the door. Some servant had piled old furniture from the servants' rooms across the door as a barrier to the flood. Clambering across this rough obstacle Walter managed to get to the door, but found it locked and bolted shut, as though ironmongery could turn back the flood.

By piling a chair on a table on a chest of drawers Walter was able to clamber up to the miniature castellations which decorated the top edge of the canopy over the door. Once on this platform he swung himself up the canopy and from there onto the broad window ledge of the Princess's boudoir. With a well aimed boot he shattered one of the bottom panes in the sash window. After winding a handkerchief over his knuckles, he broke away the sharpest pieces of glass, reached a hand in and unfastened the sash. He was then able to lift the bottom part of the window and clamber into the room.

The noise of the breaking window had alerted Marie the maid to the presence of an intruder. She had just about climbed the stairs when Walter brushed her out of the way. She shrunk back from this dripping, wild-eyed maniac, hardly recognising him as the man she had spat on in the cellar a few days previously. There was a more formidable opponent waiting at the bottom of the stairs, the monstrous servant, Piotr. The servant stood solid and impassive, daring Walter to try to get past him.

'Get out of my way!' Walter shouted out. Getting no reaction he repeated the command in French, but with no more effect than before. The man just stood there like an immovable object. Walter tried to go to either side but Piotr just blocked him, still not offering violence; still silent. When Walter tried to force his way past a huge arm firstly blocked him, then sent him spinning across the tiled hallway towards the front door. There was a stand for umbrellas and walking sticks by the door and it contained a heavy stick with a knob head, made of some dense and slow-growing bog wood. Walter grabbed this and ran at Piotr, swinging the knob end at Piotr's head. The servant easily blocked the blow with a massive forearm and pushed Walter in the chest, this time sending him crashing into the right-hand upright of the door. Walter struck his head, enough to open up a scalp wound which bled easily but was not serious.

Shaking himself back to full consciousness Walter clambered to his feet and looked around for a better weapon, but could see none. He didn't have to wonder why Piotr didn't attack him. The man had only been ordered to stop anyone getting to the Princess. This called for a change of tactic. Walter pretended to aim a blow with the stick onto Piotr's head. When the servant lifted his arm to protect his head Walter reversed the stick and drove the point of it into Piotr's belly. It sunk in several inches with little apparent resistance. Piotr grunted, but seemed very little hurt by this. He brought his arm down, now within reach and landed a stinging blow with the flat of his hand onto the side of Walter's head. Clearing his head of the fog the slap had caused him, Walter rose groggily to his feet. Piotr picked up the walking stick and snapped it like a twig. He threw the pieces at Walter, who had to duck to avoid them.

There was a small bench of some dark wood, deeply carved, under one of the windows. Walter picked it up and advanced more slowly until he was almost within range. Piotr laughed to see the clumsiness of this weapon. Walter sent it to skimming across the floor to Piotr's right side, then, while the man's attention was on the bench, he sidestepped Piotr to his left in a deftly performed rugby manoeuvre. Piotr bellowed like an angry water buffalo, turned and pursued Walter down the corridor to the kitchen. Walter had only a few seconds lead, but when Piotr entered the room he was hit on the back of the head with edge of a large cast iron skillet. The brittle metal broke with a crack far louder than the dull thud it had caused when it hit the servant's head. He turned round to face Walter, growled, then he started to sway before he crashed to the floor, causing a small cloud of dust to rise from the scrubbed floorboards.

The only rope of any kind that Walter could find was the string used to tie up the meat before roasting. Only by folding it several times could Walter create cord which would offer any resistance to anyone as strong as Piotr. It was the best Walter could do, and he trussed up the man quickly before trying to find the Princess.

The door to the cellar was locked and there was no obvious way to break it down. Walter ran back to the kitchen and searched Piotr's pockets for the key, but failed to find it. He then ran back up the stairs and tried to locate Marie the ugly maid. She had locked herself in the Princess's room. The lock was feeble compared to the one to the cellar and Walter easily crashed it open with a shoulder charge. Marie was standing in the centre of the room, and was pointing an antique duelling pistol at his chest, needing both hands to hold it steady. Walter made a dive to his left and heard the crack of the bullet leaving the barrel. The recoil from the pistol threw the maid back and onto the chaise longue. Walter was up in a moment and grabbed the maid by the throat.

'Where is the key?' he demanded to know.

'I don't know, I don't know. Let me go!' Marie screamed in impotent rage.

Walter gave her a small slap, but she was made of stern stuff and merely glared at him. An idea came to him. It wasn't right to hit a woman, but there were other ways.

'Give me the key or I will tickle you,' he said, wiggling his fingers.

Down in the Flood

Marie didn't seem to approve of this and squirmed in anticipation and dread. He pushed the fingers of both hands into her waist and began to tickle her slowly, thoroughly and mercilessly. She squirmed and cried and he was unable to distinguish whether her cries were from laughter, rage or pain. After more than a minute she begged for mercy and meekly handed over a large iron key and a smaller brass one from an inside pocket. She afterwards collapsed limp and unresisting on the chaise longue, utterly defeated.

Walter took the steps three at a time and ran to the cellar door. It opened quite easily with a half turn of the large key. The water had risen most of the way up the cellar stairs. Wading more than waist deep he forced his way through the rising flood. Water was pouring through the vents in the back wall of the house. Having been knocked out with chloroform on his previous visit, Walter did not have an exact remembrance of the layout of the cellar. It was only when he got to the third chamber that he found the Princess shackled to the wall with only her neck and head above the level of the water. She looked at Walter with unfocussed eyes. Taking the smaller key he unlocked the shackles that bound her wrists and was able to help her to stand. Taking a deep breath he plunged his head into the water and felt for the shackles round her ankles. He dropped the key at one point and spent precious seconds finding it again in the murky water. Eventually he managed to locate the keyhole and open the shackles. Then he threw the key away, hoisted the Princess on his shoulder in a fireman's lift and waded out of the cellar, careful not to bang her head on the walls and beams as he passed.

It was a struggle getting up the cellar steps but much easier when he came to the hallway. The key was still in the front door lock and it was easy to get out of this house of pain. He kicked away the furniture and waded to where the boat was moored. It was going to take a supreme effort of will to manoeuvre this dead weight around the high gates and into the boat. It was at that point that another, larger, boat came into view. Standing in the prow of the boat, looking like a ship's figurehead was Godiva. She shouted a greeting at him. Two strong policemen were rowing and a third man was working the tiller. In a minute the boat had moored besides the one Walter had borrowed.

With the help of the policemen, Walter was able to get the nearly unconscious body of the Princess into the larger boat. Godiva rubbed her wrists and found some smelling salts in her handbag which she placed under the Princess's nose. She coughed, groaned but did not revive.

'We have to get this woman to a doctor right away. She's suffering from the cold,' Godiva said in her best commanding English. Walter translated for the benefit of the policemen. Godiva then took off her own coat and wrapped the Princess in it. The man at the tiller found a small flask of brandy and a small amount was dribbled into the Princess's mouth, causing her to breathe more rapidly. The larger boat was then rowed away, leaving Walter to climb into the smaller one and follow on behind. He had to keep turning his head to see which way they were headed. He bumped into several pieces of street furniture but was able to keep pace well enough. After some minutes they came to the edge of the flood on the south side of the river, in a road where several doctors were known to practice. After drawing the boats up, the policemen carried the Princess to the largest of the surgeries and lifted her inside.

A bustling female receptionist dashed to find a doctor who hurried down to see what the commotion was about. He instantly ordered a hot bath to be prepared. The Princess was carried upstairs to the bathroom and her sodden clothes were cut off with a scalpel by a nurse before she was immersed in the bath with Godiva's help. Her skin was blue and wrinkled, having been in the cold river water for so long. Some oil was dropped into the bath water to help replace that which had been lost from her skin. Within a few minutes the

Princess began to shiver uncontrollably. Then she began to cry, waving her hands as though they were causing her great pain. Water cascaded over the side of the bath. Gradually the thrashing stopped and she began to focus her eyes.

Godiva leaned over and took her hand. Then she smiled reassuringly.

'You're safe, now,' Godiva said

'Where am I?' the Princess asked, blinking several times.

'At a doctor's house,' Godiva answered, patting her hand.

'The water was coming in. I couldn't get away,' the Princess said, and she started crying softly.

'Walter came to rescue you,' Godiva explained.

'You said I was safe before, but they found me and locked me up,' the Princess sobbed.

'They won't get you now. Walter will make sure of that,' Godiva said.

'Walter, where is he? I must thank him,' the Princess said, and she was ceasing to cry.

'He's downstairs, Eugenie. You can see him in a few minutes, when you've got some clothes on,' Godiva urged.

'I want to see him now. Get him for me. I want to see him,' the Princess said, half hysterical.

'Of course, I'll get him now,' Godiva agreed. She walked swiftly out of the room and grabbed Walter who was enjoying a well-earned cigarette in the waiting room, dragging him upstairs and into the bathroom.

'Walter!' the Princess shouted in joy, holding out her arms.

Walter ran over to her and received a very wet embrace.

'I am so very glad that you have recovered,' he said, smiling at her.

'You saved me. You darling man, you saved me,' she gushed.

'That was only because I was feeling guilty for putting you in that danger in the first place,' Walter said, laughing with relief, 'Anyway, you've got no clothes on. I really shouldn't be here.'

'I forgive you, and, anyway, you've seen me naked before!' the Princess said, laughing herself.

'Really, Eugenie!' Godiva tutted from the other side of the room.

Walter stood up, walked briskly over to Godiva and embraced her fondly, wetting the back of her blouse with the water dripping from his sleeves.

'Oh, Walter! You really are the limit,' she laughed at him.

◊

Walter took Skinner with him to the Bolshevik cafe to see another side of Parisian life. The American looked puzzled and a little out of his emotional depth. The Russians were in their usual state of behaviour, seesawing between depression and elation, sometimes making occasional stops between these extremes. Walter bought a bottle of rough Polish vodka and took it over to the table, together with several shot glasses. He invited Igor over to join them, knowing his command of English was good and that he would be able to talk to Skinner.

'Ah, wodka!' Igor said, beaming, 'Once you open the bottle it has to be finished before you leave the table.' He poured out three full measures and gestured that they should all pick up their drinks. 'Now we drink the Russian way. You drink it down in one and bang your glass on the table. Now, Cheers!'

They all downed the fiery liquid in one gulp. The burning effect of the vodka on Walter's oesophagus made his eyes water. Skinner coughed, went red in the face and started to hiccough. Igor refilled the glasses and handed them round. It took a full minute for Skinner to recover sufficiently to attempt the second drink, half of which he spluttered out. Igor laughed heartily, his beard rising and falling with the movement of his chest. Third measures were handed out in quick order.

'Nasdrovi!' Igor toasted them as he downed the third measure. Skinner was looking breathless and a little distressed after this shot, though Walter was getting used to it.

'It's so hot!' Skinner protested.

'It is the way we like it in Russia,' Igor laughed.

'Well, we don't like it this way in America,' Skinner said, his voice sounding strained, 'And I didn't know the British liked it, either.'

'I share a flat with a man from India. He likes to eat chilli pickle that would blow your socks off. I can manage that, and this is nowhere hear so hot,' Walter said with a grin.

'What is chilli pickle?' Igor asked.

'You put a little on your plate and dip the food in it, to make it more spicy,' Walter explained.

'That sounds very good. I must get some of this, err, cheelee peeckle. Can I get this in Paris?' Igor asked.

'I shouldn't think so. I'll send you some when I get back to London,' Walter answered.

'Then you must have my address,' Igor said. He took a notebook and pencil from an inside pocket and scrawled something before ripping the portion of the page with the writing from the book and handing it to Walter, who folded it and put it in an inside pocket.

'Now, tell me, who is your young American friend?'

'Oh, yes, I should have made the introductions. Igor, this is Franklin Skinner, and visa versa,' Walter said.

'Pleased to make your acquaintance, Igor,' Skinner said. Igor grabbed the proffered hand and shook it heartily between his two hairy paws. 'Say, I could get used to this stuff. Let's have another glass.'

More measures were poured out and duly dispatched. Skinner blew out his cheeks. The bottle was now two thirds gone.

'Are we celebrating something?' Igor asked, 'Not that there has to be an excuse to drink wodka.'

'Well, I am leaving Paris in a few days, and Franklin here is probably going back to America soon. I thought I'd look up my old friends before I left. And I won't forget to send you the chilli pickle when I get home,' Walter answered.

'Say, are you fellows all Russian revolutionaries?' Skinner asked, sounding a little drunk.

'Yes, I suppose we are,' Igor answered with a shrug.

'It's just that I always read that you are really dangerous men, desperate men, but you all seem to be jolly fellows,' Skinner slurred.

'Oh, you must look out, we are very dangerous men, all of us,' Igor said with a deep and rich laugh, like rolling thunder. He poured out more measures of vodka.

'To the revolution!' Skinner toasted. They knocked back the vodka in unison and banged the glasses on the table. He was beginning to look through glazed, drooping eyes.

'How is your friend, the policeman?' Igor asked Walter in French.

'He isn't quite a policeman, and he was very well the last time I saw him,' Walter said.

'If he isn't quite a policeman, what is he?' Igor asked.

'He works against the criminal gangs in Paris,' Walter explained, 'He isn't political.'

'There are plenty of criminals among us,' Igor acknowledged, 'I think it is wrong to act in that way if another country is generous enough to give you a home. So, Walter are you some kind of policeman yourself?'

'I'm no kind of policeman. I'm just a sort of adventurer,' Walter answered.

Down in the Flood

'And you are working on a case of some kind of art theft or forgery. I'm sure you won't be able to tell me exactly what it is. It doesn't matter. There are all sorts of people watching us, I know that. The newspapers say we are some kind of monsters and the government has to do something. I understand that. There are people here in this cafe who inform for the Okhrana. You are not an informant. I think you are quite sympathetic to some of our aims. Being an exile you learn to judge people quite quickly. I like you, Walter, You should think about changing your employment. Now, let us finish off this vodka,' Igor said quietly, leaning forward as he spoke. The last drops of the bottle were poured and drunk. Skinner was barely capable of raising the glass to his lips. After drinking he slumped back on the chair and closed his eyes.

'That is the way of it,' Walter said to Igor, 'The vodka hits you very hard. The first three glasses, nothing happens, then the alcohol hits all at once.'

'Yet you are not drunk, or no more drunk than I am,' Igor said.

'Mr Skinner drinks too much. There is probably a lot of alcohol from last night still in his body,' Walter mused, 'And I am a lot bigger than he is. It takes a bit more than his limit to get me very drunk.'

'It is also a matter of the will to stay sober. Do not drink like Franklin here. It is not good for anyone,' Igor pronounced.

'I have other vices,' Walter said.

'If we had more wodka I would toast to your wirtues and your wices,' Igor said.

'Then take my hand instead, and let us hope we meet again, quite soon,' Walter said, proffering his hand.

'You have my address. Do not be afraid to call on me,' Igor said.

◊

Inessa Armand welcomed Walter into her apartment, ushering him in and sitting him on a chair in the living room. Ulyanov was sitting on a chair opposite him, looking serious, his bald head shiny. Inessa left the room and shut the door behind her.

'Monsieur Oulianoff, It is good to see you again,' Walter said.

'Where is the Princess Pechorinova?' Ulyanov demanded, and he banged his hand on the arm of the chair. His voice was that of someone who was used to giving commands and having them obeyed.

'She is safe now, though she has suffered a good deal. Her husband commanded the Okhrana here in Paris. He had her taken after she left here and locked her in a cellar which flooded last night. I managed to get her out. It was a mistake to bring her here. I should have realised the house was being watched,' Walter answered.

'I want her brought here. She will be very useful to our cause,' Ulyanov stated.

'She is a person in her own right. She would not be safe here. Doesn't she have a right to be safe?' Walter asked.

'Do you know how embarrassing it would be to the Czar to tell the world how his servants act?' Ulyanov asked in return.

'My concern is solely for the welfare of the Princess. She has suffered enough, and deserves some time to make up her own mind about what she is going to do. You just want to use her to further your revolution,' Walter said.

'How dare you talk to me like that. Don't you know who I am? The whole fate of the Russian people rests on my shoulders. This is a great cause, and if some people get hurt in the process, we must look to History to say if what we did was right,' Lenin said.

'There I disagree with you. You cannot separate ends and means. If you try to achieve good by an act of evil it devalues the good. There are only individuals. If you deny justice to anyone or any group you are acting as the worst kind of despot. I won't let you use the Princess for your own ends,' Walter replied with quiet determination.

Down in the Flood

'You disappoint me. You have no determination. Our cause is great and the most worthwhile there could be. Without discipline there can be no success. There are things we do for the greater good. If we backslide the Russian people will be condemned to generations of servitude.'

'What I want is a proper revolution, where the people can tell their government what to do, where they can vote them in and out,' Walter said.

'The people are petty and selfish and act like children. They need to be led and educated. Only after that education is completed can there truly be justice,' Ulyanov said, banging his right fist into his cupped left hand.

'And what if the people never learn properly? What if the teachers become the new masters? What is the point of replacing one despot with another? You underestimate the people; they know well enough what they want, and it is not up to you to insist that you know better,' Walter said, only raising his voice very slightly.

'You are a revisionist, you wish to stop the revolution. I will not allow such opinions to be expressed. There is only one way to achieve the revolution, and there is no-one else who is capable of leading it!' Ulyanov shouted, banging his fist on the arm of the chair and raising puffs of dust. Walter cut in as he was taking another deep breath and launching into another speech.

'No man should be irreplaceable,' Walter said quietly.

'Then we have nothing more to say. Get out, now!' Ulyanov shouted.

Walter stood up, nodded towards Ulyanov, opened the door and left the room. Inessa was waiting for him in the hallway.

'How is Eugenie?' she asked.

'She is getting better. She should recover in a few days. The Prince had her locked in a cellar near the river and she nearly drowned in freezing water. She is safe and warm and dry now, but she can't come back here, she wouldn't be safe,' Walter explained.

'Monsieur Oulianoff wants her here,' Inessa said in a voice that was not her own, 'He is a very great man.'

'But I am not a great man, and I will not allow her to come here,' Walter said.

Inessa nodded dumbly. Walter held her gently by the shoulders and pressed a kiss on her forehead before he left the apartment. Outside, the sky was brightening a little.

Friday 27th January

Princess Eugenie Pechorinova had been moved to a modest clinic sited high on one of the low hills to the south of the city, where the air was comparatively clean. With all the land near the Seine still deep under water, arrangements had been made to ferry people across in boats if they had urgent business on the other side of the river. Godiva and LaDavide had used one of these temporary ferries to take them across to the south bank. A black Renault with gold lines around the coachwork was waiting for them. They had picked Walter up from his room and were taking him to see the invalid.

'This is rather like my father's car,' Walter remarked as they sped along the drying roads.

'Has your father managed to get the car repaired, yet?' Godiva asked.

'I'm not sure. I suppose he has. If it's still being fixed he would have hired another in the meantime,' Walter said, 'Mind you, if he's away for the winter he may not pick it up until the spring.'

'You father must be quite rich if he owns a car like this,' LaDavide added.

'He is quite rich, but he doesn't give much to Walter,' Godiva said, wryly.

'Will you tell me how your father came to crash his car?' LaDavide asked, curious despite himself.

'He didn't crash it. This is all to do with a previous adventure. It was a German agent who stole it and crashed it when I chased him,' Walter explained.

'Do you have a car?'

'I can't even drive. I was riding a horse at the time,' Walter answered.

'Then there was that chase after the aeroplane,' Godiva added, stifling a giggle.

'Are you having a joke?' LaDavide asked.

'No, but Godiva shouldn't laugh about it. A man died.'

'But he was a spy and a murderer,' Godiva explained.

'You had better stop telling me about this,' LaDavide said, but he sounded impressed. 'It sounds like an interesting way to make a living.'

'I think I might be able to earn a decent living for myself, now,' Walter said, 'with my paintings. Did I tell you I had sold a few?'

'Of course you did. Mind you, you can't rely on Etienne to give you a good reference,' Godiva said.

'That's alright, I'll get Skinner to provide me with a suitable introduction to a London gallery. If I can find him sober, that is.'

'Mr Skinner's mother has already left for America,' LaDavide said, with a note of regret in his voice.

'I suppose the floods kept you busy yesterday,' Walter said.

'Yes, we were rather busy. Not so busy as the gendarmerie, but busy nonetheless. We managed to catch several Apaches as they tried to move stolen goods from their warehouses. It was a very successful day for us,' LaDavide said with some satisfaction.

The car pulled in to the front of the clinic and they climbed out of the interior into pale winter sunshine. It was almost blinding in comparison with the grey skies that had enveloped the city for weeks. They walked up the steps to the front of the clinic. LaDavide had found some flowers and Godiva had somehow located some fresh fruit. Walter had brought along the wrapped picture of Eugenie in the nude.

Her room was on the first floor, overlooking a courtyard garden at the rear. She was sitting, propped up with pillows in a functional steel framed bed with white enamelled steel bars. The cool bleached linen sheets were folded as precisely as any piece of engineering. She was wearing a warm bed jacket of pale pink wool over her nightdress. Looking up from a copy of Madame Bovary she smiled broadly to see them. Godiva embraced her with some warmth and then LaDavide and Walter kissed her on the cheeks. They all presented their gifts. When Walter explained what his gift was she left the painting tightly wrapped.

'How are you doing, Eugenie?' Godiva asked solicitously.

'I am feeling almost well. I still have pains in my hands and feet, and I did not sleep well last night. The doctor tells me that I am doing very well. It is very good to be warm again, but the food here is horrible. It may be good for you, but it doesn't taste good,' she said with a smile.

'I should have brought you chocolates instead,' Godiva said.

'You can bring me some when you come next time,' Eugenie said, and she rested a hand on Godiva's arm.

'Are they going to keep you here long?' Walter asked, realising after he had said it that the question sounded a little terse.

'No, I should only be here a day or two more,' she answered, looking more serious.

'And have you decided where you will be staying after you get out?' Walter continued.

'I don't think I can go back to Inessa's house after what happened. I think I shall have to find somewhere else to stay,' Eugenie replied.

'You are very welcome to come to London, if you like. I'm sure we can find you somewhere to stay. I'll set my father to find you somewhere. It will be among intellectuals, very liberal people. I'm sure they will make you very welcome,' Godiva offered.

'Would that be far enough away from my husband?' Eugenie enquired, looking a little worried.

'Your husband is the subject of an enquiry by our Ministry of Justice. There is likely to be an official complaint. When the Russian Embassy receive that letter, he will be sent back to Russia in disgrace. If they try to argue we will release details of what he has done to the press. No-one wants to start any diplomatic disputes. He will be back in Russia very shortly,' LaDavide said reassuringly. Eugenie nodded thoughtfully.

'I think the Okhrana will still want to get to me if I stay in Paris. Perhaps it is better if I come to London,' she said.

'Good,' Walter said with some enthusiasm, 'We will be able to see each other when I am in town.'

'Do you travel a good deal?' Eugenie asked.

'I imagine that I shall be travelling a good deal from now on,' Walter admitted.

'But don't worry. I'll be around all the time. You won't be alone,' Godiva said breezily.

'Then I will accept your offer gratefully,' Eugenie decided with a smile broad enough to show her even white teeth.

'Excellent,' Walter said, smiling back.

'You can travel with us to London on Monday,' Godiva said, 'I'll arrange all the documents so that they are ready in time.'

'You are so kind to me,' Eugenie said, 'But I will need some kind of a job once I get to London.'

'I'm sure I can find you some work as a translator,' Godiva said, 'and I'm sure that my father would like to have his books translated into Russian.'

'That is good. It seems my education will be of some use to me at last,' Eugenie said.

◊

As they were driving away, Walter turned to Godiva and asked her a question which was nagging at him.

'You don't think we'll use the Princess the way that Ulyanov wanted to, do you?'

'If they try I won't let them. If she decides she wants to help us then I will allow her to do that, but I won't have her forced into doing anything,' Godiva answered.

'I'll hold you to that,' Walter said.

'You know I always keep my word,' Godiva said with absolute certainty. Walter would not have dared to contradict her. When compared to her, Ulyanov still had a lot to learn about steely-eyed determination.

'So, what shall we do tonight?' LaDavide asked, 'After all, you only have two more nights in Paris.'

'We're still here tomorrow night,' Godiva protested.

'Yes, but all of the shows will be very crowded on a Saturday,' LaDavide explained.

'How about the Bobino?' Walter asked at a sudden whim.

'That sounds a bit serious to me' Godiva said, 'I think I feel like being a bit frivolous tonight.'

'Well, how about a second rate night-club called the Blue Barge?' Walter suggested.

'But I don't think it will be very entertaining,' LaDavide said without enthusiasm.

'No, I think it sounds absolutely perfect,' Godiva responded.

'It that case We'll meet up there at a bit after eight,' Walter said.

'Where is it?' Godiva asked.

'It's just round the corner from where I live,' Walter said.

'What kind of show do they have?' Godiva asked.

'Well, there's a woman called Rosa Languedoc who does the most extraordinary dance,' Walter said, smiling.

'Alright, then, it's a date. Are you coming along? Godiva asked of LaDavide.

'Why not? But I warn you, it is not the most sophisticated kind of entertainment,' LaDavide replied.

'Then it's absolutely perfect,' Godiva said.

◊

Skinner had decided to go to the Bobino where he thought he might meet up with Brigitte and Sylvie, so he declined Walter's invitation to join them at the Blue Barge. The place was filling rapidly as they arrived and it was only LaDavide's prompt action in showing his government card which allowed them to get a table. Godiva was persuaded by him to try the absinthe, though Walter drank only brandy and LaDavide had red wine. She only had lemonade after the absinthe and began to act like a naughty schoolgirl. Walter had never seen her tipsy before. The turns who had made it through the flood-water came onstage, did their brief acts, and departed to applause that seemed greater than usual. The floods were beginning to recede and everyone present seemed relieved to have survived them.

Rosa Languedoc performed her act later than usual, with the added elements Walter had watched her rehearse. Godiva sat and watched with an expression somewhere between fascination and anger.

'She's taking her clothes off!' she said rather too loudly.

'That's largely what her act consists of,' Walter said.

'I don't think I really approve of this act,' Godiva stated very firmly, sounding tipsy.

'But she's a woman who lives her own life and makes a good living doing what she does,' Walter said teasingly.

'I just think it might give men the wrong idea,' Godiva continued.

'It would not be the wrong idea. Rosa Languedoc really is a, a...,' 'LaDavide said, searching for the right word.

'A tart,' Walter said, completing the sentence for him.

'Yes, a tart. She has sex with men for money, and this is the way she gets to meet new customers,' LaDavide said.

'Well, for pleasure as well as for money,' Walter corrected him.

'Well, that's alright then,' Godiva said sarcastically.

Saturday 28th January

Inessa Armand argued with the concierge.

'Do you need payment to take the message to Mr Davies?'

'I cannot leave my post. You can go up to the room if you like. He's had so many visitors since he came here I've lost count. I'm not showing anyone else up to the room. It's up three flights of stairs and my old legs won't take it,' the concierge grumbled, and she crossed her arms defiantly.

'Very well, then, I'll go up. You really are very unhelpful.' Inessa complained.

'It's not my job to deliver messages for that young man,' the concierge said through thin lips, 'And you're not the first woman to go to his room, not by any means.'

'I'm sure he has other lady friends' Inessa said, trying to stay calm under provocation.

'Then you can find him yourself!' the concierge replied, shutting the sliding panel to end the conversation. Her coffee was going cold.

Inessa sighed and started to make her way up the stairs, past smells of food and body odour. The poor fit of the windows meant that the air at the top of the house was reasonably fresh. She hadn't meant to see Walter in person. To do so and to be found out doing so might cause friction between her and Ulyanov.

She knocked and Walter's voice from within said 'Entré!'.

Walter was trying to shave in the lukewarm water which was the best available. The temperature of the water, the chipped and stained enamel bowl it stood in and the fogged and spotted mirror made the ceremony a poor imitation of a proper shave with hot towels. Walter owned one of the new-fangled safety razors, and it gave an unsatisfactory result when compared to a proper cut-throat one. Soon he would be back in London and could get a decent shave from his manservant, Dorkins. He was standing with his shirtsleeves rolled up, half his face still covered in soapy foam.

'Hello, Walter,' Inessa said, smiling at Walter's attempt at grooming.

'Oh, hello Inessa. Welcome back to my humble room,' Walter said, looking at his reflection in the mirror, 'Mind if I finish shaving?'

'Of course not. Please carry on,' Inessa graciously replied, sitting down on the edge of the bed.

It only took a minute for Walter to finish. He then splashed the remaining soap off and dried his face and hands on a hard, thin towel.

'What can I do for you?' Walter asked, turning round to face his guest. He rolled his sleeves back down and fastened the buttons on the cuffs of his shirt. Back in London he would be wearing proper cufflinks. The buttons marked the garment as being that of a working man.

'I understand that you will soon be returning to England,' Inessa said.

'Yes, I'll be going in a day or two. Is there anything I can do for you before I go?' Walter said.

'I think I owe you an apology. When I agreed to have Eugenie come to stay with me I thought that I should be able to look after her. I had hoped to protect her from anyone who wanted to make use of her. Monsieur Oulianoff is a very great man, but he only sees the bigger picture. His whole life is directed to the cause. He is impatient to see change, and he thought he could use Eugenie's plight to the advantage of the cause. Eugenie needs time to recover from what she has been through. I understand that. It pains me to say it, but she needs somewhere else to stay until she has recovered. You were right not to allow her to stay with me. I heard your argument with Monsieur Oulianoff and though he was right in what he said, it did not show sufficient care for Eugenie's welfare,' Inessa explained, for once not fluent in her delivery.

'Thank you,' Walter said after a few seconds of thought. 'I hope I didn't sound too self-righteous when I was talking to Monsieur Oulianoff, or should I call him Lenin?'

'So you know the name he uses when writing.'

'People talk to me, I've spoken to other Bolsheviks. They seem to think that Monsieur Oulianoff is a bit of a dictator,' Walter said.

'No, it's not that way at all. It's just that he is not very tolerant of people who do not see the bigger picture, the way he sees it, the way it is. If he was a woman he would understand that small acts of kindness are as important as big ideas. It is unusual for me to find a man who understands that. Now, Walter, I understand that you are a spy of some kind. I think the British sent you, but I am sure that you do not want to persecute us. I don't think you are that kind of a man. You want some kind of information. If I can help, and the information does not damage our cause, I would be willing to speak openly to you.'

'Thank you, again. What I really want to know about is what some Latvian anarchists are doing. We don't mind the Bolsheviks meeting and living in London. All are welcome, provided they don't go around robbing and killing people. What we have is a group of Latvians who are well, err, robbing and killing. It would be to the benefit of all the other exiles to get rid of this group. Otherwise you will just play to the prejudices of the popular press. We do try to be tolerant, and we have a good deal of sympathy for the cause of change in Russia, and for any exiles from tyranny,' Walter said.

'Do you have any names for the people in this group?' Inessa asked.

'The only one I know is Peter the Painter. That is one of the names he goes under,' Walter said.

'To be completely honest with you, I know nothing of this man or this group. If I hear of anything I will get in touch. You will have to give me an address where I can write to you,' Inessa said, looking a little nervous.

'I can't give my home address, but you can get a message to me when you need to. It is not the address of any office, it is just a place where you can get in touch with me,' Walter said, and he wrote down the address of his club in St James. He handed the sheet of paper to Inessa. She folded it in two and put it in her handbag.

'Is Walter Davies your real name?' Inessa asked.

'No, but we all use other names at times, don't we?' Walter answered with a tolerant smile.

'I suppose you have as many enemies as we do. We do not work for the same cause, but I believe you are mostly a good man. I trust you, Walter. And I trust that you will in your turn repay my trust,' Inessa said, looking a little pleadingly at Walter.

'I promise that nothing I do will ever put you or your family or friends in any danger or even anything which might lead to further investigation. I know that you are dedicated to the revolution, and I can understand why. But please don't worship Monsieur Oulianoff. It doesn't do us men any good to be looked at in that way, it makes us arrogant,' Walter said, slightly embarrassed by his own sincerity.

Inessa came over and hugged him tightly for some minutes. Then she pulled apart, smoothed down her skirts and hair, smiled and left. Walter shook his head as though he could not quite believe what had just occurred.

◊

The restaurant was crowded with diners. Many of the other restaurants were still recovering from the flooding, and those that were still operating were almost always fully booked. It had taken a little persuasion from LaDavide and a flash of his warrant card to the Maitre D before a place was found for them. Godiva had never been in such a palace of conspicuous consumption. Busy waiters bustled around collecting orders and fetching and carrying plates.

Their talk was discrete but when combined with what was going on at the other tables it was sufficient to make their conversations private.

'What is happening with le Baron's son?' Walter asked.

'He has been charged with Pascale's murder. If it goes to court he will be found guilty and he will go to the guillotine,' LaDavide answered with a rueful smile.

'What do you mean by 'if he goes to court'?' Godiva asked, picking up on the important phrase.

'Politics,' LaDavide said with a shrug, but looking mutinous.

'What will you do if it doesn't come to court?' Walter asked.

'I think I would find it difficult to remain in the Tigers,' LaDavide mused, 'Other than that I don't know what I'll do. Pascale was a good friend of mine. I cannot let his murderer go free.'

'I hope you're not planning to do anything illegal,' Godiva said in a firm tone.

'At the moment I have no idea what will happen. Someone high up may want to avoid embarrassing the government. All I can say is that if this happens a full account of what happened will appear in certain newspapers,' LaDavide said with a slight smile.

'Look, if you need to speak to anyone about some work, have a talk with me,' Godiva said handing over a card she retrieved from her handbag. LaDavide looked at the details on the card and then placed it in his waistcoat pocket.

'Prince Pechorin is continuing to protest to the ministry about what you did in rescuing his wife. He calls it kidnapping, and he says that you assaulted his servant with a skillet and beat up a man he had following you,' LaDavide said to Walter.

'Then I plead guilty to all those charges,' Walter replied, 'But I still don't feel that I have managed to really cause the Prince enough discomfort.'

'You shouldn't worry about that, Walter,' Godiva said, 'I understand that he has been recalled to Russia. He won't have a career or any influence at court. Isn't that enough?'

'Somehow I don't quite feel it is,' Walter said, 'He needs some little act that shows that he is disgraced.'

'I suggest that just for once you leave things as they are,' LaDavide suggested.

'Oh, very well then;' Walter agreed, 'Are we all going to see Eugenie before we go?'

'Unfortunately I must be somewhere else very soon,' LaDavide said sadly, 'And I have some family duties tonight. I shall see you off at the Gare du Nord tomorrow morning.'

'Then we had better go and see Eugenie, then,' Godiva said, 'Come on, Walter, we need to go now.'

LaDavide paid the bill, kissed Godiva on the cheek, embraced Walter warmly and left. Walter and Godiva decided to walk to the clinic as the Metro system was still not operating fully under the Seine. The weather was cold and dry and a good walk would be of benefit after the lunch they had just eaten. Life was coming back to the streets and people were milling around the shops. Gangs of workmen were clearing mud and debris from the low lying roads. Householders and servants were brushing the muddy water from floors and out of doors. Others were carrying furniture. After the near silence of the floods it felt like the whole city was wakening from hibernation.

Princess Eugenie Pecorinova was sitting in a chair, reading the later chapters of "Madame Bovary" when they arrived. She attempted to rise, but Godiva hurried over and persuaded her to stay sitting.

'How are you feeling today, Eugenie?' Godiva asked in a bright voice.

'I am much better, thank you. I think I shall be able to travel with you tomorrow, if that is still possible,' Eugenie replied.

'Of course it is. I have all the documents and tickets ready. We will come and collect you in the morning, if that is alright with you,' Godiva reassured her.

'Please believe me when I say that I will be most happy to come with you, and that I shall be ready at any time you want me to be. After all that has happened I won't feel safe in Paris anymore. I have never been to London. You will have to tell me what it is like,' Eugenie gushed.

'Well, from my experience it is generally safer than Paris, but the food isn't so good,' Walter answered.

'Well, I'm sure I can make friends among the exile community,' Eugenie added.

'There's certainly a variety of Russians to be found there,' Godiva agreed, 'Almost as many as there are in Paris, but rather fewer revolutionaries.'

'I rather liked Inessa Armand, I think I shall write to her,' Eugenie said a little wistfully.

'Well, just be careful that she doesn't try to use you again for Monsieur Oulianoff's revolution,' Godiva cautioned.

'I'll campaign for all sorts of changes in Russia, but I'll be very careful. I'll make sure that I'm working with the right people,' Eugenie assured her.

'And we'll have to find you somewhere to stay,' Godiva said.

'Will that be difficult?' Eugenie asked.

'I would have liked you to stay with me, but I'm just moving to a new place myself,' Godiva said.

'That's news to me,' Walter remarked, 'Does that mean you are moving out of the apartment?'

'I've got a little flat in Chelsea that will be ready in a few days. I've been meaning to tell you. I've been most grateful to you for allowing me to stay, but Mehmet will be back sometime and I really had to find my own place. I thought you would be glad to be rid of me, anyway,' Godiva said, blushing slightly.

'Well, I take your point about Mehmet coming back, but that won't be for some weeks. I was thinking that Eugenie might stay with you for a while,' Walter said.

'Unfortunately the new flat only has one bedroom. There is literally no room to put another bed in it. I'm sorry, Eugenie, but I think you will have to be in a hotel for a few days until we can find you a place. It shouldn't take long,' Godiva apologised.

'That's alright. It will give me time to decide what sort of place I want, or who I want to live with. You must both agree to visit me when I am in the hotel, or I will be very lonely,' Eugenie said in a sing-song voice.

'Of course I shall visit,' Godiva agreed.

'I'll do my best, but it rather depends where they send me,' Walter said, 'They'll probably allow me a few days in London before they send me elsewhere, so you should be seeing me.'

'That's very good. I shall look forward to seeing both of you,' Eugenie said with a smile, 'what time is it that we leave tomorrow?'

'We'll collect you at about nine o'clock,' Godiva informed her.

There were noises of shouting outside the Princess's room door. A man was shouting and a woman was protesting. Then there came a dull thud a moment before a cry of pain. Walter and Godiva jumped up out of their chairs. The door burst open and Prince Pechorin appeared in the frame, his moustache twitching. There was a small pistol in his hand, a Luger P08 semi automatic. His eyes were wild and his clothing was less than immaculate. He looked mad with rage.

'You will come with me,' he screamed at the Princess. The pistol wavered in his hand.

'Go away!' the Princess screamed back at him.

'Come here now or I will kill your friends!' he ordered.

The Princess threw her book at him, striking him painfully on the upper arm, but not the one he was using to hold the pistol. This proved sufficient distraction for Walter to leap forward and to deliver a good straight left to the side of the Prince's jaw. The punch pushed the Prince into the door frame, where he struck his head a dizzying blow. He slumped to the ground. Behind him, in the corridor was a nurse who was just raising herself from a prone position, blood pouring from a wound on her scalp, inflicted by the butt of the pistol. Godiva leapt over the body of the Prince and went to the aid of the nurse.

'Does she have any bandages on her?' Walter asked.

Godiva put the question to the nurse, who pointed to a stock cupboard in reply. The cupboard was only a few steps away and Godiva quickly returned with lint pads and bandages which she gave to the nurse.

'Could you throw me a roll of bandage, please?' Walter asked a little testily. Godiva obliged with this request.

Walter tied the Prince's wrists and ankles with several layers of bandage before picking up the pistol and putting it in his pocket. The safety catch was still on. The nurse had recovered enough to go to a wash room after making a call to the Police. Godiva came back in to the room to see what she could do to help. The Prince was just coming round and his eyes were glassy rather than wild.

'I don't suppose you have a pair of scissors in your bag, do you?' Walter asked.

'I've got some nail scissors. Will they do?' Godiva said, fishing in her handbag and finally finding the small blunt scissors. She handed them to Walter, expecting him to use them to cut the end of the bandages. Instead, Walter took them and cut the Princes' moustaches almost back to the lip, leaving an uneven and ugly stubble. The Princess clapped in pleasure.

'That is very good. He was very proud of his moustaches. It will take several months for them to grow again. He will not want to appear in public without them,' she said, grinning.

'Oh, Walter, did you have to do that?' Godiva asked, not expecting a reply.

'It made me feel better,' was Walter's answer.

◊

'What about that drink we were going to have?' Skinner asked, 'By the way you are packing, it looks like you are going to leave tomorrow.'

'As soon as I finish we can go out to the cafe and get some food. Anyway, I thought you were seeing Brigitte tonight,' Walter replied, as he folded a shirt and placed it in the borrowed, battered suitcase.

'Why don't we get together with Sylvie and make a foursome? I'm sure Sylvie would be keen to see you,' Skinner suggested, playing with the paint tubes which lay on the window sill.

'That sounds good to me. As it's my last night here, the treat is on me. Why don't you go round and invite the girls to dinner as well. We'll go to a restaurant and do it properly. You go and see the girls and I'll make a booking. I'll see you back here in about an hour,' Walter suggested.

'Yeah, I'll do that right away,' Skinner answered.

'And I'll finish this packing and then find a telephone,' Walter said.

'Mind you, I'll need to get on the old best bib and tucker,' Skinner mused, laughingly.

◊

They had eaten a very good meal, though it had taken Walter a good deal of persuasion to get Sylvie to order one of the more expensive dishes on the menu. Skinner and Brigitte seemed to have no problem in spending Walter's money and ordered champagne and dishes with truffles. Walter himself ate more expensively than he had over recent weeks, but ordered the more luxurious forms of the peasant food he had enjoyed so much. There was still plenty of money left over after the meal was paid for.

'Walter, are we going on to the Blue Barge or the Bobino now?' Skinner asked.

'I'm not sure about that. I have a question to ask Sylvie, first. But please feel free to go yourself, and take Brigitte and take some money if you like,' Walter said. He turned to Sylvie and whispered in her ear. 'I've booked a room at a hotel for the night, if you would care to come along.'

'Mais oui!' Sylvie agreed, as though this was the best suggestion she had ever heard.

'I think Sylvie's coming with me. I'll catch up with you in the morning. Here's a few francs. Enjoy yourself,' Walter said as he passed over a handful of Francs in a magnanimous gesture.

A taxi took them to the hotel where Godiva was staying and to a grand room on the top floor where an ice bucket with a bottle of champagne was waiting for them. Walter had organised a wake-up call for eight o'clock the following morning. Tomorrow he had to leave for London, but tonight he had a large and comfortable bed, a bottle of champagne and the enthusiastic company of Sylvie.

Sunday 29th January

Walter leaned over the bed and kissed Sylvie softly on the lips. She looked up sleepily and a gradual smile came over her face.

'Bonjour Sylvie,' Walter said, 'I'm very sorry but I have to go now. I just want to thank you for a wonderful night. I'm afraid that I have to leave right now, as a taxi is waiting for me. Please send my love to Brigitte. I've left some money in case you need a taxi back to your place.'

'I had a wonderful night too. You are the best lover I have known. And I always knew that you would be leaving, so I won't ask your address in London. I think you are a gentleman without any prejudice towards the working people, which is a rare thing. Now, kiss me again, and close the door as you leave,' she said, raising her arms to embrace him, so revealing her breasts. They kissed more warmly, then she released him and turned over in the bed.

Godiva was waiting for him at the reception desk. She had evidently paid the outstanding bill as she was placing he purse back into her handbag. She had two other bags with her and her trusty umbrella was rolled up and strapped to the larger bag.

'Hello Walter. I trust you had a good night,' she said, 'Are you ready to go now? I can't see any luggage, so I suppose we shall have to go via your room.'

'That sounds wonderful. Have you paid for the room?' Walter replied.

'It's all taken care of. As there is a taxi waiting, I think we ought to leave,' she said in a brisk fashion. Walter followed her out to the taxi, the bags being carried by a porter. He fished in a pocket and handed over an unnecessarily large tip.

The taxi juddered off and headed across the river in the direction of Walter's rented room. The level of the water in the river had fallen below the banks but it was still flowing brown and turbid. On the walls of flooded buildings close to the river the level the water had reached was marked in chalk. The mud and the debris from the flood stained the lower parts of the walls of these. The main thoroughfares were now clear and busy with traffic.

It took Walter two trips to fetch his luggage from the room. The main items to carry were the paintings, but he now possessed a spare overcoat and jacket, which were both bulky. Skinner must have spent the night with Brigitte as he wasn't in his room and the farewells given on the previous evening would have to suffice. The concierge barely acknowledged him when he handed in his key. The room had been paid for another week, and she would no doubt rent it again before the day was out.

The next stop was at the clinic, where Eugenie was waiting for them, seated in a chair near the entrance, her legs covered with a blanket. She greeted both of them warmly but remained seated until the taxi driver had loaded her bags into the car. Godiva helped her to her feet and then to the car, using the same blanket to keep her warm once she was seated.

The rest of the journey to the Gare du Nord was marked with short snatches of conversation without any real form. After their adventures they found little to discuss. It was as though they knew their shared experiences were coming to an end, like the last day of a holiday. None of them was as cheerful or outgoing as they had been the previous day.

LaDavide was waiting for them at the station. He was carrying sprays of hot-house flowers for the ladies and a bottle of good brandy for Walter. As he had both hands occupied he was unable to tip his hat as they approached. They all greeted him and received their gifts. A porter pushing a trolley grumbled as he had to stop the vehicle as the group chatted. After a minute or so they walked to the first class carriage they were to travel in and into a compartment reserved for them. LaDavide gallantly helped to carry in the ladies' luggage and whispered something to Godiva as she sat which could not be overheard by the others. He then turned to Eugenie.

'Ah, Princess, I must tell you that your husband has been taken back to Russia. He was deported yesterday evening. This means that we have no more complaints about Walter to deal with. The case is closed as far as the Tigers are concerned. I only have one small question to ask, and that concerns the whereabouts of the pistol the Prince was waving around,' LaDavide said to the compartment in general.

'I have it right here,' Walter admitted ruefully, patting his pocket where the pistol remained.

'Then I suggest that you keep it there in case you need it to defend these ladies. And I did not hear what you just said. The gun must, by now, be in the hands of some cursed Apache gang,' LaDavide suggested.

A porter came round to announce the imminent departure of the train. LaDavide kissed the ladies on both cheeks and shook Walter's hand strongly before getting off the train. He did not stay to wave them off but strode purposefully down the platform.

'What was that he whispered to you?' Walter asked of Godiva as the train pulled away.

'Nothing you need to be told about,' Godiva answered firmly.

◊

It was dark by the time they pulled into London Victoria Station on the boat train. Unlike his previous crossing, Walter found the channel as flat as it could get in winter, but the Princess had been affected badly by the motion of the boat and had been sick twice. Dover had looked more cheerful in full sunlight, although the famous White Cliffs looked disappointingly stained with rust.

Detective Fitch was waiting for them when they arrived at the station and quickly ushered them through the ticket barrier and through to the dimly lit street into a waiting taxi.

'Good to see you again, Miss Williams, and you, Sir. And very nice to meet you too, Madam,' Fitch said as the vehicle pulled away.

'Which hotel have you booked Eugenie, I mean the Princess Pechorinova into?' Godiva asked.

'I took the liberty of selecting the Palatine. The booking is under the name of Madam Surikov. I thought it better not to use real names,' Fitch answered. He repeated the message in perfect Russian for the benefit of Eugenie.

'That is very discrete of you,' Walter said.

'Is this a good hotel?' Eugenie asked, 'Do you know it?'

'I must admit that I know it quite well,' Walter said, 'So you will please excuse me if I don't take you to your room. I'm also known to the manager, so it is best that I stay away.'

'They might remember me there too, but I'll just have to take that chance,' Godiva said.

'I am sensing something here,' Eugenie said thoughtfully.

'Walter has used the hotel in the past for his romantic liaisons,' Godiva said with a disapproving half smile.

'So, they would know his real name, then?' Eugenie asked. Walter and Godiva looked at one another, but neither answered.

'Are you still based at the flat, or have you gone back to your father's house?' Walter asked Godiva.

'Oh, I'm still at the flat for the time being. Well, someone has to give Dorkins something to do. I promise I won't get in your way,' she replied.

'I do believe that I could do with a decent bath and shave, and a change into some decent clothes. Then I think I'll pop round to my club,' Walter announced.

The taxi pulled up outside the pristine entrance to the Palatine Hotel. As the ladies got out they were saluted extravagantly by the uniformed doorman. A porter took charge of the Princess's bags.

The ladies followed him into the reception hall. Fitch took the opportunity of their absence to speak to Walter.

'Congratulations on arriving back alive. I understand that you have been rather busy over the last few weeks. There will be a debriefing for you tomorrow at ten a.m. at the offices. Please don't be late,' he said rather formally.

'I'll look forward to that,' Walter said.

'If you could bring along your notes and any receipts you might need to claim against, that would be helpful,' Fitch added.

'Right, I'll do that, then,' Walter grunted in reply.

The two men sat in silence until Godiva returned a few minutes later.

'Where to now, Miss?' Fitch asked.

'I suppose you had better take us to Walter's flat,' she said. Fitch passed the instruction to the driver who set off again.

Walter's flat was just a few minutes' drive from the hotel. Fitch and the driver helped Walter to carry all the luggage and the paintings up to the flat before Fitch bade them a good night and left.

'Oh, welcome back, Mr Walter,' Dorkins gushed at Walter, 'and Miss Godiva,' he added with less enthusiasm.

'Good to see you again, Dorkins,' Walter said, and he patted Dorkins on the shoulder.

'Don't worry too much, Dorkins, I'll be out of here in a few days time,' Godiva said.

'Just as well, Miss, seeing as how Mr Mehmet will be arriving back next week. I opened the letter he sent to Mr Walter. I hope you don't mind, I recognised the handwriting. He asked for the place to be made ready. He's on the steamer from Cape Town as we speak,' Dorkins explained.

'Never mind that now,' Walter said, 'What I really want is a hot bath and one of your special shaves. Then I'll put on some decent clothes and go off to my club.'

'Well, I didn't like to comment on the way you were dressed, Sir, seeing as you've been travelling, but it's really not up to your normal standard,' Dorkins said, archly, 'I'll go and run your bath now.'

'Is there any food in the kitchen?' Godiva asked.

'I'll get something ready for you as soon as I've run Mr Walter's bath,' Dorkins answered.

'No, I didn't mean that. I'm quite capable of cooking something for myself,' Godiva said.

'Just as you wish, Miss. There's some chops and potatoes and some bread and cheese,' Dorkins said sniffily, as though he regarded the kitchen as his domain, even though he was a terrible cook.

'Ah, well, back to normal,' Walter remarked.

'Go and have your bath, Walter,' Godiva said in a bossy voice. Walter obeyed.

Monday 30th January

Kell and Cumming were still sharing an office. Both had large desks and Walter had to sit cramped on a hard chair in the little available space.

'Look, now, we'll read your report later, but if you could give us some idea what you have been up to we'll let you go and get a proper debriefing with Major Savage,' Cumming said, lighting a pipe-full of an aromatic blend of tobacco.

'Well, I fulfilled my first brief in that I got to know Ulyanov's mistress, Inessa Armand. In fact we should be in correspondence soon. She wasn't able to tell me anything about the Latvians, but if she learns of anything, I should get to know,' Walter answered.

'Did you get to seduce her?' Kell asked with a look of distaste on his face.

'I had her in my bed, which is what I suppose you meant, but she is a woman who is able to separate out her sexual needs from her emotions. She's not in love with me, but she thinks I'm a good man,' Walter replied.

'Losing the magic touch are you, old boy,' Cumming said with a guffaw.

'She's a very independent woman. I liked her a lot, and I think we can trust her. She's not jealous or the obsessive type. If she wasn't mixed up in all this business I'd recommend her to someone as an ideal wife,' Walter explained.

'Let's just hope she comes through with some information. It's not costing us much, anyway,' Kell said, 'Unlike that Russian woman you've got in a very expensive hotel.'

'That was a bit of an accident. I was introduced to the woman's husband, who was nominally head of the Okhrana in Paris. He tried to get her to seduce me, but I saw what he was doing. The Princess Eugenie Pechorinova is a very well-connected young woman. She used to be mistress to the Czar's cousin and she knows the court well. From what I have seen, I think we need to know at least as much about the court as we do about the Bolsheviks,' Walter said.

'That is for us to decide. You've exceeded your brief and put the mission in danger,' Kell said through thin lips.

'I must say, I think I rather agree with Walter,' Cumming said, 'if they would just introduce a reasonable level of reform we could avoid almost all of this nastiness.'

'That's not something we should be discussing now,' Kell said, looking a little exasperated, 'We're just trying to find out why he did what he did. Now, tell me, why did you get mixed up in all this gang warfare in Paris?'

'I was working with an agent in the Tigers, and I just happened to arrest the son of one of the gang leaders. I wasn't even taking part in the raid, but he was escaping, and I thought I'd help out,' Walter replied. Kell clucked disapprovingly.

'That was a bit silly of you,' Cumming commented.

'I didn't mean to get involved, but it did help out in various ways. I got to know Ulyanov's wife and then Ulyanov himself. I can't say as I took to the man. He's a bit of a cold fish, but his wife is a good woman in her way. And I became quite close to the Tiger agent and I hope he'll help us out with some more information,' Walter continued.

'Then there is the art smuggling and the American connection,' Kell growled.

'As for that, well, the forger was connected to the Bolsheviks. I had no idea where that path was going to lead me. As it turned out, it might put us in a good light with the Russians who collect art,' Walter suggested.

'And what about this extraordinary business where you kidnapped the Prince's wife, not once but twice, assaulted his servants and clipped off the Prince's moustache?' Kell said with a snort.

'There I admit it got a bit personal. The Prince had me drugged, kidnapped, imprisoned and assaulted. He also locked up and beat up his wife. It's fair to say that I did take a bit of personal revenge, but he is a very nasty and cruel man, as well as being stupid.' Walter admitted. Cumming laughed heartily.

'The reason I employed you was because you like to shake the tree and see what falls out. So I won't complain if something unexpected happens. As it stands, I don't think there is any irreparable damage done, and you may have found us some useful sources of information. Now, it's time for me to argue this out with Major Kell. So run along and see Major Savage, will you? He's somewhere on the third floor,' Cumming said.

Walter left the room without offering a salute. If they didn't give him a good commission he'd not acknowledge them in a formal way. Anyway, neither man seemed to notice.

It took Walter some minutes to find where Major Savage's office was in the warren of rooms on the third floor. When he did eventually locate the office, it proved to be even smaller than the room he had just come from, but neat as a sea captain's writing desk. Major Savage turned out to be the same man who had spoken to him at the training camp in Hampshire more than three weeks previously. The Major's sun-tan was beginning to fade.

'Look, don't bother me with the details, I can read the report for those, just let me know of anything which happened which you couldn't explain,' Savage said. Walter had to think for a minute before answering.

'Well, one thing which confused me was that when I was imprisoned the Okhrana man there knew exactly who I was and who I was working for. I caught up with him later and beat the information out of him. He said there was a man at the German

Embassy who had identified me. This agent was also working for the Germans, you see. I thought at the time that someone I met at a party, an acquaintance from London, had told someone else and that is how the information got out. It turned out that this German already knew who I was, and I was wondering how he had managed that. The only name I got for the German was Tolcher, but I'm sure it's not his real name. Anyway, I found that rather worrying,' Walter admitted.

'Miss Williams passed that information back to us, but we still haven't identified the man. All I can suggest is that your cousin, Siegfried, passed the information about you to his masters in Berlin. You are a little identifiable, if only by your height, looks and talents. If the Tigers let slip to the Prince that you were a British agent and this Okhrana man was also reporting to Tolcher it would not have been too difficult to make the connection. We'll have to get you a better identity next time. Mind you, we'll have more time to get your story and papers in order. Now, was there any other issue that is on your mind?' Savage said in a patient and even voice.

'Probably quite a lot. I presume that Godiva, Miss Williams, I mean, has told you that she is trying to recruit one of the Tigers, a very good man called LaDavide, to work for us,' Walter said.

'She did suggest something of the sort,' Savage said.

'Then there was this Mexican man I met at the party. I didn't get his real name, but he seemed to be doing some kind of intelligence work. I could tell by the way he looked around the room and listened. Oh, yes, he's quite young but almost completely bald,' Walter said.

'That's Manolo Santiago, and we've already put in a bid for his services,' Savage said, a little dismissively, 'now, is there anything else you wanted to know or to tell me?'

'Well, I would be slightly interested in what became of the Countess Podolski,' Walter ventured.

'She took the SS Laurentic from Southampton yesterday and had her husband with her. What she was doing is probably not exactly illegal in the US, so I don't think we'll have any way of getting her back to France to face charges. I understand that your room was next door to her son's. She'll probably bring him back to America soon,' Savage answered.

'Then I don't think I have any more questions at the moment,' Walter said.

'In that case, write up your report. Use a stenographer from the top floor if it's of any use. I'm afraid that Miss Williams will be unavailable, as she has something of a back-log of work to deal with. And you may be interested to know that I shall be asking your friend, the Princess Pechorinova, a few questions tomorrow. I shall get Detective Fitch to help me,' Savage said.

'Please be gentle with her, she's been through quite a lot,' Walter said, a note of concern in his voice.

'Don't worry. We're not in any great hurry, though we really must find her some employment and a cheaper place to stay. Major Kell is particularly anxious to spend money wisely,' Savage assured Walter.

'I'll bet he is,' Walter said, and he turned and left.

There was no stenographer available for Walter that day, so he decided to go to his club for some lunch and then look up some old friends.

◊

It was around teatime that Walter knocked at the door of the town house of his old friends, Charles and Emily Gurney-Stewart. Charles was at work at the ministry but Emily was in residence and not occupied by visitors or events. She invited Walter into a small sitting room and sent the maid to fetch some tea and cakes.

'How have you been, Walter?' Emily asked.

'Oh, much as usual,' Walter said, 'I've just got back from Paris.'

Down in the Flood

'Goodness! Hasn't there been a dreadful flood there?' she continued in a conversational way.

'Yes, it was pretty bad, but I was staying well above the river and managed to keep dry most of the time,' he replied.

'Do tell me, what were you up to in Paris?' was her next question for him.

'I was doing some painting and getting paid pretty well for it, among other things,' he answered with a twisted little smile.

'Knowing you as I do, I'd better not ask what else you've been up to. Anyway, I've some news for you. Walter, I'm expecting,' she said, dropping this particular bombshell without any sign of lighting the fuse.

'When is the baby due?' Walter asked, trying to remember just when he had known carnal relations with Emily.

'The doctor says it's July. Oh, Walter, I'm so excited!' she gushed, and she slopped some tea into her saucer.

'Well, that's wonderful news. I'm very happy for you both,' Walter said, stumblingly.

'I have a feeling that Charles wants you to be godfather,' Emily said with a broad smile.

'Then he'd better ask me nearer to the time. Look I couldn't be happier for you. But, Emily, are you sure it is Charles' and not mine?' Walter asked, trying to find the right words. She fixed him with a steely stare.

'It's Charles' baby. Remember that, Walter. You are not the father and have no claim on the child. Now, do you understand that?'

'I understand you completely,' Walter confirmed.

'Good, I'm glad to hear it. We'll talk no more about that. Now, tell me, how is your friend Godiva?' she said with great precision.

'She was very well when I saw her yesterday evening,' Walter replied.

'And how is the new job going?'

'The answer to that question is one I need to be discrete about,' Walter said, and they both laughed.

◊

Walter and Godiva dined in the Princess's room that evening. Eugenie was dressed in her finest silks and looked completely well and very attractive with some show of the pale skin at the top of her breasts. Plates of food were crammed onto the small round table in the room and two additional bedroom chairs had been brought in to seat the guests. The meal was quite good and the wine had been more than acceptable. Walter thought that Kell would not be willing to fund too many more meals in this style. When Godiva left to find a washroom before they left the Princess leaned forward to talk to Walter.

'You would be most welcome to stay tonight,' she suggested with a mischievous smile.

'Well, thank you for that offer,' Walter said, trying to judge if this was something he wanted to do, 'But I'm not sure about making love to you tonight for several reasons. The first thing is that I heard some news today about a friend that has rather shaken me. And secondly, it is because of the way we have got to know each other. Because your husband forced you to try to seduce me and then I had to rescue you from that cellar, I feel more like a friend or a brother than I do a potential lover. If I wanted to, I could make an excuse about having to share an apartment with Godiva, but there are always ways to get around that.'

'You make it sound as if everything just happens to me,' she said quite angrily, 'I am quite able to make my own decisions. I am quite able to live my own life. And I could be useful to you. We could work together. I still have friends in Russia, though my enemies are more powerful at the moment. Things are going to change there.'

'I'm sure things will change whether or not we become involved. I think it is more the plans of people like Mr Ulyanov that will change the course of history. You are talking to the wrong person here, you know. I really don't have any influence on policy. The Service will send me where they want to, to do jobs for them. And I will just do what they tell me to do,' Walter said, distancing himself from the research and planning areas of the business.

'You can never just obey orders. That is not the kind of man you are. When I said we could work together I did not mean we could work through your security services. There is other work we can do,' she said in a meaningful way.

'I will only do work which is not distasteful to me, and I will only work for my country,' Walter insisted. A few seconds of silence followed during which they both considered what had been said.

'In that case, I suppose we had better just be friends,' Eugenie said, looking both sad and amused.

'My advice to you is that you should be very careful about doing anything which concerns Russia while you are in London. There are people of all political persuasions who might not want you to be involved. You must take good care of yourself: I am very fond of you,' Walter said, looking rather serious. Eugenie nodded and leaned back in her chair.

Godiva walked back into the room and noted the thoughtful expression on both of their faces.

'Come on, Walter, it's time for us to leave. Thank you so much for a lovely evening, Eugenie. I'm sure we shall be seeing each other very shortly. Now, where did I leave my hat? I can see my coat on the stand. Ah, there it is, over there. Now, good night, and I will call in again tomorrow.'

As they walked down the corridor, after the door had been closed behind them, Godiva stopped Walter by grabbing his arm, just where the wound was finally healing.

'What was that all about?' she asked him in a fierce whisper.

'I'm not exactly sure. She invited me to stay the night, and when I turned her down she changed tack and asked me to work with her. She wasn't talking about both of us working for the service, but something different. To be frank, I'm not sure exactly what it was she had in mind. What I would say is that it would not be wise to underestimate her. She works by manipulating people,' Walter said, describing what had happened as honestly as he could.

'Then we shall have to be a bit subtle in our dealings with her,' Godiva mused, 'Though it seems that you are proof against her charms.'

'I much prefer a bit more of a challenge,' Walter said, 'But I don't like to refuse a lady.'

'There's something else on your mind,' Godiva observed as they started walking again.

'Oh, yes, Emily's pregnant,' Walter answered her.

'I see,' Godiva said, and neither of them spoke for some time.

Down in the Flood

Jon Wakeham

Lightning Source UK Ltd.
Milton Keynes UK
UKOW04f1320230214

227007UK00001B/1/P